Introduction

In the beginning, I had to start somewhere.
I had this idea that almost everything has an opposite.

Justice - Injustice	Right – Left	Light – Dark
Inside – Outside	Dirty – Clean	Fire - Ice
Peace - Conflict	Happy – Sad	Land – Water
Female – Male	Love – Hate	Birth - Death
Positive – Negative	Win – Lose	Wet – Dry

My theory suggests that if we have a black universe, why not a white universe somewhere out there?

I had an intriguing thought: What if instead of the Big Bang theory, our planets originated from a white hole?

With a black hole, nothing emerges from it, whereas with a white hole, nothing can enter it because it essentially births new worlds and stars.

Scientists have proposed that the Big Bang resulted from the collision of dark matter and anti-matter, which are opposites. This aligns with my theory, as it raises questions about what existed before and where the Big Bang originated from.

If the Big Bang occurred, it would imply the existence of a pre-existing universe of some kind.

My theory suggests that our planet and all the stars surrounding it were drawn into a black hole, only to emerge from a white hole into our current universe.

My Theory

Cosmic Odyssey

Journey to the Heart of the Milky Way

THE BLACK HOLE

Foreword

Welcome to my science fiction story, a journey that has been both exhilarating and enlightening to undertake. AI has been instrumental in refining certain sentences, but crafting this tale has been an adventure. From brainstorming characters and plotlines to fleshing out intricate details, every aspect required careful consideration and creative input.

Throughout the writing process, I found myself constantly Engaging with the AI involved providing guidance on the characters' roles and relationships, as well as refining the storyline to ensure coherence and depth. Additionally, discussions delved into the pros and cons of several types of propellants used in spaceships, exploring their efficacy, safety, and environmental impact in the vast expanse of space.

It is remarkable how technology can complement and enhance the creative process, yet at the same time, it underscores the importance of human imagination and ingenuity.

One of the most rewarding aspects of drafting this story has been the opportunity to explore themes of discovery, friendship, and the boundless potential of the human spirit. As the characters venture into the unknown depths of space, they encounter challenges and obstacles that test their resolve and unity. Yet, it is their unwavering determination and camaraderie that propels them forward, illuminating the resilience of the human spirit in the face of adversity.

While the journey may have been arduous at times, the result is a testament to the power of collaboration and creativity. I hope that you will find as much enjoyment in reading this story as I did in writing it. May it inspire you to embrace the wonders of imagination and embark on your own adventures, wherever they may lead.

Thank you for joining me on this journey through the cosmos. Let us explore the stars together.

I have had the privilege of delving into the world of storytelling for quite some time now, and while the tools may have changed over the years, the joy of crafting narratives remains the same. In the early days, it was just me and my trusty typewriter, tapping away at keys to bring my ideas to life. It was a slower process, yes, but there was a certain charm to it, a sense of connection to the words as they appeared on the page.

I have also had the pleasure of seeing my work make a difference beyond the realm of fiction. There was a time when a tragic event shook a community, and I felt compelled to contribute in any way I could. So, I turned to my writing and penned a poem, hoping to offer solace and support to those affected.

It was humbling to see the poem published and sold, with the proceeds going towards aiding the families of the firefighters who lost their lives. It reminded me of the power of words to unite us, to offer comfort in times of sorrow, and to inspire action for a greater cause.

Reflecting on these experiences, I'm reminded that writing isn't just about the stories we tell; it's about the connections we forge and the impact we have on the world around us. Whether it's through a tale of adventure or a heartfelt poem, each word holds the potential to uplift, to educate, and to heal. And as I continue my writing journey, I carry with me the knowledge that even the smallest story can make a difference in someone's life.

I'm currently in the process of writing two more books, both forming a trilogy set on Mars. I'm excited to dive into the third book soon, continuing the adventure and exploration of the Black Hole.

As for myself, I'm enjoying retirement by pursuing my passions for art and writing. I find solace in painting as an artist, pouring my creativity onto the canvas. Additionally, I thoroughly enjoy the process of writing, letting my imagination run wild as I craft stories. I also sell some of my computer-de- signed artwork, with a focus on reaching audiences across America. It's a fulfilling journey, blending my love for creativity and storytelling into every endeavor.

Signed,

Roger G. Carpenter

Prologue

In the vast expanse of the cosmos, where stars twinkle like distant beacons and galaxies spiral in an endless dance, a group of intrepid astronauts embarked on a journey that would defy the boundaries of space and time.

Their mission was bold and unprecedented: to traverse the enigmatic depths of a black hole and emerge into a universe bathed in ethereal white light—a realm of wonder and mystery beyond imagination.

As their spacecraft hurtled through the swirling maelstrom of the black hole's event horizon, they braced themselves for the unknown, their hearts pounding with excitement and trepidation. And then, in a blinding flash of light, they crossed the threshold into the whiter universe beyond.

Emerging from the depths of the black hole, they found themselves surrounded by a dazzling panorama of celestial wonders—planets bathed in hues of silver and gold, nebulae swirling with iridescent gases, and stars twinkling like diamonds in the velvet expanse of space.

But their journey was far from over. Guided by their insatiable curiosity and boundless spirit of exploration, they set out to chart the uncharted realms of this new universe, venturing from one exoplanet to another in search of knowledge, adventure, and even friendship.

Yet, amidst the breathtaking beauty of the cosmos, they encountered challenges and dangers that tested their courage and resolve. Some alien beings welcomed them with open arms, eager to share their wisdom and culture. Others, however, viewed them with suspicion and hostility, their intentions shrouded in darkness and mystery.

Undeterred by adversity, the astronauts pressed on, forging alliances with newfound allies and facing adversity with bravery and determination. And as they journeyed through the whiter universe, they discovered that the bonds of friendship and camaraderie could transcend the vastness of space and unite beings from worlds apart.

Contents

Chapter 1:	*Scouting the Black Hole*
Chapter 2:	*The Test*
Chapter 3:	*The Mission*
Chapter 4:	*Departure from the Moon Base*
Chapter 5:	*Intergalactic Travel*
Chapter 6:	*Approaching the Event Horizon*
Chapter 7:	*A Journey Through Spacetime*
Chapter 8:	*Beyond the Event Horizon*
Chapter 9:	*White Universe*
Chapter 10:	*The Planet*
Chapter 11:	*Underground City*
Chapter 12:	*Night Underground*
Chapter 13:	*Second Planet*
Chapter 14:	*Third Planet*
Chapter 15:	*Zorvex from Planet Bole*
Chapter 16:	*Fourth Planet*
Chapter 17:	*Meeting of Earth's Future*
Chapter 18:	*Where is the White Hole?*
Chapter 19:	*Going through the Black Hole*
Chapter 20:	*Return to the Unknown*
Chapter 21:	*The Saviors*
Chapter 22:	*Distress Signal*
Chapter 23:	*Flying Saucers*
Chapter 24:	*Returning Home*
Chapter 25:	*The Home Coming*
Epilogue:	*A Cosmic Legacy*

Chapter 1:
Scouting the Black Hole

In the dimly lit halls of the world's most advanced observatories, scientists huddle over their monitors, their brows furrowed in concentration as they pore over the latest data streaming in from the depths of space.

Among them, a team of researchers has set their sights on the most enigmatic phenomenon in the cosmos: Sagittarius A* the black hole. Located in the center of our Milky Way galaxy.

Driven by an insatiable thirst for knowledge, the scientific community has mobilized to unlock the secrets of these cosmic behemoths.

Recognizing the limitations of even the most powerful telescopes, they have put forward a bold plan to send two robotic craft into the heart of the darkness itself, to gather data that no instrument on Earth could hope to capture.

Both the Moon base's largest telescope's, a marvel of engineering perched on the lunar surface, swiveled gracefully to focus its powerful lenses on the distant enigma. With each sweep of its gaze, it captured vast swathes of data, revealing tantalizing glimpses of the black hole's immense power and potential.

Among the findings were hints of exotic particles and energies that hinted at a revolutionary source of propulsion for future spacecraft.

Excitement rippled through the lunar facility as scientists pored over the data, their minds ablaze with possibilities. Discussions buzzed with speculation about the implications of harnessing the black hole's energy, with visions of interstellar travel and boundless exploration dancing in their heads.

Yet, amidst the fervor of discovery, a sobering reality set in the data, while rich in promise, lacked the depth and nuance required to fully understand the black hole's inner workings.

The scientists knew that to unlock its true potential, they needed more detail — more precise measurements, more comprehensive observations, more insights into the fundamental forces at play within its voracious maw.

Years of meticulous observation and analysis had yielded tantalizing glimpses into the black hole's secrets, but questions remained unanswered, mysteries unsolved.

Determined to unveil the truth hidden within its dark embrace, the Moon base embarked on an audacious mission: to send not one, but two spacecraft to venture closer to the black hole than ever before.

These robotic emissaries, equipped with state-of-the-art. sensors and innovative technology, are tasked with venturing into the perilous vicinity of the black hole, where time itself warps and reality bends. Their mission is clear: to gather as much data as possible, to unravel the mysteries of these cosmic giants and shed light on the fundamental workings of the universe.

As the robotic craft embark on their journey into the unknown, the scientific community holds its breath, knowing that the data they gather could revolutionize our understanding of the cosmos. For in the darkness of space, amidst the swirling maelstrom of gravity and radiation, lies the key to unlocking the greatest secrets of the universe.

As the two robotic craft ventured into the ominous threshold of the black hole's event horizon, the scientists at the moon base eagerly awaited the data streaming back from their intrepid explorers.

Initial transmissions provided glimpses into the mysterious depths of the black hole, but the information received was perplexing, defying conventional understanding and challenging the very laws of physics.

Despite their best efforts to interpret the data, the scientists found themselves faced with an enigma that grew more complex with each passing moment. Measurements fluctuated unpredictably, gravitational forces warped in ways beyond explanation, and time itself appeared to bend and twist in ways that defied comprehension.

Even as they grappled with the puzzling nature of the information, the scientists remained determined to unravel the mysteries hidden within the black hole's depths.

But their hopes were dashed when, suddenly and without warning, contact with both robotic craft was lost, plunging the moon base into a state of uncertainty and concern.

However, the setback did not deter the professors. Recognizing the importance of continuing their exploration, albeit with caution, they authorized the launch of two more robotic craft. This time, however, they implemented strict controls to ensure they did not venture too close to the black hole's event horizon.

The loss of the previous craft was a sobering reminder of the dangers that lurked in the depths of space, and the professors were determined not to repeat past mistakes.

With bated breath, the scientists monitored the progress of the new missions, their hopes tempered by the knowledge of the risks involved. But as the robotic craft ventured further into the unknown, gathering data and transmitting their findings back to the moon base, a sense of optimism began to take hold once more.

For even in the face of adversity, the spirit of exploration burned brightly, driving humanity ever forward in its quest to unlock the secrets of the universe.

Meanwhile, back on Earth, scientists and engineers pored over the streams of data transmitted by the spacecraft, analyzing every byte, scrutinizing every anomaly. The insights gleaned from these missions were invaluable, laying the groundwork for what would come next.

Undeterred by the daunting challenge ahead, the researchers redoubled their efforts, devising new strategies and technologies to probe deeper into the heart of the cosmic abyss.

They knew that their quest for knowledge would be fraught with peril and uncertainty, but they were driven by a shared determination to unravel the mysteries of the universe and push the boundaries of human understanding.

And so, against the backdrop of the cold expanse of space and the stark beauty of the lunar landscape, the Moon base stood as a beacon of scientific progress and human ingenuity, its inhabitants united in their quest to unlock the secrets of the cosmos and chart a course towards a brighter future for all humanity.

With the loss of contact with the first two robotic probes, the scientists at the moon base had sent two more faced a dilemma. While the data collected had been invaluable, it was clear that a more direct approach was needed to unravel the mysteries of the black hole.

After much deliberation and careful consideration of the risks involved, the scientific community unanimously agreed that a crewed mission, though perilous, offered the best chance of unlocking the secrets hidden within the enigmatic depths of the black hole.

The decision was not made lightly. Countless simulations were run, risk assessments conducted, and contingencies planned, but in the end, the scientists were adamant that the potential rewards outweighed the dangers.

Sending a crewed mission to the vicinity of the black hole, while avoiding the event horizon itself, held the promise of gathering unprecedented levels of detail and insight into the nature of these cosmic phenomena.

Preparations for the mission began in earnest, with teams of engineers and technicians working tirelessly to retrofit spacecraft, develop advanced navigation systems, and train the intrepid astronauts who would embark on this historic journey.

Every aspect of the mission was scrutinized and refined to ensure the safety and success of the crew, but the inherent risks of venturing into the unknown loomed large in the minds of all involved.

Despite the challenges ahead, the scientific community remained undeterred in their pursuit of knowledge. For they understood that the quest to understand the mysteries of the universe required courage, determination, and a willingness to push the boundaries of human exploration.

And so, with resolve and determination, they prepared to embark on a journey that would take them closer to the heart of Sagittarius A* than ever before, in search of answers that had eluded humanity for millennia.

The first spacecraft, equipped with state-of-the-art instruments and manned by a crew of fearless astronauts, soared towards the black hole, its mission clear: gather data, chart the surrounding terrain, and pave the way for future exploration. This time, the mission was even bolder: to journey to the edge of the black hole itself and come home safely.

With meticulous planning and unwavering determination, the crew embarked on their historic voyage. Their spacecraft, a marvel of human ingenuity, hurtled towards the gaping maw of the black hole, its engines roaring with defiance in the face of the unknown.

As the spacecraft ventured deeper into the cosmic abyss, the crew encountered a myriad of challenges unlike anything they had faced before.

The gravitational pull of Sagittarius A* threatened to swallow them whole, while swirling clouds of space debris posed a constant hazard to their journey.

With nerves of steel and quick thinking, the crew navigated their way through the treacherous environment, their spacecraft twisting and turning as they fought against the forces of gravity.

Each collision with space debris sent shudders through the hull, but the crew remained steadfast in their determination to press forward.

Despite the chaos and uncertainty, they refused to succumb to fear or despair. Guided by their training and the collective expertise of the scientific community back on Earth, they worked together tirelessly to regain control of the spacecraft and steer it away from the clutches of the black hole.

Finally, after what felt like an eternity, the spacecraft emerged from the chaos of the black hole's vicinity, battered but unbroken.

With a collective sigh of relief, the crew gathered their bearings and turned their attention to the task at hand: observing the black hole from a safe distance and gathering the data they had risked so much to obtain.

Their journey had been harrowing, fraught with danger at every turn, but as they gazed out into the vast expanse of space, they knew that their bravery and resilience had brought them one step closer to unlocking the secrets of the universe.

And though the road ahead would be long and arduous, they were more determined than ever to continue their quest for knowledge, wherever it may lead.

Upon their return from the perilous journey of observing the black hole from a safe distance, the crew found themselves battered and weary, yet grateful to be alive.

Their spacecraft, however, bore the scars of their harrowing passage at the edge of the black hole. The once sleek vessel now bore the marks of its ordeal: scorched hull plating, malfunctioning systems, and structural weaknesses that threatened to compromise its integrity.

As the crew emerged from their damaged craft, they were met with a sense of relief mingled with trepidation.

While they had survived their journey, it was clear that the ship would need extensive repairs before it could undertake another mission.

Discussions quickly turned to the need for stronger alloys and more robust engines to withstand the rigors of interstellar travel.

Back at the Moon base, engineers and scientists worked

tirelessly to analyze the data gathered from the damaged spacecraft and devise solutions to improve future missions.

They pored over blueprints and conducted simulations, brainstorming ideas for reinforced hulls, advanced propulsion systems, and enhanced navigation technologies.

Amidst the flurry of activity, one thing became clear: if humanity were to continue its exploration of the cosmos and unlock the secrets of the universe, it would need spacecraft capable of withstanding the extreme conditions of space travel.

The crew's return from the black hole served as a stark reminder of the challenges that lay ahead, but also as a testament to the resilience and determination of the human spirit.

And so, fueled by the promise of discovery and the spirit of exploration, they pressed on, forging ahead towards a future among the stars.

In the heart of the lunar base, nestled among the rugged craters and vast plains of dust, a team of scientists and engineers gathered in the research laboratory. Their mission: to perfect a stronger, lighter alloy for spacecraft construction using the abundant resources of the Moon.

Dr. Elena Garcia, a materials scientist, peered intently at

the holographic display of lunar regolith composition. "We have everything we need right here," she exclaimed, excitement lighting up her eyes. "Iron, aluminum, titanium, silicon... the key ingredients for our new alloy."

With determination fueling their efforts, the team set to work, meticulously extracting, and refining the raw materials from the lunar soil. They employed advanced techniques, including nanoscale manipulation and molecular synthesis, to craft the perfect alloy with enhanced strength and durability.

Days turned into weeks and weeks turned into months as the scientists conducted countless experiments, tweaking the composition and structure of the alloy to achieve optimal results.

They faced challenges along the way, navigating the complexities of lunar resource extraction and refining processes. But with each setback came new insights, pushing them closer to their goal.

Finally, after tireless effort and collaboration, a breakthrough was achieved. The team unveiled their masterpiece: a revolutionary alloy that surpassed all expectations.

Not only was it stronger and more durable than any previous spacecraft material, but it was also remarkably lightweight, offering significant fuel savings for future missions.

As news of their achievement spread throughout the lunar base, excitement rippled through the scientific community. The prospect of spacecraft constructed from lunar-derived materials promised to revolutionize space exploration, opening up new frontiers and pushing the boundaries of human ingenuity.

With their newfound alloy paving the way for the next generation of spacecraft, the scientists looked to the stars with renewed hope and determination. For on the surface of the Moon, they had unlocked the key to a future among the cosmos.

In their relentless pursuit of progress, the scientific community focused their efforts on developing even smaller nuclear reactors for spacecraft propulsion.

This ambitious endeavor aimed to create a compact yet powerful reactor capable of providing the necessary energy for long-distance space missions.

Researchers poured their expertise into refining existing designs and exploring innovative technologies to achieve this goal. The quest for a smaller nuclear reactor held the potential to revolutionize space exploration, enabling faster and more efficient journeys across the cosmos.

The development of revolutionary nuclear reactors for spacecraft propulsion represents a monumental leap forward in our quest for exploration beyond Earth's boundaries.

These reactors harness the incredible power of nuclear fusion, a process in which atomic nuclei combine to release vast amounts of energy, far exceeding the capabilities of conventional chemical propulsion systems.

One of the key advantages of nuclear fusion is its unparalleled energy density. Unlike chemical reactions that involve the combustion of fuel, nuclear fusion unleashes orders of magnitude more energy from a given mass of fuel.

This enables spacecraft equipped with nuclear reactors to achieve higher velocities and traverse interstellar distances in significantly shorter time frames.

The design and construction of these nuclear reactors require advanced materials capable of withstanding the extreme conditions of space and the intense heat and radiation generated by nuclear fusion.

Engineers utilize cutting-edge ceramics, composites, and alloys that exhibit exceptional heat resistance, structural integrity, and radiation tolerance.

These materials are carefully engineered to endure prolonged exposure to the harsh environment of space, ensuring the reliability and longevity of the reactors throughout the duration of the mission.

In addition to propulsion, nuclear reactors also serve as the primary power source for the spacecraft's onboard systems.

Through sophisticated energy conversion mechanisms, the heat generated by nuclear fusion is efficiently converted into electrical energy, powering vital systems such as life support, communications, and scientific instrumentation.

This self-sustaining power generation capability enables the spacecraft to operate autonomously for extended periods, eliminating the need for frequent refueling or reliance on external power sources.

Furthermore, advancements in reactor miniaturization have resulted in compact and efficient designs that maximize power output while minimizing space and weight requirements.

This allows for seamless integration into the spacecraft's overall architecture, optimizing payload capacity and mission flexibility. The compactness of these nuclear reactors also reduces the spacecraft's environmental footprint, contributing to a more sustainable approach to space exploration.

Overall, the development of revolutionary nuclear reactors represents a transformative milestone in our ability to explore the cosmos.

With their unparalleled power and efficiency, these reactors propel humanity further into the depths of space, unlocking new frontiers of knowledge and discovery that were once beyond our reach.

As the final pieces of the spacecraft come together and preparations for launch reach their culmination, the realization dawns that this monumental achievement represents more than just a technological triumph—it is a testament to the boundless ingenuity and indomitable spirit of the human race.

With the power of nuclear fusion propelling them forward, humanity stands poised to embark on a journey of discovery that will forever alter our understanding of the universe and our place within it.

With the construction of the advanced spacecraft equipped with nuclear reactors complete, humanity's aspirations for interstellar exploration take flight.

Chapter 2:
The Test

After years of tireless research and meticulous planning, the day had finally arrived. At the bustling spaceport nestled on the lunar surface, a sense of anticipation hung in the air as the first spacecraft.

As the sun cast long shadows across the lunar landscape, engineers in crisp white lab coats hurried about, making final adjustments to the sleek spacecraft poised on the launchpad. The hum of machinery filled the air, intermingling with the excited chatter of scientists and technicians bustling about their final preparations.

Inside the spacecraft, Commander Sarah Reynolds and Lieutenant Jackson sat side by side in the cockpit, conducting last-minute checks. Their faces mirrored the mix of nerves and excitement felt by all as they prepared to embark on this historic journey.

As the countdown commenced, a hush fell over the spaceport, anticipation reaching a crescendo with each passing second. Then, with a deafening roar, the engines ignited, propelling the spacecraft skyward in a blaze of light and sound.

Onlookers erupted into cheers and applause as the spacecraft soared gracefully into the heavens, leaving behind a trail of smoke and fire. For Sarah and her crew, this mission was more than just a voyage—it was a testament to human perseverance and the boundless spirit of exploration that drove them to push the limits of what was possible.

As the spacecraft disappeared from view, vanishing into the vast expanse of space, a sense of awe and wonder washed over those who had witnessed its departure.

For in that moment, humanity had taken another giant leap towards the stars, propelled by the boundless spirit of exploration and the unwavering determination to reach ever further into the cosmos.

"Commander Reynolds, this is Moon base. We are considering pushing the ship to its fastest speed, but we need to ensure it remains within communication range.

Commander Reynolds acknowledged the message from Moon base, her voice calm and assured despite the gravity of the decision at hand. "Understood, Moon base," she responded over the crackling radio transmission. "We'll assess the situation and provide you with our recommendations shortly."

Inside the spacecraft's command module, Commander Reynolds turned to Lieutenant Jackson, her expression thoughtful. "Jackson, run a diagnostic check on our propulsion systems. I want to know if we can safely increase our speed without jeopardizing our mission."

Lieutenant Jackson nodded, his fingers flying across the control panel as he initiated the diagnostic sequence. "Roger that, Commander," he replied, his tone focused. "I'll have the results for you in just a moment."

As the diagnostic check commenced, tension mounted in the command module. Every second felt like an eternity as the crew awaited the crucial information that would determine their course of action.

Finally, Lieutenant Jackson's voice broke through the silence. "Commander, the diagnostic check is complete. Our propulsion systems are operating within normal parameters, and it looks like we can safely increase our speed without any significant risk."

Commander Reynolds nodded, her mind racing with calculations and considerations. "Moon base, this is Commander Reynolds," she radioed, her voice steady. "We've completed our assessment, and it appears that we can proceed with increasing our speed. However, we'll need to maintain regular communication to ensure we remain within range."

A sense of anticipation filled the air as the crew awaited Moon base's response. With their decision made, they prepared to push the boundaries of exploration, propelled by the unwavering determination to unlock the mysteries of the cosmos.

Our new infrared communication systems have not been

tested yet. What are your thoughts?" came the voice of the mission control operator through the speakers.

Commander Reynolds took a moment to consult with her crew, including Ensign Tom Watts, whose expertise in communications systems made him an invaluable asset to the mission. Together, they analyzed the situation, weighing the potential risks and benefits of utilizing the untested infrared communication systems.

Ensign Tom Watts leaned over his console, furrowing his brow in deep concentration as he reviewed the specifications of the new communication technology. "Commander," he began, his voice measured, "while the infrared systems haven't undergone full testing, initial simulations suggest that they should be capable of maintaining communication even at higher speeds."

Commander Reynolds nodded, impressed by Ensign Tom Watts' analysis. "Thank you, Tom," she replied, her tone conveying both gratitude and confidence. "Let's proceed with activating the infrared communication systems and increasing our speed. We'll monitor their performance closely and adjust as necessary."

With Ensign Tom Watts at the helm of the communication systems, the crew worked swiftly to implement the necessary adjustments. As the spacecraft surged forward, propelled by the power of its engines, the crew held their breath, their eyes fixed on the monitors displaying vital telemetry data. With a unanimous agreement from her crew, Commander Reynolds relayed the command to the Moon base, and preparations were made to increase the spacecraft's velocity.

Despite the initial apprehension, the infrared communication systems proved their worth, maintaining a stable connection with the Moon base as the spacecraft accelerated to unprecedented speeds. Commander Reynolds exchanged a relieved smile with her crew, grateful for their teamwork and resourcefulness in navigating this pivotal moment in their journey through the cosmos.

As the engines roared to life once more, propelling the vessel forward at unprecedented speeds, the crew held their breath, knowing that each moment brought them closer to the edge of the known universe—and to the limits of their own ingenuity.

As the spacecraft hurtled through the void of space, the Moon base once again reached out to Commander Sarah Reynolds and her crew, this time to gather feedback on the ship's speed and communication capabilities.

"Speed is holding steady at the increased velocity," Commander Reynolds reported, her voice calm and composed despite the weight of responsibility resting on her shoulders. "The spacecraft is performing admirably, and the communication systems are holding up remarkably well, thanks to Ensign Tom Watts' expertise."

Ensign Tom Watts acknowledged the compliment with a nod of appreciation, his focus unwavering as he monitored the intricate array of communication instruments before him.

"But we're encountering some minor fluctuations in the sensor readings," Lieutenant Jackson chimed in, his brow furrowed in concern as he analyzed the data streaming across his console. "Nothing critical, but worth keeping an eye on."

Commander Reynolds nodded, taking note of Lieutenant Jackson's observation. "Understood," she replied, her mind already racing through potential solutions to address the fluctuations. "We'll continue to monitor the situation and provide regular updates."

As the conversation with the Moon base concluded, Commander Reynolds shared a reassuring smile with her crew, a silent reminder of their shared commitment to the success of their mission. Together, they forged ahead into the vast expanse of space, their resolve unshaken by the challenges that lay ahead.

The speed is impressive, but we have noticed a few glitches in the communication systems. There have been intermittent delays in transmission, and we have had to make adjustments to compensate. Overall, though, the systems are holding up well."

Commander Reynolds acknowledged the crew's concerns with a thoughtful nod, her mind already working through potential solutions to address the communication glitches.

"Understood," she replied, her voice steady and reassuring. "Let's run a diagnostic check on the communication systems and see if we can pinpoint the source of the delays. Ensign Watts, Lieutenant Jackson, I want you both to focus on troubleshooting the issue and report back with your findings."

Ensign Watts and Lieutenant Jackson nodded in response; their expressions focused as they prepared to tackle the challenge at hand.

With the crew mobilized to address the issue, Commander Reynolds turned her attention back to the task of piloting the spacecraft through the vast expanse of space. Despite the setbacks, she remained confident in their ability to overcome any obstacles they encountered on their journey.

As they continued their mission, the crew's determination and resourcefulness shone brightly, driving them forward towards the unknown with unwavering resolve. And with each passing moment, they drew closer to uncovering the secrets that awaited them in the depths of space.

The crew murmured in agreement, nodding at

Commander Reynolds' assessment. However, Ensign Watts, and Lieutenant Jackson chimed in, "There's definitely room for improvement, especially in reducing latency and ensuring more consistent signal strength."

Commander Reynolds listened intently to Ensign Watts and Lieutenant Jackson's assessments, recognizing the critical importance of refining the communication systems for the success of future missions.

"Thank you, Ensign Watts, Lieutenant Jackson," she said, acknowledging their input. "Moon base, this is Commander Reynolds. Ensign Watts and Lieutenant Jackson have identified areas for improvement in our communication systems. We need to focus on reducing latency and ensuring more consistent signal strength."

The response from mission control was swift, with technicians at the Moon base immediately springing into action to analyze the data and devise strategies for optimizing the communication systems.

Meanwhile, onboard the spacecraft, Ensign Watts and Lieutenant Jackson worked tirelessly to implement temporary fixes while awaiting further instructions from mission control. Their expertise and dedication were instrumental in maintaining open lines of communication amidst the vastness of space.

As the crew continued their journey, Commander Reynolds remained hopeful that the challenges they faced would ultimately lead to valuable insights and advancements, paving the way for smoother and more efficient interstellar communication in the future.

"Moon base, it seems we've made significant progress, but there's still work to be done," Commander Reynolds reported, her voice steady and determined. "Let's focus on addressing these issues to enhance the efficiency and reliability of our communications."

The response from the Moon base was encouraging, with the mission control team expressing their commitment to resolving the remaining challenges. "Commander Reynolds, this is Moon base," came the reply. "We're glad to hear about the progress. We're fine-tuning the communication systems on our end to ensure smoother operation."

As the spacecraft continued its journey through the cosmos, the crew remained in regular communication with the Moon base, providing updates on their progress and receiving guidance on troubleshooting any lingering issues. Together, they forged ahead, united in their mission to overcome obstacles and pave the way for future interstellar exploration.

With each passing day, the communication systems improved, thanks to the collaborative efforts of the crew onboard and the dedicated team at the Moon base. Their shared commitment to excellence propelled them forward, bringing them one step closer to unlocking the mysteries of the universe.

After weeks of exploration in the far reaches of space, Commander Reynolds and her crew were finally ready to return home.

"Moon base, this is Commander Reynolds. We are preparing to initiate our return trajectory. Is there anything else you need from us before we head back?" Commander Reynolds radioed back to the control center on the Moon.

A voice crackled over the intercom, "Understood, Commander Reynolds. Safe travels on your return journey. We'll be standing by to receive your full report once you're back at base."

Then, a moment of silence followed before the voice from the Moon base spoke again, "Commander Reynolds, before you head back, we have one final request. We would like you to conduct a visual survey of the asteroid belt along your return trajectory. Any data you can gather would be invaluable for our ongoing research."

Commander Reynolds nodded in acknowledgment. "Copy that, Moon base. We will make the necessary arrangements to conduct the survey. Reynolds out." With a sense of purpose, the crew prepared to fulfil their final task before journeying back to the Moon, knowing that their efforts would contribute to humanity's ever-expanding knowledge of the cosmos.

With their return trajectory set, Commander Reynolds and her crew prepared to conduct a visual survey of the asteroid belt. As they approached the belt, the vast expanse of space became littered with rocky debris, a celestial obstacle course stretching out before them.

"Ensign Watts, prepare the imaging sensors for the survey," Commander Reynolds instructed, her voice calm and decisive. "Lieutenant Jackson, plot a course through the asteroid belt, ensuring we maintain a safe distance from any potential hazards."

Ensign Watts nodded in acknowledgment, swiftly configuring the spacecraft's sensors for optimal data collection. Meanwhile, Lieutenant Jackson meticulously charted a course, navigating through the treacherous terrain of the asteroid belt with precision and caution.

As they ventured deeper into the asteroid belt, the crew marveled at the diverse array of celestial bodies that surrounded some asteroids were small, irregular chunks of rock, while others were massive behemoths, their surfaces scarred by eons of cosmic collisions.

"Commander, we're approaching a particularly dense region of the asteroid belt," Lieutenant Jackson reported, his tone tinged with caution. "I recommend we proceed with extra vigilance."

Commander Reynolds nodded in agreement; her focus unwavering as she monitored the spacecraft's instruments. With each passing moment, the crew scanned the asteroid belt, capturing detailed images and data that would provide invaluable insights into the composition and structure of these ancient remnants of the solar system.

As they navigated through the asteroid belt, the crew remained alert, ready to respond to any unexpected challenges that might arise. Despite the inherent dangers of their surroundings, they pressed on, driven by the pursuit of knowledge and discovery that defined their mission.

Hours passed as the spacecraft weaved its way through the asteroid belt, the crew's efforts culminating in a comprehensive survey of this enigmatic region of space. With their mission accomplished, Commander Reynolds and her crew set a course back to the Moon, their hearts filled with a sense of fulfilment and excitement for the discoveries that awaited them upon their return.

With practiced efficiency, the crew completed their tasks, ensuring that every component was secured for the journey back to the Moon. Commander Reynolds monitored the status updates from her crew, her confidence in their abilities unwavering.

"Ensign Watts, confirm that all imaging sensors are offline and stowed," she instructed, her voice steady as she double-checked the readiness of their equipment.

Ensign Watts nodded, quickly verifying the status of the sensors before reporting back to the commander. "All sensors are offline and secured, Commander. We're ready to disengage."

Lieutenant Jackson, stationed at the navigation console, confirmed their trajectory back to the Moon. "Course plotted for return," he announced, his fingers dancing across the controls with practiced ease.

Commander Reynolds nodded in approval, a sense of anticipation building as they prepared to depart from the asteroid belt and journey homeward. "Initiate disengagement procedures," she commanded, her gaze fixed on the viewscreen that displayed the vast expanse of space before them.

With a series of commands, the spacecraft disengaged from its position among the asteroids, its engines roaring to life as it set course for the Moon. As they left the asteroid belt behind, the crew felt a surge of satisfaction, knowing that they had completed their mission with precision and professionalism.

As the journey back to the Moon commenced, Commander Reynolds and her crew settled in for the return trip, their minds already turning to the next chapter of their exploration of the cosmos.

As the spacecraft approached the Moon, the crew marveled at the sight of their lunar destination growing larger in the viewscreen. Commander Reynolds could not help but feel a sense of pride as they drew nearer to their lunar home once again.

"Lieutenant Jackson, prepare for lunar orbit insertion," she instructed, her voice tinged with anticipation.

"Aye, Commander," Lieutenant Jackson responded, swiftly inputting the commands to adjust their trajectory for a stable orbit around the Moon.

The spacecraft smoothly transitioned into lunar orbit, its engines adjusting to the weaker gravitational pull of Earth's celestial companion. The crew watched with anticipation as the rugged landscape of the Moon came into clearer view, the familiar craters and valleys marking their return to this celestial neighbor.

"We've made it back," Ensign Watts remarked, a sense of relief evident in his voice as he took in the sight before them.

Commander Reynolds nodded in agreement, a smile tugging at the corners of her lips. "Yes, Ensign. We have made it home," she replied, her tone filled with satisfaction.

As they prepared to descend to the lunar surface, the crew reflected on the challenges they had overcome and the discoveries they had made during their mission. Despite the vastness of space and the unknown that lay beyond, they knew that the Moon would always be a familiar and welcoming sight, guiding them safely back to Earth."

Chapter 3: The Mission

As the broadcast reverberated through the expansive halls of space agencies worldwide, thousands of astronauts listened with bated breath to the solemn yet electrifying words emanating from mission control.

The atmosphere crackled with a palpable blend of anticipation and trepidation; each word spoken by the announcer carrying the weight of the monumental mission that lay ahead—the audacious voyage into the unfathomable depths of a black hole.

With meticulous detail, the broadcast delved into the unprecedented risks and challenges that awaited the intrepid souls who would dare to venture into the cosmic abyss.

It painted a vivid portrait of the hostile environment within the black hole's event horizon, where the laws of physics appeared to undergo a bewildering metamorphosis. Extreme gravitational forces capable of distorting space and time, time dilation effects that could warp the very fabric of reality, and enigmatic phenomena shrouded in mystery were all starkly highlighted as potential hazards that loomed ominously over the mission.

Despite the daunting odds and the inherent dangers that

permeated every aspect of the mission, the call for volunteers resounded with unwavering clarity.

Mission control articulated their unwavering pursuit of individuals possessing unparalleled courage, unwavering skill, and indomitable determination—astronauts willing to push the boundaries of human exploration to their limits and beyond, prepared to sacrifice everything in the relentless pursuit of knowledge and discovery.

For many who listened to the broadcast, the decision to volunteer. Represented a momentous crossroads, a choice fraught with uncertainty and profound implications.

Each aspiring astronaut meticulously weighed the risks against the potential rewards, grappling with the daunting prospect of journeying into the unknown. Yet, propelled by an unyielding sense of duty, an insatiable thirst for knowledge, and an irrepressible spirit of adventure that coursed through their veins, a multitude stepped forward, eager to inscribe their names in the annals of history.

As the broadcast drew to a close, the air was thick with a heady mixture of anticipation and resolve, as thousands of hopeful volunteers began to steel themselves for the monumental odyssey that awaited them.

Among them, those who would ultimately be chosen to comprise the final crew of four would embark on a perilous journey into the heart of the black hole, destined to navigate the uncharted realms of the cosmos and confront the mysteries of the universe head-on.

Behind the scenes, mission control confronted the formidable challenge of meticulously vetting each candidate, sifting through the deluge of applicants to handpick the select few who possessed the requisite combination of skills, expertise, and fortitude to undertake the harrowing mission.

Teams of seasoned experts embarked on a rigorous and exhaustive vetting process, subjecting each candidate to a battery of interviews, tests, and evaluations designed to assess their physical resilience, mental acuity, and emotional stability.

Only those who demonstrated exceptional aptitude, unwavering determination, and an unshakable resolve to confront the unknown with courage and conviction would be deemed worthy of ascending to the stars.

For the chosen few, the path ahead would be fraught with peril and uncertainty, yet it would also offer the promise of unparalleled discovery, pushing the boundaries of human exploration to unprecedented heights and unlocking the secrets of the cosmos that lay hidden within the inky depths of space.

For many of the volunteers, the prospect of being selected for the mission was both exhilarating and nerve-wracking.

Each candidate knew that they were vying for the opportunity to make history—to journey to the very edge of human knowledge and explore the mysteries of the cosmos firsthand.

Yet, they also understood the immense risks involved, and the weight of responsibility that would rest upon their shoulders should they be chosen.

As the vetting process progressed, mission control worked tirelessly to whittle down the pool of candidates, carefully evaluating each individual against a set of stringent criteria.

While only four would ultimately be selected for the mission, those who were not chosen would not be forgotten—they would be given priority consideration for future missions, ensuring that their contributions to the cause of space exploration would not go unrecognized.

Finally, after months of exhaustive deliberation, mission control announced the names of the four astronauts who had been chosen to undertake the historic mission into the black hole.

For these intrepid explorers, it was a moment of triumph and validation— a culmination of years of training, sacrifice, and unwavering dedication to the pursuit of knowledge.

And as they prepared to embark on their journey into the unknown, they did so with a sense of pride and purpose, knowing that they were about to make history in the annals of human space exploration.

The perilous journey through a black hole presented a daunting challenge, one that required the utmost courage and determination from those who volunteered for the mission.

Despite the inherent risks and uncertainties, a diverse group of individuals stepped forward, driven by a shared sense of curiosity and a pioneering spirit that transcended fear.

Among the volunteers were seasoned astronauts with years of experience in space exploration, eager to push the boundaries of human knowledge and understanding. Their expertise in piloting spacecraft and navigating through the cosmos would prove invaluable during the perilous journey through the black hole's event horizon.

Joining them were scientists and researchers from various disciplines, working on the moon for this very mission, drawn to the opportunity to unlock the mysteries of the universe firsthand.

Their expertise in astrophysics, quantum mechanics, and other fields of study would play a crucial role in interpreting the data collected during the mission and unravelling the secrets hidden within the depths of the black hole.

Also among the volunteers were engineers and technicians, tasked with ensuring the spacecraft's systems were operating at peak efficiency for the journey. Their skill and ingenuity would be put to the test as they worked to overcome the myriad challenges posed by the extreme conditions encountered near the black hole.

Despite the uncertainty of what lay ahead, each volunteer shared a common bond—a steadfast commitment to humanity's collective quest for knowledge and discovery. With their hearts set on the stars and their minds focused on the challenges ahead, they embarked on a journey that would forever alter our understanding of the cosmos and our place within it.

Commander Dr. Elizabeth Hayes, Lieutenant Commander Mark Thompson, Dr. Emily Chen, Ph.D., and Lieutenant Sarah Johnson formed the core crew of the mission, each bringing their unique skills and expertise to the endeavor. Dr. Hayes, with her extensive experience in space exploration and leadership, was chosen as the mission commander, responsible for guiding the crew through the complexities of the journey and making critical decisions under pressure.

Commander Dr. Elizabeth Hayes, a seasoned astronaut and astrophysicist, brings a wealth of knowledge and leadership to the mission.

Born into a family of scientists, her passion for space exploration ignited at an early age. With a Ph.D. in astrophysics from a prestigious university, she quickly rose through the ranks of the space program, earning a reputation for her exceptional leadership skills and unwavering dedication to the pursuit of knowledge.

As the commander of the mission, she is responsible for overseeing preparations, ensuring the crew is adequately trained, and meticulously planning every aspect of the mission.

She understands the gravity of the task ahead and recognizes the immense challenges and risks involved in journeying into the heart of a black hole.

Despite the uncertainties and dangers, remains focused and determined, drawing on her years of experience and expertise to guide her team through the complexities of space exploration.

With her calm demeanor and sharp intellect, Dr. Hayes instils confidence in her team, inspiring them to push the boundaries of human knowledge.

As the countdown to launch approaches, she remains steadfast in her leadership, inspiring confidence in her crewmates and instilling a sense of purpose in their mission. Dr. Hayes knows that the success of the endeavor depends on their collective efforts and unwavering commitment to the pursuit of scientific inquiry.

When the time comes for the crew to embark on their historic journey into the black hole, Dr. Hayes will lead them with courage, resilience, and a steadfast determination to unlock the secrets of the universe.

Until then, she continues to prepare, ensuring that they are ready for whatever challenges may lie ahead.

Lieutenant Commander Mark Thompson, a seasoned pilot and engineer, had a distinguished career as an aerospace engineer, specializing in spacecraft propulsion systems and design.

His journey began with academic excellence, pursuing aerospace engineering from a prestigious institution. During his studies, Mark demonstrated exceptional talent and interest in space exploration, leading to advanced training in spacecraft propulsion systems.

Mark's expertise quickly garnered attention, and he was recruited by leading aerospace companies for cutting-edge projects, designing and testing propulsion systems for spacecraft.

Alongside his engineering work, Mark obtained a pilot's license, logging countless flight hours, providing valuable insights for his astronaut role.

Driven by a desire for exploration, Mark applied to become an astronaut, leveraging his engineering and piloting background to join the mission team.

As launch approached, Mark, the second-in-command, remained focused, ready to embark on a journey into space's unknown depths.

As a skilled technician and communication specialist, Mark ensured crew connectivity with mission control and loved ones. His calm demeanor and problem-solving skills proved invaluable, making him a stalwart asset in navigating space's complexities.

A veteran astronaut and engineer, grew up on a remote farm, fostering a fascination with technology and aviation. Joining the space program as a pilot, he quickly distinguished himself with flying skills and problem- solving abilities, becoming a trusted leader amidst the mission's unknown dangers.

Dr. Emily Chen, Ph.D., a brilliant astrophysicist specializing in black hole research, dedicated years to advanced studies culminating in her doctorate from a prestigious institution renowned for its contributions to the field.

Throughout her academic journey, she delved deep into the cosmos' mysteries, focusing on black holes, gravitational dynamics, and fundamental aspects of the universe.

Her expertise quickly distinguished her as a leading expert, with numerous publications in prestigious scientific journals and presentations at international conferences.

Emily's research focused on understanding black holes' behavior, gravitational waves, and other cosmic phenomena, shedding light on the universe's enigmatic mysteries.

As the chief scientist onboard the spacecraft, Dr. Emily Chen brings her insatiable curiosity and keen intellect to drive the crew's quest for discovery. With her background in research and academia, she plays a vital role in unravelling the cosmos' mysteries and unlocking space's secrets.

Lieutenant Sarah Johnson brings a diverse background in technical disciplines to her role as communications and systems specialist on the mission.

Raised in a military family, she developed a strong sense of duty and discipline from an early age. Her journey into the space program began with rigorous education and hands-on practical experience, earning certifications in aerospace engineering and telecommunications.
Sarah's expertise spans a broad spectrum of technological domains, including satellite communication protocols, spacecraft telemetry systems, and emergency response procedures.

This comprehensive background equips her with the knowledge and proficiency needed to excel in her field, ensuring the seamless operation of critical systems and facilitating effective communication in various contexts.

As the communications and systems specialist, Sarah ensures seamless coordination between the crew and mission control. Her technical expertise and unwavering determination keep the spacecraft's vital systems running smoothly. With proficiency in communications systems and spacecraft operations, she plays a critical role in ensuring the mission's success.

With the countdown to launch underway, Sarah stands ready, knowing that her skills will be crucial in navigating the challenges ahead.

As the spacecraft embarks on its historic journey into the depths of a black hole, Sarah's dedication and expertise will be instrumental in guiding the crew safely through the unknown.

Together with her formidable team, including seasoned pilot and engineer Lieutenant Commander Mark Thompson, Dr. Chen leads scientific investigations onboard, analyzing data to unravel the mysteries of the cosmic abyss. United in their determination to push the boundaries of human exploration, they embark on a historic journey, ready to confront whatever challenges the cosmos has in store.

Standing together on the lunar surface, surrounded by the desolate expanse of the moon's landscape, the crew of the moon base finds themselves enveloped in the eerie glow of distant stars against the pitch-black canvas of space.

Commander Dr. Elizabeth Hayes leads the team, her resolve unwavering as they prepare to embark on a historic journey into the unknown.

Despite the absence of Earth's direct light, the crew feels a palpable sense of connection to their distant home planet, knowing it lies beyond the moon's horizon.

United by their shared passion for exploration and thirst for knowledge, they stand ready to confront the challenges that await them. For the past few years, they have devoted themselves to rigorous training, immersing themselves in simulations, physical conditioning, and mental preparation.

Each member of the crew has honed their skills, mastering the intricacies of spacecraft operation and the nuances of navigating through space.

Their mission is anything but ordinary—it represents the culmination of decades of scientific inquiry and technological innovation. The prospect of venturing into the heart of a black hole, where the laws of physics are pushed to their limits, fills the crew with a mixture of excitement and trepidation.

Yet, it is precisely this sense of awe-inspiring challenge that drives them forward. Together, Commander Hayes, Lieutenant Commander Thompson, Dr. Chen, and Lieutenant Johnson form a formidable team, ready to confront the mysteries of the cosmos and push the boundaries of human knowledge.

As they stand beneath the towering spires of the moon base, a silent witness to the audacious endeavor about to unfold, the crew feels a profound sense of awe mingled with anticipation.

The lunar landscape stretches out before them, a vast expanse of rugged terrain and barren plains, serving as a poignant reminder of the vastness and unforgiving nature of space.

Yet, amidst this desolate backdrop, the crew finds a sense of purpose and unity—a shared commitment to explore the uncharted realms of the cosmos and unravel the mysteries that lie beyond.
Each member of the team feels a deep connection to the stars, fueled by a burning curiosity and an insatiable thirst for knowledge.

Their journey will take them to the very edge of human understanding, where the fabric of space and time bends and warps in ways that defy comprehension. They will confront extreme gravitational forces, time dilation effects, and the unknown phenomena that lurk within the depths of the black hole. But they will also embrace the boundless potential for discovery and enlightenment that awaits them—a chance to peer into the cosmic unknown and glimpse the secrets of the universe.

As they make their final preparations, checking and double-checking every system and procedure, the crew is keenly aware of the risks that lie ahead.

They know that their mission is fraught with danger, and that success is far from guaranteed. Yet, they also know that the pursuit of knowledge requires courage, determination, and a willingness to confront the unknown head-on.

With hearts full of hope and minds ablaze with possibility, they stand ready to embark on the greatest adventure of their lives—a journey into the cosmic abyss, where humanity's dreams of exploration and discovery will take flight once more.

Together, they will push the boundaries of what is known and venture into the unknown, carrying with them the hopes and aspirations of all humankind.

Chapter 4:
Departure from Moon Base

The lunar base is a marvel of modern engineering, carefully constructed to withstand the harsh conditions of the lunar environment while serving as a hub for humanity's exploration of space. Situated amidst the desolate grandeur of the lunar landscape, the base represents a beacon of progress and possibility, offering a gateway to the stars.

From the outside, the base's sleek, metallic structures gleam in the sunlight, their futuristic design standing out against the barren expanse of the lunar surface. These structures have been meticulously engineered to provide a safe and habitable environment for the crew, with reinforced walls and advanced life support systems to protect against the vacuum of space and the extremes of temperature on the moon.

Solar panels adorn the surface of the base, their photovoltaic cells soaking up the sun's energy and converting it into electricity to power the base's operations. These panels are a vital lifeline for the crew, providing the energy needed to run essential systems, such as lighting, heating, and life support, as well as to recharge the batteries of the rovers used for exploration.

Rising above the base are communication antennas, their

slender forms reaching skyward like outstretched arms. These antennas serve as the lifeline between the lunar outpost and mission control on Earth via the satellite's, enabling real-time communication and data transmission between the three locations. Through these antennas, the crew can stay connected with their colleagues on Earth, receive critical updates and instructions, and share their discoveries and experiences with the rest of humanity.

Despite the harsh and inhospitable nature of the lunar environment, the base stands as a testament to human ingenuity and determination. It represents a symbol of our species' relentless pursuit of knowledge and exploration, as well as our capacity to overcome the most daunting challenges in our quest to reach for the stars. And as humanity's next great adventure begins to unfold, the lunar base stands ready to serve as a launching pad for the dreams and aspirations of generations to come.

In the bustling hub of the moon base, where organized chaos reigns supreme, there is an unmistakable buzz of anticipation and vitality. Engineers dart back and forth with purpose, their actions precise and methodical as they put the finishing touches on equipment and conduct meticulous checks to ensure everything is in perfect working order.

Each movement is a testament to their expertise and dedication, fueled by the knowledge that the success of the upcoming mission depends on their meticulous preparations.

Meanwhile, one group of scientists congregates around computer terminals, their focus laser sharp as they pore over data and run simulations in anticipation of what lies ahead.

With eyes fixed on the screens before them, they dissect every piece of information, searching for insights and patterns that could prove invaluable once they embark on their journey into the unknown depths of space.

In a quiet corner of the bustling hub, a team of astronauts gathers around a holographic map, their expressions a mixture of excitement and determination. They discuss strategy and review mission objectives with a sense of purpose, each member bringing their unique expertise to the table.

Despite the weight of the task that lies ahead, there is an undeniable camaraderie among the crew, forged through years of training and shared experiences.
As they prepare to venture into the uncharted territory of the cosmos, the astronauts draw strength from one another, knowing that they are part of something greater than themselves.

Theirs is a mission fueled not only by a thirst for discovery but also by a deep sense of camaraderie and unity—a bond that will carry them through the trials and tribulations that await them on their epic journey into the unknown.

In the heart of the bustling command center lies a spacious recreational area, meticulously designed to cater to the diverse interests and preferences of the astronauts stationed at the moon base.

Here, amidst the hum of activity and the glow of monitors, crew members find sanctuary from the rigors of their mission, engaging in a variety of leisure pursuits to unwind and rejuvenate.

At the center of this dynamic space sits a grand chessboard, its polished surface gleaming under the soft glow of overhead lights. Magnetic chess pieces rest upon the board, poised for battle, each move a strategic calculation in the timeless game of intellect and skill. Surrounding the chessboard are comfortable seating arrangements, inviting crew members to gather and engage in friendly matches that test their tactical prowess and strategic acumen.

Adjacent to the chess area, a vibrant games room buzzes with energy as crew members come together to partake in a myriad of recreational activities. Zero-gravity basketball hoops hang from the ceiling, providing the backdrop for exhilarating matches where players defy gravity to score points and showcase their agility and coordination.

Nearby, virtual reality consoles transport participants to

immersive digital worlds, offering an escape from the confines of their lunar surroundings and a chance to explore fantastical realms limited only by imagination.

In another corner of the recreational space, a serene activity room provides a peaceful retreat for crew members seeking moments of introspection and relaxation.

Here, amidst tranquil surroundings, astronauts can engage in quiet pursuits such as reading, painting, or practicing mindfulness exercises like yoga and meditation. The soft lighting and comfortable furnishings create an atmosphere conducive to reflection and rejuvenation, allowing crew members to recharge their spirits and find balance amidst the demands of their mission.

Throughout the recreational center, camaraderie flourishes as crew members bond over shared experiences and interests. Whether engaging in spirited competition on the chessboard, testing their skills in the games room, or finding solace in the quiet tranquility of the activity room, astronauts forge deep connections that transcend the challenges of space exploration.

In this vibrant hub of leisure and camaraderie, the bonds of friendship grow stronger, uniting the crew as they embark on their journey through the cosmos.

In the midst of the lunar base's bustling operations, a proposal emerged from the science community, captivating the attention of mission control.

The idea? The construction of a multi-purpose underground facility right there on the lunar surface. While the lunar base had already been established for practical purposes, this proposal promised to elevate its significance to new heights.

The scientists presented a compelling case for the underground facility, emphasizing its potential to not only enhance the physical fitness and wellbeing of lunar inhabitants but also to serve as a center for scientific exploration and research.

They highlighted the unique opportunity to study human performance in low-gravity environments, providing invaluable insights for future space missions and habitat design.

As the proposal took shape, discussions in mission control buzzed with excitement and anticipation. Engineers and scientists collaborated to flesh out the details, envisioning a facility equipped with cutting-edge research equipment and versatile recreational spaces.

Plans were drawn up to ensure that the facility could accommodate a diverse range of sports and physical activities, fostering a sense of community and camaraderie among lunar residents.

The underground facility was not just seen as a practical

addition to the lunar base—it was viewed as a beacon of innovation and progress, symbolizing humanity's relentless pursuit of knowledge and exploration.

With each step forward, the vision of the multi-purpose underground facility grew clearer, promising to transform the lunar base into a hub of scientific discovery and human ingenuity amidst the vast lunar landscape.

In the bustling hub of the moon base, anticipation hangs thick in the air, electrifying the atmosphere with an undeniable energy. Every corner of the space hums with activity as crew members prepare for the impending mission.

Engineers conduct final checks on equipment, ensuring that every component is in optimal condition for the journey ahead.

Meanwhile, astronauts don their suits and perform last-minute readiness drills, mentally preparing themselves for the challenges that lie ahead.

Commander Dr. Elizabeth Hayes stands at the center of it all, a commanding figure amidst the bustling activity of the mission preparations. Her presence radiates authority and leadership, anchoring the team with her unwavering determination and expertise. As she oversees the final preparations and discussions, her calm demeanor instils confidence and reassurance in her crew.

With each directive she issues, Commander Hayes's voice carries a sense of clarity and purpose, cutting through the chaos of the moment.

Her years of experience in space exploration are evident in every word and gesture, guiding her team with a steady hand and a sharp mind. As she addresses her crew, her words resonate with wisdom and insight, inspiring them to rise to the challenges that lie ahead.

Amidst the flurry of activity, Commander Hayes remains a steadfast presence, her unwavering focus a testament to her commitment to the mission's success. With her at the helm, the crew finds strength and determination, ready to embark on their journey into the unknown under her steady guidance.

While on board the spacecraft, Commander Dr. Elizabeth Hayes maintains a vigilant watch over every aspect of the mission. From the control center of the spacecraft, she oversees the crew's activities and monitors the vital systems with meticulous attention to detail.

Beside her, Lieutenant Commander Mark Thompson moves with the quiet efficiency of a seasoned professional, his hands deftly navigating the controls of their spacecraft. As the mission's second-in-command, Lieutenant Commander Thompson brings a wealth of knowledge and expertise to the table, his sharp mind and quick reflexes honed through years of training and experience. With a keen eye for detail and a knack for problem-solving, he ensures that every aspect of the mission is meticulously planned and executed, leaving nothing to chance.

Dr. Emily Chen, Ph.D., the mission's chief scientist, is deeply engrossed in her work, her mind a whirlwind of calculations and hypotheses. Surrounded by banks of computer screens and scientific equipment, she pores over reams of data, analyzing every piece of information with laser- like focus.

Her passion for astrophysics and her insatiable curiosity drives her to push the boundaries of human knowledge, eager to unlock the secrets of the universe that lie beyond the reaches of the moon.

Together, the crew of four stands on the threshold of history, poised to embark on a journey that will push the boundaries of human exploration.

As they make their final preparations, the anticipation builds a palpable energy that fuels their determination to chart a course into the unknown depths of space. With hearts full of courage and minds ablaze with possibility, they are ready to embark on their unprecedented mission, ready to make their mark on the annals of space exploration.

The crew members exchange final nods and words of encouragement as they strap themselves into their seats, their hearts beating with a mix of excitement and apprehension. Outside the spacecraft's windows, the lunar landscape stretches out in all directions, a stark reminder of the unforgiving environment they are leaving behind.

Inside the cramped confines of the spacecraft's cockpit, the air is exciting with anticipation as the crew runs through their pre-flight checklists one last time.

But even as she marvels at the celestial spectacle before her, Dr. Chen remains grounded in her purpose. With a deep breath, she turns away from the viewport and refocuses her attention on her console, the array of instruments and monitors awaiting her command.

As the mission's chief scientist, she carries the weight of responsibility on her shoulders—the responsibility to unlock the secrets of the universe and further humanity's understanding of the cosmos.

With steady hands and a sharp mind, Dr. Chen begins her work, initiating data collection protocols and conducting experiments that will yield valuable insights into the nature of the cosmos.

Each observation, each measurement, brings humanity one step closer to unravelling the mysteries of the universe, and Dr. Chen is determined to make every moment count.

As she delves deeper into her research, Dr. Chen's passion for discovery burns brightly within her, driving her to push the boundaries of human knowledge and understanding. With each new discovery, she knows that she is contributing to something greater than herself—to a legacy of exploration and enlightenment that will endure long after she has returned home. And so, with a sense of purpose and determination, Dr. Chen sets out to chart a course through the stars, guided by her insatiable curiosity and her unwavering commitment to the pursuit of truth.

Lieutenant Sarah Johnson sits at her station, her gaze focused on the array of controls before her. With practiced precision, her fingers hover over the communications panel, ready to spring into action at a moment's notice.

As the designated communications and systems specialist, she understands the critical role she plays in keeping the crew connected and informed throughout their perilous journey.

With a nod of silent determination, Lieutenant Johnson reaffirms her commitment to the task at hand. She knows that the success of the mission depends on her ability to maintain clear and constant communication with mission control and her fellow crew members.

In the vast expanse of space, where danger lurks around every corner, the ability to relay vital information and coordinate actions is paramount. As the countdown to liftoff ticks steadily onward, the hub becomes a hive of focused activity.

Each member of the crew is keenly aware of the significance of the mission, and their determination to succeed fuels their every action. Despite the gravity of the task at hand, there is an undeniable sense of excitement and possibility in the air—a shared belief that, together, they are embarking on a journey that will change the course of history.

As the countdown to launch ticks away, Lieutenant Johnson remains vigilant, her focus unwavering as she monitors the intricate network of communication systems.

Each beep and blip that emanates from the control panel is a testament to her diligence and expertise, a reminder of the vital role she plays in the success of the mission.

With steady hands and a calm demeanor, Lieutenant Johnson stands ready to face whatever challenges lie ahead. She knows that the journey into the unknown will test her resolve and her skills like never before, but she is prepared to rise to the occasion.

With her fingers poised over the controls, she awaits the call to action, ready to fulfil her duty and ensure the safety and success of her fellow crew members. As the countdown reaches its ultimate moments, a palpable sense of anticipation fills the cramped confines of the cockpit.

The crew members exchange determined glances, their hearts pounding in unison as they brace themselves for the momentous journey ahead. With a resolute nod, Lieutenant Commander Thompson takes his position at the controls, his hands steady and his focus unwavering.

As the last moments of the countdown tick away, a palpable tension grips the hub, each second feeling like an eternity. Then, with a thunderous roar that reverberates through the chamber, the spacecraft's engines ignite, casting a brilliant glow against the lunar surface.

The crew feels the powerful surge of acceleration as the craft begins its graceful ascent, leaving behind a trail of dust and debris in its wake.

Inside the cockpit, the crew's hearts race with a heady mix of anticipation, excitement, and a tinge of apprehension. They have trained for this moment tirelessly, honing their skills and preparing for the challenges that lie ahead.

As the moon base shrinks into the distance below, they are acutely aware of the magnitude of their mission. They are not just leaving the moon's surface; they are embarking on a journey that will push the boundaries of human exploration and redefine our understanding of the cosmos.

In the control room, cheers erupt as the spacecraft lifts off successfully, marking the beginning of a new chapter in humanity's quest for knowledge.

But amidst the celebration, there is a sense of solemnity, a recognition of the risks and uncertainties that accompany space travel. The crew knows that they are venturing into the unknown, where every decision could mean the difference between success and failure.

As the spacecraft climbs higher into the lunar sky, the crew cannot help but marvel at the breathtaking view unfolding before them.

The rugged terrain of the moon stretches out below, bathed in the soft glow of Earth's distant light. It is a sight that never fails to inspire awe, a reminder of the beauty and majesty of the universe.

But there is no time to dwell on the scenery. With the engines roaring and the spacecraft hurtling through space, the crew's focus shifts to the tasks at hand.

They must ensure that every system is functioning perfectly, that every maneuver is executed with precision. Their training has prepared them for this moment, but they know that the real challenges lie ahead, as they journey deeper into the cosmos, into the unknown.

With every passing moment, the moon's surface grows smaller below them, gradually fading into the distance as they soar higher into the cosmos. The stars twinkle in the darkness beyond the viewport, their distant light beckoning the crew onward towards the unknown.

As the spacecraft climbs higher and higher, leaving the lunar surface far behind, a sense of awe and wonder washes over the crew, mingled with a steely resolve to face whatever challenges lie ahead.

For Lieutenant Commander Thompson, this is more than just a mission— it is a testament to the indomitable spirit of human exploration. With each passing moment, he steers the spacecraft ever closer to their destination, his hands steady and his determination unyielding. As they hurtle through the void of space, he remains the steadfast guide, leading his crew towards the ultimate frontier with courage and conviction.

As the spacecraft leaves the familiar lunar landscape behind and ventures deeper into the uncharted depths of space towards Sagittarius A*, the supermassive black hole at the heart of the Milky Way galaxy, the crew's anticipation and apprehension mingle with a sense of awe and determination.

In the vast expanse of space, where the laws of physics bend and reality itself seems to warp, the crew knows that they are embarking on a journey that will push the limits of human exploration to their very edge.

They understand the immense risks and challenges that lie ahead, yet they are undeterred, powered by their shared passion for discovery and their unwavering commitment to advancing the frontiers of knowledge.

Each member of the crew is acutely aware of the gravity of their mission— both literally and figuratively.

As they hurtle through the void of space towards the enigmatic black hole, they know that they are venturing into the unknown, where the very fabric of space and time is warped beyond comprehension.

Yet, amidst the uncertainty and the ever-present dangers that lurk in the cosmic abyss, there is also a palpable sense of excitement and possibility. For the crew, this mission represents the culmination of years of training, preparation, and sacrifice—a chance to make history and unravel the greatest mysteries of the universe.

As they journey deeper into the heart of the galaxy, the crew draws strength from their shared sense of purpose and camaraderie. Each member brings their own unique skills and expertise to the table, contributing to the collective effort to unlock the secrets of Sagittarius A* and broaden humanity's understanding of the cosmos.

Together, they press onward, their resolve unshakable,

their spirits undaunted. For they know that beyond the event horizon of the black hole lies a realm of infinite possibility, where the boundaries of what is known and what is possible blur into insignificance.

And it is there, in the shadowy depths of the cosmic abyss, that they will find the answers they seek, waiting to be discovered amidst the swirling maelstrom of space and time.

Commander Dr. Elizabeth Hayes, her voice calm and resolute, guides the crew with steady assurance, instilling confidence, and unity among her team. As the leader of the mission, she understands the importance of maintaining morale and ensuring that each member of the crew feels supported and cared for.

Lieutenant Commander Mark Thompson, his hands steady on the controls, navigates the spacecraft with precision and skill, charting a course through the cosmic unknown with unwavering focus. His expertise in piloting and engineering proves invaluable as the crew traverses the vast expanse of space towards their destination.

As the hours stretch by and the journey to Sagittarius A* stretches on, Commander Hayes takes a moment to address the crew on the intercom. "Attention, everyone," she announces, her voice calm but authoritative.

"I know it's going to be a long journey, and we still have a way to go before we reach our destination. But I wanted to remind you all to take care of yourselves. It's important to stay hydrated and nourished, even in the midst of our mission."

She pauses, allowing her words to sink in before continuing. "Lieutenant Johnson, could you please arrange for some food and drinks to be brought to the crew quarters? Let's make sure everyone has a chance to refuel and recharge before we press on, put it on auto Pilot for now."

With a nod of acknowledgment, Lieutenant Johnson sets to work, coordinating with the rest of the crew to ensure that everyone's needs are met.

As the crew members take a moment to eat, drink, and relax, they are reminded of the importance of looking out for one another and supporting each other through the challenges that lie ahead.

And with renewed energy and determination, they prepare to continue their journey into the cosmic unknown, united in their quest to unlock the secrets of the universe.

Dr. Emily Chen, Ph.D., her mind ablaze with scientific curiosity, eagerly awaits the opportunity to study the black hole up close.

As the mission's chief scientist, her expertise in astrophysics is poised to unlock the secrets of this enigmatic cosmic phenomenon. With each passing moment, Dr. Chen's anticipation grows, fueled by the prospect of analyzing data and conducting experiments that could reshape humanity's understanding of the universe.

Lieutenant Sarah Johnson, her technical prowess matched only by her unwavering determination, plays a critical role in ensuring the spacecraft's vital systems remain stable amidst the turbulent forces of space.

As the communications and systems specialist, she maintains constant vigilance, monitoring every aspect of the spacecraft's functionality with meticulous attention to detail. With her steady hand and quick thinking, Lieutenant Johnson instils confidence in her fellow crew members, knowing that their safety and success depend on her expertise and unwavering commitment to duty.

As the ship ventures into space, the crew maintains constant radio contact thanks to the innovative infrared radio technology onboard.

This innovative communication system ensures seamless communication between the spacecraft and mission control on the moon and Earth, allowing for real-time updates, coordination of activities, and immediate responses to any unforeseen challenges or emergencies.

With the reliability of the infrared radio, the crew can stay connected with ground control throughout their journey, providing reassurance and support as they push further into the depths of space.

Together, the crew of the spacecraft presses onward, their hearts filled with a sense of purpose and adventure as they journey towards the black hole.

With each passing moment, they draw closer to the ultimate frontier of human exploration, ready to confront whatever challenges and mysteries await them in the depths of Sagittarius A*.

Chapter 5:
Intergalactic Travel

From the lunar base three ships were commissioned and prepared for voyages to distant planets within our galaxy and beyond.

Each spacecraft represents the pinnacle of human engineering and ingenuity, meticulously designed, and outfitted for the rigors of long- duration space travel.

Powered by the revolutionary nuclear reactors developed for the Lunar Advanced Telescope project, these ships boast unprecedented range and endurance, capable of traversing the vast distances between celestial bodies with remarkable speed and efficiency.

As the crews of these pioneering vessels prepare for their journeys, anticipation and excitement fill the air.

For the astronauts selected to embark on these historic missions, the opportunity to explore distant planets represents the culmination of a lifetime of training and dedication. With their expertise in a wide range of scientific disciplines, from astronomy and geology to biology and robotics, these intrepid explorers stand ready to unlock the mysteries of the cosmos and chart a course towards humanity's future among the stars.

Each ship was equipped with two reactors, ensuring redundancy and reliability in the event of unforeseen challenges during the voyage.

This redundancy was essential for maintaining power and propulsion systems throughout the mission, providing the crews with the confidence and reassurance needed to undertake the monumental task of interstellar exploration.

With their nuclear reactors as the beating heart of their vessels, the crews set forth into the unknown, propelled by the boundless spirit of human curiosity and the relentless pursuit of knowledge.

From the frozen wastes of ice-covered moons to the scorching deserts of distant exoplanets, each destination offers its own unique challenges and opportunities for discovery.

Whether searching for signs of extraterrestrial life, studying the geology and climate of alien worlds, or prospecting for valuable resources to support future colonization efforts, the crews of these interstellar vessels are prepared to expand our understanding of the universe and pave the way for humanity's continued exploration and expansion into space.

As the countdown to launch begins and the engines roar to life, the crews of these interstellar ships embark on a journey into the unknown, driven by an insatiable thirst for knowledge and a boundless spirit of adventure.

With the vast expanse of the cosmos stretching out before them, they set their course for distant planets and uncharted territories, ready to push the boundaries of human exploration and unlock the secrets of the universe.

These sleek spacecrafts, their hulls gleaming in the lunar sunlight, stand poised at the launchpad of the moon base, ready to embark on humanity's boldest adventure yet. Each vessel represents the pinnacle of human engineering, outfitted with advanced propulsion systems, state-of-the-art navigation equipment, and a complement of innovative scientific instruments.

With their crews assembled and their mission objectives set, they prepare to leave the safety of Earth's orbit behind and venture into the unknown depths of space.

Onboard the first spacecraft, named the "Venturer," a crew of seasoned astronauts awaits the signal for liftoff.

Commander Andy Spear is a seasoned veteran of space exploration, having dedicated his life to unravelling the mysteries of the cosmos.

With decades of experience in astrophysics and deep space missions, he brings a wealth of knowledge and expertise to the team.
Born and raised with a fascination for the stars, he

pursued a career in astronomy, earning advanced degrees in astrophysics from prestigious universities.

His passion for space exploration led him to join the ranks of elite astronauts, where he quickly distinguished himself as a natural leader and visionary thinker.

Throughout his illustrious career, has participated in numerous groundbreaking missions, from studying distant galaxies to exploring the outer reaches of the solar system.

His contributions to the field of astrophysics have earned him widespread acclaim and recognition, solidifying his reputation as one of the foremost experts in his field.

As the leader of the interstellar exploration team, Commander Spear brings a steady hand and calm demeanor to even the most challenging situations.

His ability to remain focused under pressure and make quick, informed decisions has earned him the respect and admiration of his colleagues.

Beyond his technical expertise, he is known for his unwavering dedication to the mission and the well-being of his crew. He fosters a culture of teamwork and collaboration, encouraging open communication and mutual support among team members.

With Commander Spear at the helm, the interstellar

exploration team is poised for success, ready to embark on a journey of discovery that will push the boundaries of human knowledge and redefine our understanding of the universe.

Lieutenant Mary Spiers is a distinguished geologist with a passion for unravelling the geological mysteries of celestial bodies.

With a keen eye for detail and a deep understanding of planetary processes, she is well-equipped to analyze the lunar surface and beyond. Her expertise in identifying rock formations, studying crater morphology, and interpreting geological features makes her an invaluable asset to the mission.

Dr. Mira Lucas is a robotics engineer of exceptional talent, specializing in the design and operation of advanced spacecraft systems.

With her technical prowess and problem-solving skills, she ensures the smooth operation of the spacecraft's intricate systems, from propulsion and navigation to life support and communications.

Her ability to troubleshoot technical challenges in real-time is crucial for the success of the mission, enabling the crew to overcome any obstacles they may encounter along the way.

Dr. Robert Vaughan is a renowned atmospheric scientist,

renowned for his expertise in studying the atmospheric dynamics and weather patterns of celestial bodies.

With his deep understanding of atmospheric processes, he provides invaluable insights into the environmental conditions of the planets and moons they may encounter during the mission.

His research informs critical decisions regarding landing site selection, atmospheric entry and exit strategies, and environmental monitoring, ensuring the safety and success of the crew's exploration efforts.

Together, this extraordinary team is poised to push the boundaries of human exploration, venturing into the unknown depths of space in search of new worlds, new discoveries, and perhaps even new forms of life.

As they embark on this monumental journey, they carry with them the hopes and aspirations of all humanity, united in their quest to unlock the secrets of the universe and chart a course towards a brighter future among the stars.

Onboard the second spacecraft, known as the "Pathfinder 2," a diverse and skilled crew of explorers eagerly awaits the commencement of their journey into the unknown.

Captain Miguel Diaz, a veteran space farer with numerous missions under his belt, brings a wealth of experience and expertise to the crew of the "Pathfinder

2." With a background in planetary geology, he has a keen eye for detail and a profound understanding of the geological processes that shape celestial bodies.

Having explored diverse terrains across the solar system, from the icy plains of Europa to the rugged mountains of Mars, he is well-equipped to lead the crew on their journey into the unknown.

His calm demeanor and decisive leadership style inspire confidence among his crewmates, instilling a sense of unity and purpose as they embark on their interstellar voyage.

As the captain of the "Pathfinder 2," he is responsible for overseeing all aspects of the mission, from navigation and resource management to crew morale and safety. His leadership is characterized by a careful balance of pragmatism and optimism, ensuring that the crew remains focused and motivated even in the face of adversity.

Beyond his role as captain, he also serves as the crew's resident expert in planetary geology, offering valuable insights into the geological features and formations they may encounter during their journey.

His knowledge of rock formations, crater morphology, and surface composition will prove invaluable in selecting landing sites and conducting scientific analyses of distant worlds.

With Captain Diaz at the helm, the crew of the "Pathfinder 2" is well- prepared to confront the challenges and opportunities that await them on their journey into the unknown. Together, they stand ready to push the boundaries of human exploration and expand humanity's understanding of the cosmos.

Lieutenant Commander Anna Patel, a highly skilled pilot and engineer, brings a wealth of technical expertise and a sharp intellect to the crew of the spacecraft.
With her extensive experience in spacecraft operations and engineering, she plays a critical role in ensuring the smooth operation of the spacecraft's intricate systems.

Her meticulous attention to detail and problem-solving abilities makes her an invaluable asset to the mission, as she navigates the challenges of interstellar travel with precision and efficiency.

Dr. Hiroto Oyama, Ph.D., an esteemed biologist specializing in exobiology, eagerly anticipates the opportunity to study potential extraterrestrial life forms and the unique ecosystems they may encounter during the mission.

With a keen interest in the origins of life and the potential for life beyond Earth he brings a deep understanding of biology and evolution to the crew, as well as a sense of wonder and curiosity about the mysteries of the cosmos.

His expertise will be instrumental in analyzing samples collected from distant worlds and identifying any signs of life or habitability.

Lieutenant Emma Rodriguez, a talented robotics engineer, stands ready to deploy and maintain the spacecraft's robotic explorers, leveraging her expertise to navigate and investigate the uncharted territories they will traverse.

With her keen problem-solving skills and innovative approach to robotics, she ensures that the spacecraft's robotic systems operate effectively in the harsh conditions of space, enabling the crew to gather valuable data and conduct scientific experiments with precision and accuracy.

Together, this dynamic and multidisciplinary team embodies humanity's spirit of exploration and collaboration, poised to push the boundaries of knowledge, and embark on a voyage of discovery that will shape the course of history.

With their diverse backgrounds and complementary skills, they stand ready to confront the challenges and opportunities of interstellar travel, united in their pursuit of unlocking the secrets of the universe.

Their mission: to venture to one of the exoplanets, seeking answers to age- old questions about the possibility of life beyond our solar system and expanding humanity's understanding of the cosmos.

Onboard the third spacecraft, christened the "Voyager," a seasoned crew of intrepid explorers prepares to embark on their extraordinary voyage into the depths of space.

At the helm of the spacecraft stands *Captain Alexei Ivanov*, a seasoned test pilot whose reputation precedes him in the annals of space exploration.

With a career marked by daring missions and remarkable feats of courage, he has earned a reputation as one of the finest pilots in the cosmos.

His steady hand and exceptional leadership have guided countless expeditions through the depths of space, earning him the trust and respect of his fellow crew members.

His journey to the helm of the spacecraft is a testament to his unwavering dedication and relentless pursuit of excellence.

Born and raised in a family of cosmonauts, he inherited a passion for space exploration from an early age. From his first flight in a homemade rocket to his years of training at the prestigious Cosmonaut Academy, he has always dreamed of reaching for the stars and exploring the unknown reaches of the universe.

Throughout his illustrious career, he has faced numerous challenges and overcome countless obstacles, demonstrating a resilience and determination that have become his trademark.

Whether navigating through treacherous asteroid fields or braving the intense radiation of a solar flare, he has always risen to the occasion with courage and grace, inspiring those around him to push the boundaries of human achievement.

Being the leader of the spacecraft's mission, his leadership is put to the test like never before.

With the fate of the crew and the success of the mission resting on his shoulders, he must draw upon all of his experience and expertise to guide the spacecraft safely through the hazards of space and towards the distant stars beyond.

With his unwavering courage and exceptional leadership, Captain Ivanov stands ready to lead his crew into the unknown and write the next chapter in the history of space exploration.

Assisting him in navigating the vast expanse of space is *Lieutenant Commander Li Wei*, a consummate professional with a knack for charting precise courses through the cosmos.

With a background in both navigation and engineering,

he brings a unique blend of technical expertise and strategic thinking to the mission. His meticulous approach to planning and execution ensures the crew's safe passage through the myriad hazards of space, from asteroid fields to gravitational anomalies.

Dr. Natalia Petrovna, Ph.D., adds a wealth of scientific expertise to the team as the mission's atmospheric scientist.

With a deep understanding of atmospheric dynamics and climate science, she is eager to study the atmospheres of distant worlds and unravel the mysteries of their weather patterns.

Her keen analytical mind and insatiable curiosity drive her quest to uncover the secrets hidden within the swirling clouds and turbulent winds of alien worlds.

Last but not least is *Lieutenant Zhang Wei*, a specialist in remote sensing and data analysis. With a keen eye for detail and a talent for interpreting complex data sets, he plays a crucial role in collecting and analyzing the vast amounts of information gathered during the mission.

From mapping the surface features of distant planets to monitoring changes in their atmospheric composition, his expertise ensures that no detail goes unnoticed in the quest to unravel the mysteries of the universe.

Together, they form a formidable team of explorers,

united by their shared determination to push the boundaries of human knowledge and unravel the mysteries of the universe.

With their combined skills and expertise, they stand ready to embark on humanity's boldest adventure yet, charting a course through the cosmos in search of answers to the deepest questions of existence.

As they prepare to embark on their voyage of discovery, they stand ready to confront the challenges and wonders that await them, forging a path into the unknown with courage, curiosity, and camaraderie.

Their mission: to explore an exoplanet, expanding humanity's understanding of the cosmos. As the countdown reaches its last moments and the engines roar to life.

With a thunderous roar, the vessels lift off from the lunar surface, leaving behind a plume of dust and debris as they ascend into the star-speckled expanse of space.

Guided by the unwavering spirit of exploration and fueled by the promise of discovery, the crews of the Venturer, Pathfinder, and Voyager set their sights on the distant planets that await them, ready to embark on an epic journey into the unknown.

Together, they represent humanity's boundless ambition and insatiable curiosity, poised to push the boundaries of human knowledge, and unlock the secrets of the cosmos.

With each spacecraft carrying a diverse and skilled crew, equipped with advanced technology, and fueled by a shared sense of purpose, they venture forth into the vast expanse of space, prepared to face the challenges and wonders that lie ahead.

Their mission is not just a voyage of exploration, but a testament to the enduring spirit of humanity's quest for understanding and discovery.

Chapter 6:
Approaching the Event Horizon

As the crew's spacecraft edges closer to the colossal presence of the black hole, they are enveloped in a surreal panorama of cosmic grandeur.

The event horizon looms ominously before them, a boundary that marks the point of no return, where the laws of physics begin to unravel in the face of unfathomable gravitational forces.

The crew members can sense the Immense power emanating from the black hole, its gravitational pull tugging at their very essence. Space itself seems to warp and distort around them, as if the fabric of reality is being stretched to its limits.

Despite the inherent dangers and uncertainties that lie ahead, the crew is filled with a mixture of awe and excitement. They understand the magnitude of the moment, realizing that they are on the cusp of a discovery that could reshape their understanding of the universe.

Each member of the crew is acutely aware of the historic significance of their mission. They are not just embarking on a journey into the unknown; they are charting new frontiers of human knowledge and exploration.

And as they stand on the precipice of the black hole's event horizon, they are ready to face whatever challenges may come their way in their quest for understanding and discovery.

As the crew approaches the black hole, Dr. Emily Chen, Ph.D., meticulously analyses the data and proposes a strategic course of action.

Her suggestion to position the spacecraft at the center of the gravitational singularity resonates with the crew, as they recognize the critical importance of such a maneuver.

Commander Dr. Elizabeth Hayes wholeheartedly supports Dr. Chen's plan, acknowledging its significance for the success and safety of their mission.

Her authoritative tone reassures the crew, instilling confidence in their leader's decision-making.

Lieutenant Commander Thompson, entrusted with the responsibility of adjusting the spacecraft's trajectory, responds with precision and efficiency.

With each calculated maneuver, he navigates the crew closer to their objective, ensuring they remain on course to reach the center of the black hole's gravitational pull unscathed.

As the crew stands on the precipice of the black hole's

domain, a profound sense of awe and trepidation washes over them. They are acutely aware of the gravity of their mission, both metaphorically and literally, as they prepare to venture into the unknown depths of Sagittarius A*, the supermassive black hole at the heart of the Milky Way galaxy.

In this pivotal moment, surrounded by the vast expanse of space, each member of the crew takes a moment to reflect on the magnitude of what lies ahead. They understand that they are on the verge of embarking on a journey that will test the limits of human understanding and redefine the boundaries of exploration. It is a journey that promises to unveil the secrets of the universe and reshape our perception of reality itself.

As the spacecraft approaches the unfathomable depths of the black hole, the crew senses the gravitational forces intensifying, drawing them closer to the ominous event horizon—the boundary beyond which no escape is possible.

The fabric of space-time itself seems to contort and bend around them, distorting their perceptions and challenging their understanding of the laws of physics.

With the gravity of the black hole looming ominously ahead, the crew realizes that it is time to relay their findings and status to mission control. Despite the trepidation coursing through their veins, they maintain their composure and initiate contact with ground control.

Half-hourly check-ins take on a newfound urgency as the crew updates mission control on their proximity to the black hole and the increasingly intense gravitational forces affecting their spacecraft.

Through the veil of distortion and uncertainty, the crew relies on both traditional radio and advanced infrared communication systems to convey the gravity of their situation.

For the crew, the reassuring voices of mission control provide a semblance of stability amidst the chaos of their descent towards the event horizon.

With each transmission, they draw strength from the unwavering support and expertise of their counterparts on Earth, knowing that they are not alone in confronting the mysteries and perils of the cosmos.

Yet, amidst the turmoil of cosmic forces, the crew remains resolute. They are driven by a shared sense of purpose and a collective thirst for knowledge.

Each member understands the risks involved, but they are undeterred, their spirits buoyed by the possibility of making groundbreaking discoveries that will shape the course of humanity's future.

With every passing moment, the crew draws closer to the threshold of the black hole, their hearts beating in unison with the rhythm of the universe itself.

They are prepared to confront whatever challenges await them, knowing that their journey holds the potential to unlock the mysteries of existence and illuminate the darkest corners of the cosmos.

Inside the vessel, the crew braces themselves for the disorienting sensation of crossing into the black hole's domain. As they peer out through the viewports, the surrounding space undergoes a surreal transformation. The stars, once distant points of light, now streak past in long arcs, their trajectories warped by the immense gravitational field of the black hole.

The spacecraft shudders as it encounters the boundary of the event horizon, the point of no return.

Gravity pulls relentlessly at the vessel, distorting its shape and sending ripples through its hull.

The crew members feel the weight of the universe pressing down upon them, their bodies subjected to forces beyond comprehension.

Suddenly, the spacecraft lurches, its trajectory veering off course as it succumbs to the black hole's gravitational grip.

The crew members cling to their seats, their senses overwhelmed by the disorienting motion. Outside, the stars blur into streaks of light, swirling around the spacecraft in a mesmerizing dance orchestrated by the forces of spacetime.

Despite the chaos unfolding around them, the crew remains focused on their mission. They know that they are on the threshold of a monumental discovery, and they are determined to see it through to the end.

With nerves of steel and unwavering resolve, they steel themselves for the challenges that lie ahead as they plunge deeper into the heart of the black hole.

The gravitational forces intensify, pulling at the fabric of their spacecraft and distorting the very essence of space and time around them.

Yet, even as they confront the terrifying unknown that lies ahead, they remain resolute in their determination to unlock the secrets of the cosmos, prepared to face whatever challenges await them on the other side.

As they approach the event horizon, the crew witnesses a mesmerizing transformation in the surrounding space.

The light emitted by distant stars and galaxies undergoes a profound metamorphosis as it struggles against the relentless grip of the black hole's gravity.

What was once a steady stream of photons now appearing fragmented and scattered, bent by the curvature of spacetime like a river flowing around a massive boulder.

It is a surreal spectacle, a visual testament to the immense power wielded by the cosmic behemoth before them.

Despite the awe-inspiring and somewhat terrifying nature of their surroundings, the crew remains focused on their mission.

Their hearts beat with determination, their minds sharpened by the anticipation of discovery.

They know that they are on the brink of a momentous breakthrough—one that could revolutionize humanity's understanding of the cosmos and reshape the course of scientific history. With nerves of steel and unwavering resolve, they press forward, ready to confront whatever challenges and revelations await them on the other side of the event horizon.

For in the face of the unknown, it is their courage and curiosity that will guide them through the depths of the cosmic abyss.

As they venture deeper into the unknown, the crew members feel the subtle yet profound effects of the black hole's gravitational field permeating their spacecraft.

The instruments aboard the vessel buzz with activity, registering fluctuations and anomalies in the surrounding space. Commander Hayes, her brow furrowed in concentration, leads the team with a steady hand, making calculated adjustments to their course to navigate through the turbulent currents of spacetime.

Inside the spacecraft, tension hangs palpably in the air, mingling with the electric anticipation of discovery.

Each crew member is acutely aware of the gravity of their mission—both figuratively and literally—as they inch closer to the event horizon, the threshold of the black hole's domain.

Yet, despite the weight of the moment, their spirits remain buoyant with the thrill of exploration and the promise of unveiling the secrets of the cosmos.

Outside the viewports, the fabric of space warps and bends, distorting the familiar backdrop of stars and galaxies into surreal shapes and patterns.

The crew members watch in awe as the laws of physics appear to unravel before their eyes, a testament to the unfathomable power wielded by the celestial giant looming before them.

With each passing moment, their resolve is tested, yet strengthened by the enormity of the challenge they face. They are pioneers, daring to venture where few have gone before, driven by an unyielding determination to unravel the mysteries of the universe and expand the boundaries of human knowledge.

And so, with hearts filled with anticipation and minds honed with focus, they press onward, ready to confront whatever mysteries await them beyond the event horizon of the black hole.

For they are not merely passengers on this cosmic journey—they are explorers, driven by an insatiable thirst for knowledge and a boundless curiosity about the universe and all its wonders.

Commander Hayes's voice cuts through the tense silence inside the spacecraft, her words echoing with a sense of urgency and determination. "We're approaching the critical point," she announces, her eyes fixed on the swirling vortex of the black hole ahead.

"This is where we encounter Spaghettification—the phenomenon where the immense gravitational forces stretch any object, including our spacecraft, into long, thin strands like spaghetti. Hence the name."

The crew exchanges nervous glances, fully aware of the peril that lies ahead. Lieutenant Johnson's fingers hover over the control panel, ready to implement the commander's orders at a moment's notice.

"We'll need to divert all available power to the warp engines," Commander Hayes continues, her voice unwavering.

"We cannot afford to linger here. If we are to have any chance of navigating through this without being torn apart, we need to go through at warp speed."

As Commander Hayes speaks, the crew members' training kicks in, and they spring into action, swiftly adjusting the spacecraft's systems for the imminent encounter with Spaghettification.

With each member keenly aware that the mission's success hinges on flawless execution under immense pressure, they work with determination and steely resolve.

With a collective nod, they synchronize their efforts, each member conducting their assigned tasks with precision and focus. Lieutenant Johnson directs power to the warp engines, while Dr. Chen diligently monitors the spacecraft's structural integrity, ensuring it can withstand the forthcoming onslaught of forces.

United in purpose, they stand ready to confront whatever challenges the black hole may present, determined to emerge victorious.

As the spacecraft hurtles towards the event horizon, the crew braces themselves for the intense ordeal ahead. The gravitational forces grow stronger with each passing moment, threatening to tear them apart at the molecular level.

As Commander Hayes presses the button to increase speed, the spacecraft responds with a surge of acceleration, propelling them deeper into the gravitational well of the black hole.

Inside the vessel, the crew members feel the subtle shift in momentum, a sensation akin to being pushed back into their seats as the spacecraft hurtles forward.

As they plunge deeper into the black hole's domain, the crew is confronted with a surreal spectacle unlike anything they have ever experienced. Reality itself seems to warp and twist around them, with space and time intertwining in a mesmerizing dance of cosmic proportions.

Outside the viewports, the stars blur and streak, their light distorted into strange, mesmerizing patterns by the intense gravitational forces at play.

Inside the spacecraft, the crew watches in awe as the fabric of spacetime contorts and bends, creating a kaleidoscope of colors and shapes that defy comprehension.

Yet, despite the overwhelming strangeness of their surroundings, the crew remains focused on their mission, their resolve unyielding in the face of uncertainty.

With each passing moment, they draw nearer to the heart

of the black hole, driven by an insatiable thirst for knowledge and discovery.

As they hurtle towards the unknown depths of the black hole, Commander Hayes's voice cuts through the tension inside the spacecraft, her words a steady anchor amidst the chaos. "Hold on tight, everyone," she says, her tone calm yet determined.

"We're about to venture into uncharted territory, but together, we'll face whatever lies ahead." Despite the increasing intensity of the forces at play, Commander Hayes remains focused, her hands steady on the controls as she navigates the spacecraft through the swirling chaos of the black hole's gravitational field.

With each passing moment, the event horizon draws nearer, its ominous presence looming large on the viewscreens.

Lieutenant Commander Mark Thompson monitors the instrumentation, his eyes scanning the readouts for any signs of instability or danger.

Dr. Emily Chen, Ph.D., analyses the data streaming in from the sensors, her mind racing as she tries to make sense of the complex phenomena they are witnessing.

Lieutenant Sarah Johnson, her fingers flying across the control panel, ensures that the spacecraft's vital systems remain operational amidst the chaotic forces that surround them.

Together, they navigate through the cosmic minefield, their hearts filled with a mix of trepidation and excitement as they draw ever closer to the heart of the black hole.

Inside the spacecraft, the crew members feel the gravitational forces intensify, pressing down on them with an almost palpable weight.

Despite the immense strain, they remain focused on their tasks, their training and expertise guiding them through the treacherous environment of the black hole's domain.

Outside the viewports, the stars blur and streak, their light warped and distorted by the immense gravitational forces.

Space itself seems to twist and contort, bending around the spacecraft in strange and unpredictable ways.

Yet, amidst the chaos, the crew maintains their composure, their determination unwavering in the face of the unknown.

As the crew pushes deeper into the heart, the fabric of spacetime itself seems to warp and twist around them, distorting their perceptions of reality. Outside the viewports, the stars streak past in a dizzying blur, their light stretched and bent by the gravitational forces at play.

Yet, amidst the chaos and uncertainty, the crew remains resolute, united in their determination to unravel the mysteries of the black hole and emerge victorious on the other side.

With Commander Hayes at the helm, guiding them with skill and precision, they press forward into the unknown, their spirits undaunted by the challenges that lie ahead.

They are on the brink of entering a realm where the laws of physics cease to apply, where time and space become fluid concepts, and where the very nature of reality is called into question.

Through the viewport, the crew witnesses the surreal spectacle of the surrounding space warping and distorting, the stars and galaxies contorted into strange and unfamiliar shapes.

It is a sight that defies comprehension, challenging their understanding of the universe and pushing the limits of their imagination.

But even as they confront the unknown, the crew's resolve remains unshakeable. They are explorers, adventurers, driven by an insatiable curiosity to push the boundaries of human knowledge and understanding. And as they stand on the threshold of the black hole's event horizon, they know that they are on the cusp of a discovery that will change the course of history.

But despite the dangers that lie ahead, they press on, driven by an insatiable thirst for knowledge and a shared determination to unlock the mysteries of the universe.

For they know that beyond the event horizon lies the promise of enlightenment, the chance to glimpse the very fabric of reality itself, and the opportunity to make discoveries that will forever change our understanding of the cosmos.

As Commander Dr. Elizabeth Hayes gazes ahead, her focus sharpens on the swirling darkness that looms before them. Excitement pulses through her veins, tempered by a flicker of apprehension, as she realizes the gravity of their upcoming journey.

Beside her, Lieutenant Commander Mark Thompson exudes a calm demeanor, his experienced hands poised over the controls, prepared to navigate the treacherous currents of the gravitational maelstrom enveloping the black hole.

Despite the thrill of exploration, a sense of danger hangs heavy in the air. The crew knows that they are venturing into uncharted territory, where the laws of physics bend and warp under the immense gravitational pull of the black hole.

Each member of the crew understands the risks

involved, but they also recognize the significance of their mission. They are pioneers, venturing into realms yet unseen, and their courage and determination will pave the way for future generations of explorers.

As they prepare to cross the threshold into the unknown, the crew shares a silent moment of reflection, drawing strength from each other and the knowledge that they are not alone in their quest for discovery. With hearts full of anticipation and minds focused on the task at hand, they stand ready to face whatever challenges the black hole may present, knowing that their journey will be remembered throughout history.

Lieutenant Commander Thompson's fingers dance across the controls, his movements precise as he adjusts their trajectory, guiding the spacecraft with unwavering determination. Dr. Emily Chen, Ph.D., monitors their instruments with keen attention, her expertise in astrophysics providing invaluable insights into the shifting dynamics of their surroundings.

Lieutenant Sarah Johnson is ready at the communications console, her focus trained on maintaining contact with mission control and relaying vital updates to the crew.

Together, they form a cohesive unit, united by a shared sense of purpose and an unwavering commitment to the mission at hand.

Chapter 7:
A Journey Through Spacetime

As the crew's spacecraft breaches the threshold of the black hole's domain, they are immediately engulfed by an overwhelming maelstrom of darkness and distortion. The once serene expanse of space outside now transforms into a tumultuous whirlpool of cosmic forces, where the laws of physics seem to unravel at the seams.

Inside the spacecraft, tension mounts as the crew grapples with the disorienting effects of their descent into the abyss. Communication with mission control is abruptly lost, leaving them isolated in the void of space.

Commander Dr. Elizabeth Hayes exchanges a glance with her crew, her expression a mix of determination and concern. Lieutenant Commander Mark Thompson furrows his brow, his hands moving swiftly over the controls in a desperate attempt to stabilize their trajectory.

Dr. Emily Chen, Ph.D., scans the readouts, her mind racing to make sense of the chaotic data streaming in from their instruments. Lieutenant Sarah Johnson frantically attempts to reestablish contact with mission control, her fingers flying across the console in a frantic dance.

But the silence persists, punctuated only by the eerie

hum of the spacecraft's systems and the distant roar of the black hole's gravitational pull. As they plunge deeper into the heart of the cosmic tempest, the crew braces themselves for the unknown, their resolve tested by the relentless forces that surround them. With each passing moment, they cling to the hope that they will emerge from the darkness unscathed, ready to face whatever challenges lie ahead in their quest for discovery.

Inside the cockpit, the crew members cling to their seats as the spacecraft is buffeted by unseen energies, their instruments spinning wildly as they struggle to make sense of the chaos around them.

Outside the viewport, the stars themselves seem to warp and distort; twisted into unrecognizable shapes by the black hole's immense gravitational pull.

Commander Dr. Elizabeth Hayes grits her teeth against the relentless onslaught, her hands flying across the control panel as she fights to keep the spacecraft on course.

Lieutenant Commander Mark Thompson peers anxiously out the viewport, his eyes wide with awe and apprehension as he watches the fabric of spacetime bend and warp before his eyes. Dr. Emily Chen, Ph.D., frantically scans the data readouts, her mind racing to comprehend the incomprehensible as she grapples with the implications of their journey into the heart of a black hole.

And Lieutenant Sarah Johnson, her fingers flying across the console with practiced precision, works tirelessly to maintain the integrity of the spacecraft's systems amidst the chaos of their surroundings. Together, the crew braces themselves against the relentless forces of the black hole, their resolve unyielding in the face of the unknown.

For they know that beyond this maelstrom of darkness and distortion lies the promise of discovery, the chance to unlock the secrets of the universe and uncover the mysteries that lie hidden within the depths of spacetime itself. And with every passing moment, they inch closer to the truth, their spirits undaunted by the daunting challenges that lie ahead.

Commander Hayes, her voice strained yet resolute, issues commands to her crew as they navigate through the chaotic maelstrom. Lieutenant Commander Thompson, his hands steady on the controls, adjusts their trajectory with precision, guiding the spacecraft through the turbulent currents of spacetime with unwavering focus.

Dr. Chen, her mind racing with scientific curiosity, studies the strange phenomena unfolding around them, eager to unravel the mysteries of the black hole's domain. Lieutenant Johnson, her eyes fixed on the monitors before her, monitors the spacecraft's vital systems with meticulous commitment to detail, ensuring that every component remains operational amidst the chaos.

As they hurtle deeper past the heart of the black hole, the crew is filled with a sense of awe and trepidation. They know that they are venturing into uncharted territory, where the very fabric of reality is stretched to its limits. Yet, amidst the chaos and uncertainty, they remain steadfast in their quest for knowledge, drawing on their training and expertise to navigate through the unknown.

For they understand that beyond the darkness lies the promise of enlightenment, the chance to unlock the secrets of the universe and gain a deeper understanding of the mysteries that lie at the heart of existence. And so, with courage and determination, they press on, ready to confront whatever challenges and revelations await them in the infinite depths of the black hole's domain.

Commander Dr. Elizabeth Hayes, her voice a steady anchor amidst the chaos, issues commands to her crew with unwavering resolve.

Her years of experience as an astronaut and astrophysicist have prepared her for this moment, and she navigates the spacecraft through the swirling darkness with a calm determination born of necessity.

Lieutenant Commander Mark Thompson, her trusted second-in-command, sits at her side, his hands poised over the controls as he adjusts the spacecraft's trajectory with precision.

His background as a pilot and engineer serves him well in this moment of crisis, and he charts a course through the shifting tides of the cosmic vortex with a steady hand.

Dr. Emily Chen, Ph.D., the mission's chief scientist, is at her workstation, surrounded by monitors displaying reams of data streaming in from the ship's sensors.

Her mind races with a mixture of excitement and trepidation as she studies the strange phenomena unfolding around them, eager to unravel the mysteries of the black hole's domain.

Lieutenant Sarah Johnson, the mission's communications and systems specialist, sits at her station, her focus unwavering despite the surreal surroundings.

She monitors the spacecraft's vital systems with meticulous attention to detail, ensuring that every component remains operational amidst the chaotic forces that threaten to tear them apart.

With each passing moment, the crew finds themselves confronting the limits of human understanding. Time bends and twists, stretching into impossible loops that defy logic.

Space warps and contorts around them, folding in on

itself in ways that challenge the very foundations of their perception. Yet amidst the disorienting whirlwind of cosmic chaos, they cling to their purpose with unwavering determination.

As the spacecraft hurtles deeper into the swirling depths of the black hole, an unexpected phenomenon occurs: the rotation of the vessel abruptly reverses direction, shifting from anti-clockwise to clockwise.

The sudden reversal catches the crew off guard, sending a ripple of confusion through their ranks.

Commander Hayes furrows her brow in concern, her mind racing to comprehend the inexplicable change.

"What's happening?" Lieutenant Johnson asks, her voice tinged with apprehension as she struggles to stabilize the spacecraft's trajectory.

Dr. Chen frantically checks the onboard instruments, searching for any clues as to the cause of the unexpected rotation.

"It's as if the very fabric of spacetime is twisting around us," she remarks, her expression reflecting a mixture of awe and uncertainty.

Despite the disorienting effects of the sudden change, the crew remains focused on their mission, their training and camaraderie serving as a steadfast anchor amidst the chaos.

With a collective effort, they work together to regain control of the spacecraft, adjusting their course to navigate the unfamiliar currents of the black hole.

As they press onward into the unknown, the crew braces themselves for whatever challenges lie ahead, their determination unyielding in the face of adversity.

For they know that beyond the chaos lies the promise of enlightenment— the chance to uncover the secrets of the universe hidden within the depths of the cosmic abyss.

Every twist and turn of their journey brings them closer to the truth, driving them onward with a sense of urgency and purpose.

Commander Hayes, her voice a steady anchor amidst the storm, issues commands to her crew with unwavering resolve. Lieutenant Commander Thompson, his hands steady on the controls, navigates the spacecraft through the shifting currents of spacetime with precision and skill.

Dr. Chen, her mind ablaze with curiosity, analyses the data streaming in from their sensors, searching for clues amidst the chaos.

And Lieutenant Johnson, her focus unwavering despite the surreal surroundings, ensures that the spacecraft's vital systems remain operational amidst the tumultuous forces that threaten to tear them apart.

As they continue their journey into the unknown, the crew is filled with a sense of anticipation and excitement.

They know that they are on the verge of a discovery that will change the course of human history—a revelation that will unlock the secrets of the cosmos and reshape our understanding of the universe.

Within the black hole's unfathomable grasp, the crew is subjected to a surreal barrage of cosmic phenomena that defies all conventional understanding.

Spacetime itself seems to warp and distort, stretching and compressing in ways that are utterly incomprehensible to the human mind. The crew finds themselves caught in a turbulent dance of gravity and energy, buffeted by forces beyond their wildest imaginings.

Commander Hayes, her voice tinged with awe and determination, issues commands to her crew as they navigate through the dizzying maelstrom of cosmic chaos.

Lieutenant Commander Thompson, his hands steady on the controls, adjusts their trajectory with precision, guiding the spacecraft through the ever-shifting currents of spacetime.

Dr. Chen, her mind ablaze with scientific curiosity, studies the strange phenomena unfolding around them, seeking to unravel the mysteries of the black hole's domain.

Lieutenant Johnson, her eyes darting between monitors and controls, monitors the spacecraft's vital systems with meticulous notice to detail, ensuring that every component remains operational amidst the chaos.

As they journey deeper into the heart of the black hole, the crew finds themselves confronting phenomena that defy all known laws of physics.

Space itself seems to bend and twist around them, folding in on itself in ways that challenge their understanding of reality. Time becomes a fluid concept, stretching and compressing in unpredictable patterns that make it impossible to discern past from present, or future from past.

As they venture deeper into the black hole's domain, the crew experiences the mind-bending effects of spacetime dilation with increasing intensity.

Minutes stretch into hours, hours into days, and days into what feels like an eternity, yet somehow, the passage of time remains subjective, a fluid concept that eludes their grasp.

They find themselves caught in a surreal dance of temporal distortion, where moments both linger and rush by in a bewildering blur. Reality itself twists and bends around them, revealing glimpses of alternate dimensions and parallel realities that challenge their perceptions of the universe.

Commander Hayes at the helm of the spacecraft, her voice cutting through the din of the chaotic spacetime labyrinth with authoritative clarity.

"Lieutenant Commander Thompson, adjust our trajectory by 15 degrees starboard to avoid that gravitational anomaly," she commands, her tone firm and decisive.

Lieutenant Commander Thompson responds immediately, his hands moving with practiced precision over the controls.

With a series of deft maneuvers, he recalibrates the spacecraft's course, veering it away from the looming danger with calculated finesse. "Trajectory adjusted, Commander," he reports, his voice calm and assured as he steers them clear of the gravitational distortion.

Meanwhile, Dr. Chen, her eyes glued to the sensor readings, alerts the crew to potential hazards lurking in the cosmic abyss.

"Commander, we've detected a cluster of debris ahead," she interjects, her voice tinged with urgency. "Recommend altering our course to avoid collision."

Commander Hayes nods in acknowledgment, her focus unwavering as she weighs Dr. Chen's assessment. "Lieutenant Johnson, prepare to execute a course correction to avoid the debris field," she orders, her confidence instilling a sense of calm amidst the tension.

Lieutenant Johnson acknowledges the command springing into action, her fingers flying across the control panel with practiced ease. With swift precision, she orchestrates the necessary adjustments, guiding the spacecraft on a safe path through the perilous maze of space-time.

As the crew works together seamlessly to navigate through the bewildering labyrinth of spacetime, their collective expertise and unwavering determination serve as beacons of hope amidst the chaos.

Each member plays a crucial role in ensuring their safe passage through the treacherous expanse, their efforts a testament to the power of teamwork and ingenuity in the face of adversity.

And with Commander Hayes at the helm, leading them with unwavering resolve, they press onward, steadfast in their mission to unlock the secrets of the cosmos.

Dr. Chen, her mind racing with scientific curiosity, studies the strange phenomena unfolding around them, eager to unlock the secrets hidden within the black hole's domain.

Lieutenant Johnson, his eyes darting between monitors and controls, monitors the spacecraft's vital systems with unwavering focus, ensuring that every component remains operational amidst the mind-bending effects of spacetime dilation.

Dr. Emily Chen, Ph.D., pores over the data streaming in from the ship's sensors, her brow furrowed in concentration as she grapples with the incomprehensible nature of their surroundings.

"The data... it's unlike anything I've ever seen," she murmurs, her voice tinged with a mixture of awe and uncertainty. "It's as if the laws of physics as we know them no longer apply here."

Lieutenant Commander Mark Thompson nods in agreement, his usually stoic demeanor betraying a sense of unease. "It's as if we've entered a realm beyond our understanding," he observes, his voice hushed with reverence. "A place where time and space are mere illusions, and reality is but a fleeting shadow."

Commander Dr. Elizabeth Hayes, her gaze fixed on the swirling abyss before them, senses the weight of their predicament. "We've ventured into uncharted territory," she declares, her voice steady despite the gravity of the situation. "But we must press on. Our mission demands it."

Lieutenant Sarah Johnson, her hands poised over the controls with a mix of determination and trepidation, braces herself for whatever challenges lie ahead. "We knew the risks when we embarked on this journey," she remarks, her voice tinged with resolve. "But if there's one thing humanity has always excelled at, it's pushing the boundaries of what is possible."

The crew confronts the limits of human comprehension, they draw strength from their shared determination to unravel the mysteries of the cosmos.

Though the journey may be perilous and the path ahead uncertain, they press onward, driven by an insatiable thirst for knowledge and discovery.

For they know that it is only by daring to venture into the unknown that they can hope to unlock the secrets that lie hidden within the depths of the black hole's enigmatic domain.

Gravitational tidal forces buffet the spacecraft relentlessly, subjecting it to immense pressures that threaten to tear it apart at the seams. The crew feels the weight of the universe bearing down upon them, a crushing force that assesses their physical and mental endurance to its limits.

Commander Hayes, her voice strained yet resolute, issues commands to her crew as they struggle to maintain control amidst the tumultuous onslaught of gravitational forces.

Lieutenant Commander Thompson, his hands gripping the controls with white-knuckled determination, fights to keep the spacecraft on course despite the relentless buffeting it endures.

Dr. Chen, her mind racing with scientific curiosity, studies the data streaming in from their instruments, searching for any signs of weakness or vulnerability in the spacecraft's hull.

Lieutenant Johnson, her eyes darting between monitors and controls, works tirelessly to ensure that every system remains operational amidst the chaos.

As the crew battles against the gravitational forces threatening to tear them apart, they draw on every ounce of strength and resilience they possess. Every fiber of their being is assessed as they struggle to maintain their grip on reality in the face of overwhelming adversity.

Amidst the chaos and uncertainty, the crew remains steadfast in their quest for knowledge. Commander Hayes, her voice a beacon of calm amidst the storm, issues commands to her crew with unwavering determination. Lieutenant Commander Thompson, his hands steady on the controls, navigates the spacecraft through the swirling abyss with a precision born of necessity.

Dr. Chen, ablaze with curiosity, studies the strange phenomena unfolding around them, eager to unravel the mysteries of the black hole's domain.

Lieutenant Johnson, her focus unwavering despite the surreal surroundings, monitors the spacecraft's vital systems with meticulous diligence, ensuring that every component remains operational amidst the chaos.

As they journey deeper into the unknown, the crew is filled with a sense of awe and wonder at the sheer magnitude of the cosmic forces that surround them.

For they know that beyond the chaos lies the promise of discovery, the chance to uncover the secrets of the universe hidden within the depths of the black hole's grasp.

And so, with courage and determination, they press on, ready to confront whatever challenges and revelations await them on the other side.

Lieutenant Sarah Johnson's hands tremble as she desperately toggles switches and adjusts frequencies, trying to reestablish contact with mission control.

With each passing moment, her anxiety mounts as the

silence from the other end persists, indicating a complete loss of communication.

Commander Dr. Elizabeth Hayes observes Lieutenant Johnson's efforts, her brow furrowed with concern.

She knows that maintaining contact with mission control is vital for the success and safety of their mission. Without it, they are left adrift in the vast expanse of space, cut off from the guidance and support of their colleagues back on the moon base.

Lieutenant Commander Mark Thompson joins Lieutenant Johnson at the communication console, his expression grim as he attempts to troubleshoot the issue alongside her.

They try every possible method to establish a connection, but all their efforts are met with the same ominous silence.

As the realization sinks in that they have lost contact completely, a heavy silence descends upon the spacecraft. The crew exchanges worried glances, grappling with the gravity of the situation.

Without the ability to communicate with mission control, they are left to navigate the challenges of deep space exploration alone, with no guidance or support from Earth.

Commander Hayes takes a deep breath, her mind racing with the implications of their predicament.

She knows that they must remain calm and focused, relying on their training and expertise to navigate the uncertainties that lie ahead. With determination in her voice, she addresses the crew.

"We may have lost contact with mission control, but we haven't lost hope," she says, her voice steady despite the tension in the air.
"We will continue to press forward, relying on our training and teamwork to overcome whatever challenges come our way. Together, we will find a way to navigate this situation and ensure the success of our mission."

The crew nods in silent agreement, their resolve strengthened by their commander's words. Despite the uncertainty of their circumstances, they know that they must remain united and resilient in the face of adversity as they forge ahead into the unknown.

Chapter 8:
Beyond the Event Horizon

As the crew's spacecraft approaches the central singularity of the black hole, a sense of anticipation hangs heavy in the air.

Commander Hayes stands at the forefront, her voice a beacon of authority amidst the impending chaos. "Prepare for the final approach," she commands, her tone steady and resolute.

Lieutenant Commander Thompson nods in acknowledgment, his hands poised over the controls with unwavering focus.

With each passing moment, the gravitational pull grows weaker, tugging at the fabric of spacetime and threatening to engulf them in its formidable embrace. Yet, Thompson remains steadfast, his determination unwavering as he steers the spacecraft with precision and skill.

Dr. Chen pores over the data with feverish intensity, her scientific curiosity driving her to unravel the mysteries of the singularity. "We're gathering invaluable insights into the nature of this phenomenon," she reports, her voice tinged with excitement. "But we must proceed with caution."

Lieutenant Johnson monitors the spacecraft's vital systems with meticulous diligence, ensuring that they remain operational amidst the overwhelming forces that surround them.

"All systems are holding steady," she confirms, her voice calm and composed despite the magnitude of the situation.

As they stand on the brink of the unknown, the crew knows that they are about to embark on a journey that will forever alter their understanding of the cosmos. With each passing moment, they draw closer to the singularity, their hearts racing with anticipation as they prepare to confront the deepest secrets of the universe head-on. And though the path ahead may be fraught with peril, they face it with unwavering courage and determination, united in their quest for knowledge and discovery.

Within the confines of their spacecraft, the crew braces themselves for the impending encounter with the singularity, a moment that will test the limits of their courage and resolve.

Commander Hayes, her voice calm yet tinged with a hint of urgency, issues final instructions to her crew. "Prepare for impact," she commands, her words echoing through the tense silence of the cabin.

Lieutenant Commander Thompson nods in

acknowledgment, his hands steady as he maneuvers the spacecraft with precision through the turbulent currents of spacetime.

Despite the overwhelming forces at play, he remains focused, determined to guide them safely through the maelstrom of the singularity's gravitational pull.

Dr. Chen, her eyes fixed on the swirling vortex of darkness outside their viewport, feels a surge of adrenaline coursing through her veins.

"This is it," she murmurs to herself, her scientific curiosity piqued by the prospect of what lies beyond the event horizon. Anxiously, she awaits the defining moment, eager to witness firsthand the secrets that the singularity holds.

Lieutenant Johnson monitors the spacecraft's vital systems with unwavering diligence, her steady hands ensuring that every component remains operational amidst the chaos of their surroundings.

Despite the palpable tension in the air, she remains calm and composed, her focus unwavering as they hurtle towards the unknown.

As the spacecraft breaches the threshold of the singularity, the crew is enveloped by a surreal cacophony of sound and light. Reality itself seems to unravel before their eyes, twisting and distorting in ways that defy all logic and reason.

Yet amidst the chaos, there is also a profound sense of awe and wonder— a recognition that they are on the brink of an extraordinary discovery that could reshape our understanding of the cosmos.

With each passing moment, they draw closer to the heart of the singularity, their hearts pounding with anticipation as they prepare to confront the mysteries that lie beyond.

For they know that beyond the event horizon lies the promise of enlightenment—a chance to glimpse the very fabric of reality itself and unlock the secrets of the universe.

And so, with courage and determination, they press onward, ready to confront whatever challenges and revelations await them on the other side.

Dr. Chen, her mind ablaze with curiosity and anticipation, delves deep into the data flooding in from the ship's sensors.

Each piece of information is a puzzle waiting to be explained, offering potential insights into the nature of the black hole's central core.

Lieutenant Johnson, her gaze fixed on the array of monitors before her, meticulously monitors the spacecraft's vital systems, ensuring that they remain operational as they approach the point of no return.

As the crew inches closer to the singularity, a palpable sense of awe and trepidation fills the spacecraft. They are on the brink of a momentous encounter, one that may redefine their understanding of the universe itself.

The very fabric of reality seems to ripple and warp around them as they draw nearer, a testament to the immense gravitational forces at play.

As the spacecraft breaches the threshold of the singularity, the crew is thrust into a realm where the laws of physics cease to hold sway. Reality itself seems to dissolve into a kaleidoscope of swirling chaos, as time and space lose all meaning.

Alternate dimensions and parallel realities shimmer into view, offering tantalizing glimpses of the infinite possibilities that lie beyond the event horizon.

Amidst the disorienting maelstrom of cosmic forces, the crew remains resolute in their quest for knowledge and understanding. For they know that beyond the singularity lies the promise of enlightenment—a chance to unravel the mysteries of the universe and glimpse the very essence of existence itself.

Commander Hayes, her voice a steady anchor amidst the chaos, issues commands to her crew as they navigate through the shifting currents of spacetime.

Lieutenant Commander Thompson, his hands gripping the controls with unwavering determination, guides the spacecraft with precision, deftly maneuvering through the swirling chaos.

Dr. Chen, her mind ablaze with scientific curiosity, studies the strange phenomena unfolding around them, eager to unlock the secrets hidden within the singularity's domain.

Lieutenant Johnson, her eyes darting between monitors and controls, monitors the spacecraft's vital systems with meticulous diligence, ensuring that every component remains operational amidst the tumultuous forces that threaten to tear them apart.

With courage and determination, they press on, ready to confront whatever challenges and revelations await them in the infinite depths of the black hole's central singularity.

For they are explorers, pioneers, driven by an insatiable thirst for truth and discovery, and they will stop at nothing to unlock the secrets of the cosmos.

Dr. Emily Chen, Ph.D., the mission's chief scientist, is at her workstation, surrounded by monitors displaying reams of data streaming in from the ship's sensors.

Her brow furrows in concentration as she tries to make

sense of the complex gravitational dynamics at play, her mind racing with theories and calculations about what they might encounter as they approach the event horizon.

Meanwhile, Lieutenant Sarah Johnson, the mission's expert in communications and systems, remains vigilant at her station. With a seasoned gaze, she oversees the spacecraft's critical systems, ensuring each component operates seamlessly amidst the formidable forces of the black hole. As the crew's vessel travels an unexpected anomaly catches their attention: a disturbance in spacetime that challenges all known theories.

Instead of the expected crushing gravitational forces and spaghettification, they find themselves drawn towards a shimmering portal, resembling a tunnel of swirling energy.

Commander Hayes, recognizing the potential danger, orders an increase in warp speed, hoping to navigate the gravitational currents without succumbing to the extreme tidal forces. With each passing moment, the crew braces themselves for the unknown as they hurtle towards the wormhole's entrance.

As they cross the threshold, a profound sense of disorientation washes over them, accompanied by a kaleidoscope of colors and sensations that defy description. The laws of physics seem to warp and bend around them, distorting reality in ways they could never have imagined.

Inside the wormhole, time and space become fluid concepts, with the crew experiencing a surreal journey through a labyrinth of interconnected dimensions. Their senses are overwhelmed by the sheer magnitude of the experience, as they traverse through regions of spacetime previously thought unreachable.

Despite the chaos and uncertainty, Commander Hayes remains steadfast, guiding the spacecraft with unwavering determination.

Miraculously, against all odds, the crew emerges from the black hole's grip, their spacecraft battered and worn, but their spirits soaring with the weight of the profound experiences they have undergone.

Expecting to find themselves in the depths of a void of darkness, they are instead greeted by a sight that defies comprehension.

Before them stretches a realm of boundless light and energy, a dazzling tapestry of colors that dance and shimmer with an otherworldly brilliance.

It is a stark contrast to the darkness they had anticipated, a testament to the wondrous diversity of the universe and the infinite possibilities that lie beyond the confines of their understanding.

Commander Dr. Elizabeth Hayes, recognizing the

urgency of the situation, issues a decisive order to the crew.

"Stop all engines," she commands, her voice steady and authoritative.

"We need to log our current location, ensuring that we have a record of our position in the vastness of space, should we need to return in the future so log our and assess our situation before we proceed any further."

Outside the viewport, the dazzling tapestry of colors continues to dance and shimmer, casting an ethereal glow upon the spacecraft's hull.

It is a sight unlike anything they have ever seen, a testament to the boundless beauty and complexity of the universe.

And so, with hearts full of wonder and minds ablaze with curiosity, the crew prepares to embark on the next chapter of their journey, ready to explore the endless depths of this wondrous realm and unlock the secrets that lie within. For they know that the universe is a place of infinite beauty and complexity, and they are determined to chart its uncharted territories, one discovery at a time.

"Attention, Moon Base. This is Commander Dr. Elizabeth Hayes of the Explore spacecraft expedition team. We have successfully emerged from the black hole's grip and are now on the other side. Please confirm if you are receiving this message. Over."

Concerned about the lack of response from Moon Base, Commander Hayes furrows her brow, contemplating their next course of action.

She turns to Lieutenant Johnson, the communications specialist, and nods in silent understanding. "Keep trying to establish contact," she instructs, her voice tinged with urgency. "We need to make sure they receive our message."

With a sense of determination, Lieutenant Johnson adjusts the communication settings and begins sending repeated signals to Moon Base, hoping for a response.

Meanwhile, the rest of the crew stands by their hearts heavy with worry as they await any sign of communication from their home base.

With each passing moment, their resolve strengthens, fueled by the knowledge that they are on the brink of something truly extraordinary.

They understand the magnitude of the task ahead, but they also embrace the exhilarating challenge that lies before them. Every step they take into the unknown brings them closer to unravelling the mysteries of the cosmos, and they are eager to embrace whatever wonders and challenges await them.

Frustration mounts among the crew as their attempts to establish contact with Moon Base continue to yield no response. Commander Hayes furrows her brow, considering their options in the face of this unexpected silence.

As the crew works together to troubleshoot the communication issue and gather information, a sense of urgency hangs heavy in the air. With each passing moment, the need to establish contact with Moon Base grows more pressing, and the crew's determination to find a solution only intensifies.

Commander Dr. Elizabeth Hayes, her voice filled with awe and wonder, feels relieved as she gazes upon this celestial spectacle. For a moment, she is at a loss for words, struck by the sheer beauty and majesty of their surroundings.

Lieutenant Commander Mark Thompson, his eyes wide with disbelief, can only shake his head in amazement at the sheer scale of what they are witnessing. It is a moment that will stay with him forever, a reminder of the awe-inspiring wonders that lie beyond the reaches of human comprehension.

Dr. Chen chimes in, her gaze fixed on the navigation console. "In the meantime, let's gather as much data as we can about our surroundings," she suggests. "We may be in uncharted territory, but every piece of information we collect brings us closer to understanding where we are."

In the boundless expanse of the cosmos, our courageous voyagers find themselves enveloped by an infinite sea of radiant white.

This celestial hue, stretching endlessly in every direction, bathes the universe in a soft, luminous glow, accentuating the splendor of the cosmic wonders that adorn the celestial canvas.

Brilliant stars, akin to distant jewels, twinkle with ethereal brilliance against this backdrop of pristine whiteness, their shimmering light punctuating the vast expanse with celestial brilliance.

Clusters of galaxies, vast and sprawling, adorn the cosmic horizon, each a majestic congregation of billions of stars.

Their cores aglow with radiant energy, they cast warm, inviting hues across the cosmic tapestry. Nebulae, vast clouds of interstellar gas and dust, drift gracefully through the cosmic ballet, their ethereal forms illuminated by the gentle white light that suffuses the universe.

Amidst this luminous spectacle, planets emerge as enigmatic silhouettes against the radiant backdrop of space. Their darkened forms stand in stark contrast to the brilliance surrounding them, casting subtle shadows upon the celestial canvas. From a distance, they appear as silent sentinels, guardians of the cosmic secrets concealed within their depths.

Yet, beneath their somber exterior, these darkened worlds teem with life and possibility. Concealed within their shadowy embrace, entire ecosystems thrive, hidden from prying eyes by the cloak of darkness.

Each planet holds the promise of discovery, offering tantalizing glimpses into the rich tapestry of life that flourishes throughout the cosmos.

As the crew gazes out into the vastness of space, they are mesmerized by the sheer diversity and beauty of the stars that adorn the cosmic landscape. Some shine with a soft, gentle glow, while others burn with a fierce intensity, their luminosity rivalling that of the sun itself. Each star tells a story of cosmic evolution and stellar birth, a testament to the immense forces that shape the universe.

Against this backdrop of celestial splendor, iridescent nebulae weave their ethereal dance across the cosmic stage, their swirling clouds of gas and dust illuminated by the light of nearby stars. Shades of emerald, green, sapphire blue, and ruby red mingle and blend in a mesmerizing display of color, creating a spectacle that is both breathtaking and awe-inspiring.

They find themselves immersed in a world of

unparalleled beauty and wonder; their senses overwhelmed by the sheer grandeur of the White Universe.

Here, amidst the brilliance of the cosmos, they are reminded of the boundless mysteries that lie beyond the reaches of human comprehension, beckoning them ever onward in their quest for discovery and understanding.

Dr. Emily Chen, Ph.D., her scientific curiosity piqued to new heights, scrambles to collect data from their sensors, eager to unravel the mysteries of this enigmatic realm. Every piece of information she gathers is a puzzle waiting to be solved, a clue that may help unlock the secrets of the universe.

Lieutenant Sarah Johnson, her fingers flying across the control panel with a mix of excitement and trepidation, ensures that the spacecraft remains stable amidst the sea of energy that surrounds them. It is a task that requires all her skill and expertise, but she approaches it with a calm determination that belies the chaos of their surroundings.

As they take in the breathtaking sights before them, the crew is overcome with a profound sense of humility and gratitude. They realize that they have been granted a rare glimpse into the true nature of the cosmos, a privilege reserved for only the most intrepid explorers.
For beyond the black hole's event horizon lies not just darkness and oblivion, but a realm of boundless possibility and infinite wonder. It is a reminder that the

universe is vast and mysterious, filled with wonders beyond imagining, waiting to be discovered by those brave enough to venture into the unknown.

Chapter 9:
The White Universe

Commander Dr. Elizabeth Hayes's voice cuts through the tension, offering a moment of respite amidst the uncertainty. "While we've paused to assess our situation, I believe it's prudent to regroup," she states, her tone steady and resolute.

"Let's take a moment for refreshments and then conduct a thorough examination of the spacecraft, both inside and out. Our priority is to ensure all critical systems, including the reactors, are intact and functioning properly."

Following her lead, the crew takes a moment to replenish their energy, sharing a brief meal before gearing up in their space gear.

Venturing outside the spacecraft, they meticulously inspect its exterior, finding a few areas in need of repair. Fortunately, they have brought enough spare shields inside the ship to address the damage.

Commander Hayes leads the inspection with precision, ensuring no detail escapes their scrutiny.

Lieutenant Commander Mark Thompson coordinates the inspection of the ship's reactors his expertise in engineering proving invaluable as he meticulously examines each component for signs of damage or malfunction meticulously examining the reactors to ensure their stability and functionality.

While Sarah Johnson persists in her efforts to establish communication with mission control, her determination unyielding despite the challenges they face.

As the crew works together to address any potential issues, a sense of unity and purpose drives them forward in their mission to navigate the mysteries of the cosmos.

Meanwhile, Dr. Emily Chen, Ph.D., oversees the analysis of the spacecraft's external hull, her keen eye for detail ensuring that no potential vulnerabilities are overlooked.

As the crew works diligently to assess the condition of their vessel, Commander Hayes remains vigilant, her gaze scanning the surrounding expanse of space for any signs of danger.

Despite the tranquility that now envelops them, she knows that they are not out of harm's way yet, and she remains ever vigilant against the unknown threats that may lurk anywhere.

Meanwhile, Lieutenant Sarah Johnson continues her attempts to re- establish contact with mission control, her determination unwavering despite the lack of response thus far.

As the crew works together to assess their situation, a sense of focus and determination fills the cockpit, driving them forward even in the face of uncertainty.

Commander Dr. Elizabeth Hayes stands at the helm of the spacecraft, her eyes scanning the mesmerizing vista before her with a mixture of awe and wonder.

Beside her, Lieutenant Commander Mark Thompson watches in silent reverence as the cosmic panorama unfolds, his breath caught in his throat at the sheer beauty of their surroundings.

"Look at that," Commander Hayes whispers, her voice barely audible above the gentle hum of the spacecraft's engines, her eyes wide with wonder as she gazes out into the cosmic expanse. "It's like nothing I've ever seen before."

Lieutenant Commander Thompson nods in silent agreement, his expression awestruck as he fixes his gaze on a distant galaxy that shimmers with an otherworldly brilliance. "It's breathtaking," he murmurs, his voice filled with reverence for the celestial spectacle unfolding before them.

Unable to tear his eyes away from the mesmerizing display, he feels a sense of profound connection to the vastness of the universe.

The two officers stand in companionable silence, lost in the grandeur of the cosmos unfolding before them. In that moment, they feel a profound connection to the universe, a sense of awe and insignificance that transcends words.

For here, amidst the vast expanse of space, they are but small specks in the tapestry of creation, witnesses to the beauty and majesty of the cosmos. Commander Hayes comments on the darker hue of the planets, observing their subdued presence against the backdrop of the surrounding cosmos.

Lieutenant Commander Thompson acknowledges the observation, concurring with the commander's assessment of the planets' darker appearance. As they look further into the heart of the White Universe, the crew finds themselves immersed in a world of cosmic harmony and tranquility. Cosmic structures stretch out before them in symmetrical patterns, their forms bathed in a soft, ethereal light that seems to emanate from within.

Dr. Emily Chen, Ph.D., renowned astrophysicist, stands transfixed at the viewport, her eyes alight with excitement as she takes in the breathtaking celestial wonders that surround them. Her heart races with exhilaration, her mind buzzing with the sheer magnitude of what lies before her. "This is incredible," she exclaims, her voice tinged with awe. "I've never seen anything like it."

Her words hang in the air, filled with a sense of wonder and reverence for the cosmic spectacle unfolding before them. For Dr. Chen, this moment represents the culmination of a lifetime of study and exploration — a chance to witness firsthand the beauty and majesty of the universe she has devoted her career to understanding.

As she continues to gaze out into the boundless expanse of space, Dr. Chen feels a deep sense of connection to the cosmos, a profound appreciation for the intricate dance of galaxies, stars, and nebulae that fills the void. In this moment, she is reminded of the limitless potential of human curiosity and the enduring quest for knowledge that drives us ever onward into the unknown.

Lieutenant Sarah Johnson, a seasoned astronaut and engineer, nods in agreement, her eyes wide with wonder as she takes in the ethereal beauty of their surroundings. "It's like we've entered a realm of pure imagination," she says, her voice filled with reverence.

Her words echo through the spacecraft, resonating with a sense of awe and respect for the cosmic wonders that surround them. For Lieutenant Johnson, this moment is a testament to the boundless creativity and majesty of the universe — a reminder of the endless possibilities that lie beyond the confines of human understanding.

As she continues to marvel at the celestial spectacle

unfolding before her, Lieutenant Johnson feels a profound sense of humility and gratitude.

In this vast and wondrous expanse of space, she is but a tiny speck in the grand tapestry of the cosmos, yet she is filled with a sense of purpose and wonder that transcends the boundaries of her own existence. In the presence of such magnificence, Lieutenant Johnson is reminded of the power of exploration and discovery to inspire and uplift the human spirit.

With each passing moment, she finds herself drawn deeper into the mysteries of the universe, eager to uncover its secrets and unlock the mysteries that lie hidden within its depths.

"Right," Commander Hayes declared, her voice commanding attention in the dimly lit bridge of the spacecraft. Her words reverberated through the vessel, cutting through the quiet hum of the ship's systems. "Let's proceed slowly and explore this part of the galaxy."

Her crew, a dedicated ensemble of explorers, snapped to attention, their eyes alight with anticipation.

Lieutenant Commander Thompson, his hands steady on the control panel, adjusted the navigation settings with precision, ensuring their course aligned with the commander's directive.

Dr. Chen, nestled at her workstation, eagerly scanned the sensors for any signs of celestial phenomena or anomalies that might pique their scientific curiosity.

Her expertise in astrophysics made her an invaluable asset to the mission, her keen eye ready to detect even the faintest glimmer of discovery.

Meanwhile, Lieutenant Johnson, stationed at the communication console, diligently attempted to establish contact with mission control back on the moon.

With focused determination, she toggled the controls, adjusting frequencies and scanning for any incoming signals. Despite her efforts, the console remained silent, devoid of the reassuring chatter of voices from their home base. Lieutenant Johnson's brow furrowed in concentration as she persisted, undeterred by the lack of response. Commander Hayes glanced over at Lieutenant Johnson, her expression conveying both empathy and encouragement.

"Keep trying, Lieutenant," she said, her voice carrying a note of reassurance. "We'll make contact soon enough."

With renewed determination, Lieutenant Johnson continued her efforts, her resolve unwavering as she remained vigilant in her quest to establish communication with mission control.

Each attempt brought them one step closer to

reconnecting with their terrestrial counterparts and ensuring the success of their mission.

As the spacecraft glided through the cosmos at a leisurely pace, the crew found themselves immersed in the beauty of the stellar landscape that unfolded before them.

Nebulae painted vibrant swirls of color against the velvet backdrop of space, while distant stars twinkled like diamonds scattered across an endless expanse.

With Commander Hayes leading the way, they embarked on a journey of exploration and discovery, venturing deeper into the uncharted reaches of the galaxy.

Each moment brought the promise of new horizons and untold wonders, driving the crew forward in their quest to unravel the mysteries of the cosmos.

As they continue their journey through the White Universe, the crew encounters ethereal phenomena that defy explanation. Glowing auroras dance across the cosmic horizon, their colors shifting and swirling in a mesmerizing display of celestial beauty.

Commander Dr. Elizabeth Hayes stands at the viewport, her eyes transfixed on the luminous spectacle unfolding before her. "It's like watching a symphony of light," she murmurs, her voice filled with wonder.

Beside her, Lieutenant Commander Mark Thompson nods in agreement, his gaze locked on the mesmerizing dance of colors. "I'll say it again, I've never seen anything quite like it," he says, his tone tinged with awe.

Dr. Emily Chen, Ph.D., joins them at the viewport, her scientific curiosity piqued by the celestial phenomenon. "These auroras must be generated by some form of exotic energy source," she muses, her mind already racing with theories and hypotheses.

As the crew continues to marvel at the celestial display, they are filled with a sense of awe and wonder at the beauty of the universe.

In this strange and wondrous realm, they are reminded of the boundless mysteries that lie beyond the reaches of human knowledge, and the endless possibilities that await those who dare to explore.

Dr. Chen furrows her brow in concentration as she studies the phenomena unfolding before them. "These auroras are unlike any I've ever seen," she muses, her mind racing with possibilities. "I wonder what causes them."

Commander Dr. Elizabeth Hayes nods in agreement, her curiosity piqued by Dr. Chen's observation. "Indeed," she responds, her voice tinged with intrigue. "It's as if we've stumbled upon a whole new realm of physics."

Lieutenant Commander Mark Thompson joins the conversation, his eyes alight with scientific curiosity. "Perhaps it's related to the unique properties of the White Universe," he suggests, his tone thoughtful. "We'll need to collect data and run simulations to unravel the mystery."

As the crew discusses possible explanations for the phenomenon, they prepare to deploy instruments and sensors to gather data. In the midst of their exploration, they are reminded once again of the vastness of the cosmos and the endless wonders that await discovery.

Commander Hayes nods thoughtfully, her gaze lingering on the shimmering lights that dance across the cosmic expanse. "Perhaps it's a manifestation of the universe's energy," she suggests, her voice tinged with curiosity. "A reminder of the vast mysteries that lie beyond our understanding."

As they journey deeper into the heart of the White Universe, the crew is filled with a sense of reverence and wonder. Here, amidst the brilliance of the cosmos, they find themselves on a journey of exploration and discovery unlike any other, united in their quest to unravel the secrets of the universe and unlock the mysteries of the White Universe.

As the crew's spacecraft navigates through the expansive reaches of the White Universe, their instruments pick up the presence of a distant celestial object on the horizon.

This planet emerges as a radiant sphere amidst the cosmic panorama, its surface illuminated by an otherworldly glow that distinguishes it from the surrounding void.

Commander Dr. Elizabeth Hayes, her eyes riveted to the mesmerizing image of the planet displayed on the view screen, leans forward with a mix of curiosity and anticipation.

Her voice, tinged with an undercurrent of excitement, carries a note of authority as she turns to her crew for answers, eager to unravel the mysteries of this enigmatic world.

"Gather all available data," she commands, her tone firm yet tinged with a sense of urgency, "We need to understand everything we can about this planet before we proceed."

Lieutenant Commander Mark Thompson, his eyes focused intently on the array of data readouts displayed before him, sifts through the streams of information with practiced precision.

Each line of data holds clues to the nature of the planet they are approaching, and Thompson's expertise as a pilot and engineer is instrumental in deciphering its secrets.

As he analyses the preliminary findings, Thompson's brow furrows in concentration, his mind racing to interpret the implications of the data. The readings indicate that the planet boasts a breathable atmosphere, a revelation that sparks a ripple of excitement among the crew.

It suggests the potential for habitability, hinting at the tantalizing possibility of life existing beyond the confines of Earth.

Further analysis reveals another promising sign: moderate temperatures. This detail is crucial, as it indicates conditions conducive to sustaining life as we know it.

The presence of liquid water on the surface, indicated by subtle fluctuations in the planet's thermal signatures, further bolsters the case for habitability.

Thompson's voice resonates with a mix of professional detachment and cautious optimism as he relays the findings to the commander and the rest of the crew. "Preliminary analysis indicates favorable conditions for life," he reports, his tone measured yet tinged with a hint of excitement. "But we'll need to gather more data to confirm our initial observations."

Dr. Emily Chen, Ph.D., adds her expertise to the discussion, her astrophysical insights illuminating the crew's understanding of the planet's composition and potential.

With her background in research and a keen eye for detail, Dr. Chen delves deeper into the data, uncovering fascinating similarities between the newfound world and Earth.

As she pores over the intricate details revealed by their sensors, Dr. Chen identifies a myriad of geological formations dotting the planet's surface.

From rugged mountain ranges to sprawling plains and winding rivers, the landscape paints a picture of geological diversity reminiscent of their home planet.

These features hint at a rich history of geological processes and natural phenomena, offering tantalizing clues to the planet's past and present.

But it's not just the terrain that captivates Dr. Chen's attention. Her keen observation skills detect subtle hints of life within the planet's ecosystem. The presence of diverse biological signatures, ranging from complex organic compounds to atmospheric gases indicative of metabolic activity, suggests that the planet may indeed be teeming with life in various forms.

Excitement bubbles within Dr. Chen as she shares her findings with the crew, her voice alive with the thrill of discovery.

"The planet exhibits a composition reminiscent of Earth's," she explains, her words tinged with enthusiasm. "It showcases a variety of geological formations and hosts a diverse ecosystem, making it a promising prospect for in-depth exploration and scientific investigation."

Her words resonate with the crew, igniting a spark of curiosity and anticipation as they prepare to embark on a journey of exploration and discovery unlike any they have undertaken before.

With Dr. Chen's expertise guiding their efforts, they stand ready to unlock the secrets of this enigmatic world and unravel the mysteries that lie hidden within its depths.

As the crew remains enveloped in silence from mission control, a palpable sense of self-reliance settles over the spacecraft. Without external guidance, they understand that they must rely on their training, ingenuity, and collective expertise to navigate the challenges ahead.

Commander Dr. Elizabeth Hayes, recognizing the gravity of their situation, takes charge with a steady hand and a clear mind.

She reaffirms to her team that they are capable and well-prepared to handle whatever obstacles may arise, emphasizing the importance of staying focused and working together as a cohesive unit.

Lieutenant Commander Mark Thompson, undeterred by the lack of communication, remains vigilant at his post, monitoring the spacecraft's systems with meticulous attention to detail. Dr. Emily Chen, Ph.D., channels her scientific curiosity into analyzing the data they have collected, searching for insights that may aid them in their exploration of the unknown planet.

Lieutenant Sarah Johnson, recognizing the importance of maintaining their autonomy, ensures that the spacecraft's communications systems are functioning optimally, ready to relay any critical information amongst the crew.

As they venture into uncharted territory without the guidance of mission control, the crew finds strength in their unity and resolve.

With each passing moment, they draw closer to the mysterious planet looming on the horizon, their determination unwavering as they prepare to embark on this unprecedented journey into the unknown.

Chapter 10: The Planet

As the crew's spacecraft descends through the planet's atmosphere, a sense of anticipation fills the air, mingling with the hum of the ship's engines.

Outside the viewport, the barren landscape unfolds before them like a monochromatic canvas, with vast expanses of dusty plains and rugged rock formations stretching to the distant horizon.

Commander Dr. Elizabeth Hayes stands at the forefront of the control room, her eyes fixed on the panoramic view of the desolate terrain below.

With a furrowed brow, she directs the crew to activate the scanning equipment, their mission clear: to search for any traces of past civilizations or structures amidst the stark emptiness of the planet's surface.

Lieutenant Commander Mark Thompson, his hands steady on the controls, guides the spacecraft with precision as it descends towards the barren landscape below.

With each passing moment, the rugged terrain looms ever closer, its jagged contours revealing little about the secrets that lie hidden beneath the surface.

Dr. Emily Chen, Ph.D., hovers over the data consoles, her keen intellect focused on interpreting the streams of information pouring in from the scanning instruments.

Her fingers fly across the controls as she sifts through the data, searching for anomalies or irregularities that may hint at the presence of ancient civilizations or artifacts.

Lieutenant Sarah Johnson, her eyes fixed on the communication panel, stands ready to relay any findings to the rest of the crew. Despite the starkness of the landscape unfolding before them, she remains vigilant, knowing that the answers they seek may lie buried deep within the planet's rocky crust.

Together, the crew remains poised on the brink of discovery, their senses heightened as they prepare to unravel the mysteries of this alien world.

With each passing moment, the anticipation mounts, building towards the moment when they will finally uncover the secrets hidden beneath the desolate surface of the planet below.

Lieutenant Commander Mark Thompson, his attention fixed on the sensor data, delivers his report with a mix of surprise and intrigue.

"Initial scans have indeed detected signs of life," he

announces, his voice tinged with excitement. "Though faint, there are unmistakable traces of biological activity present on the planet's surface."

Dr. Emily Chen, Ph.D., leans in closer to examine the data, her scientific curiosity piqued by the revelation. "These readings suggest the presence of microbial organisms or possibly primitive plant life," she muses, her tone reflecting a sense of wonder.

"It's a remarkable discovery and opens up intriguing possibilities for further exploration." With their expectations surpassed by the unexpected discovery, the crew prepares to delve deeper into the mysteries of this newfound life-form.

Armed with a sense of anticipation and a thirst for knowledge, they eagerly await the opportunity to explore the planet's surface and unravel the secrets hidden within its biosphere.

As the crew prepares to make their descent to the planet's surface, Dr. Emily Chen, Ph.D., takes charge of activating the spacecraft's sophisticated atmospheric sensors.

With a series of deft movements, she initiates the data collection process, her fingers dancing across the control panel with practiced precision.

The sensors spring to life, their delicate instruments

poised to sample the planet's atmosphere and analyses its composition. Within moments, streams of data begin to flood the onboard systems, providing a detailed snapshot of the air surrounding the spacecraft.

Dr. Chen's trained eye scans the incoming data, interpreting the complex readings with a mix of expertise and anticipation. As the analysis unfolds, she scrutinizes each parameter, searching for any indications of gases or particulates that could pose a threat to the crew's safety.

After a tense moment of analysis, Dr. Chen's expression relaxes into a satisfied smile.

"The atmospheric conditions appear to be within acceptable parameters," she announces, her voice laced with relief. "Oxygen levels are sufficient for human respiration, and there are no harmful pollutants present."

With the all-clear from Dr. Chen, the crew breathes a collective sigh of relief, their confidence bolstered by the reassurance of their expert scientist.

As they prepare for their mission to explore the planet's surface, the crew eagerly readies themselves for the adventure ahead. With each member equipped with the necessary gear and supplies, they stand poised at the ready, anticipation coursing through their veins.

Upon touchdown, the crew members brace themselves as the spacecraft's hatch opens, revealing the alien landscape beyond. Stepping out onto the planet's surface, they are immediately struck by the stark and desolate panorama before them.

Barren plains of dust and rock stretch out in all directions, devoid of any signs of vegetation or animal life. The terrain is rugged and unforgiving, with jagged peaks and deep crevices creating an otherworldly landscape that seems frozen in time.

Despite the harsh conditions, the crew remains undeterred, their spirits buoyed by the thrill of exploration and the promise of discovery. With each step they take, they inch closer to unravelling the mysteries of this alien world, forging ahead with determination and resolve.

As they prepare to embark on their mission to explore the planet's surface, they do so with the knowledge that they are stepping into an environment that is both hospitable and ripe for discovery.

As the crew steps out onto the planet's surface, they are immediately struck by the stark and desolate landscape that stretches out before them. Barren plains of dust and rock extend to the horizon, devoid of any signs of vegetation or animal life. The terrain is rugged and uneven, with jagged peaks and deep crevices carving intricate patterns into the surface.

The air is eerily still, with no hint of breeze to stir the

dust that coats the ground. Despite the barrenness of their surroundings, there is a palpable sense of anticipation and excitement among the crew as they prepare to explore this alien terrain.

Every rock and crevice holds the promise of discovery, beckoning them to unravel the secrets hidden within the planet's ancient geology. With each step, they move forward into the unknown, eager to uncover the mysteries that lie beneath the surface of this enigmatic world.

Lieutenant Sarah Johnson, the team's experienced astronaut and engineer, takes the lead in deploying a series of probes equipped with advanced environmental sensors designed to gather data on the planet's atmosphere.

With precision and expertise, she oversees the deployment, ensuring each probe is positioned strategically to capture comprehensive readings.

After meticulously analyzing the gathered data, Lieutenant Johnson relays her findings to the rest of the crew.

"The atmosphere appears to consist predominantly of nitrogen and oxygen, mirroring the composition of Earth's atmosphere," she reports. "However, there are indications of trace elements and potential contaminants that warrant further investigation and caution."

The crew exchanges thoughtful glances, their minds abuzz with speculation and curiosity. Could this planet have once harbored a flourishing ecosystem, now lost to time and circumstance? Or perhaps there are deeper, more enigmatic forces at work, shaping the planet's atmosphere and history in ways yet to be understood.

Undeterred by the mysteries that surround them, the crew presses forward with their exploration, their senses heightened, and their resolve strengthened by the knowledge that even the most barren landscapes can conceal untold secrets waiting to be uncovered.

With each step, they inch closer to unravelling the mysteries of this enigmatic world and unlocking the truth hidden within its ancient terrain.

Commander Dr. Elizabeth Hayes issues a reminder to the team, emphasizing the paramount importance of safety protocols as they embark on their exploration of the planet's surface.

Stressing the need to remain within a safe distance from the spacecraft at all times, she underscores the significance of communication and cohesion to ensure the crew's well-being in this unfamiliar environment.

With these directives in mind, the crew sets out on their exploration, dividing into small groups equipped with specialized gear and communication devices to facilitate seamless coordination.

They move with precision and vigilance, methodically scanning their surroundings for any signs of activity or anomalies that may warrant further investigation. Each step is taken with caution, guided by the imperative to prioritize safety while unravelling the mysteries of this alien terrain.

As they traverse the landscape, the crew maintains constant communication, sharing observations and insights as they navigate the uncharted territory together.

Their collective efforts serve as a testament to their professionalism and dedication, ensuring that every precaution is taken to safeguard their mission and each other amidst the inherent uncertainties of planetary exploration.

As the crew delves deeper into their exploration, they meticulously document their findings, collecting samples of soil and rock formations while capturing detailed images of the alien landscape for further analysis.

Despite the stark desolation that surrounds them, an undercurrent of excitement pulses through the crew as they uncover each new discovery, each piece of data offering a potential key to unlocking the mysteries of this enigmatic world.

With each sample collected and image captured, the crew edges closer to understanding the secrets that lie hidden beneath the planet's barren surface.

Every anomaly observed and every detail documented serves as a breadcrumb in their quest for knowledge, propelling them forward with a sense of purpose and determination.

Amidst the solitude of their surroundings, the crew's camaraderie and shared sense of exploration serve as a beacon of light, illuminating the path ahead as they navigate the uncharted terrain together.

Each revelation sparks lively discussions and debates among the team, fueling their curiosity and driving them to delve deeper into the unknown.

As they continue to uncover clues and piece together the puzzle of this enigmatic world, the crew remains steadfast in their mission, driven by the relentless pursuit of discovery and the unwavering belief that every step forward brings them closer to unravelling the secrets of the universe.

Lieutenant Sarah Johnson's body tenses as her keen eyes detect a faint movement in the distance. With a subtle gesture, she signals to her companions to halt, their footsteps coming to an abrupt stop on the barren terrain.

Silently, they watch, their senses on high alert, as they strain to identify the origin of the elusive motion against the backdrop of the desolate landscape.

Time seems to slow as they wait, the only sound echoing through the stillness is the faint rustle of the planet's atmosphere. Each member of the crew holds their breath, anticipation mounting with each passing moment, as they remain poised for any further signs of activity.

In the quiet intensity of the moment, their minds race with possibilities, their imaginations conjuring scenarios of what might lie hidden amidst the silent expanse of the planet's surface.

With hearts pounding and adrenaline coursing through their veins, they stand ready, prepared to face whatever revelation awaits them in the vast unknown.

As the enigmatic figure draws closer, the crew members exchange cautious glances, their hearts pounding with a mixture of anticipation and trepidation. Each step the figure takes brings it into sharper focus, revealing its humanoid form draped in flowing, tattered robes that sway gently in the planet's eerie light.

Commander Dr. Elizabeth Hayes takes the lead, her posture poised yet alert as she prepares to engage with the mysterious visitor.

With a voice that carries a blend of warmth and wariness, Commander Hayes addresses the approaching figure.

"Greetings," she calls out, her words echoing softly across the barren landscape. "We come in peace. Are you a resident of this planet?"

The other being's features begin to emerge from the shadows, illuminated by the subtle glow of the planet's light.

Its eyes, deep and penetrating, seem to hold a wisdom beyond mortal comprehension, while its movements possess an otherworldly grace that sets it apart from anything the crew has encountered before.

Sensing the tension in the air, Lieutenant Sarah Johnson takes a cautious step back, her hand instinctively reaching for the communicator at her side.

"Commander, we're not getting any response," she reports, her voice tinged with a hint of unease.

Commander Hayes acknowledges the report with a nod, her gaze remaining fixed on the enigmatic figure before them. "Stay alert, but don't make any sudden movements," she advises, her tone steady and composed. "Let's observe and see what it does."

Anxiously, the crew watches as the mysterious being draws closer, its intentions cloaked in secrecy, leaving them to ponder the enigma that stands before them in the vast expanse of the alien landscape.

Lieutenant Commander Mark Thompson's agreement is punctuated by a solemn nod, his gaze unwavering as he observes the enigmatic being before them.

"It's plausible that its mode of communication differs from ours," he suggests, his voice a steady anchor amidst the uncertainty. "Remaining open-minded and observant could be key to deciphering its intentions."

Dr. Emily Chen, Ph.D., furrows her brow in contemplation, her analytical mind already racing through potential solutions.

"If verbal communication proves futile, we must explore alternative methods of connection," she muses, her voice tinged with determination.

Commander Dr. Elizabeth Hayes echoes their sentiments with a nod of affirmation. "Let's extend a gesture of goodwill," she suggests, her tone imbued with cautious optimism.

"Perhaps a symbol of our peaceful intentions will pave the way for mutual understanding."

With a shared resolve, the crew prepares to signal their peaceful intentions to the enigmatic being, hopeful that their efforts will bridge the gap between their worlds and pave the way for meaningful communication amidst the vast expanse of the White Universe.

As the enigmatic beings materialize from the shadows, their presence casts a palpable sense of unease among the crew, who exchange wary glances, uncertain of the intentions behind this mysterious encounter.

Commander Dr. Elizabeth Hayes maintains a composed demeanor, her voice cutting through the tension with unwavering authority.

"We come in peace," she declares, her words echoing in the stillness of the alien landscape.

"We Harbor no ill intentions towards you. We are but humble explorers, traversing the depths of the cosmos in search of knowledge and understanding."

The air crackles with anticipation as the crew awaits a response, their senses heightened in anticipation of the enigmatic beings' reaction to their diplomatic overture.

In the silence that follows, the weight of the moment hangs heavy, teetering on the precipice of discovery or discord amidst the vast expanse of the unknown.

As Lieutenant Commander Mark Thompson stands beside Commander Dr. Elizabeth Hayes, his hand subtly resting on the hilt of his sidearm, a silent reminder of the need for caution in the face of uncertainty.

Dr. Emily Chen, Ph.D., and Lieutenant Sarah Johnson maintain a cautious distance, their eyes darting between the strange beings and their commanding officers, ready to act at a moment's notice.

In the charged atmosphere, the air crackles with anticipation, each member of the crew keenly aware of the delicate balance that hangs in the balance. They hope for a peaceful resolution to this unexpected encounter in the depths of the White Universe, their hearts pounding with a mixture of apprehension and curiosity as they await the beings' response.

An elderly leader takes a deliberate step forward, his figure seems to fill the space around him with an aura of presence and authority.

His eyes, deep and penetrating, hold within them the accumulated wisdom of countless ages, yet they sparkle with a curious twinkle, as if perpetually eager to learn and discover.

Despite the weight of his years, there is a vitality about him, an energy that seems to radiate from every inch of his being.

"We extend our most sincere greetings to you, travelers from realms beyond," he begins, his voice resonating with a serene tranquility that seems to soothe the tension in the air.

"I am known among our people as Ark, an elder whose years have been enriched by the vast tapestry of experiences woven throughout our history.

We have observed your journey with great interest, curious about the beings who dare to venture into our sacred domain."

Commander Dr. Elizabeth Hayes steps forward, her presence commanding attention as she extends her hand in a gesture of friendship.

"I am Commander Elizabeth Hayes," she introduces herself with a warm smile, her voice steady and respectful. "We are honored to meet you, Ark.

We seek to learn about your world and forge a connection between our peoples."

Commander Dr. Elizabeth Hayes requests, "You speak our language?" However, the other individual appears puzzled, indicating a lack of understanding.

Ark nods thoughtfully, comprehending the Commander's inquiry. "Our language may not perfectly align with yours," he begins, his voice infused with reverence for the history he's about to unveil.

"But our records, transmitted across generations, tell of ancient connections with civilizations from far-flung worlds, perhaps even including your own."

He gestures towards the sprawling landscape stretching out before them, where remnants of ancient structures and artifacts lie scattered amidst the alien terrain.

"Here, on the surface of our world, we hold traces of our shared heritage with the Pharaohs," Ark explains, his gaze sweeping over the ancient ruins.

"These remnants, though weathered by time, serve as a testament to the connections between our peoples, forged across the vast expanse of time and space."

As Ark speaks, the Commander and her crew take in the sights before them, sensing the profound significance of their surroundings.

In the silence that follows, a newfound understanding begins to dawn, bridging the gap between their disparate worlds and laying the foundation for a deeper connection forged through shared history and exploration.

Ark acknowledges their presence with a nod, his demeanor exuding a sense of thoughtful consideration.

"There exists considerable potential for mutual learning and understanding between our respective peoples," he suggests.

"I extend an invitation for you to accompany me to our dwelling, where we can embark on a journey of exploration together. By pooling our knowledge and resources, we may unlock the mysteries of the cosmos and strengthen the bonds between our civilizations."

With Ark taking the lead towards his home, the crew follows closely behind, their minds brimming with excitement and anticipation for the revelations awaiting them in the enigmatic realm of the White Universe.

Chapter 11:
The Underground City

As Ark guides the crew deeper into the cavern, the temperature gradually drops, and a chill permeates the air, sending shivers down their spines.

The narrow passageways twist and turn, leading them further into the bowels of the planet. The soft glow of their headlamps illuminates the rugged walls, revealing intricate patterns etched into the ancient rock formations.

The silence of the cavern is broken only by the echoing sounds of their footsteps, reverberating off the walls and creating an otherworldly ambiance.

Every now and then, they catch glimpses of mysterious shadows darting across the rocky surfaces, heightening the sense of unease that hangs in the air.

Despite the eerie surroundings, the crew presses on, their curiosity driving them forward into the unknown depths of the cave. With each step, they draw closer to uncovering the secrets that lie hidden within the ancient rock, eager to unravel the mysteries of this enigmatic realm.

As the crew marvels at the intricate carvings in the chamber, Ark gestures towards them with pride.

"These are the records of our people," he explains, his voice echoing in the expansive space. "They chronicle only a part of our history—the tales of our forebears, their struggles, and triumphs."

However, Ark's revelation does not end there. "But there is more," he continues, leading the crew deeper into the cavern. "In another chamber, we have preserved thousands of books, each filled with the knowledge and wisdom of our ancestors. They are a testament to our enduring quest for understanding and discovery."

As they follow Ark into the next chamber, the crew's excitement grows. They realize that within these ancient tomes lies the key to unlocking even more of the mysteries of the cosmos.

With eager anticipation, they prepare to delve into the wealth of knowledge that awaits them, ready to uncover the secrets that have been hidden for generations.

As the crew gazes upon the ancient artifacts, Dr. Emily Chen's scientific curiosity sparks to life.

She meticulously examines the intricate carvings, noting their remarkable resemblance to the ancient hieroglyphs discovered on Earth, suggesting a shared heritage with the Pharaoh people.

"These symbols bear a striking resemblance to ancient Earth languages," she remarks, her voice tinged with excitement. "It's fascinating to consider that civilizations from different corners of the universe could share such similarities in their written language.

Perhaps the Pharaohs were travelers through space," she speculates, her imagination fueled by the possibility of interstellar connections.

Ark nods in agreement, his expression contemplative. "Indeed, the universe is vast, yet interconnected in ways we are only beginning to grasp," he reflects.

"Perhaps our encounter today is evidence of the bonds that transcend time and space." His words carry a sense of awe, highlighting the profound mysteries that link disparate worlds and civilizations across the cosmos.

As they venture further into the depths of the cave, the crew's footsteps echo softly against the walls, creating an eerie yet mesmerizing ambiance.

Shafts of soft light filter through narrow crevices, casting intricate patterns on the cavern floor and illuminating the ancient artifacts that line the rocky walls.

The air is thick with a sense of anticipation as they move deeper into the heart of the cavern, each step forward revealing new wonders.

The crew members pause at intervals, their eyes tracing the contours of the carvings and the delicate details etched into the stone. They marvel at the intricacy of the designs and the skill of the ancient craftsmen who created them, sensing the weight of history that permeates the chamber.

With each artifact they encounter, the crew gains a deeper insight into the culture and traditions of the civilization that once flourished here.

They speculate about the stories and knowledge encoded within these timeless relics, piecing together fragments of a bygone era as they traverse the ancient passageways of the underground city.

Driven by a sense of curiosity and awe, the crew presses on, eager to unlock the secrets that lie hidden within the labyrinthine passages of the cave. Each step forward brings them closer to unravelling the mysteries of the ancient civilization that once called this underground city home.

As they traverse the winding corridors and explore the shadowy alcoves, the crew's senses are inundated with sights, sounds, and sensations unlike anything they have experienced before. Shafts of light filter through fissures in the rock, illuminating ancient artifacts and revealing glimpses of a lost world frozen in time.

The air is thick with the scent of this planet's age-old

secrets, stirring something primal within the crew members as they navigate the maze-like tunnels.

Every discovery sparks new questions and fuels their determination to uncover the truth behind the enigmatic relics that surround them.

Despite the challenges and uncertainties that lie ahead, the crew's spirits remain buoyant as they embrace the adventure unfolding before them.

With Ark as their guide and ally, they stand ready to confront whatever obstacles may arise, united in their quest for knowledge and discovery in the boundless expanse of the White Universe.

Commander Hayes addresses Ark with a mixture of curiosity and concern. "Ark, we couldn't help but notice that your people don't seem to live on the surface. What happened?"

Commander Hayes' inquiry hangs in the air, her words laced with a blend of curiosity and concern as she directs her gaze towards Ark, the elder of the enigmatic civilization.

Ark stops; his expression softens, and eyes reflecting a hint of sorrow as he recounts the tale of his people's exodus from the surface of their planet.

"Our ancestors once dwelled on the surface, under the

open skies," Ark begins, his voice resonating with the weight of generations past. "But as the ages passed, our world underwent great upheavals. Catastrophic events ravaged the surface, rendering it uninhabitable.

Faced with the threat of extinction, our ancestors sought refuge underground, where they could shelter from the harsh conditions above."

As Ark's gaze drifts towards the cavern walls adorned with ancient carvings, Commander Hayes can sense the depth of emotion behind his words. "These walls hold the stories of our people's struggle to adapt and endure," he continues, his voice steady despite the somber undertones. "Though our existence may be hidden from the light of day, we have found solace and safety in the depths of our planet."

The crew listens intently, their hearts heavy with empathy for Ark and his people. Despite the challenges they have faced, Ark's resilience and determination shine through, a testament to the indomitable spirit of his civilization.

As the echoes of Ark's words fade into the silence of the cavern, Commander Hayes offers a word of solidarity. "Your resilience is a testament to the strength of your people," she says, her voice filled with admiration. "We are honored to stand beside you as allies and friends in the face of adversity."

Ark's words resonate through the cavern, carrying the weight of generations of resilience and adaptation. The crew listens intently, struck by the solemnity of his tone and the depth of his commitment to his people's survival.

"For generations, we have lived beneath the surface, adapting to our new environment and striving to preserve our way of life," Ark continues, his voice steady despite the weight of his words. "Though the surface may be inhospitable, we have found solace and sustenance in the depths of our world, forging a new existence amidst the darkness."

His words evoke a sense of reverence for his people's endurance, their ability to thrive in the face of adversity. The crew feels a profound respect for Ark and his community, admiring their resilience and determination to persevere against all odds.

As Ark's gaze lingers on the ancient carvings, the crew senses a glimmer of hope in his eyes. "For generations, we have lived here in isolation, preserving our culture and our way of life. But now, with your arrival, perhaps there is hope for a new beginning."

The crew exchanges glances, a silent understanding passing between them. They realize that their encounter with Ark and his people is more than just a chance meeting—it's an opportunity to forge connections, to learn from one another, and to embark on a journey of mutual discovery.

With renewed determination, the crew prepares to accompany Ark deeper into the heart of his underground world, eager to uncover the secrets that lie hidden within the labyrinthine passages of the cave. As they follow him into the darkness, they carry with them a sense of purpose and possibility, ready to embrace whatever the future may hold.

Commander Hayes's words resonate with genuine compassion, her empathy palpable as she addresses Ark and his people. Her commitment to assisting them shines through, a beacon of hope in the midst of uncertainty.

"We understand," she says, her voice a soothing balm in the cavern's solemn atmosphere. "We may be from different worlds, but we share a common bond as fellow inhabitants of the cosmos. We will do everything in our power to assist you and your people."

Ark nods, a sense of gratitude evident in his expression as he meets Commander Hayes's gaze. "Your offer of assistance is deeply appreciated," he replies, his voice tinged with emotion. "We have faced many challenges in our journey, but with your help, perhaps we can overcome them together."

The crew members exchange nods of agreement, their determination to aid Ark and his community unwavering. They know that their journey together will be fraught with challenges, but they are ready to face them head-on, united in their quest for understanding and discovery.

Commander Hayes inquires once more, her voice gentle yet insistent, "Ark, forgive me for pressing, but was it volcanic activity that forced your people to seek shelter in these caves?"

Commander Hayes's inquiry delves deeper, probing into the precise nature of the cataclysmic events that precipitated Ark's people's retreat into the subterranean depths. She seeks to understand the full extent of the challenges they faced and the decisions they were forced to make in order to ensure their survival.

Ark's response is measured, his voice carrying the weight of centuries-old sorrow and loss. "Yes, Commander," he acknowledges, his tone heavy with resignation. "It was not only volcanic activity but also a series of environmental catastrophes that befell our world. Rising temperatures, shifting tectonic plates, and devastating storms wreaked havoc on the surface, making it increasingly inhospitable for our people."

He pauses, a somber silence settling over the chamber as the echoes of his words linger in the air. "Faced with the relentless onslaught of these disasters, we had no choice but to seek refuge underground, where we could shelter from the harsh conditions above and safeguard our way of life."

Ark's words paint a vivid picture of the trials and tribulations that his people endured; their resilience tested by the unforgiving forces of nature. Yet, despite the hardships they faced, there is a quiet determination in Ark's demeanor, a steadfast resolve to persevere against the odds and rebuild their shattered world.

Commander Hayes listens intently, her heart heavy with empathy for Ark and his people. She understands the gravity of their situation and is determined to offer whatever assistance she can to help them overcome the challenges they face.

With a solemn nod, Ark acknowledges her words, grateful for the understanding and compassion shown by the crew. Together, they stand on the threshold of a new chapter, united in their determination to overcome the challenges that lie ahead and forge a path towards a brighter future for Ark and his community.

As the crew follows Ark deeper into the cave, they come upon a set of stairs leading downward into the darkness below. The air grows cooler, and a faint echo reverberates off the stone walls, creating an eerie atmosphere that sends shivers down their spines.

Commander Hayes, her curiosity piqued, approaches the stairs with caution, her gaze fixed on the descending path ahead. "Ark, where do these stairs lead?" she inquires, her voice carrying a mixture of fascination and apprehension.

Ark nods solemnly, his expression reflecting the gravity of their journey. "These stairs lead to the heart of our underground city," he explains, his voice tinged with reverence. "It is where our people have made their home for generations, seeking refuge from the unforgiving forces of the surface world."

Lieutenant Commander Thompson casts a wary glance down the stairwell, his hand instinctively reaching for the flashlight at his side. "Are you sure it's safe down there?" he asks, his voice tinged with apprehension. Ark nods reassuringly. "Yes, Commander. Our city is well-protected and secure," he assures them. "You have nothing to fear."

Despite Lieutenant Commander Thompson's apprehension, he nods in acknowledgment of Ark's reassurance, his trust in their newfound ally evident. "Very well," he replies, his tone steady despite the lingering sense of unease. "Lead the way, Ark. We trust you."

With Ark taking the lead, with a nod of agreement from Commander Hayes, the crew begins their descent down the stairs, their footsteps echoing softly against the cold stone walls. As they disappear into the depths below, they brace themselves for the mysteries that await them in the heart of Ark's underground city.

As they descend further into the depths, the air grows

cooler, and a sense of anticipation builds within the crew. Each step brings them closer to the heart of Ark's civilization, where untold wonders and ancient secrets await discovery.

The dim glow of lanterns illuminates the path ahead, casting long shadows that dance across the ancient walls. The air is thick with the scent of earth and minerals, mingling with the faint aroma of cooking fires and the distant hum of activity.

Despite the unfamiliar surroundings, the crew is filled with a sense of wonder and curiosity as they navigate the winding corridors of the underground city. With each passing moment, they draw closer to unlocking the secrets that lie hidden within its ancient walls, eager to learn more about the enigmatic civilization that calls this place home.

With each footfall, the crew's excitement mounts, tempered by a profound sense of respect for the history and heritage of Ark's people. They are about to embark on a journey into the heart of the unknown, where the mysteries of the past and the possibilities of the future converge in a timeless dance of exploration and discovery.

The crew emerges from the darkness of the cave into the vibrant heart of the underground city, greeted by a spectacle unlike anything they have ever seen.

Towering structures rise up around them, their walls adorned with intricate carvings depicting scenes from ancient legends and myths. Colorful murals decorate the facades, depicting vibrant landscapes and celestial phenomena, adding a sense of life and vibrancy to the underground world.

Winding streets snake through the city, bustling with activity as residents go about their daily lives. Merchants peddle their wares in bustling marketplaces, their stalls overflowing with exotic goods and rare treasures from across the cosmos.

Aromas of exotic spices and freshly cooked meals waft through the air, enticing the crew with the promise of culinary delights waiting to be savored.

As they wander through the labyrinthine streets, the crew encounters a diverse array of beings, each with their own unique features and customs.

Some move with grace and elegance, their attire adorned with intricate patterns and jewels, while others boast rugged features and stoic demeanors, hinting at lives shaped by hardship and resilience.

Throughout the city, the hum of conversation fills the air, punctuated by bursts of laughter and the occasional melodious tune drifting from street performers.

Despite the underground setting, there is a sense of

warmth and community that permeates every corner of the city, binding its inhabitants together in a shared sense of purpose and camaraderie.

As the crew takes in the sights and sounds of the underground metropolis, they can't help but feel a sense of wonder and awe at the vibrant tapestry of life that thrives beneath the surface of this planet.

With each passing moment, they are drawn deeper into the heart of the city, eager to uncover its secrets and learn more about the civilization that calls it home.

Commander Hayes, her eyes wide with wonder, takes in the sights and sounds of the bustling cityscape. "This is remarkable," she remarks, her voice filled with awe. "To think that an entire civilization exists beneath the surface of this planet."

Ark pauses, his gaze thoughtful as he considers Commander Hayes' question. "Our community is not large," he begins, his voice carrying a hint of introspection. "We are a close-knit group, descendants of those who sought refuge underground generations ago. While our numbers may be modest, each member plays a vital role in our collective survival."

He gestures towards the winding tunnels that stretch out before them, the echoes of their footsteps reverberating softly in the cavernous space. "In these depths, we have forged a home, a sanctuary where we support one another and strive to thrive amidst the challenges of our environment."

Ark's expression softens, a sense of pride shining through the somberness of his words. "Though we may be few in number, we are bound by a shared history and a shared purpose," he concludes. "And together, we face the future with determination and hope."

Ark nods proudly, gesturing toward the various buildings and landmarks that populate the city. "Welcome to our home," he says, a hint of pride in his voice. "Here, you will find everything you need to sustain and support our way of life."

The crew marvels at the ingenuity and resourcefulness of Ark's people, as they navigate the labyrinthine streets, taking in the sights and sounds of this hidden world. Everywhere they turn, there are signs of life and activity, from bustling marketplaces where merchants peddle their wares, to workshops where artisans ply their trade.

As they explore further, they encounter residents going about their daily lives, their faces filled with warmth and hospitality as they welcome the crew into their midst. Despite the challenges they face living in the underground, there is a sense of resilience and community that binds Ark's people together, forging bonds that transcend the darkness that surrounds them.

For Commander Hayes and the crew, it is a humbling

experience, a reminder of the resilience of the human spirit and the power of unity in the face of adversity.

As they continue their journey through the underground city, they are filled with a renewed sense of purpose and determination, eager to learn more about this hidden civilization and the mysteries it holds.

Lieutenant Commander Thompson marvels at the ingenuity and resilience of Ark's people as he observes the bustling streets and lively marketplaces. "It's incredible how you've managed to thrive in this environment," he remarks, his voice tinged with admiration.

Ark smiles warmly, his eyes shining with pride. "We are a resilient people," he says. "And we owe it to our ancestors, who built this city generations ago to escape the dangers of the surface."

As the crew explores the bustling streets and vibrant marketplaces of the underground city, they cannot help but feel a sense of wonder and fascination at the ingenuity and resourcefulness of Ark's people.

Everywhere they look, there are signs of life and activity, from artisans crafting intricate goods to farmers tending to lush underground gardens.

As the crew delves deeper into the underground city, they encounter a remarkable sight: lush greenery thriving amidst the urban landscape. Commander Hayes and her team marvel at the advanced agricultural techniques employed by the inhabitants.

Dr. Chen's keen scientific eye detects the presence of Photon Growth illuminators illuminating the underground farms. She explains how these sophisticated lighting systems provide the optimal spectrum of light for photosynthesis, enabling the plants to grow and flourish without natural sunlight.

Dr. Chen inquires, "How do you pollinate flowers and crops without bees?"

Ark, considering Dr. Chen's inquiry about pollination in the absence of natural sunlight and bity, Ark nods in agreement with Dr. Chen's inquiry and begins his explanation. "Indeed, Dr. Chen, 'bity' refers to your bees, the small insects that buzz. Let me show you." Ark leads Dr. Chen's attention to a picture hanging on the wall beside the garden.

In the image, intricate illustrations portray buzzing bees with vibrant colors, showcasing their distinct appearance. "These are our 'bity'," Ark explains, pointing to the depiction of bees. "They are vital insects known for their buzzing sound and their crucial role in pollination."

Continuing, Ark says, "In our community, 'bity' are highly esteemed for their pollination capabilities and for producing honey, an esteemed resource." He underscores the importance of 'bity' in their underground society's agriculture and ecosystem.

"So, as you rightly identified, Dr. Chen," Ark concludes, "these buzzing insects are indeed our 'bity,' commonly known to you as bees, essential to the thriving of our underground gardens and agricultural endeavors."

He gestures toward a nearby section of the illuminated farm where workers are delicately hand-pollinating the flowers. "Firstly, we employ manual pollination techniques," Ark explains. "Our skilled workers carefully transfer pollen from the stamen to the pistil of each flower, mimicking the role of natural pollinators like bity."

Ark then points to small robotic drones buzzing around the farm. "In addition to manual pollination, we've developed specialized drones equipped with soft brushes," he continues. "These drones mimic the flight patterns of bity, gently brushing against the flowers to transfer pollen from one bloom to another."

He smiles, proud of their innovative approach. "By combining manual intervention with technological solutions, we ensure that our crops receive the pollination they need to thrive, even in the absence of natural sunlight and we have a small number of bity to give us our honey."

Meanwhile, Lieutenant Johnson observes the hydroponic and aeroponic systems with fascination. She recognizes how these innovative farming methods allow the residents to cultivate crops without the need for traditional soil, using nutrient-rich water solutions instead. It's a testament to their ingenuity and adaptability in creating sustainable food sources in their subterranean environment.

Commander Hayes's observation resonates with the crew as they navigate through the bustling underground city. They witness firsthand the ingenuity and determination of Ark's people as they go about their daily lives.

Dr. Chen nods in agreement, impressed by the advanced technologies and sustainable practices that support life beneath the surface. "It's remarkable how they've overcome the challenges of their environment," she remarks. "Their ability to adapt and innovate is truly inspiring."

Lieutenant Johnson echoes their sentiments, noting the sense of community and cooperation that permeates the underground city. "Despite the limitations of their surroundings, they've built a thriving community," she observes. "It's a testament to their resilience and strength."

As they continue their exploration, the crew gains a newfound appreciation for the resilience and resourcefulness of Ark's people. They realize that despite the differences in their worlds, they share a common bond as fellow inhabitants of the cosmos, united by their shared determination to overcome adversity and thrive in the face of challenges.

Commander Hayes and her crew follow Ark through the bustling streets of the underground city until they reach his home.

The dwelling, though modest by their standards, exudes a sense of warmth and hospitality. Ark introduces them to his family—a kind-hearted wife and three curious children who greet the visitors with wide-eyed wonder.

As they step inside, the crew is welcomed by the comforting aroma of a hearty meal cooking on the stove. Ark's wife, a gracious host, invites them to join them at the table, where they share stories and laughter over a delicious meal made from the bountiful harvest of their underground farms.

As they share a meal together, Commander Hayes and her crew are struck by the sense of community and camaraderie that permeates Ark's household.

Despite the challenges they face living underground, Ark and his family radiate a sense of resilience and determination, embodying the spirit of unity and cooperation that defines their society.

Amidst the warm atmosphere, Ark's family serves a

refreshing herbal tea, brewed with care from the aromatic herbs grown in their underground gardens. As the crew sips the fragrant beverage, Mark wonders aloud if there is any sugar available to sweeten his tea.

Ark, ever hospitable, smiles warmly and nods, his curiosity piqued by the mention of sugar. "Sugar?" he repeats, a thoughtful expression on his face. "I'm not familiar with that term. Could you tell me more about it?"

Mark explains, "Sugar is a sweet substance commonly used to add sweetness to food and drinks. It's often derived from sugarcane or sugar beets and comes in various forms, such as granulated sugar, brown sugar, and powdered sugar."

Ark listens intently, intrigued by this new concept. "Ah, I see," he responds, nodding thoughtfully, "and food what is that may I ask."

Dr Hayes replied, "It is what you grow and feed yourself with like the meal we just had."

"While we don't have sugar in the traditional sense, we do have honey harvested from our underground apiaries, it's a natural sweetener, and it pairs wonderfully with the herbal tea, and as for food we call it khat."

"Well thank you for the lovely khat it was most welcome" said dr Hayes.

Gratefully, Mark accepts a dollop of honey to stir into his tea, savoring the delicate sweetness it imparts. In this simple act of sharing a meal and enjoying a comforting drink, the bonds of friendship between the crew and Ark's family deepen, bridging the gap between their two worlds and reinforcing the spirit of cooperation that unites them in their journey through the cosmos.

Around the table, stories are exchanged, laughter fills the air, and bonds of friendship are forged. Ark's wife regales them with tales of life in the underground city, sharing anecdotes of triumphs and challenges, while the children eagerly ask questions about life beyond their subterranean home.

As they dine on the fruits of the underground farms, the crew can't help but feel a sense of gratitude for the hospitality shown to them by Ark and his family. In this moment, surrounded by warmth and companionship, they find solace and comfort in the midst of their interstellar journey.

Through shared experiences and shared meals, Commander Hayes and her crew come to understand the true meaning of community and connection, realizing that no matter where they may travel in the cosmos, the bonds of friendship and solidarity will always endure.

As the evening draws to a close, Commander Hayes expresses her gratitude to Ark and his family for their hospitality. Though their time together is brief, the connection forged between the two groups serves as a poignant reminder of the bonds that transcend language and culture, uniting all beings in the vast tapestry of the universe.

As the evening deepens Ark extends a gracious invitation to Commander Hayes and her crew to stay the night. His warm hospitality touches the hearts of the weary travelers, offering them a respite from their journey through the cosmos.

Commander Hayes considers the offer, grateful for the chance to rest and replenish their energy before embarking on the next leg of their adventure. She exchanges a glance with her crew, who nod in silent agreement, their expressions reflecting a mix of appreciation and relief.

"We would be honored to accept your kind invitation," Commander Hayes replies, her voice conveying their collective gratitude. "Thank you for welcoming us into your home."

With Ark's guidance, Commander Hayes and her crew settle into their temporary lodgings, grateful for the opportunity to rest and rejuvenate in the midst of their cosmic odyssey. As they drift off to sleep, their dreams are filled with visions of distant stars and undiscovered worlds, carried on the gentle embrace of Ark's hospitality.

Chapter 12:
Night Underground

The next morning, as the first light of dawn kisses the horizon, Commander Hayes and her crew awaken to the comforting aroma of breakfast prepared by Ark's wife. The tantalizing scent of freshly cooked food fills the air, stirring their senses and beckoning them to the communal table.

With a smile of gratitude, Ark's wife welcomes the weary travelers, her warmth and hospitality shining through her gentle demeanor. She gestures for them to take a seat, offering a spread of food that reflects the rich Flavors and culinary traditions of their home world.

Commander Hayes and her crew gather around the table, their spirits lifted by the prospect of a hearty meal shared in the company of newfound friends. They express they're thanks to Ark's wife for her generous hospitality, savoring each bite of the delicious food set before them.

As they eat, conversation flows effortlessly between the two groups, bridging the gap between their worlds and fostering a sense of camaraderie that transcends language and culture.

Together, they share stories of their respective journeys and discoveries, finding common ground in their shared love for exploration and adventure.

As the meal draws to a close, Commander Hayes and her crew express their gratitude once more to Ark's wife for her kindness and generosity. "Thank you so much for your hospitality," Commander Hayes said warmly. "Your kindness has truly made our stay memorable."

As the meal wound down, Commander Hayes and her crew turned to Ark's wife with a sense of gratitude. Ark's wife smiled warmly, her eyes sparkling with genuine warmth. "It was our pleasure to host you," she replied. "You are always welcome here."

With renewed energy and a sense of camaraderie, the crew rose from the table, eager to explore the city that had welcomed them so graciously. "Do you mind if we have a look around your city?" Commander Hayes asked, her tone respectful.

Ark's wife nodded, her smile widening. "Of course not," she said. "Feel free to explore to your heart's content. And if you need anything, don't hesitate to ask."

With a final expression of gratitude, Commander Hayes and her crew bid farewell to Ark's family and set out to explore the bustling streets of the alien city.

As they wandered through the vibrant thoroughfares, they could not help but marvel at the sights and sounds of this new world, grateful for the opportunity to immerse themselves in its rich culture and history.

As Commander Hayes and her crew ventured through the underground city, they were enveloped in a world of dimly lit tunnels and caverns. The walls, hewn from solid rock, bore intricate carvings and symbols that spoke of a rich cultural history.

Navigating through the labyrinthine passages, they encountered bustling marketplaces illuminated by softly glowing crystals embedded in the walls. Merchants called out to passersby, their voices echoing off the rough-hewn stone as they showcased their wares.

They passed by workshops where artisans crafted intricate sculptures and artifacts, their skilled hands bringing to life the stories and legends of their people. The air was filled with the rhythmic clinking of hammers and the soft whispers of creativity. As they delved deeper into the city, they stumbled upon communal gathering spaces where residents congregated to share meals and stories.

The flickering light of torches cast dancing shadows across the faces of the gathered crowd as they laughed and conversed in their native tongue.

Occasionally, they caught glimpses of children playing in the narrow alleyways, their laughter echoing through the caverns as they chased one another in a carefree game.

Despite the unfamiliar surroundings, Commander Hayes and her crew felt a sense of kinship with the inhabitants of the underground city. As they explored its depths, they marveled at the resilience and ingenuity of the alien civilization that had made it their home.

And with each step they took, they knew that they were uncovering a wealth of knowledge and understanding that would forever shape their perception of the universe.

Ark approached Commander Hayes and her crew with a warm smile, his presence a reassuring sight in the labyrinthine tunnels of the underground city. "Welcome, travelers," he greeted them, his voice echoing softly off the cavern walls. "I hope you are finding our city to your liking."

Commander Hayes returned Ark's smile with a nod of gratitude. "We are grateful for your hospitality, Ark," she replied. "Your city is truly remarkable, a testament to the ingenuity of your people."

Ark's eyes sparkled with pride as he gestured for them to follow him. "I'm glad you think so," he said. "There is much more to see, if you are interested. Allow me to show you around."

With Ark as their guide, Commander Hayes and her crew embarked on a journey of discovery through the winding passageways and hidden alcoves of the underground city. Along the way, Ark regaled them with stories of his people's history and traditions, painting a vivid picture of life beneath the surface of the planet.

As they walked, Commander Hayes could not help but be struck by the resilience and unity of the underground community. Despite the challenges they faced, the inhabitants of the city had built a thriving civilization in the depths of the planet, their spirit unbroken by the harshness of their environment.

With each step, Commander Hayes and her crew gained a deeper appreciation for the strength and resilience of the alien civilization they had encountered.

And as they continued their exploration, they knew that they were forging bonds that would transcend the boundaries of language and culture, connecting them to the people of this remarkable underground city in ways they had never imagined.

As they stepped into the library, Commander Hayes and her crew were greeted by the sight of towering shelves filled with ancient tomes and illuminated manuscripts.

The air was thick with the scent of old parchment and ink, lending an air of reverence to the space.

Ark led them through the rows of books, pointing out notable volumes and sharing stories of the knowledge contained within their pages.

"Our library is one of the oldest and most cherished institutions in our city," he explained, his voice filled with pride. "It holds the collective wisdom of our ancestors, passed down through generations."

Commander Hayes ran her fingers along the spines of the books, marveling at the wealth of knowledge contained within their weathered pages. "It's truly remarkable," she murmured, her eyes scanning the titles with fascination. "I can only imagine the stories these books hold."

Ark nodded in agreement, his gaze lingering on a particularly ornate tome. "Indeed," he said. "Our history, our culture, our very essence is preserved within these walls. It is a privilege to be their custodians."

As they explored the library, Commander Hayes and her crew were struck by the depth of knowledge and wisdom contained within its shelves. Each book was a testament to the ingenuity and creativity of Ark's people, a reminder of the power of learning and discovery.

As Ark carefully opened the ancient tome, Commander Hayes and her crew gathered around, their eyes alight with curiosity.

The pages were weathered and yellowed with age, each one filled with intricate symbols and faded illustrations that spoke of a distant time and place.

"This book has been passed down through generations, a relic from the time of the Pharaohs," Ark explained, his voice tinged with reverence.

"They were our ancestors, travelers from a distant world who brought with them the seeds of knowledge and wisdom."

Commander Hayes leaned in closer, studying the elaborate script that adorned the pages. "It's incredible to think that this book has survived for so long," she remarked, her voice hushed with awe. "What secrets does it hold?"

Ark smiled knowingly, his eyes reflecting the ancient knowledge contained within the tome.

"The Pharaohs were scholars and explorers, seekers of truth and enlightenment," he explained. "This book contains their teachings, their stories, and their visions for the future."

As they turned the pages, Commander Hayes and her crew were transported to a world of wonder and discovery.

The words of the Pharaohs spoke of distant galaxies and uncharted stars, of mysteries waiting to be unraveled and adventures waiting to be had.

"We are but custodians of their legacy," Ark said

solemnly, his hand resting on the open page. "It is our duty to preserve their wisdom and carry their torch into the future."

As Commander Hayes scanned the pages of the ancient tome, her eyes narrowed with concentration. "What does it say about where they came from?" she inquired; her voice tinged with anticipation.

Ark's brow furrowed as he studied the intricate symbols on the page. "The Pharaohs spoke of a distant star system, far beyond the reaches of our own," he explained, his voice grave with reverence.

"They called it the Cradle of Light, a place of boundless energy and infinite possibility."

Commander Hayes's heart quickened with excitement at the mention of a distant star system. "Do they provide any clues about how to find it?" she pressed; her curiosity piqued.

Ark shook his head regretfully. "The secrets of the Cradle of Light remain shrouded in mystery," he admitted. "But perhaps with time and perseverance, you may uncover the truth hidden within these ancient pages."

As Commander Hayes and her crew absorbed this revelation, they felt a renewed sense of purpose coursing through their veins. The Cradle of Light beckoned to them from across the vast expanse of space, promising untold wonders and revelations beyond imagination.

Lieutenant Johnson asked, "What could this Cradle of Light signify? Could it mean our Sun?"

"Lieutenant Johnson might be onto something," Commander Hayes remarked, her eyes alight with realization. "The Cradle of Light could indeed refer to our sun, the source of warmth and life in our solar system."

Dr. Chen nodded in agreement, her mind racing with possibilities. "If the Pharaohs originated from a star system similar to ours, it could provide valuable insights into their culture and technological advancements," she mused, her voice filled with excitement.

Mark Thompson furrowed his brow, deep in thought. "But what led them to leave their home and embark on a journey across the cosmos?" he wondered aloud; his curiosity piqued by the enigmatic origins of the Pharaohs.

Commander Hayes considered his question carefully, her gaze drifting back to the ancient tome in Ark's hands. "That's a question we'll have to explore further," she replied, her tone resolute. "But for now, let's focus on deciphering the rest of the text and uncovering the truth behind the Pharaohs' legacy."

With renewed determination, Commander Hayes and her

crew returned their attention to the ancient tome, eager to unravel the mysteries that lay hidden within its pages.

As they delved deeper into the Pharaohs' ancient wisdom, they knew that their journey was only just beginning, and that the secrets of the universe awaited them on the path ahead.

As the hours passed, Commander Hayes and her crew poured over the ancient text, deciphering its cryptic symbols, and piecing together fragments of the Pharaohs' history.

With each revelation, they gained a deeper understanding of the enigmatic beings who had once roamed the cosmos.

Suddenly, Dr. Chen let out an exclamation of excitement, her finger tracing a passage in the tome. "Look at this," she exclaimed, her voice tinged with awe. "It mentions a distant planet, a world teeming with life and brimming with energy."

Dr. Chen's gaze fell upon the page of the ancient tome, her fingers tracing the intricate lines of the hieroglyphic inscription. With a furrowed brow, she pondered the meaning of the symbol before her, a circle with a dot in its center.

"I studied a little about hieroglyphics at university," she murmured to herself, her voice barely above a whisper.

"That symbol... it means 'sun'."

As the words escaped her lips, Dr. Chen felt a surge of excitement coursing through her veins. Here, in the pages of this ancient book, lay the secrets of a civilization long gone, waiting to be deciphered and understood. With renewed determination, she delved deeper into the text, eager to unlock the mysteries hidden within its pages.

Commander Hayes leaned in closer, her eyes scanning the text with keen interest. "Could this be a reference to Earth?" she wondered aloud, her mind racing with possibilities. "If so, it suggests that the Pharaohs were not only travelers of the stars but also observers of our own world."

Mark Thompson nodded in agreement; his gaze focused on the ancient script before him. "It's remarkable to think that beings from another corner of the universe were aware of our existence," he mused, his voice filled with wonder.

With newfound determination, Commander Hayes and her crew continued their exploration of the ancient tome, eager to uncover more clues about the Pharaohs' connection to Earth.

As they delved deeper into the text, they knew that their journey would lead them not only to the far reaches of the cosmos but also back to their own home planet, where the threads of destiny awaited to be unraveled.

Ark interrupted their intense discussion with a gentle smile. "Would anyone care for some refreshments?" he offered warmly, his voice echoing through the library.

Commander Hayes glanced up from the ancient tome, grateful for the interruption. "That would be much appreciated, Ark," she replied with a nod. "Thank you for your hospitality."

The crew exchanged glances; their curiosity piqued by the prospect of sampling the local cuisine. Dr. Chen's eyes sparkled with excitement as she eagerly accepted Ark's offer. "I would love to try some of your traditional dishes," she exclaimed, her voice filled with enthusiasm for new experiences.

Mark Thompson nodded in agreement, his stomach rumbling in anticipation. "A drink sounds great, thank you," he said, his tone grateful for the chance to take a break from their research.

Sarah Johnson smiled warmly; her curiosity piqued by the opportunity to learn more about the culture of their gracious hosts. "I'm curious to see what delicacies you have to offer," she remarked, her voice friendly and inviting.

With their preferences expressed, Ark nodded in understanding. "Very well, please follow me to the dining area," he said, gesturing for the crew to accompany him. "I'll show you to some of our finest culinary delights."

As Commander Hayes and her crew followed Ark out of the library, their minds buzzing with excitement, they couldn't help but feel grateful for the chance to experience the hospitality of the inhabitants of this mysterious underground city. And as they prepared to embark on this new adventure, they knew that their journey would only grow richer with each new encounter along the way.

In the cozy ambiance of the communal dining area, Commander Hayes and her crew sat around a table laden with an array of exotic dishes and beverages. Each member of the crew had selected a different meal and drink, eager to sample the culinary delights of their gracious hosts.

Dr. Chen savored a dish of Savory vegetable stew, her taste buds tingling with delight as she explored the intricate flavors and textures of the hearty meal. Beside her, Mark Thompson enjoyed a plate of roasted meats and vegetables, relishing the smoky aroma and tender juiciness of the dish.

Meanwhile, Sarah Johnson delighted in a bowl of fragrant rice and aromatic spices, her senses tingling with the bold flavors and tantalizing aromas of the exotic cuisine. And Commander Hayes sampled a traditional soup made with local herbs and spices, savoring each spoonful as she immersed herself in the rich culinary tapestry of Ark's culture.

As they dined, the crew exchanged friendly banter and shared stories of their past adventures, their laughter filling the air with warmth and camaraderie. With each bite and sip, they discovered new flavors and experiences, forging deeper connections with each other.

As the meal drew to a close, Commander Hayes raised her glass in a toast to their hosts. "To new friendships and shared adventures," she declared, her voice filled with gratitude and goodwill.

The crew echoed her sentiment, clinking their glasses together in a gesture of camaraderie and solidarity. In that moment, as they basked in the glow of newfound friendships and the warmth of shared experiences, they knew that their journey had brought them to a place of true belonging—a place where the bonds of friendship transcended language and culture, uniting them in a shared vision of exploration and discovery.

Mark Thompson raised an eyebrow as he surveyed the tantalizing spread of roasted meats before him. "I couldn't help but notice," he began, his tone curious, "I haven't seen any animals during our time here. Yet, you've prepared this delightful array of meats. How is that possible?"

Mark Thompson 's observation prompted a thoughtful pause among the crew. Commander Hayes glanced around the dining area, taking in the absence of any visible signs of animal life. "That's an interesting observation, Mark," she remarked, her brow furrowing slightly. "It does seem curious that we haven't encountered any animals during our time here."

Ark, their gracious host, nodded in understanding. "Our planet is home to a diverse array of flora and fauna," he explained, his voice calm and reassuring. "However, the animals you see on your plate are not native to our world. They are cultivated and prepared using alternative methods to meet the dietary preferences of our guests."

Commander Hayes and her crew exchanged surprised glances, intrigued by Ark's explanation. "So, you're saying that these 'roasted meats' are actually synthetic or lab-grown?" Sarah Johnson inquired; her curiosity piqued by the revelation.

Ark nodded in confirmation. "Yes, that's correct," he confirmed. "We've developed advanced technologies that allow us to create sustainable khat sources without the need for traditional animal farming. It's part of our commitment to environmental stewardship and ethical dining practices."

Dr. Chen's eyes sparkled with interest as she considered the implications of Ark's words. "That's truly remarkable," she exclaimed, her voice filled with admiration. "It's a testament to your society's ingenuity and dedication to sustainability."

As they continued their meal, Commander Hayes and her crew marveled at the innovative culinary creations before them, appreciating not only the delicious flavors but also the ethical and environmental considerations that went into their preparation.

In that moment, they gained a newfound appreciation for the ingenuity and resourcefulness of their hosts, deepening their respect for the culture and values of the people of Ark's world.

Commander Hayes addressed Ark with a warm smile. "We're truly grateful for your hospitality and the opportunity to explore your city and culture," she began, her voice filled with appreciation. "However, we must also remember our mission and the need to return home. We've been away from our own planet for quite some time now, and it's essential that we continue our journey."

Commander Hayes, intrigued by the unique civilization she has encountered, poses a question to Ark before they depart. "Ark, are there other underground cities like yours scattered across this planet?"

Ark's expression grows solemn as he considers the question. "Yes, Commander," he responds, his voice tinged with a sense of melancholy. "There are other underground settlements, remnants of our once-thriving civilization. But they are scattered and isolated, each community facing its own challenges and struggles."

Commander Hayes nods thoughtfully, absorbing Ark's words. "Thank you for sharing that with us," she says, her tone filled with empathy. "Perhaps one day, we can work together to help these communities thrive once again."

With a final nod of understanding, Ark bids farewell to the crew as they prepare to depart, leaving behind a world filled with untold stories and hidden wonders.

As the visit concludes, one of the inhabitants graciously offers to escort Commander Hayes and her crew back to their spacecraft. They traverse the winding pathways of the underground city, illuminated by softly glowing crystals embedded in the walls.

With each step, they carry with them memories of friendship, warmth, and shared experiences, knowing that their encounter with Ark and his people will forever remain etched in their hearts.

As they bid farewell to their newfound friends and prepare to depart, they are filled with a renewed sense of purpose and unity, ready to continue their journey through the cosmos with open hearts and minds.

Along the way, the crew members exchange glances,

each reflecting on the profound encounter they have just experienced. Despite the differences in their worlds, they cannot help but feel a sense of kinship with Ark and his community.

Upon reaching the entrance to the cavernous chamber where their spacecraft awaits, Commander Hayes extends her heartfelt thanks to their guide. With a warm smile, the inhabitant nods in understanding, bidding them farewell with a gesture of goodwill.

As they board their ship and prepare for departure, the crew carries with them the memories of their extraordinary encounter with Ark and his people.

Though their journey through the White Universe has been filled with wonders beyond imagination, it is the unexpected connections forged along the way that leave the deepest impression on their hearts and minds.

As the engines hum to life and the spacecraft lifts off from the surface of the planet, the crew looks back one last time, gazing upon the underground city with a mixture of gratitude and longing.

Though they must continue their voyage through the cosmos, they know that they carry with them the spirit of friendship and unity that they found in the depths of the White Universe.

And as they soar through the stars, they are filled with

hope for the future, knowing that wherever their journey may lead, they will always cherish the memories of their time spent with Ark and his people.

Chapter 13:
Second Planet

As Lieutenant Commander Mark Thompson and Dr. Emily Chen contemplated their recent encounter with the inhabitants of the planet, they could not shake the lingering question: are there more worlds like the one they had visited?

The sense of wonder and amazement that accompanied their discovery fueled a deep curiosity about the diversity of life and civilizations that might exist beyond their own.

In quiet moments aboard the spacecraft, Mark and Emily engaged in discussions, speculating about the possibilities that awaited them in the vast reaches of space.

They pondered the potential for encountering other advanced societies, each with its own unique culture, technology, and way of life. Their imaginations soared as they envisioned exploring new worlds, forging connections with other beings, and unravelling the mysteries of the cosmos.

Despite the challenges and uncertainties that lay ahead,

Mark and Emily shared a sense of excitement and anticipation for the adventures yet to come. With their spirits buoyed by the prospect of further exploration, they eagerly awaited the next leg of their journey, eager to uncover the secrets of the universe and expand humanity's understanding of its place in the cosmos.

As they stood together, Commander Dr. Elizabeth Hayes could sense the undercurrent of excitement in their conversation. She leaned in slightly, her interest piqued by their discussion.

Mark's eyes gleamed with curiosity as he elaborated, "We were considering the implications of our encounter with Ark and his people. It's remarkable to think about the possibility of other underground civilizations like theirs. What if there are entire worlds out there, hidden beneath the surface, waiting to be discovered?"

Emily nodded thoughtfully, her mind already racing with possibilities. "Exactly," she chimed in. "And even beyond underground civilizations, we've barely scratched the surface of what lies beyond our own galaxy. Who knows what other forms of life might exist in the countless stars and planets we have yet to explore?"

Their conversation sparked a lively exchange of ideas, as they delved into theories about the potential diversity of life in the universe and the myriad of civilizations that might exist beyond their own. With each passing moment, their sense of wonder and curiosity deepened, fueling their anticipation for the adventures that lay ahead in the uncharted realms of space.

As they delved deeper into their discussion, Commander Hayes, Lieutenant Commander Thompson, and Dr. Chen found themselves enthralled by the vastness of the universe and the myriad of possibilities it held. They speculated about encountering civilizations with advanced technologies, uncovering ancient relics left behind by long-forgotten races, and unravelling the secrets of distant galaxies.

With each passing moment, their excitement grew, fueling their determination to push forward in their exploration of the cosmos. They exchanged ideas and theories, their imaginations soaring as they contemplated the wonders that awaited them on their journey through the stars.

As they gazed out into the endless expanse of space, Commander Hayes could not help but feel a sense of awe and gratitude for the opportunity to embark on such an extraordinary adventure. With a renewed sense of purpose, she turned to her companions, a bright smile lighting up her face.

"Let's continue to chart our course through the stars," she said, her voice filled with enthusiasm. "Together, there's no limit to what we can discover and accomplish. Onward, to new horizons!"

Lieutenant Commander Mark Thompson nods in response to Commander Hayes' question. "Yes, Commander, I've attempted to send a message to base, but we're still experiencing communication issues. It seems our signals are being disrupted by the unique properties of this region of space."

Acknowledging the challenging situation they face; Commander Hayes suggests putting their options to a vote. Gathering the crew, they discuss their priorities and weigh the risks and benefits of each course of action. United in their determination, they reach a consensus and prepare to face the challenges ahead, ready to adapt and respond to whatever awaits them in space.

With a sense of urgency, the crew convenes to weigh their options and decide on the best path forward. Each member presents their perspective, highlighting the risks and benefits of various choices, from continuing their journey to conserving resources and awaiting assistance from base. As the discussion unfolds, it becomes clear that the decision will shape the course of their mission and determine their fate in the vast expanse of the cosmos.

Commander Dr. Elizabeth Hayes:
For: Advocates for exploring nearby planets to assess their habitability and potential resources. Emphasizes the importance of finding a sustainable environment for the crew and securing additional supplies to ensure their

long-term survival.

Against: Expresses concerns about the risks involved in venturing into unknown territory and the possibility of encountering hostile environments or unforeseen dangers. Prioritizes caution and safety over the potential benefits of finding a habitable planet.

Lieutenant Commander Mark Thompson:
For: Supports the idea of searching for habitable planets as a proactive measure to secure the crew's future. Argues that finding a suitable environment could provide a stable base of operations and access to essential resources, reducing their reliance on limited supplies.

Against: Expresses reservations about the feasibility of finding habitable planets within their reach and the potential dangers of exploring unknown regions of space. Stresses the importance of conserving resources and prioritizing safety over the uncertain prospect of finding a habitable planet.

Dr. Emily Chen, Ph.D.:
For: Advocates for scientific exploration and discovery, emphasizing the potential benefits of finding habitable planets for research and colonization. Argues that expanding humanity's knowledge of the cosmos and finding new habitats is essential for long-term survival and progress.

Against: Acknowledges the challenges and uncertainties of searching for habitable planets in uncharted space. Expresses concerns about the risks involved in exploring unknown environments and the potential strain on resources and morale if their efforts prove fruitless.

Lieutenant Sarah Johnson:
For: Supports the idea of searching for habitable planets as a proactive measure to secure the crew's future and increase their chances of long-term survival. Emphasizes the importance of exploring all available options to ensure the crew's safety and well-being.
Against: Expresses concerns about the practicalities of finding habitable planets within their reach and the potential dangers of venturing into unknown territory. Stresses the need for caution and careful consideration of the risks and benefits involved in the search for habitable planets.

After careful consideration and deliberation, the crew comes to a unified conclusion regarding their decision to search for more habitable planets. Despite the inherent risks and uncertainties, they agree that exploring new worlds is essential for their long-term survival and the advancement of human knowledge.

They recognize that the challenges they may face are outweighed by the potential benefits of finding a suitable environment to establish a stable base of operations.

Commander Hayes gathers the crew together in the ship's main conference room, her voice steady and authoritative as she addresses them. "Team, as we prepare to venture further into the unknown, it's imperative that we ensure the integrity of our ship's reactors. They are our lifeline in this vast expanse of space, and any malfunction could jeopardize not only our mission but our very survival."

She assigns specific tasks to each crew member, outlining a comprehensive plan to thoroughly inspect and test the ship's reactors. Lieutenant Commander Mark Thompson and Dr. Emily Chen are tasked with conducting diagnostic checks on the reactor systems, analyzing their performance, and identifying any anomalies.

Lieutenant Sarah Johnson is responsible for monitoring the reactor's energy output and radiation levels, ensuring they remain within safe parameters. Meanwhile, Commander Hayes oversees the entire operation, coordinating efforts and making critical decisions to address any issues that may arise.

With their mission clear and their objectives set, the crew sets to work, methodically inspecting and testing every component of the ship's reactors. Each member understands the importance of their role in this crucial task, knowing that the safety and success of their mission depend on their diligence and expertise.

As they work tirelessly to ensure the reactors are in optimal condition, a sense of camaraderie and determination fills the air. They know that their efforts today will pave the way for their journey into the depths of the white space, where new adventures and discoveries await.

With their decision made, the crew wastes no time in setting their plan into motion. Lieutenant Commander Mark Thompson begins analyzing the data from their navigational systems, plotting a course that will take them through uncharted regions of space in search of potentially habitable planets.

Meanwhile, Dr. Emily Chen, Ph.D., focuses her efforts on refining their criteria for identifying suitable candidates for exploration. Drawing on her expertise in astrobiology, she considers factors such as atmospheric composition, surface conditions, and the presence of water—essential elements for sustaining life.

Lieutenant Sarah Johnson takes charge of coordinating their communications and monitoring vital systems, ensuring that their spacecraft remains operational and capable of supporting their mission for the long haul.

As they venture deeper into the cosmos, each member of the crew is filled with a sense of anticipation and excitement for the discoveries that lie ahead. With a shared sense of purpose and determination, they are ready to face whatever challenges come their way as they journey into the unknown, united in their quest to unlock the secrets of the universe and secure humanity's future among the stars.

The crew conducts a thorough assessment of the spacecraft's reactor power to determine their available resources before embarking on their next mission. They calculate the remaining power reserves and consider several factors such as energy consumption, propulsion requirements, and life support systems.

With their analysis revealing no issues with power in the white universe, the crew of the Explorer turned their attention to other critical aspects of their mission. They understood the importance of navigating this unfamiliar realm with caution and precision.

With this understanding, they proceeded to plan their mission accordingly, mindful of the challenges they may encounter in the white universe. Their primary objective remained the exploration and study of this enigmatic environment, seeking to unravel its mysteries and expand humanity's understanding of the cosmos.

Every decision was made with careful consideration of the unique characteristics of the white universe. The crew leveraged their expertise and the advanced technology of the Explorer to gather data and conduct experiments, shedding light on the nature of this extraordinary realm.

As they ventured deeper into the white universe, the crew remained vigilant, ready to adapt to any unexpected developments or phenomena they encountered. They knew that their journey through this ethereal landscape would be unlike any other, and they embraced the opportunity to explore the unknown with open minds and unwavering determination.

With each passing moment, the crew of the Explorer pressed forward, their spirits buoyed by the thrill of discovery and the boundless possibilities that lay ahead. In the vast expanse of the white universe, they found inspiration and wonder, united in their quest to unlock its secrets and chart a course into the uncharted depths of the cosmos.

With the available reactor power assessed and their decision to explore further planets solidified, the crew engages in a discussion to determine their next destination. They consider a range of factors such as proximity, potential habitability, and the likelihood of encountering new forms of life or valuable resources. After deliberation, they reach a consensus to prioritize nearby star systems that show promising signs of habitability.

These star systems may offer the best chance of discovering new worlds that could support human life or provide valuable insights into the diversity of planetary environments across the cosmos. With their destination chosen, the crew sets a course for the nearest promising star system, eager to continue their quest for exploration and discovery.

As their spacecraft traverses the vast expanse of space, the crew's sensors detect several planets with striking similarities to Earth. These worlds exhibit familiar features such as temperate climates, abundant water sources, and a diverse range of ecosystems. Excitement courses through the crew as they realize the potential significance of these discoveries and the possibility of finding habitable environments beyond their home planet.

Commander Dr. Elizabeth Hayes, ever the pragmatist, sees the discovery of Earth-like planets as a promising sign for the future of humanity. She emphasizes the importance of thorough exploration and scientific analysis to determine the true habitability and potential of these newfound worlds. Despite her cautious approach, she acknowledges the profound impact that finding habitable planets could have on humanity's understanding of the cosmos.

Lieutenant Commander Mark Thompson, with his background in engineering and resource management, sees the discovery of habitable planets as a potential solution to the long-term challenges of sustaining human civilization. He advocates for thorough surveys of these planets to assess their suitability for colonization and resource extraction, believing that they could provide valuable resources and opportunities for expansion beyond Earth.

Dr. Emily Chen, Ph.D., the astrophysicist on board, is fascinated by the discovery of Earth-like planets and sees it as a chance to study the conditions necessary for life to thrive in the universe. She eagerly proposes detailed observations and analyses of these planets' atmospheres, geology, and potential signs of life, hoping to unlock the secrets of their formation and evolution.

Lieutenant Sarah Johnson, with her expertise in astronautics and exploration, is filled with a sense of wonder and adventure at the prospect of exploring new worlds. She advocates for sending probes and reconnaissance missions to these planets to gather data and assess the suitability for future human exploration. She believes that the discovery of habitable planets represents a new frontier for humanity to explore and colonize.

Together, the crew recognizes the significance of their discovery and the potential it holds for the future of humanity. With their combined expertise and determination, they are prepared to embark on a new chapter of exploration and discovery, venturing forth into the unknown to unravel the mysteries of these Earth-like planets and unlock the secrets of the cosmos.

With the decision made to gather more information about one of the Earth- like planets, the crew prepares to deploy a reconnaissance pod to conduct a detailed analysis of its surface and atmosphere. The pod, equipped with advanced sensors and imaging equipment, will provide valuable data to assess the planet's potential habitability and suitability for human exploration.

Commander Dr. Elizabeth Hayes coordinates the mission,

ensuring that all necessary precautions are taken to minimize risks and maximize the effectiveness of the reconnaissance operation. She emphasizes the importance of thorough planning and careful execution to gather accurate and comprehensive data about the planet.

Lieutenant Commander Mark Thompson oversees the preparation and deployment of the reconnaissance pod, ensuring that it is equipped with all the necessary instruments and systems for the mission ahead. His expertise in engineering and logistics proves invaluable in ensuring the success of the operation.

Dr. Emily Chen, Ph.D., provides guidance on the scientific objectives of the reconnaissance mission, identifying key areas of interest for data collection and analysis. Her expertise in astrophysics and planetary science helps to inform the selection of observation targets and prioritize the collection of relevant data.

Lieutenant Sarah Johnson, with her expertise in astronautics and spacecraft operations, assumes the responsibility of overseeing the deployment and control of the reconnaissance pod from the spacecraft. With meticulous precision and unwavering focus, she guides the pod through the vast expanse of space towards its designated destination.

Using advanced navigational tools and her extensive knowledge of spacecraft systems, Lieutenant Johnson ensures that the pod follows its intended trajectory with pinpoint accuracy. She monitors every aspect of the deployment process, from the pod's propulsion systems to its communication channels, to ensure a smooth and successful mission.

As the reconnaissance pod journeys deeper into space, Lieutenant Johnson remains vigilant, ready to address any challenges or obstacles that may arise along the way. Her calm demeanor and decisive actions inspire confidence in the rest of the crew, knowing that their mission is in capable hands.

With Lieutenant Johnson at the helm, the reconnaissance pod executes its mission flawlessly, gathering valuable data and insights from the far reaches of the cosmos. Her expertise and dedication play a vital role in the success of their exploratory endeavors, paving the way for new discoveries and adventures beyond the stars.

As the reconnaissance pod gracefully descends towards the Earth-like planet below, the crew watches intently from their spacecraft, their excitement palpable. Each member is keenly aware of the importance of the data the pod will collect and the potential discoveries it may yield.

Lieutenant Sarah Johnson, stationed at the control panel, monitors the pod's descent with precision, adjusting its trajectory as needed to ensure a safe landing. Her expertise in spacecraft operations proves invaluable as she navigates the pod through the planet's atmosphere, skillfully maneuvering around any obstacles that may arise.

Commander Dr. Elizabeth Hayes observes the proceedings with a mix of anticipation, her mind already racing with the possibilities of what they may uncover. With each passing moment, they draw closer to unlocking the secrets of this alien world and expanding humanity's understanding of the cosmos.

As the reconnaissance pod touches down on the planet's surface, a sense of excitement fills the spacecraft. The crew eagerly awaits the transmission of data, eager to analyses the information and glean insights into the planet's geography, atmosphere, and potential for life.

With their expertise and teamwork, the crew is poised to embark on a journey of discovery that will further humanity's quest to explore the cosmos and uncover the mysteries of the universe.

As the data streams in from the reconnaissance pod, revealing the presence of cyanide in the atmosphere of the Earth-like planet, a hushed tension settles over the crew. Commander Dr. Elizabeth Hayes furrows her brow, her mind racing as she considers the implications of this discovery.

"These changes things," she murmurs, her voice laced with concern. "Cyanide is highly toxic, and it poses a significant risk to any potential exploration efforts. We need to proceed with extreme caution."

Lieutenant Sarah Johnson nods in agreement, her fingers flying across the control panel as she analyses the incoming data. "We can't afford to take any chances," she says, her tone resolute. "We need to gather more information before we make any decisions."

With a shared sense of urgency, the crew initiates a comprehensive analysis of the reconnaissance data, scouring it for any additional insights into the planet's atmosphere and composition. Meanwhile, Dr. Emily Chen, Ph.D., delves into the scientific literature, researching the potential effects of cyanide exposure and formulating a plan to ensure the safety of the crew.

After careful consideration, the crew reaches a unanimous decision: they will not risk landing or further exploration until they can gather more information and assess the situation thoroughly. With their safety as the top priority, they prepare to recalibrate their approach and continue their mission with caution and vigilance.

Commander Dr. Elizabeth Hayes leads the crew in formulating a plan to study the planet remotely, using their spacecraft's sensors and imaging equipment to gather data from a safe distance. She emphasizes the importance of thorough analysis and careful consideration before making any decisions about future exploration efforts.

Lieutenant Commander Mark Thompson coordinates the efforts to gather remote data, ensuring that the spacecraft's instruments are calibrated and optimized for detecting and analyzing cyanide levels in the planet's atmosphere. His attention to detail and expertise in spacecraft operations prove invaluable in ensuring the success of the remote study.

Lieutenant Sarah Johnson oversees the remote data collection process, monitoring the spacecraft's systems and ensuring that the gathered data is accurate and reliable. Her diligence and expertise in spacecraft operations play a crucial role in the crew's efforts to study the planet safely from orbit.

As the crew conducts their remote study of the planet, they remain vigilant and cautious, prioritizing safety and scientific rigor in their exploration efforts. While the discovery of cyanide presents a challenge, they are determined to overcome it with careful analysis and prudent decision- making, ensuring that their journey of exploration continues safely.

Dr. Chen's keen eye detects a promising celestial body on the edge of their sensor range, sparking excitement among the crew.

Chapter 14:
Third Planet

Intrigued by Dr. Emily Chen's discovery, the crew of the Explorer set their sights on the planet she had spotted. With their power concerns alleviated in the white universe, they eagerly directed their attention toward this new destination, eager to explore its potential and uncover any secrets it might hold.

As they approached the planet, the crew prepared their instruments and sensors, eager to gather data and learn more about this uncharted world. Dr. Chen's initial observations had hinted at the possibility of unique geological formations or perhaps even signs of life, sparking excitement and anticipation among the crew.

As the Explorer drew closer, the planet's features came into sharper focus, revealing a diverse landscape of rugged terrain and swirling clouds. The crew observed with fascination as they scanned the planet's surface, searching for any anomalies or points of interest that might warrant further investigation.

With each passing moment, the crew's anticipation grew, their curiosity driving them to delve deeper into the mysteries of this unexplored world. They knew that their journey was fraught with uncertainty, but they embraced the challenge with determination and resolve, eager to unlock the secrets that lay hidden beneath the planet's surface.

As they continued their observations, the crew remained vigilant, ready to respond to any unexpected developments or discoveries. For in the vast expanse of the cosmos, every planet held the potential to yield new insights and expand humanity's understanding of the universe.

With their eyes fixed on the horizon and their hearts filled with excitement, the crew of the Explorer pressed onward, united in their quest for knowledge and discovery. And as they charted their course toward the mysterious planet before them, they knew that their journey was just beginning, and that the wonders of the cosmos awaited them with each passing moment.

Excited by the prospect of exploring the mysterious planet, the crew of the Explorer quickly set to work preparing a pod for descent. Equipped with a suite of sensors and instruments, the pod would gather vital data about the planet's composition, including readings of carbon levels and other key elements.

With meticulous care, the crew ensured that the pod was ready for its de- scent, conducting final checks and calibrations to ensure its instruments were functioning optimally. Once satisfied with their preparations, they initiated the launch sequence, guiding the pod toward the planet's surface with precision and skill.

As the pod descended through the planet's atmosphere, the crew monitored its progress closely, eagerly awaiting the data it would collect. Atmospheric pressure, temperature, and chemical composition were all recorded in real-time, providing valuable insights into the planet's environmental conditions.

Upon reaching the surface, the pod began its survey, systematically gathering readings of carbon levels and other elemental compositions. Each data point transmitted back to the Explorer was met with anticipation and excitement, as the crew eagerly analyzed the findings in search of clues about the planet's past and potential for life.

Hours passed as the pod continued its mission, traversing the planet's surface and collecting a wealth of data. As it prepared to return to the Explorer, the crew eagerly awaited its final transmission, eager to delve deeper into the mysteries of this enigmatic world.

With the pod safely back on board, the crew wasted no time in analyzing the data it had collected. Carbon levels, atmospheric conditions, and geo- logical formations were all scrutinized in detail, as the crew worked to un- ravel the secrets of the planet and unlock its potential for further exploration.

As the data poured in, the crew of the Explorer found themselves filled with a sense of awe and wonder, realizing that they had only scratched the surface of what this mysterious planet had to offer. With each discovery, their determination to uncover the truth about this enigmatic world grew stronger, driving them ever forward in their quest for knowledge and understanding.

Dr. Chen's observation piqued the curiosity of the crew even further. If the readings indeed resembled those of their own planet, it could indicate the potential for habitability or at least conditions conducive to life.

As they meticulously analyzed the data collected by the pod, the crew's excitement grew. The carbon levels, atmospheric composition, and other readings bore striking similarities to those of Earth, suggesting the possibility of familiar environmental conditions.

The implications of such findings were profound. If this planet harbored conditions similar to Earth's, it could signify the presence of life or the potential for colonization in the future. The crew's sense of wonder and anticipation soared as they contemplated the implications of their discovery.

With renewed determination, the crew resolved to further explore the planet and uncover any signs of life or evidence of habitability. They knew that their mission had taken on new significance, as they ventured deeper into the mysteries of this remarkable world.

As they charted their course for further exploration, the

crew of the Explorer felt a sense of awe and humility. In the vast expanse of the cosmos, they had stumbled upon a planet that bore striking resemblance to their own, a reminder of the interconnectedness of the universe and the infinite possibilities that lay beyond. With each passing moment, their determination to unlock the secrets of this enigmatic world grew stronger, driving them ever onward in their quest for discovery and understanding.

With Commander Hayes's prudent suggestion of landing on the planet, the crew of the Explorer felt a sense of relief. They knew safety was para- mount, especially considering the potential significance of the planet's re- semblance to Earth. Mark, their skilled navigator, was tasked with identifying a landing spot that would offer both safety and opportunity.

Mark, with his expertise and precision, meticulously analyzed the data collected by the pod. After careful consideration, he pinpointed a location that appeared promising—a vast plain nestled between rolling hills, with no apparent signs of danger or instability.

As the Explorer descended toward the chosen landing spot, the tension onboard gradually eased. The crew prepared for touchdown, their excitement building as they anticipated setting foot on the alien terrain below.

With Commander Hayes's approval, the final descent began. The crew held their breath as the Explorer approached the surface, their eyes fixed on the viewport, eager to catch the first glimpse of their new surroundings.

With a gentle thud, the Explorer touched down on the planet's surface, its landing gear absorbing the impact with ease. A cheer erupted among the crew as they realized they had safely arrived at their destination.

Stepping out onto the alien landscape, Commander Hayes and her crew were greeted by a scene of awe-inspiring beauty. The air was crisp and invigorating, and the landscape stretched out before them in all its grandeur.

With the Explorer safely grounded, the crew wasted no time in preparing to explore their new surroundings. They donned their suits and equipped themselves with scientific instruments, eager to begin their investigation of this remarkable world.

As they ventured out onto the planet's surface, the crew felt a sense of exhilaration and anticipation. They knew that their journey had only just begun, and that countless discoveries awaited them on the horizon. With each step they took, they forged a path into the unknown, ready to unlock the secrets of this enigmatic planet and uncover the mysteries that lay hidden within its depths.

As the crew of the Explorer ventured further into the alien landscape, their senses were inundated with new sights and sounds. Among the verdant foliage and towering trees, they caught glimpses of movement—graceful forms darting between the shadows.

Commander Hayes and her team halted; their attention drawn to a group of creatures grazing in a nearby clearing. With wide eyes and hushed whispers, they observed as the animals moved with a serene elegance, their slender bodies reminiscent of Earth's deer.

Eager to learn more about these newfound inhabitants of the planet, the crew carefully approached, taking care not to startle the creatures. As they drew closer, they marveled at the intricate patterns adorning their fur and the gentle curiosity in their eyes.

Dr. Chen, the ship's biologist, eagerly began documenting their observations, noting the creatures' behavior and interactions. She speculated about their ecological role and evolutionary history, drawing comparisons to similar species on Earth.

The crew remained captivated by the sight of the creatures, their presence serving as a poignant reminder of the diversity and wonder of life in the cosmos. For Commander Hayes and her team, this encounter was a testament to the importance of exploration and discovery, reaffirming their commitment to uncovering the secrets of this remarkable planet.

As they continued their exploration, the crew

encountered other fascinating species, each one offering new insights into the planet's ecosystem and evolutionary processes. With each discovery, their sense of wonder and awe only deepened, fueling their determination to unlock the mysteries of this alien world and expand humanity's understanding of the universe.

As the crew of the Explorer traversed further into the alien landscape, their eyes widened with astonishment as they stumbled upon a towering structure that stretched toward the sky. Rising above the verdant canopy, the building stood as a testament to an advanced civilization that once inhabited the planet.

Commander Hayes and her team approached the structure cautiously, their hearts racing with excitement and curiosity. Its transparent walls shimmered in the sunlight, reflecting the colors of the surrounding flora and fauna. It was a sight unlike anything they had ever seen—a monument to the ingenuity and creativity of an ancient civilization.

As they drew nearer, the crew marveled at the intricacy of the building's design. Its sleek lines and graceful curves spoke of an advanced under- standing of architecture and engineering, while its transparent façade al- lowed glimpses into its interior, revealing a space filled with intricate pat- terns and structures.

Dr. Chen, the ship's scientist, eagerly speculated about the purpose of the building and the civilization that had constructed it. She hypothesized about the technology and culture of the planet's ancient inhabitants, drawing parallels to human history and civilization.

With cautious optimism, Commander Hayes led her team inside the building, their footsteps echoing against the polished floors. As they explored its interior, they discovered chambers filled with artifacts and relics—testaments to the achievements and aspirations of a bygone era.

Each discovery fueled their determination to unravel the mysteries of this ancient civilization, to uncover the secrets that lay buried within the ruins of their world. For Commander Hayes and her team, the discovery of the building was a reminder of the boundless potential of exploration and the enduring legacy of those who came before.

As they delved deeper into the structure, the crew remained ever vigilant, their senses attuned to any signs of danger or discovery. For in the heart of this alien world, they knew that every step held the promise of new revelations and unforeseen challenges, driving them ever onward in their quest for knowledge and understanding.

With each step, the crew of the Explorer proceeded cautiously through the intricate chambers of the towering glass building. Every room they entered revealed more about the mysterious civilization that once inhabited the planet, yet also heightened their awareness of the unknown.

Commander Hayes led her team with purpose, their senses sharp and alert for any signs of activity or surveillance. Dr. Chen meticulously catalogued the artifacts they encountered.
As they ascended the stairs to the upper levels of the building, a sense of anticipation gripped the crew. Each floor held the promise of new discoveries, yet also the potential for unforeseen dangers. They moved with silent determination, their eyes scanning the shadows for any sign of movement.

With each room they searched, the crew remained on high alert, their instincts finely tuned to the slightest disturbance. They knew that they were exploring uncharted territory, and the possibility of encountering unknown inhabitants or surveillance systems loomed ever present in their minds.

Undeterred by the unknowns that lay ahead, the crew of the Explorer pressed on, their determination unwavering in the face of uncertainty. With each step forward, they drew closer to unravelling the mysteries of the ancient civilization that awaited them.

Driven by their insatiable curiosity and thirst for knowledge, they pushed aside any doubts or fears that threatened to hold them back. For they knew that they were on the brink of discovering something truly extraordinary a treasure trove of wisdom and history that had remained hidden for eons.

As they journeyed deeper into the heart of the unknown, the crew remained steadfast in their resolve, their spirits buoyed by the anticipation of what lay ahead. For them, the challenges they faced were merely steppingstones on the path to enlightenment, guiding them ever closer to the truth they sought.

And though the road ahead was fraught with obstacles and dangers, the crew pressed on, united by a shared sense of purpose and a belief in the power of discovery. For they knew that the secrets they sought were worth any sacrifice, and that their journey would ultimately lead them to the answers they sought.

As they continued to explore, the crew remained vigilant, their senses heightened by the knowledge that they could be watched at any moment. Yet, with each room they searched and each artifact they uncovered, they grew ever closer to unravelling the mysteries of the glass building and the enigmatic civilization that had once called this planet home. And as they ventured deeper into the unknown, they knew that their journey was far from over, with countless discoveries still awaiting them in the depths of the ancient ruins.

Commander Hayes stood at the entrance of the towering glass structure; her gaze transfixed by the intricate patterns etched into its transparent walls. Beside her, the crew of the Explorer marveled at the alien architecture, their minds buzzing with questions and excitement.

Mark chimed in, breaking the momentary silence. "This place is truly fascinating, but there's so much more to discover beyond these walls." Commander Hayes turned to face her crew, a spark of excitement igniting in her eyes. "You're absolutely right, Mark," she replied, her voice filled with determination. "We've only scratched the surface of what lies within this ancient structure. There's no telling what wonders await us as we delve deeper into its mysteries."

Dr. Chen nodded in agreement; her scientific curiosity piqued by the possibilities that lay before them. "I can't wait to start analyzing the artifacts and deciphering the inscriptions," she exclaimed, her enthusiasm contagious.

Sarah, the communications specialist, glanced around the chamber, her senses heightened by the aura of discovery that permeated the air. "I'll set up a communication relay back to the ship," she said, already beginning to unpack her equipment.

With the crew's roles defined and their objectives clear, Commander Hayes felt a surge of confidence wash over her. "Let's get to work, everyone," she declared, her voice echoing with determination. "There's a wealth of knowledge waiting to be uncovered, and it's up to us to unlock its secrets."

And with that, the crew of the Explorer stepped forward, ready to embark on the adventure of a lifetime, united in their quest to unravel the mysteries of the towering glass structure and the civilization that had built it.

Commander Hayes nodded in agreement, her eyes scanning the horizon with a sense of anticipation. "Indeed," she replied, her voice filled with determination. "Let us venture forth and explore more of the outside."

With a sense of purpose, the crew of the Explorer gathered their gear and prepared to depart. Dr. Chen adjusted her scanner, eager to capture any new data they might encounter.

Stepping out into the open air, the crew was greeted by a landscape unlike anything they had seen before. Towering trees swayed gently in the breeze, their leaves shimmering in the soft light of the alien sun. Strange creatures scurried among the underbrush, their calls echoing through the tranquil forest.

Chapter 15:
Zorvex from Planet Bole

As Commander Hayes and her crew ventured deeper into the alien wilderness, their exploration was abruptly interrupted by the sudden appearance of a flying car. The sleek vehicle descended gracefully before them, its engines humming softly as it came to a halt.

Surprised by the unexpected encounter, the crew watched with a mixture of curiosity and caution as the car's canopy slid open, revealing its occupants. They were tall and slender, with luminous eyes that seemed to gleam with intelligence.

As the beings stepped out of the flying car, the crew of the Explorer noticed peculiar devices attached to their garments. These devices emitted a soft glow and appeared to be some form of advanced technology.

Dr. Chen, always eager to learn and understand, approached one of the beings cautiously. "Excuse me," she began tentatively, "are those translator devices? They seem quite advanced."

The being nodded in acknowledgment, a faint smile playing across its lips. "Yes," it replied, its voice emanating from the device on its garment. "Our translator devices allow us to communicate with visitors from other worlds, such as yourselves. Here are some for you while you are here."

Commander Hayes said, "They will very much."

Commander Hayes and her crew exchanged looks of amazement, marvel- ling at the ingenuity of the beings' technology. With the aid of the translator devices, communication between the two groups became effortless, opening the door to a deeper exchange of knowledge and understanding.

As they conversed, Commander Hayes and her crew learned more about the beings' civilization and their connection to the planet. They discovered that the beings were guardians tasked with preserving the secrets of their ancestors, including the ancient ruins scattered across the landscape.

With the aid of the translator devices, the conversation flowed smoothly, bridging the gap between two vastly different cultures. Commander Hayes and her crew shared stories of their own world and their mission to explore the cosmos, forging a bond of friendship and mutual respect with their newfound acquaintances.

As the encounter drew to a close, the beings extended an invitation to Commander Hayes and her crew to visit their settlement and learn more about their culture and history. Eager to continue their exploration and deepen their understanding of this enigmatic world, the crew accepted the invitation with gratitude and anticipation.

With the aid of the translator devices, Commander Hayes and her crew embarked on a journey of discovery, guided by their newfound friends into the heart of the beings' civilization. And as they ventured forth into the unknown, they knew that their encounter with the beings and their remark- able technology would forever shape their understanding of the universe and their place within it.

As Commander Hayes and her crew entered the sprawling building, they were greeted by the sight of a bustling gathering of beings, their forms illuminated by the soft glow of ambient light. The vast chamber echoed with the hum of conversation and the rustle of movement as the beings went about their activities.

The crew of the Explorer exchanged astonished looks, taking in the scene before them. Never before had they encountered such a diverse and vibrant community, and the sheer number of beings gathered in the building was staggering.

Dr. Chen's eyes widened with wonder as she surveyed the crowd, her curiosity piqued by the sight of so many different individuals. "It's incredible," she whispered to her companions, her voice filled with awe. "I've never seen anything like it."

Commander Hayes nodded in agreement, her gaze sweeping over the gathering with a mixture of admiration and caution. "Stay alert, everyone," she reminded her crew, her voice low but firm. "We're guests here, but we mustn't forget that we're still in an unfamiliar environment."

With that, the crew of the Explorer followed their hosts deeper into the building, their footsteps echoing against the polished floors. As they moved through the throng of beings, they exchanged greetings and nods of acknowledgment, their interactions facilitated by the translator devices provided by their hosts.

The beings welcomed Commander Hayes and her crew with open arms, eager to share their culture and traditions with their newfound friends. They led the crew through the bustling corridors of the building, offering glimpses into their way of life and the customs that defined their society.

As they journeyed deeper into the heart of the settlement, the crew of the Explorer felt a sense of wonder and excitement at the prospect of exploring this vibrant new world. With each passing moment, they knew that they were embarking on an adventure unlike any they had experienced before, guided by the spirit of curiosity and discovery that had brought them to this distant corner of the cosmos.

As Commander Hayes and her crew entered the expansive meeting room, their attention was immediately drawn to the striking sight at its center— a large table surrounded by chairs suspended in mid-air. Each chair hovered effortlessly, seemingly defying the laws of gravity, arranged in a perfect circle around the table.

The crew exchanged astonished glances, marveling at the surreal display before them. Dr. Chen stepped forward; her scientific curiosity piqued by the unusual phenomenon. "This is incredible," she breathed, her eyes wide with wonder. "I've never seen anything like it."

Commander Hayes nodded in agreement; her gaze fixed on the suspended chairs. "It's as if they're floating," she observed, her voice tinged with amazement.

Their hosts approached, offering explanations for the extraordinary sight. "These chairs are a symbol of unity and equality in our society," one of the beings explained, their voice resonating with pride. "They represent the importance of collaboration and cooperation in our discussions and decision-making processes."

As one of the beings introduced themselves as Zorvex, a sense of reverence filled the air, accompanied by the announcement of their home planet's name—Bole. Commander Hayes and her crew exchanged glances, acknowledging the significance of the moment. Zorvex's introduction pro- vided insight into the unique culture and identity of the planet they had come to explore.

As Zorvex, the representative of the planet Bole, introduced himself, each member of Commander Hayes's crew followed suit, reciprocating the gesture of mutual respect and camaraderie.

Commander Hayes stepped forward, her posture exuding authority and confidence. "I am Commander Sarah Hayes, leader of the Explorer mission," she declared, her voice steady and resolute.

Dr. Emily Chen, the team's scientist, followed, her eyes alight with curiosity and wonder. "I am Dr. Emily Chen," she said, her tone filled with enthusiasm for discovery.

Lieutenant Commander Mark Thompson, the skilled navigator, and engineer, nodded in greeting. " Lieutenant Commander Mark Thompson," he stated simply, his demeanor calm and focused.

Lastly, Lieutenant Sarah Johnson, the communications specialist, offered a warm smile. "I'm Lieutenant Sarah Johnson," she chimed in, her voice friendly and inviting.

With introductions complete, the atmosphere brimmed with a sense of unity and purpose as the two groups prepared to embark on a journey of exploration and understanding together.

As Zorvex initiated the introductions, the other beings

followed suit, each offering their names with a sense of pride and hospitality.

One being, with a regal bearing, stepped forward. "I am Xandar, the keeper of knowledge," they announced, their voice carrying an air of wisdom.

Another being, smaller in stature but exuding warmth, introduced them- selves next. "I am Vela, the caretaker of our natural world," they said, their eyes twinkling with kindness.

A third being, with a keen gaze and an aura of determination, spoke up. "I am Thalor, the guardian of our traditions and customs," they declared, their voice resonating with resolve.

Lastly, a being with a gentle demeanor approached, their presence calming yet powerful. "I am Rynna, the healer and empath of our community," they said, their voice soothing like a melody.

With each introduction, the bond between the two groups strengthened, united by a shared sense of curiosity and respect. Commander Hayes and her crew greeted their new acquaintances with open minds and eager hearts, ready to embark on a journey of discovery alongside their new- found allies.

As the crew circled the table, their hosts gestured for them to take a seat in the floating chairs. With a mixture of excitement and trepidation, Commander Hayes and her crew settled into the suspended seats, feeling the gentle support beneath them as they adjusted to the weightless sensation.

Sitting around the table, the crew felt a sense of camaraderie and solidarity, united by the shared experience of exploration and discovery. They listened intently as their hosts spoke of the history and traditions surrounding the floating chairs, gaining a deeper understanding of the culture and values of the beings.

As the meeting progressed, Commander Hayes and her crew found themselves fully immersed in the conversation, exchanging ideas and insights with their hosts. The surreal setting of the floating chairs seemed to enhance the atmosphere of collaboration and mutual respect, fostering a sense of unity among all who gathered around the table.

And as they discussed plans for future exploration and cooperation, the crew of the Explorer couldn't help but feel grateful for the opportunity to be part of such a remarkable experience. In the presence of the floating chairs and the beings who had created them, they knew that they were on the verge of uncovering extraordinary discoveries and forging lasting bonds that would transcend the boundaries of space and time.

As the introductions concluded, Zorvex turned to Commander Hayes and her crew with a hospitable gesture. "Would any of you care for a drink or some food?" he inquired, his tone warm and welcoming.

Commander Hayes exchanged a glance with her crew, a faint smile touching her lips. "Thank you, Zorvex. We would be grateful for some refreshments," she replied, expressing their collective appreciation for the offer.

Dr. Chen's eyes sparkled with curiosity as she spoke up. "I'd love to try some of your local cuisine," she said eagerly, her scientific mind already curious about the culinary delights of Bole.

Mark nodded in agreement, "thank you," he said, his voice betraying his excitement at the prospect of sampling something new.

Sarah smiled warmly; her curiosity piqued. "I'll have whatever you recommend," she said, her tone friendly and open to new experiences.

With their preferences expressed, Zorvex nodded in understanding. "Very well, please follow me," he said, gesturing for the crew to accompany him to a nearby dining area where they could enjoy the hospitality of the beings of Bole.

As Commander Hayes and her crew settled into the dining area of the beings' settlement on Bole, they eagerly awaited the refreshments offered by Zorvex and his companions. However, as the food and drink were presented before them, the crew exchanged curious glances, realizing that their expectations had not aligned with the reality of what was served.

The food was unlike anything they had encountered before—exotic dishes with vibrant colors and unusual textures that piqued their curiosity. Dr. Chen leaned forward; her scientific interest piqued as she examined the ingredients with fascination. "This is fascinating," she remarked, her excitement palpable. "I've never seen anything like it."

Mark hesitated before taking a sip of the drink offered to him, his brow furrowing slightly in surprise at the unexpected flavor. "It's... different," he admitted, trying to mask his uncertainty with a polite smile.

Sarah, ever diplomatic, took a small bite of the food, her expression a mixture of surprise and intrigue. "It's certainly... unique," she commented diplomatically, trying to find something positive to say.

Commander Hayes, always the leader, maintained a composed demeanor as she sampled the offerings before her. "Thank you for your hospitality," she said graciously, recognizing the effort that had gone into preparing the meal. "We appreciate the opportunity to experience your culture firsthand."

As they continued their meal, the crew of the Explorer embraced the unfamiliar flavors and textures, embracing the spirit of exploration and discovery that had brought them to this distant corner of the cosmos. And though the food and drink may not have been what they had expected, they were grateful for the chance to broaden their horizons and learn more about the beings of Bole.

As the meal concluded, Zorvex rose from his seat with a gracious smile. "It's time we return you to your ship," he announced, his tone warm and accommodating.

Commander Hayes and her crew nodded in agreement, expressing their gratitude for the hospitality they had received. "Thank you, Zorvex. We appreciate your kindness," Commander Hayes said, her voice conveying their sincere appreciation.

Zorvex gestured towards the exit, leading the way to the settlement's transportation hub. "Please, follow me. I will take you to your ship," he offered, his demeanor friendly and reassuring.

As they arrived at the landing platform, the crew's eyes widened in awe as they beheld the sight of a sleek, futuristic flying car awaiting them. Sarah's face lit up with excitement, while Mark marveled at the advanced technology before them.

Zorvex gestured for them to board the vehicle, his expression one of genuine hospitality. "Please, allow me to give you a ride," he insisted, his offer a gesture of goodwill and friendship.

Commander Hayes instructed everyone to hand their translator devices to Zorvex. they all said, "Thank you."

With a sense of anticipation, Commander Hayes and her crew climbed aboard the flying car, ready to embark on the next leg of their journey. As they soared through the skies of Bole, they could not help but feel grateful for the unforgettable experiences they had shared and the bonds of friendship they had forged with the beings of this remarkable planet.

As the flying car gently descended, Commander Hayes and her crew stepped out onto the solid ground of Bole once more. Zorvex approached them, holding out a small device in his outstretched hand.

"Before you go, please take these," he said, offering each member of the crew a translator device. "These will come in handy during your explorations of other worlds. They will allow you to communicate with beings who speak different languages."

Grateful for the thoughtful gesture, the crew accepted the translator de- vices with nods of appreciation. Commander Hayes thanked Zorvex warmly. "This is incredibly generous of you, Zorvex. We will make good use of these," she promised, her voice sincere.

Zorvex smiled warmly, his eyes reflecting a sense of camaraderie and shared purpose. "Safe travels, Commander Hayes. May your journey be filled with discovery and wonder," he said, his words carrying a genuine wish for their success.

With a final wave goodbye, Commander Hayes and her crew watched as Zorvex and the flying car disappeared into the distance. As they prepared to continue their exploration of the cosmos, they knew that the translator devices would be invaluable tools, helping them bridge the gap between cultures and forge new connections with the beings they encountered along the way.

Chapter 16:
The Fourth Planet

As the crew of the Explorer bid farewell to the enigmatic planet of Bole, they could not shake the sense of wonder and excitement that lingered in their minds. With their translator devices in hand, courtesy of their gracious hosts, they embarked on their next journey through the white universe, eager to explore new horizons and uncover the mysteries that awaited them.

As the spacecraft soared through the vast expanse of space, Dr. Emily Chen kept a watchful eye on the navigation systems, scanning the surrounding area for any signs of celestial bodies that might warrant further investigation. It was not long before her efforts were rewarded, as a distant planet appeared on the ship's sensors, bathed in the soft glow of distant stars.

"Commander Hayes, Lieutenant Commander Thompson, I've detected a planet on our scanners," Dr. Chen announced, her voice filled with excitement. "It seems to be similar in size and composition to Earth, with a breathable atmosphere and a diverse array of ecosystems. Shall we set a course for further exploration?"

Commander Hayes and Lieutenant Commander Thompson exchanged a glance, their expressions reflecting a shared sense of anticipation. "Absolutely," Commander Hayes replied, her voice tinged with excitement. "Plot a course for the planet and prepare to conduct a thorough survey of its surface. Let's see what secrets it holds."

With Lieutenant Sarah Johnson at the helm, the Explorer altered its trajectory, setting a course for the newly discovered planet. As they drew closer, the crew marveled at the sight of its lush landscapes and shimmering oceans, a stark contrast to the barren expanse of space they had traversed just moments before.

Eager to delve into the mysteries of the planet, the crew of the Explorer swiftly begins readying a pod for descent.

Once the pod safely returned to the Explorer, the crew wasted no time in analyzing the collected data. They meticulously examined carbon levels, atmospheric conditions, and geological formations, striving to unlock the planet's secrets and pave the way for further exploration.

As they immersed themselves in the data, a sense of awe and wonder filled the crew of the Explorer. They realized that they had only begun to uncover the mysteries of this enigmatic planet. With each revelation, their resolve to uncover the truth strengthened.

Finally, Commander Hayes, after reviewing the findings, nods decisively. "Alright, let's make the landing," she declares, her voice filled with determination. The crew springs into action, ready to embark on the next phase of their exploration journey.

As the spacecraft descended towards the planet's surface, the crew prepared to embark on their latest adventure, eager to explore its untamed wilderness and unlock the mysteries of this alien world. For Commander Hayes and her intrepid crew, the journey into the unknown had only just begun, and they were determined to uncover the secrets that lay hidden within the depths of the cosmos.

As Commander Hayes and her crew emerged from their spacecraft onto the unfamiliar terrain of the newly discovered planet, they were greeted by a group of beings unlike any they had encountered before. The beings' alien features and imposing stature sent a shiver of apprehension down the crew's spines, and their guttural language sounded harsh and discordant to human ears.

Unease settled over the crew as they struggled to comprehend the intentions of these enigmatic beings. Lieutenant Commander Mark Thompson hastily retrieved the translator devices from the spacecraft, hoping they would shed some light on the situation.

As the crew activated the translators, they were met with a barrage of hos- tile words from the beings. Their tone was aggressive, their gestures men- acing as they surrounded the explorers, their eyes glinting with suspicion and distrust.

"Why do you trespass on our world?" demanded one of the beings, them voice dripping with hostility. "What business do you have here?"

Commander Hayes raised her hands in a gesture of peace, trying to convey their peaceful intentions. "We come in peace," she replied, her voice steady despite the tension in the air. "We are explorers, seeking to learn about new worlds and forge alliances with civilizations we encounter."

The beings were taken by surprise that Sarah could speak their language.

The beings scoffed at Commander Hayes's words, their expressions in- credulous. "Explorers, you say?" sneered another being, their tone laced with skepticism. "More like invaders, trespassing on sacred ground with- out permission."

Dr. Emily Chen, sensing the escalating tension, spoke up in an attempt to defuse the situation. "We mean no harm," she implored, her voice tinged with urgency. "We only seek knowledge and understanding. We are willing to cooperate with you and abide by your customs."

But the beings remained unmoved, their hostility unabated. "We have no need for outsiders meddling in our affairs," declared one of the beings, their voice dripping with disdain. "Leave now or face the consequences."

With tensions escalating and the situation growing increasingly dire, Commander Hayes knew they had to tread carefully. The crew exchanged worried glances, silently acknowledging the gravity of their predicament.

As they prepared to depart from the hostile planet, Commander Hayes could not shake the feeling of unease that lingered in the air. They had encountered many challenges in their journey through the cosmos, but none as formidable as the hostility of the beings they had encountered on this alien world.

As Commander Hayes and her crew departed from the hostile encounter with the strange beings, a sense of unease settled over them. The tension was palpable as they contemplated their next move, wary of what lay ahead on this enigmatic planet.

With grim determination, Commander Hayes made the decision to explore the other side of the planet, hoping to encounter friendlier inhabitants. The crew silently prepared the spacecraft for departure, their minds filled with apprehension and uncertainty.

As they emerged from the planet's shadow, their hopes of finding a more welcoming environment were quickly dashed. Instead of lush landscapes and bustling civilizations, they were met with a desolate wasteland stretching endlessly before them. There was no sign of intelligent life, no indication that they would find the answers they sought.

Lieutenant Commander Mark Thompson sighed heavily, his frustration evident in his voice. "It seems we've come to a dead end," he remarked, his tone tinged with disappointment.

Dr Emily Chen furrowed her brow, pondering their next move. "Perhaps we should continue our search," she suggested tentatively. "There may be unexplored regions of the planet that hold some promise."

Commander Hayes nodded grimly, her resolve unwavering despite the bleak circumstances. "We can't afford to give up now," she declared, her voice firm with determination. "We must exhaust every possibility before we consider leaving."

With heavy hearts, the crew set a course for uncharted territory, knowing that the path ahead would be fraught with danger and uncertainty. But they were undeterred, driven by a relentless pursuit of knowledge and discovery that propelled them ever forward into the unknown.

As they ventured deeper into the alien landscape, they remained vigilant, their senses alert for any signs of life or danger. Though the odds were stacked against them, Commander Hayes and her crew refused to abandon hope, knowing that their quest for answers was far from over.

As Commander Hayes and her crew ventured around the planet, hoping to encounter friendlier inhabitants, they soon found themselves facing a new challenge. More aliens soon halted their journey, but these were not the humanoid beings they had encountered earlier. Instead, they were confronted by a group of water-type aliens emerging from the depths of a nearby ocean.

The water aliens approached with a mix of curiosity and caution, their translucent forms shimmering in the sunlight. Commander Hayes and her crew watched warily as the strange beings drew closer, unsure of what to expect from these aquatic creatures.

Communication with the water aliens proved to be difficult at first, as their language was unlike anything the crew had encountered before. Despite their best efforts, they struggled to find common ground with the enigmatic beings.

As tensions reached a crescendo, Commander Hayes took charge, directing the crew to retreat to the safety of their spacecraft. Their hope was to regroup and formulate a plan to establish effective communication with the water aliens. However, their path back to the spacecraft was abruptly halted by the water aliens, who appeared determined to impede their departure.

Caught between the mysterious creatures and the expansive ocean, Commander Hayes and her crew realized they were in a precarious situation. With no means of communication with the water aliens and their escape route blocked, they understood the gravity of their predicament. In this dire moment, they would have to rely on their ingenuity and quick thinking to navigate through this challenge.

Just as despair threatened to engulf them, Mark felt a familiar object in his pocket. Pulling it out, he discovered a translator device tucked away. With a sense of urgency, he handed it to Commander Hayes, his eyes alight with hope. The commander's face lit up as she received the device, a glimmer of optimism breaking through the tension.

With the translator in hand, Commander Hayes activated it, hoping it would bridge the communication barrier with the water aliens. As the de- vice hummed to life, emitting a soft glow, a wave of anticipation swept over the crew. They now had a tool to facilitate dialogue and potentially find a resolution to their predicament.

As Commander Hayes activated the translator device and began to speak, a sense of wonder swept over the water aliens. They recoiled slightly, their fluid forms undulating with surprise, as if this sudden ability to understand the visitors was nothing short of magical.

Commander Hayes pressed on, her voice amplified and

translated by the device, breaking through the barrier of silence that had separated them moments before. "We come in peace," she began, her tone calm yet resolute. "We seek only to understand and explore this planet and its inhabitants."

The water aliens listened intently; their large, luminous eyes fixed on the commander as her words resonated with them through the translator. Slowly, their initial apprehension gave way to curiosity and intrigue, as they began to comprehend the intentions of the visitors from another world.

With the aid of the translator device, Commander Hayes and her crew found themselves on the brink of a breakthrough in communication with the water aliens. As the tension eased and mutual understanding began to take root, they dared to hope that a peaceful resolution to their encounter might yet be within reach.

As the water aliens began to speak, their voices overlapped in a rapid flurry of incomprehensible sounds, leaving Commander Hayes and her crew struggling to make sense of the cacophony. Sensing the need for clarity, Commander Hayes raised her hand, gesturing for the water aliens to quiet down.

"Please, one at a time," she requested, her voice amplified by the translator device. "We want to understand you, but we need to take it slowly."

As the chatter subsided, Commander Hayes seized the opportunity to ad- dress the water aliens once more. "Do you mind if my colleagues retrieve something from our ship?" she inquired politely. "It will help all of us understand each other better."

The water aliens regarded Commander Hayes with a mix of curiosity and cautious interest, their fluid forms bobbing gently in the ocean currents. After a moment of deliberation, one of them nodded in agreement, indicating their consent to the proposal.

With the water aliens' approval secured, Commander Hayes gestured for Mark to return to the spacecraft and retrieve the additional translation equipment. Mark nodded in acknowledgment and quickly made his way back to the ship, determined to assist in resolving the language barrier between them and the water aliens.

With Mark's departure, the beach fell into a tense silence, the water aliens watching closely as the crew awaited his return. Minutes passed, each one feeling like an eternity as they waited anxiously for Mark to reappear with the translator device.

Finally, after what seemed like an eternity, Mark emerged from the spacecraft, holding the translator device in his hand. With a sense of urgency, he approached Commander Hayes and handed her the device, his expression a mix of determination and relief.

"Here you go, Commander," Mark said, his voice filled with determination. "I hope this helps."

With the translator devices in hand, Commander Hayes distributed them to each member of her crew, ensuring that everyone had the means to communicate effectively with the water aliens. As she passed out the devices, she emphasized the importance of clear and respectful communication, urging her crew to use the devices wisely.

"These translator devices will allow us to understand and be understood by the water aliens," Commander Hayes explained, her voice steady and authoritative. "Let's use them to establish a dialogue and work towards finding a peaceful resolution to this situation."

Her crew nodded in agreement, their expressions reflecting a mix of determination and apprehension. With the translator devices activated and ready for use, they stood ready to engage with the water aliens and navigate the challenges that lay ahead.

Commander Hayes, utilizing the translator device to communicate effectively with the water aliens, clarified the function of the small devices held by her crew.

"These devices are translators," she explained, her voice transmitted through the device to ensure clear comprehension. "They enable us to understand your language and engage in seamless communication with one another."

The water aliens regarded the devices with evident curiosity, their fluid forms swirling with interest. After a brief moment of contemplation, one of the aliens spoke up, its voice resonating in the crew's minds through the translator device.

"Fascinating," it remarked, its tone tinged with admiration. "Your technology is truly remarkable. With these devices, we can transcend language barriers and converse freely, fostering mutual understanding between our species."

Commander Hayes nodded in agreement, expressing her appreciation. "In- deed," she affirmed, her voice conveying gratitude. "These translators serve as a conduit for dialogue and cooperation, allowing us to exchange knowledge and forge meaningful connections."

Armed with the translator devices, Commander Hayes and her crew embarked on a journey of communication and exploration, poised to deepen their understanding of the water aliens' world, and cultivate harmonious relations with their newfound aquatic counterparts.

Commander Hayes elaborated, providing additional context about the origin of the translator devices.

"These translators were graciously provided to us by

another alien species we encountered on a different world," she explained, her words relayed through the device to the attentive water aliens. "They recognized the im- portance of communication in fostering peaceful interactions between di- verse civilizations and entrusted us with these devices to facilitate our interactions with beings such as yourselves."

The water aliens listened intently, their luminous eyes reflecting a sense of understanding and appreciation. Through the translator device, they conveyed their gratitude for the generosity of the alien species who had bestowed the devices upon Commander Hayes and her crew.

Commander Hayes addressed the water aliens with a tone of curiosity and concern. "We encountered individuals from another part of your planet, but they were quite hostile towards us," she explained, her words translated by the device. "Do you have any knowledge of them? Are they a part of your society?"

The water aliens exchanged glances, their fluid forms shifting with a sense of unease. After a moment of silent communication among themselves, one of the water aliens spoke up, its voice echoing in their minds through the translator device.

"We are aware of the beings you speak of," it replied, its tone tinged with caution. "They are known to us, but they dwell in a distant region of the planet, far from our own territory. Their motives are often mysterious, and their interactions with outsiders are fraught with conflict and distrust."

Commander Hayes nodded, absorbing the information with a sense of gravity. "Thank you for your honesty," she said, her voice reflecting a mixture of apprehension and determination. "We will proceed with caution and avoid further encounters with them if possible. Our goal is peaceful exploration and understanding."

The water aliens acknowledged Commander Hayes's words with a silent nod, understanding the importance of maintaining harmony and cooperation in the face of potential threats. With this newfound knowledge, Commander Hayes and her crew prepared to continue their journey, mindful of the challenges and dangers that awaited them in the uncharted depths of the ocean.

Lieutenant Commander Mark Thompson coordinates with the team to con- duct final checks on the reactor systems, confirming that they are functioning optimally for the voyage ahead. Dr. Emily Chen, Ph.D., assists in calculating the optimal trajectory and propulsion settings for the return journey, considering the gravitational forces and celestial obstacles they may encounter along the way.

Lieutenant Sarah Johnson monitors the spacecraft's energy reserves closely, adjusting power distribution to ensure a balanced and efficient use of resources throughout the journey.

Chapter 17:
The Meeting of Earth's Future

As Commander Hayes and her crew navigated through the vast expanse of space toward their next destination, they were suddenly confronted by a sight both awe-inspiring and terrifying—a storm unlike anything they had ever seen. Swirling clouds of cosmic dust and debris danced with chaotic energy, illuminated by the crackling discharge of electrical currents arcing across the void.

With gritted teeth and steady hands, the crew fought to stabilize the spacecraft amidst the tumultuous onslaught. Outside the viewports, streaks of energy crackled across the void, a stark reminder of the unforgiving nature of space.

Amidst the chaos, Commander Hayes sought answers from Mark, her voice firm despite the urgency of the situation. "Mark, what's our status? Can we weather this storm?"

Mark's fingers flew across the console, his brow furrowed in concentration as he analyzed the data streaming in. "It's intense, Commander," he replied, his tone grave. "But we should be able to ride it out."

With determination etched on their faces, the crew worked in unison, their training and expertise guiding them through the maelstrom. Despite the overwhelming odds, they refused to yield, their resolve unyielding in the face of adversity.

As the storm raged on, battering the spacecraft with relentless fury, the crew remained steadfast, their spirits unbroken. Together, they would weather this trial, emerging stronger on the other side, ready to continue their journey into the depths of the white universe.

As the crew pressed on through the white expanse of space, Commander Hayes's voice cut through the hum of the spacecraft, her gaze fixed on the distant stars.

"We have a planet on our scope. Let us go and see," Mark relayed to Commander Hayes, his voice carrying a sense of anticipation and curiosity.

Commander Hayes nodded; her eyes fixed on the viewport displaying the distant celestial body. "Prepare for approach," she instructed, her tone resolute yet tinged with excitement.

With a series of commands, the spacecraft adjusted its trajectory, veering towards the enigmatic planet that beckoned in the depths of space. As they drew closer, the planet's features became more defined, revealing rugged terrain and swirling clouds that hinted at untold mysteries waiting to be uncovered.

Before their approach to the planet, Commander Hayes swiftly ordered the deployment of the pods for a preliminary survey. Each pod, equipped with advanced sensors, ventured into the vast expanse of space to gather crucial data about the planet's surface and atmosphere.

As the pods closed in on the planet, their sensors diligently scanned the unfamiliar terrain, capturing detailed images and readings. Commander Hayes and her crew closely monitored the incoming data, eager to decipher the planet's composition and identify any potential risks.

With the insights gleaned from the pod's observations, the crew could strategize their landing and ensure a safe descent to the planet's surface. Fueled by determination and armed with newfound knowledge, they pressed forward on their cosmic journey, prepared to uncover the mysteries that awaited them on this distant world.

"The commander asked, 'How is the information from the pods?'" Emily reported, her voice crackling over the communications system.

Sarah, stationed at the monitoring station, swiftly analyzed the incoming data. "It's coming through clear," she replied, her tone focused. "We're getting detailed scans of the planet's surface and atmosphere. No signs of any immediate dangers."

Commander Hayes nodded, a sense of relief washing over her. "Good work, team. Let us continue monitoring as we approach. We need to be pre- pared for anything."

With the crew's spirits lifted by the reassuring report, they pressed on, their anticipation growing with each passing moment as they drew closer to the enigmatic planet awaiting their exploration.

"Prepare to land, everyone in their seats," commanded Commander Hayes, her voice steady and authoritative over the intercom.

The crew members swiftly complied, securing themselves in their seats as the spacecraft descended towards the surface of the unknown planet. Tension hung in the air as they braced for the moment of touchdown, their hearts racing with anticipation and excitement for the adventure that awaited them below.

The craft descended gracefully under Mark's expert guidance, navigating through the planet's atmosphere with precision and care. With his steady hand on the controls, he ensured a smooth landing, gently setting the spacecraft down in a clearing amidst the alien terrain.

As the engines powered down and the dust settled, the crew members ex- changed relieved glances, grateful for Mark's skillful piloting that had brought them safely to their destination. With the spacecraft now grounded on the surface of the planet.

"Emily, activate the atmospheric sensors to ensure," Commander Hayes instructed, her voice steady as she glanced over at Emily, who nodded in response.

Emily swiftly accessed the controls, activating the atmospheric sensors with practiced efficiency. The instruments hummed to life, their digital dis- plays lighting up with readings as they began to scan the surrounding air for composition and pressure.

As the data streamed in, the crew members watched intently, eager to gain insight into the environment outside their spacecraft. With the atmospheric sensors in operation, they would be better equipped to assess the conditions on the planet's surface and make informed decisions about their next course of action.

Emily reports back with the atmospheric composition readings for the planet:

Nitrogen (N2): Approximately 78% - 80%. Oxygen (O2): Around 20% - 21%
These readings suggest that the planet's atmosphere is similar in composition to Earth's, which is promising for potential habitation and exploration.

"Thank you, Emily," Commander Hayes acknowledged with a nod. "Let's ensure our ship is intact and make any necessary repairs before we embark on further exploration. If the atmosphere is indeed similar to ours, there may be a possibility of life on this planet."

With a sense of anticipation, the crew prepared to assess

the condition of their spacecraft and make any required adjustments before venturing out to explore the alien world before them.

With the ship's condition confirmed and the reactors given the green light, the crew took a moment to relax and refuel with some refreshments before venturing out onto the planet's surface.

Sitting together in the ship's common area, they shared stories and ex- changed theories about what they might encounter on the planet below. Emily passed around some energy bars, while Sarah brewed a fresh pot of coffee from the ship's supplies. As they sipped their drinks and nibbled on snacks, they could not help but feel a sense of excitement tinged with apprehension for what lay ahead.

Commander Hayes, always the picture of calm and composure, took a moment to address her crew. "Alright, everyone," she said, her voice steady and reassuring. "We've prepared for this moment, and now it's time to take the next step in our journey. Let's stay vigilant and work together as we explore this new world."

With that, the crew finished their refreshments, donned their spacesuits, and made their way to the airlock, ready to embark on their expedition. As the doors hissed open and they stepped out onto the planet's surface, they were greeted by a landscape unlike anything they had ever seen before, sparking a sense of wonder and adventure in each of them.

"Have you all got your interpretation machine?" asked Commander Hayes, her tone firm yet tinged with concern. "We don't want the same thing happening here."

The crew members nodded in unison, each reaching to double-check the presence of their interpretation devices.

With their interpretation machines securely in place, the crew proceeded cautiously, mindful of the potential for miscommunication in this unfamiliar environment. As they ventured further into the alien landscape, they remained vigilant, relying on their devices to ensure clear and accurate communication with any inhabitants they might encounter.

With their safety and success at the forefront of their minds, the crew pressed on, determined to navigate this new world with caution and precision.

"Looks like a stream over there," Emily exclaimed, her excitement contagious as she pointed out the sparkling water to her companions.

With Commander Hayes's nod of approval, Emily approached the stream, her equipment ready for analysis. She meticulously tested the water, checking for any signs of contamination or danger that could jeopardize the crew's safety.

As Emily worked, the rest of the crew watched intently, eager to uncover more about this enigmatic planet and its potential for sustaining life. Their collective curiosity spurred them on, driving their quest to unravel the mysteries of this alien world.

Suddenly, Emily's instruments registered a surprising result—the water was safe for human consumption. But her attention was soon drawn to movement beneath the surface. To her amazement, she spotted fish grace- fully swimming in the pristine stream. Excited by her discovery, "Commander, come see this," Emily exclaimed, her voice filled with wonder as she gestured towards the water. "There are fish swimming in the stream!"

Commander Hayes joined Emily at the water's edge, her eyes widening in astonishment as she observed the aquatic life below. It was a remarkable sight, hinting at the possibility of a thriving ecosystem on this unexplored planet.

With the confirmation of drinkable water and the presence of fish, the crew's spirits soared. This planet held untold wonders, and they were eager to continue their exploration, eager to uncover its secrets and unlock the mysteries hidden within its depths.

As they walked a little further, the crew stumbled upon a cluster of large boulders, providing a convenient resting spot. They settled down, taking a moment to catch their breath and survey the landscape stretching out before them.

Commander Hayes broke the silence, her voice cutting through the stillness of the rugged terrain. "Has anyone spotted any signs of animal life or human habitation yet?" she inquired, her words echoing against the alien landscape. "It feels as if we're the first humans to set foot on this planet."

The crew members exchanged glances, their eyes scanning the horizon in search of any hints of movement or civilization. Despite their keen observation, the vast expanse around them remained devoid of any signs of life or human activity. It was as if they had stumbled upon a pristine world, untouched by sentient beings.

With a mixture of anticipation and curiosity, the crew readied themselves to venture deeper into the unknown, eager to unravel the mysteries that awaited them on this uncharted planet.

As the crew had rested for about 10 to 15 minutes, they were suddenly startled by the sight of a spacecraft descending to land just a short distance away. Gasps of surprise escaped their lips as they watched in awe, hardly daring to believe what they were witnessing.

Commander Hayes wasted no time in issuing orders, her voice calm yet urgent. "Everyone, be on guard and activate your interpretation machines. We'll approach slowly to avoid alarming them."

With hearts pounding with anticipation, the crew readied themselves for the encounter, their senses heightened as they prepared to meet whatever awaited them on this mysterious planet.

The hatch of the spacecraft swung open, and to the astonishment of Commander Hayes and her crew, two figures emerged. They appeared unmistakably human, their features mirroring those of Earth's inhabitants.

The surprise on both sides was palpable as the two groups locked eyes, each seemingly taken aback by the presence of the other. Tension hung in the air, mingled with a sense of curiosity, and wonder as they faced this unexpected encounter on the distant planet's surface.

With a cautious approach, Commander Hayes steps forward, extending a hand in a gesture of goodwill. "Greetings," she says, her voice calm yet filled with curiosity. "We come in peace. I'm Commander Hayes, and these are my crew members. We did not expect to encounter others here. Can we assist you in any way?"

The two individuals from the other spacecraft exchange a quick glance before one of them, a tall figure with piercing blue eyes, steps forward to meet Commander Hayes's handshake. "I'm Captain Cygnus," he responds, his voice carrying a hint of surprise. "We didn't anticipate meeting fellow travelers on this remote planet either. Our mission is to explore and gather data. Perhaps we can collaborate."

A sense of relief washes over the assembled group as the tension eases. Both crews share stories of their respective journeys and discoveries, ex- changing valuable information about the planet's environment and its potential for habitation.

As the day draws to a close, Commander Hayes and Captain Cygnus agree to continue their exploration together, pooling their resources and knowledge for the benefit of both crews. With newfound allies by their side, they embark on a journey of discovery, eager to unravel the mysteries of the planet and forge new friendships across the vast expanse of space.

As Commander Hayes absorbs Captain Cygnus's revelation, her mind races with a mixture of disbelief and fascination. "Earth... in the future?" she echoes, her voice tinged with incredulity. "But how is that possible? How far into the future are we talking?"

Captain Cygnus nods, his expression serious yet tinged with a hint of excitement. "Yes, Earth. It seems our journeys through the black holes have led us to different points in time as well as space. As for the year, on my planet, it is 2350."

The revelation leaves Commander Hayes and her crew stunned, grappling with the implications of what they have just learned. "So much has changed," Commander Hayes muses, her mind racing with possibilities. "Antimatter Engines... faster-than-light travel... it's beyond anything we could have imagined."

With a newfound sense of purpose and determination, Commander Hayes and Captain Cygnus exchange ideas and plans for their continued exploration of the universe. Despite the vast distances and the uncertainties of time and space, they find common ground in their shared quest for knowledge and discovery.

As they prepare to embark on their next journey together, Commander Hayes reflects on the incredible twists of fate that have brought them to this moment. In the vast expanse of the cosmos, where time and space intertwine in ways beyond comprehension, they stand united in their pursuit of understanding, bound by the bonds of friendship forged in the depths of space. And with each new adventure, they inch closer to unlocking the mysteries of the universe and uncovering the secrets that lie hidden among the stars.

As the day drew to a close, the crew gathered to bid farewell to Captain Cygnus and his team. Despite the whirlwind of events that had transpired, there was a sense of camaraderie and mutual respect among them all.

Commander Hayes extended her hand to Captain Cygnus, a silent acknowledgment of the bond forged between their crews during their brief but eventful encounter. "Safe travels, Captain," she said, her voice tinged with warmth and gratitude. "May our paths cross again in the vast expanse of the cosmos."

Captain Cygnus clasped her hand firmly, his gaze meeting hers with a nod of appreciation. "Indeed, Commander," he replied, his tone echoing her sentiment. "Until we meet again, may the stars guide your journey and the mysteries of the universe reveal themselves to you."

With a final exchange of farewells, Captain Cygnus and his crew departed, making their way back to their own spacecraft. As the hatch closed behind them, the crew of the Explorer watched with a mixture of nostalgia and anticipation, knowing that their paths had crossed with those of their fellow travelers from Earth's distant future.

As they prepared to resume their own journey through the cosmos, the crew of the Explorer carried with them the memories of their encounter with Captain Cygnus and the knowledge that, despite the vastness of space, they were never truly alone. And with each passing moment, they drew closer to unlocking the secrets of the universe and fulfilling their shared destiny among the stars.

As they boarded their spacecraft, the hum of anticipation filled the air, mingling with the gentle thrum of the ship's engines. Above them, the sleek vessel piloted by Captain Cygnus soared gracefully, a silent reminder of the vastness of space and the endless possibilities that lay beyond.

Commander Hayes took her seat at the helm, her hands steady on the controls as she prepared to guide their craft through the cosmic expanse. Beside her, the crew members settled into their respective stations, their focus unwavering as they awaited the command to take flight.

"Let's get ready to take off," Commander Hayes announced, her voice resonating with determination and purpose. With a flick of a switch and a surge of power, the spacecraft roared to life, its engines igniting with a brilliant burst of light.

As they ascended into the star-studded sky, the crew of the Explorer felt a surge of exhilaration course through their veins. Ahead of them, the twinkling lights of distant galaxies beckoned, promising adventure and discovery beyond imagination.

With each passing moment, they drew closer to the mysteries of the cosmos, united in their quest to explore the unknown and uncover the secrets of the universe. And as they ventured forth into the endless expanse of space, they knew that their journey had only just begun.

Lieutenant Commander Mark Thompson coordinates with the team to conduct final checks on the reactor systems, confirming that they are functioning optimally for the voyage ahead. Dr. Emily Chen, Ph.D., assists in calculating the optimal trajectory and propulsion settings for the return journey, considering the gravitational forces and celestial obstacles they may encounter along the way.

Lieutenant Sarah Johnson monitors the spacecraft's energy reserves closely, adjusting power distribution to ensure a balanced and efficient use of resources throughout the journey. With determination and teamwork, they are ready to navigate through the cosmic abyss and make their way back to the white hole, where they hope to emerge safely and continue their journey through the enigmatic realms of the universe.

Chapter 18:
Where is the White Hole?

Commander Hayes and Dr. Chen stood side by side in the command center, poised and attentive. Hayes, authoritative and resolute, surveyed the expanse of space on the main viewport. Dr. Chen, radiating confidence and expertise, mirrored the commander's focus, awaiting instructions.

The hum of the ship's systems filled the air, a constant reminder of the weight of their mission and the challenges that lay ahead. Yet, in the face of uncertainty, Commander Hayes exuded a sense of calm determination, her presence anchoring the crew amidst the boundless reaches of the cos- mos.

"Dr. Chen," Commander Hayes began, her voice steady and authoritative, "I need you to initiate a comprehensive scan of our surroundings. We must gather as much data as possible to ensure the safety and success of our mission."

Dr. Chen nodded in acknowledgment; her fingers poised over the controls with practiced precision. With a few deft movements, she activated the ship's sensors, setting them to sweep the surrounding space for any anomalies, celestial bodies, or potential hazards that might lie in their path.

As the scan commenced, Commander Hayes and Dr. Chen exchanged a brief yet meaningful glance, a silent acknowledgment of the trust and camaraderie that bound them together in their pursuit of knowledge and exploration amidst the vast unknown. With their combined expertise and un- wavering determination, they were ready to face whatever challenges awaited them on their journey through the cosmos.

Commander Hayes's voice resonated with authority as she conveyed her instructions to Lieutenant Commander Thompson. "Mark," she began, her tone firm yet measured, "your expertise in navigation is crucial at this moment. I need you to collaborate closely with Dr. Chen to ensure our map- ping process is meticulous and accurate. We cannot afford any errors in our trajectory."

Lieutenant Commander Thompson's expression hardened with resolve as he acknowledged the gravity of the task at hand. "Understood, Commander," he responded, his voice reflecting a steely determination. "I'll dedicate all my efforts to verifying our calculations and confirming our course alignment. We won't stray off course on my watch."

With a nod of assurance, Commander Hayes knew she could trust Lieu- tenant Commander Thompson to uphold the highest standards of precision and diligence in their navigation efforts. Together with Dr. Chen's expertise, they formed an indomitable team, ready to tackle the challenges of charting a course through the vast unknown of space.

Commander Hayes stood at the heart of the craft, her eyes surveying the bustling activity around her. Each crew member was engrossed in their respective tasks, working with precision and focus. The hum of machinery and the soft glow of screens filled the air, creating an atmosphere of purposeful determination.

As she observed her team in action, Commander Hayes could not help but feel a sense of pride. They were more than just colleagues; they were a cohesive unit, bound together by a shared goal and unwavering commitment to the mission. In their hands, she entrusted not only the success of their current endeavor but also the future of humanity's exploration of the cosmos.

With the mapping process underway and every member of the crew dedicated to their role, Commander Hayes allowed herself a moment of quiet optimism. Despite the vast unknown that lay ahead, she knew that they were prepared for whatever challenges they might encounter. Together, they would navigate through the depths of space, pushing the boundaries of human knowledge and discovery with each passing moment.

As they embark on their return journey, the crew of the spacecraft does not just carry themselves back to the safety of moon base; they carry with them the wisdom and knowledge acquired from their extraordinary voyage. Each light-year traversed is not just a distance covered but a step closer to a brighter future for humanity—a future forged by the profound insights gleaned from their cosmic odyssey.

With every passing moment, they carry forward the torch of enlightenment, illuminating the path for future generations to follow. Their journey serves as a testament to the indomitable spirit of exploration that defines humanity, inspiring others to reach for the stars and uncover the mysteries of the universe.

As they emerge from the depths of the cosmos, their spirits ablaze with the fire of discovery, they stand as beacons of inspiration, guiding humanity towards a destiny among the stars. And with each stride forward, they bring humanity closer to realizing its full potential and embracing the boundless possibilities that await in the vast expanse of space.

The crew receives the startling news from their onboard sensors that the white hole they had initially traversed through has shifted its position, complicating their return journey. Commander Dr. Elizabeth Hayes gathers her team to assess the situation and formulate a new plan of action.

Lieutenant Commander Mark Thompson immediately begins recalculating their navigation coordinates based on the updated position of the white hole. With precision and expertise, he adjusts their course to align with the new trajectory, ensuring that they remain on track for their return journey.

Dr. Emily Chen, Ph.D., analyses the data from their sensors to determine the potential causes behind the white hole's movement. She considers numerous factors, including gravitational disturbances and cosmic phenomena, in an attempt to understand the nature of this unexpected occurrence.

Lieutenant Sarah Johnson diligently monitors the spacecraft's energy reserves, a task that she takes on with meticulous care and precision. As she navigates the complex systems and data readings, she is acutely aware of the critical role energy optimization plays in their journey to the new location of the white hole.

While she may not have a dedicated team at her side, Lieutenant Johnson's expertise and resourcefulness allow her to collaborate effectively with the ship's engineering systems. She leverages every available tool and resource to maximize energy efficiency, ensuring that they have more than enough reserves to navigate the challenges that lie ahead.

With her steadfast dedication and unwavering focus, Lieutenant Johnson embodies the spirit of ingenuity and adaptability that is essential for their mission's success. Her tireless efforts serve as a vital component in the crew's collective endeavor to reach their destination safely and accomplish their objectives amidst the vast unknowns of space.

Lieutenant Commander Mark Thompson and Dr. Emily Chen meticulously construct a detailed map of their current position and trajectory be- fore venturing into the white hole. With their expertise in navigation and astrophysics, they utilize advanced software and data from previous scans to ensure the accuracy of their calculations.

Their primary objective is to confirm that the newly located white hole is indeed the same one from which they emerged. To achieve this, they cross- reference their current position with known celestial landmarks and the unique gravitational signatures associated with the white hole.

As they meticulously plot their course, Lieutenant Commander Thompson and Dr. Chen leave no detail unchecked, carefully analyzing each data point to verify their findings. Their thorough approach ensures that they proceed with confidence, knowing that they are on the right path to re- enter the white hole and continue their journey through the cosmos.

With the map taking shape on the spacecraft's display screens, the crew gathers around to review and compare it with their previous calculations. Each member of the team brings their expertise to the table, scrutinizing every detail to ensure accuracy and optimize their route through the cosmic expanse.

Commander Hayes nods in approval as she surveys the map, her confidence in her crew unwavering. "Excellent work, everyone," she says, her voice echoing with determination. "This map will be our guide as we venture into the unknown. Let's proceed with caution, but also with the knowledge that we are well-prepared for whatever challenges may come our way."

With their preparations complete and their route meticulously plotted, the crew stands ready to embark on the next leg of their journey. As they brace themselves for the uncertainties of the cosmic void, they draw strength from their collective expertise and determination to explore the mysteries of the universe.

As the spacecraft glides through the vast expanse of space, the crew remains vigilant, their senses attuned to any fluctuations or anomalies in their surroundings. With each passing moment, they draw closer to their destination, propelled by a shared sense of purpose and determination.

Commander Hayes monitors the ship's systems with unwavering focus, ensuring that they remain on course and prepared for any contingencies. Lieutenant Commander Thompson and Dr. Chen collaborate closely, re- fining their navigation strategies and adapting to the dynamic nature of the cosmic currents.

Meanwhile, Lieutenant Johnson continues to manage the

spacecraft's energy reserves, optimizing power usage to sustain their journey through the depths of space. With her expertise and meticulous attention to detail, she ensures that they have the necessary resources to overcome any obstacles they may encounter along the way.

Commander Hayes and Lieutenant Commander Thompson meticulously plot the trajectory, their focus sharpening with each calculation. They pore over charts and data, ensuring the accuracy of their course adjustments, mindful of potential hazards in the cosmic expanse.

Meanwhile, the rest of the crew prepares the spacecraft for the journey, conducting thorough checks on all systems and equipment to ensure they are functioning optimally. Dr. Emily Chen verifies the integrity of the navigation systems, double-checking their calculations and simulations to confirm their reliability.

Lieutenant Sarah Johnson monitors the spacecraft's energy reserves, making adjustments to power allocation to accommodate the extended journey. Her expertise in energy management proves invaluable as she optimizes the ship's resources for the long voyage ahead.

With each member of the crew fulfilling their role with unwavering dedication, the spacecraft stands ready to embark on its next chapter of exploration. As they prepare to traverse the cosmic unknown towards the new location of the white hole, their spirits are buoyed by the shared sense of purpose and the anticipation of the discoveries that await them beyond the stars.

As the spacecraft hurtled through the void of space, the crew's initial sense of awe and wonder at the white universe began to yield to a more sobering realization. Commander Dr. Elizabeth Hayes and her team had been so captivated by the beauty and strangeness of this new realm that they had failed to notice the looming danger lurking in their path.

"All hands, brace for potential impact," Commander Hayes announces, her voice steady but tinged with urgency. The crew's attention snaps to the cockpit displays, where a shadowy mass looms ominously ahead—a black hole, closer than they had anticipated.

Mixed reactions ripple through the cockpit as the crew grapples with the sudden turn of events. Some express disbelief, while others exchange anxious glances, silently processing the gravity of their situation.

"That was close. We did not see that when we came out of the white hole," remarks one crew member, breaking the tense silence with a shaky breath.

Commander Hayes nods grimly, her mind racing as she considers their next move. "Indeed, it seems our focus on the wonders of the white universe may have obscured the presence of potential hazards," she admits, her tone tinged with regret. "But we must remain vigilant. The cosmos is full of surprises, and we cannot afford to let our guard down."

Lieutenant Commander Mark Thompson, his eyes fixed on the navigational charts, offers a practical solution. "We'll need to adjust our trajectory to ensure we steer clear of any other unexpected obstacles," he suggests, his voice resolute. "We can't risk encountering another black hole or any other unknown phenomena."

Dr. Emily Chen nods in agreement, already immersed in calculations to plot a safer course. "Agreed," she affirms, her tone decisive. "Let's proceed with caution and keep a close eye on our surroundings. We must be pre- pared for anything the cosmos throws our way."

With their narrow escape serving as a stark reminder of the dangers that lurk in the depths of space, the crew redoubles their efforts, their determination unwavering as they continue their journey. Though the challenges may be daunting, they are united in their resolve to navigate the unknown and secure their passage back to familiar territory.

As the spacecraft veers away from the black hole's ominous grasp, relief washes over the crew, tempered by the realization that their journey through the cosmos is fraught with unforeseen dangers. With their resolve strengthened and their determination unwavering, they press on towards the white hole, their spirits undaunted by the challenges that lie ahead.

Before venturing into the white hole, Lieutenant Commander Mark Thompson, assisted by Dr. Emily Chen, meticulously constructs a detailed map of their current position and trajectory. Using advanced navigation software and data from previous scans of the region, they plot the course that will lead them to the newly located white hole.

As the map takes shape on the spacecraft's display screens, the crew gathers around to review and compare it with their previous calculations. They scrutinize every detail, ensuring that their route is accurate and optimized for the safest and most efficient passage through the cosmic expanse.

As the crew grappled with the unexpected presence of the black hole, another startling realization dawned upon them: the white hole they had previously entered seemed to exert a force contrary to that of a black hole. This revelation sent shockwaves through the cockpit, as the crew tried to make sense of the paradoxical nature of their surroundings.

Commander Dr. Elizabeth Hayes furrows her brow, her mind racing to comprehend the implications of this newfound knowledge. "It appears that entering the white hole was impossible due to its repulsive force, which is the opposite of what we'd expect from a black hole," she observes, her voice laced with a mixture of curiosity and concern.

Dr. Emily Chen furrows her brow, her mind racing with possibilities. "If the white hole repels matter and energy, then what does that mean for our current trajectory?" she wonders aloud, her voice filled with uncertainty.

As the crew grapples with this newfound revelation, they realize that their journey through the white universe is far more complex and enigmatic than they had ever imagined. With their understanding of the cosmos fundamentally challenged, they must now navigate through a realm where the laws of physics themselves seem to defy logic and reason.

Commander Dr. Elizabeth Hayes ponders the implications of their discovery aloud, her thoughts echoing through the cockpit. "If a black hole can serve as a gateway to this white universe, then it stands to reason that there must be white holes within our own universe," she muses, her voice tinged with a mix of curiosity and determination.

Her words spark a flurry of speculation among the crew as they contemplate the existence of white holes within their own familiar cosmos. Dr. Emily Chen, her mind racing with possibilities, chimes in, "Perhaps these white holes could offer a means of traversing vast distances in space, opening up new avenues for exploration and discovery."

Lieutenant Commander Mark Thompson nods in agreement, his gaze fixed on the swirling darkness of the black hole outside the viewport. "It's a tantalizing prospect," he says, his voice filled with a sense of wonder. "But it also raises new questions about the nature of these cosmic phenomena and their potential impact on our understanding of the universe."

As they continue to ponder the mysteries of the cosmos, the crew realizes that their journey has only just begun. With each new revelation, they are propelled further into the depths of the unknown, driven by their insatiable thirst for knowledge and their unwavering determination to unlock the secrets of the universe.

Mark's urgent voice breaks the tension in the cockpit. "We can't waste time. We need answers, fast," he declares, his eyes fixed on the swirling white hole ahead. "Let's gather data and analyze it thoroughly to understand this anomaly and its impact on our mission."

Commander Hayes nods in agreement, her expression reflecting a sense of urgency. "Agreed. We cannot afford to delay in our pursuit of answers," she declares, her voice resolute. "We need to gather as much information as we can about these white holes and their implications for our mission and our understanding of the cosmos."

With determination, the crew sets to work, deploying sensors to measure the radiation emitted by the white hole. They carefully monitor any matter or energy being ejected, noting its composition and trajectory. Simultaneously, they observe the effects of the white hole on nearby celestial bodies, studying how its presence alters their orbits and gravitational interactions.

As the data streams in, the crew meticulously analyses each piece, searching for patterns and anomalies that might offer insight into the nature of the white hole. They collaborate, sharing observations and hypotheses as they strive to unravel the mysteries of this enigmatic phenomenon.

Despite the urgency of their task, the crew remains focused and methodical, knowing that their findings could hold the key to understanding not only the white hole itself but also its implications for their mission and the universe at large.

With a renewed sense of purpose, the crew springs into action, activating sensors and instruments to study the surrounding space and gather data on the black hole and the white universe beyond. Each member of the team works tirelessly, their focus sharpened by the gravity of the situation and the importance of their mission.

As they delve deeper into their research, the crew remains ever vigilant, ready to adapt and respond to whatever challenges may arise. With their collective expertise and unwavering determination, they are determined to uncover the truth behind the enigmatic white holes and chart a course towards the answers they seek.

Sarah's voice breaks the silence, her words carrying a weighty implication. "If we were to enter the black hole, theoretically, we might emerge from a white hole," she suggests, her tone laced with uncertainty. "It's a radical idea, but it could explain our unexpected arrival in the White Universe."

The crew exchanges incredulous glances, the implications of Sarah's theory sinking in. Could it be that their journey through the black hole had indeed, led them to this enigmatic realm? The possibility hangs in the air, challenging their understanding of the cosmos and sparking a flurry of questions about the nature of their reality.

The crew exchanges cautious glances, grappling with the enormity of the decision before them. If their hypothesis holds true, their journey through the black hole could not only lead them back to familiar space but also shed light on the fundamental forces that govern the cosmos. With the weight of their choice hanging heavy in the air, they brace themselves for the challenges that lie ahead, ready to embark on a daring quest to unlock the secrets of the universe.

As the crew deliberates on their plan to traverse the black hole, Lieutenant Commander Mark Thompson steps forward, his voice steady despite the gravity of the situation. "Going through a black hole is no small feat," he begins, his tone measured. "We'll need to calculate the trajectory precisely to avoid being pulled into the singularity."

Dr. Emily Chen nods in agreement, her expression focused. "The gravitational forces near a black hole are incredibly intense," she adds. "We'll need to ensure that our spacecraft is equipped to withstand the extreme conditions we'll encounter."

Commander Hayes listens intently, her mind already racing with the logistics of such a perilous journey. "We'll need to prepare meticulously," she declares, her voice firm. "Every aspect of our mission must be scrutinized to ensure the safety of the crew and the success of our endeavor. We've already navigated through one black hole, so we know the challenges that lie ahead."

With their plan taking shape, the crew sets to work, drawing on their collective expertise to devise a strategy that will enable them to navigate the treacherous depths of the black hole and emerge unscathed on the other side. As they embark on this daring mission, they know that their courage, ingenuity, and unwavering determination will be tested like never before.

With the crew's meticulous calculations and thorough readings, they con- firm a remarkable discovery: the black hole they are facing exhibits the same characteristics as the one they traversed earlier. This realization sparks a flurry of discussion among the crew, as they grapple with the implications of this extraordinary finding.

Chapter 19:
Going through the Black Hole

As the crew's spacecraft draws nearer to the black hole, anticipation courses through their veins, mingled with memories of their previous encounter with a similar cosmic phenomenon.

Dr. Chen's gentle reminder echoes through the cockpit, cutting through the tension like a beacon of clarity. "Remember, everyone," she says, her voice calm but firm, "we must aim for the precise center of the black hole. That's our best chance of navigating through safely."

Her words serve as a sobering reminder of the gravity of their mission, grounding the crew's focus as they prepare to confront the immense forces that await them. With her guidance, they steel themselves for the daunting task ahead, each member of the team committed to the success of their daring endeavor.

Commander Hayes gazes out of the viewport, her eyes filled with wonder as she beholds the sight before them. She realizes they stand on the cusp of a discovery that could revolutionize humanity's comprehension of the cosmos—an encounter with a cosmic force that has baffled scientists for generations.

Lieutenant Commander Thompson adjusts their

trajectory with precision, guiding the spacecraft towards the heart of the black hole with expert skill. His hands move deftly over the controls, navigating through the chaotic currents of space-time with unwavering focus.

Dr. Chen, her mind ablaze with scientific curiosity, eagerly studies the data streaming in from their sensors. She knows that this encounter holds the potential to unlock new insights into the fundamental nature of the cosmos, and she is determined to capture every detail for analysis.

Lieutenant Johnson monitors the spacecraft's vital systems, ensuring that they remain stable amidst the intense gravitational forces surrounding the black hole. Her steady hand and quick thinking are crucial as they approach the threshold of this enigmatic phenomenon.

Commander Hayes's remark reflects a blend of confidence and caution as they prepare to traverse the black hole. Having successfully navigated the complexities of the black hole before, she acknowledges the inherent risks of traveling through another cosmic anomaly. However, her unwavering determination and trust in her crew's abilities reassure them that they are well-equipped to face whatever challenges may arise. With their past experiences as a guide, they brace themselves for the journey ahead, knowing that each obstacle they overcome brings them closer to their ultimate goal.

As they edge closer to the black hole's event horizon, the crew braces themselves for whatever wonders—and dangers—lie ahead.

They know that this journey into the unknown will test their resolve and challenge their understanding of the universe. But with courage and determination, they press onward, ready to unlock the secrets of this cosmic anomaly and expand the boundaries of human knowledge once more.

As the crew embarked on their journey towards the enigmatic black hole, a sense of anticipation filled the spacecraft. Commander Hayes, Dr. Chen, Lieutenant Commander Thompson, and the rest of the team were united in their determination to unlock the mysteries that awaited them. With each passing moment, the gravitational pull of the black hole grew stronger, tugging at the fabric of spacetime itself. The crew watched in awe as the surrounding stars seemed to blur and warp, distorted by the immense gravitational forces at play.

"Steady as she goes," Commander Hayes commanded, her voice calm yet resolute. "We're approaching the event horizon. Keep a close eye on our trajectory, everyone."

Dr. Chen and Lieutenant Commander Thompson worked tirelessly; their eyes fixed on the navigation instruments as they carefully plotted the spacecraft's course. Every adjustment was calculated with precision, ensuring that they maintained a safe distance from the event horizon while still getting close enough to study the black hole's properties.

As they drew nearer to their destination, the crew braced themselves for the unknown. They knew that they were venturing into uncharted territory, where the laws of physics as they knew them might no longer apply. But they also knew that their quest for knowledge and understanding drove them forward, compelling them to push the boundaries of human exploration.

With their eyes fixed on the swirling vortex of dark matter and energy ahead, the crew pressed on, ready to confront whatever wonders and challenges awaited them at the threshold of the black hole.

With each passing moment, the crew's excitement grows, fueled by the knowledge that they are about to witness a phenomenon that few have ever seen. They understand the risks involved in venturing into the unknown, but they also know that the potential rewards are immeasurable.

Commander Hayes breaks the tense silence inside the spacecraft, her voice carrying a palpable urgency and resolve. "We're nearing the critical juncture," she declares, her gaze fixed on the swirling vortex of the black hole looming ahead. "This is where we encounter Spaghettification again re- member the first time?"

"We must allocate all accessible power to the warp engines,"

As Commander Hayes issues her directives, the crew springs into action, their training guiding their swift responses to prepare the spacecraft for the impending encounter with Spaghettification. With the success of the mission contingent upon flawless execution under immense pressure, each member focuses on their assigned tasks with unwavering determination.

Lieutenant Johnson allocates power to the warp engines, while Dr. Chen meticulously monitors the spacecraft's structural integrity, verifying its ability to withstand the impending forces. Unified in purpose, they stand prepared to confront the challenges posed by the black hole, resolute in their determination to emerge triumphant.

As Commander Hayes issues her directives, the crew springs into action, swiftly adapting the spacecraft's systems for the impending encounter with Spaghettification. Each member is acutely aware of the critical nature of their tasks, their training guiding their actions with precision and determination. With a unified sense of purpose, they synchronize their efforts, ensuring that every aspect of the spacecraft is optimized for the challenges ahead.

Lieutenant Johnson channels power to the warp engines,

while Dr. Chen meticulously monitors the structural integrity of the spacecraft, preparing it to withstand the immense gravitational forces they are about to face. With their roles defined and their resolve unwavering, they stand united in their determination to navigate through the black hole's maelstrom and emerge on the other side unscathed.

As the spacecraft hurtles towards the event horizon, the crew braces themselves for the impending trial. The gravitational forces intensify with each passing moment, threatening to subject them to the unfathomable phenomenon of Spaghettification.

Upon Commander Hayes's command, the spacecraft accelerates, surging forward with increased speed, propelling itself deeper into the gravitational abyss of the black hole. Inside the vessel, the crew members experience a subtle change in momentum, akin to the sensation of being gently pushed back into their seats, as the spacecraft hurtles onward into the un- charted depths of the unknown.

Commander Dr. Elizabeth Hayes at the helm, her gaze fixed on the swirling vortex of light and energy ahead. With a sense of anticipation mingled with trepidation, she issues final commands to her crew, each member poised for the momentous task ahead. Lieutenant Commander Mark Thompson, his hands steady on the controls, navigates the spacecraft with precision, guiding them toward the heart of the black hole.

As they delve deeper into the realm of the black hole, the crew is met with an otherworldly spectacle unlike anything they have encountered before. Reality itself seems to contort and warp around them, with space and time merging in a mesmerizing display of cosmic phenomena.

Outside the viewports, the stars blur and streak, their light bending and twisting into mesmerizing patterns under the influence of the intense gravitational forces. Within the confines of the spacecraft, the crew watches in awe as the fabric of spacetime bends and distorts, creating a surreal panorama of colors and shapes that defy conventional understanding.

Despite the surrealness of their surroundings, the crew remains steadfast in their mission, their determination unshaken by the uncertainty that surrounds them. With each passing moment, they draw nearer to the heart of the black hole, driven by an insatiable curiosity and a desire to unravel the mysteries of the cosmos.

As they hurtle deeper into the unknown depths of the black hole, Commander Hayes's voice breaks through the tension within the spacecraft, her words a beacon of reassurance amid the chaos. "Hold steady, everyone," she says, her voice calm yet resolute. "We're entering uncharted territory, but together, we'll navigate through whatever challenges lie ahead."

As Dr. Emily Chen delves into her scientific analysis within the singularity's core, she meticulously compares her findings against the data collected from their encounter with the first black hole. Drawing upon her expertise and the wealth of information gathered during their previous expedition, she seeks to identify any similarities or differences between the two phenomena.

With a keen eye for detail and a deep understanding of astrophysical principles, Dr. Chen scrutinizes the gravitational signatures, spectral emissions, and structural characteristics of the singularity, comparing them to the observations made during their previous encounter. She notes any deviations or anomalies, no matter how subtle, that may indicate variations in the properties or behavior of the black holes.

As she meticulously analyses the data, Dr. Chen begins to discern patterns and correlations between the two black holes, unravelling the intricate tapestry of cosmic phenomena that govern their existence. Through careful examination and rigorous scientific inquiry, she seeks to uncover the underlying principles that govern the formation and evolution of black holes, shedding light on the fundamental mysteries of the universe.

Ultimately, Dr. Chen's comparison reveals both striking similarities and intriguing differences between the two black holes. While they share many common traits indicative of their nature as gravitational singularities, subtle variations in their properties hint at the diverse range of cosmic phenomena that can arise within the vast expanse of space. Armed with this newfound knowledge, Dr. Chen continues her investigation with renewed vigor, eager to unravel the secrets hidden within the depths of the cosmos.

Lieutenant Sarah Johnson's gaze flits across the multitude of monitors lining the control panel before her, her focus unwavering even amidst the swirling chaos of energies that envelop the spacecraft. With a deft touch, she adjusts the dials and toggles, monitoring the vital systems with meticulous precision.

Despite the tumultuous environment outside, Lieutenant Johnson remains steadfast, her expertise in spacecraft operations shining through as she maintains a delicate balance between the vessel's various subsystems. With each passing moment, she keeps a watchful eye on the readings, ready to intervene at a moment's notice should any anomalies arise.

As the crew ventures deeper into the heart of the black hole, Lieutenant Johnson's vigilance becomes all the more crucial, her steady hand guiding the spacecraft through the turbulent currents of space-time. With her un- wavering dedication to duty, she ensures that the crew can navigate the perilous journey ahead with confidence and resolve.

As they cross the threshold of the black hole's event horizon once again, the crew finds themselves enveloped in a mesmerizing display of light and energy, a dazzling array of colors painting the cosmic canvas before them. Space-time contorts and twists around their spacecraft, creating a surreal spectacle that defies comprehension.

Within this maelstrom of gravitational forces, the crew feels as though they are adrift in a sea of cosmic chaos, buffeted by waves of energy that ripple through the fabric of reality itself. Yet, amidst the disorienting whirl of colors and shapes, they remain steadfast in their mission, their resolve un- yielding in the face of the unknown.

With each passing moment, they press onward, navigating through the tumultuous currents of the black hole's domain with skill and determination. Though the journey is fraught with peril, they remain focused on their goal, drawing closer to the heart of the cosmic enigma that lies ahead.

As they venture deeper into the heart of the black hole, the crew's excitement and curiosity reach new heights. This journey represents a unique opportunity for exploration, promising to expand their knowledge of the universe and challenge their perceptions of reality.

Filled with a blend of wonder and determination, the crew pushes forward, eager to unravel the mysteries concealed within the black hole's enigmatic depths. They see themselves as intrepid explorers, driven by an insatiable thirst for discovery and a steadfast resolve to overcome any obstacles that may arise along the way.

However, their exhilaration is soon tempered by a sudden turn of events. Without warning, the ship begins to spin, setting off alarms throughout the spacecraft and sending the crew into a flurry of activity. Commander Hayes springs into action, issuing rapid-fire commands as they work to regain control of the ship.

Lieutenant Commander Thompson's voice cuts through the chaos, reporting a troubling similarity to their previous encounter with a black hole. As they grapple with this unexpected twist, the crew braces themselves for the challenges that lie ahead, drawing on their expertise and teamwork to navigate through the unknown.

Lieutenant Commander Thompson's gaze darted across the navigation console; his expression etched with concern. "It seems we've been ensnared by a gravitational eddy," he reported, his voice tight with tension. "The black hole's immense gravity is pulling us off our intended trajectory."

Dr. Chen, fully immersed in the task at hand, nodded in agreement, her fingers dancing across the control panel as she sought to stabilize their spiraling motion. "We must counteract these gravitational forces," she asserted, her determination palpable. "I'm recalculating our trajectory as we speak."

As the ship's rotation intensified, threatening to throw the crew into disarray, Commander Hayes remained steadfast, refusing to succumb to panic. With a firm grip on her composure, she rallied her team, infusing them with a renewed sense of purpose and resolve.

"We cannot allow this setback to derail us," she declared, her voice unwavering amidst the chaos. "We will find a solution and press on with our mission. Stay focused, everyone."

The crew members brace themselves as the spacecraft is jolted off its in- tended path, thrown into disarray by the unforgiving gravitational forces of the black hole. Commander Hayes springs into action, her voice a beacon of authority amid the chaos as she issues rapid commands to her team.

"We must stabilize our trajectory immediately!" she commands, her urgency evident. "Activate emergency thrusters and engage manual over- ride!"

Lieutenant Commander Thompson and Dr. Chen respond with swift precision, their hands darting across their respective control panels as they fight to regain control of the ship. With each passing second, the gravitational forces intensify, threatening to rip the spacecraft apart at its seams.

"We're losing altitude!" Lieutenant Commander Thompson's voice echoes through the cockpit, urgency collaring his tone. "We need to boost thrust to counteract the gravitational pull!" Dr. Chen nods in agreement, her focus unwavering as she inputs the necessary commands. "Boosting thrust now!" she declares, determination evident in her voice.

Amidst the frantic activity to stabilize the spacecraft, one of the crew members speaks up, voicing a nagging doubt that lingers in the back of their mind. "I don't recall this happening when we went through the other black hole," they remark, their tone tinged with uncertainty as they reflect on their previous encounter.

Commander Hayes pauses for a moment, considering the crew member's observation. Despite the urgency of their current situation, she knows the importance of addressing their concerns and maintaining transparency within the team.

"You're right," she acknowledges, her voice calm yet resolute. "This experience is different from our previous encounter. We'll need to analyze the data once we've stabilized the ship to understand what's happening."

With her words, Commander Hayes instils a sense of confidence in the crew, reassuring them that they will confront this new challenge with the same determination and resourcefulness that has carried them through countless trials before. And as they continue to work together to navigate the perils of the cosmos, they do so with a renewed sense of purpose, ready to face whatever obstacles lie ahead.

As the ship stabilized once more, a collective sigh of relief echoed through the spacecraft. Though they had faced a moment of uncertainty and danger, the crew emerged stronger and more determined than ever to press forward into the unknown. With Commander Hayes leading the way, they were ready to confront whatever challenges lay ahead as they continued their journey towards the black hole.

However, as they draw closer to the anomaly, the crew notices something unusual—a distortion in spacetime that defies all conventional understanding. Instead of the expected crushing gravitational forces and extreme distortions, they perceive a shimmering portal, reminiscent of a swirling tunnel of energy.

Commander Hayes, her brow furrowing with concern, speaks up, her voice carrying a note of confusion. "That wasn't in the other black hole when we came out, and by my recollection, we should be nearly out by now."

The crew exchanges uneasy glances, the anomaly before them presenting a baffling mystery that defies explanation. Despite their uncertainty, they know they must proceed cautiously, gathering as much data as possible to understand the nature of this unexpected phenomenon. With their resolve unshaken, they brace themselves for the challenges that lie ahead, knowing that the answers they seek may lead them to new revelations about the nature of the cosmos.

As the crew of the spacecraft navigates through the depths of the black hole, Commander Hayes and Dr. Chen exchange a meaningful glance, silently acknowledging the gravity of their situation. Despite the chaos swirling around them, they remain steadfast in their commitment to un- covering the truth behind the enigmatic phenomenon they now face.

"Dr. Chen," Commander Hayes begins, her voice steady yet tinged with urgency, "can you compare this hole with the first time we went through? I want to know what's different."

Dr. Chen's eyes light up with determination as she accepts the challenge. "Of course, Commander," she responds, her mind already racing with possibilities. "I'll analyze the data from both instances and compare them side by side. Hopefully, we'll uncover any discrepancies or anomalies that could explain the unexpected phenomenon we're witnessing now."

With a sense of purpose, Dr. Chen immerses herself in her task, pouring over the ship's records and scientific logs with meticulous attention to de- tail. As she sifts through the data, she remains focused on her objective, determined to unravel the mysteries of the black hole, and guide the crew safely through the unknown.

Meanwhile, Commander Hayes is at her side, offering support and guidance as they navigate the complexities of their situation. Together, they epitomize the resilience and determination of humanity in the face of adversity, ready to confront whatever challenges the cosmos may throw their way. And as they delve deeper into the mysteries of the black hole, they know that their journey is far from over, but with their unwavering resolve and commitment to discovery, they are prepared to face whatever lies ahead.

As Commander Hayes comes to the realization that they should avoid entering the shimmering portal, a hushed silence falls over the crew. The significance of her observation weighs heavily on their minds, stirring a mix of curiosity and apprehension.

"It seems we encountered a similar portal in the first black hole, but chose not to enter," Commander Hayes muses aloud, her voice tinged with un- certainty. "Could this mean that the portal leads to another dimension?"

Commander Hayes's realization sends a shiver of apprehension through the crew as they contemplate the implications of her words. The notion of venturing into another dimension is both exhilarating and terrifying, raising countless questions about what they might encounter on the other side.

Dr. Chen furrows her brow, her mind racing with the possibilities. "It's certainly a fascinating theory," she muses, her tone thoughtful. "But we must proceed with caution. Venturing into another dimension could lead to unknown dangers or consequences that we can't even begin to imagine."

Lieutenant Commander Thompson nods in agreement, his expression grave. "I agree, Commander. While the prospect of exploring another dimension is intriguing, we cannot afford to take unnecessary risks. We need to prioritize the safety of the crew above all else."

As they debate their options, the crew grapples with the weight of their decision. On one hand, the allure of uncovering new realms of existence beckons to their sense of adventure and curiosity. On the other hand, the unknown dangers lurking beyond the shimmering portal loom ominously, reminding them of the fragility of their existence in the vast expanse of the cosmos.

In the end, they know that the choice is theirs alone to make. With their collective expertise and unwavering resolve, they stand ready to confront whatever lies ahead, whether it be within the confines of their current reality or beyond the bounds of space and time itself.

As the spacecraft veers away from the shimmering portal, a collective sense of relief washes over the crew. They narrowly avoided what could have been a perilous journey into another dimension, guided by Commander Hayes's keen intuition and the crew's quick thinking.

With the immediate danger averted, the crew refocuses their attention on navigating through the black hole's gravitational field. Lieutenant Commander Thompson adjusts their trajectory, steering the spacecraft to the right and away from the shimmering anomaly they just narrowly missed.

Tension still lingers in the air as they continue on their path, the crew acutely aware of the precarious nature of their surroundings. Yet, there is also a renewed sense of determination and unity among them, forged through their shared experience and their mutual resolve to overcome whatever challenges lie ahead.

As they press onward, the crew remains vigilant, their eyes fixed on the swirling abyss before them. With each passing moment, they draw closer to the heart of the black hole, their minds filled with anticipation and apprehension for what awaits them on the other side. But with their trust in each other and their unwavering determination, they are ready to face whatever trials may come their way as they journey deeper into the unknown depths of the cosmos.

Chapter 20:
Return to the Unknown

As the spacecraft emerges from the black hole's grasp and finds itself in an unfamiliar region of the universe, a hushed silence falls over the crew. Commander Hayes, her brow furrowed in concern, quickly assesses their surroundings, and realizes the gravity of the situation. Without hesitation, she issues a command for the ship to come to a complete stop, halting their forward momentum and allowing them a moment to gather their thoughts.

"While we're paused to assess our location, Mark, could you please ensure the reactors are functioning properly?" Commander Hayes requested, her tone decisive yet calm. "Sarah and Emily, would you mind inspecting the exterior of the spacecraft to ensure our integrity? If you find any issues, Mark can lend a hand after he completes his inspection of the reactors."

After diligently conducting their respective tasks, the crew members re- convene inside the spacecraft. Mark, Sarah, and Emily return with reassuring reports— the reactors are functioning flawlessly, and the exterior of the spacecraft remains intact without any signs of damage or compromise.

Commander Hayes nods in satisfaction, her confidence in her crew reaffirmed. "Excellent work, everyone," she commends, a hint of relief in her voice.

"Now all we have to do is figure out where we are," Commander Hayes stated, breaking the tense silence that enveloped the crew. "Are we in a different universe, or are we simply a long way from home?"

The crew members exchanged bewildered glances, their minds racing with questions and uncertainties. How had they ended up in this distant corner of the cosmos? What cosmic forces had guided their journey, and what lay ahead in this uncharted territory?

Despite the confusion and apprehension that hung in the air, Commander Hayes remained composed, her leadership unwavering in the face of adversity. With a steady voice, she addressed her crew, urging them to remain calm and focused as they navigated this unexpected twist in their journey.

"We may be in uncharted territory, but we've faced challenges before," she reassures them, her tone resolute. "Let's gather our data and assess our options. We'll approach this with caution and precision, just as we always have." With their commander's guidance, the crew springs into action, initiating scans of their surroundings and compiling data to analyze their current position. Though the road ahead may be fraught with uncertainty, they are united in their determination to navigate through this cosmic mystery and emerge stronger on the other side.

Commander Dr. Elizabeth Hayes blinks in disbelief as she surveys their new surroundings, her mind racing with the implications of their unexpected arrival. Beside her, Lieutenant Commander Mark Thompson fur- rows his brow in concentration, recalibrating their navigational systems to determine their exact location amidst the vast expanse of space. Dr. Emily Chen, Ph.D., pores over the data streaming in from their sensors, her scientific curiosity ignited by the opportunity to unravel the mysteries of this unfamiliar region.

Meanwhile, Lieutenant Sarah Johnson remains vigilant, her eyes scanning the horizon for any signs of danger, poised to guide the crew through the challenges that lie ahead with her steady expertise. Together, they stand at the forefront of exploration, ready to confront the unknown and unlock the secrets of the cosmos.

With each passing moment, the crew's curiosity deepens, fueled by the knowledge that they are on the brink of discovery. They understand that their journey through the white hole has brought them to a realm of infinite possibility, where the unknown awaits around every corner.

As the crew gazes out at the galaxy before them, both familiar and unfamiliar, a sense of awe and uncertainty washes over them. The stars twinkle with a familiar brilliance, yet there is something different about this corner of the cosmos. As they study the celestial coordinates and com- pare them to their known charts, a startling realization dawns upon them— they are in uncharted territory.

Lieutenant Commander Mark Thompson breaks the silence with a contemplative tone. "Perhaps we should have ventured through the shimmering portal," he muses, his words carrying a hint of uncertainty. "But who knows what lies on the other side?"

Commander Hayes furrows her brow in concentration as she studies the data before her, her mind racing with possibilities. Could this be their own galaxy, viewed from a different vantage point? Or have they stumbled upon an entirely new and undiscovered corner of the universe?

Lieutenant Commander Thompson adjusts the navigation systems, double- checking their position with meticulous care, but the results only deepen the mystery. Despite their efforts, the coordinates they have gathered seem to defy all known celestial charts and databases.

The crew exchanges uncertain glances, their curiosity mingled with a sense of trepidation. They are in uncharted territory, far from the familiar stars and constellations they once relied on for navigation. As they grapple with the implications of their discovery, one thing becomes clear—whatever lies ahead will test their courage, resourcefulness, and resolve like never before.

Commander Hayes, recognizing the urgency of their situation, issues a command for the crew to attempt communication with Moon Base using the infrared radio. With their standard communication channels disrupted by the unique properties of the space they find themselves in, the infrared radio might offer a chance to establish contact with their home base.

As the crew members spring into action, configuring the infrared radio and scanning the frequencies for any sign of a response, a tense silence fills the spacecraft. Each moment feels like an eternity as they wait, their hopes riding on the possibility of reconnecting with civilization and finding answers to the myriad questions swirling in their minds.

Commander Hayes absorbs the news with a mix of disappointment and determination. She knew the odds of establishing contact were uncertain, given their unfamiliar location and the limitations of their equipment. Nevertheless, she refuses to be discouraged.

"Keep trying," she instructs the crew, her voice firm and resolute. "We can't afford to give up hope. Moon Base may be out there, waiting for our signal. We'll continue our attempts to establish communication while we explore our surroundings."

With a renewed sense of purpose, the crew redoubles

their efforts, adjusting frequencies and fine-tuning the equipment in the hopes of catching even the faintest whisper of a response from Moon Base. Each attempt brings them one step closer to unravelling the mysteries of their unexpected journey and finding a way back home.

Amidst the swirling uncertainty, Commander Hayes remains a beacon of resolve and leadership, her steady guidance anchoring the crew in their pursuit of knowledge and understanding. With each passing moment, they inch closer to unlocking the secrets of this enigmatic corner of the universe, driven by their insatiable curiosity and unwavering determination.

As the crew continues to scan the vast expanse of space for any signs of life or familiar landmarks, they remain vigilant, ever mindful of the challenges that lie ahead. With their resources dwindling and the mysteries of their surroundings deepening, they know that they must tread carefully, balancing the thrill of discovery with the need for caution.

With their attempts to contact Moon Base proving futile, the crew turns their attention to scanning the surrounding space for any signs of outposts or civilizations. Lieutenant Johnson carefully adjusts the communication systems, expanding their search parameters to encompass a wider range of frequencies and wavelengths.

Commander Hayes issues an order to halt their progress,

recognizing the need for a brief respite. "Let's take a moment to pause and refresh our- selves," she declares, her tone decisive yet compassionate. "We'll reconvene here shortly and continue our efforts to ascertain our location."

The crew members nod in agreement, grateful for the opportunity to momentarily ease the tension that hangs in the air. They gather in the space- craft's common area, pouring cups of hot tea and exchanging murmured conversations as they take a much-needed break.

After a brief interval, Commander Hayes calls the crew back to their stations. "Alright, everyone, let's resume our search," she announces, her voice resolute. "We'll navigate through this together, one step at a time."

With renewed determination, the crew returns to their tasks, ready to confront the challenges of their uncertain journey head-on. As they peer into the vast expanse of space, they remain steadfast in their commitment to unravelling the mysteries that lie ahead.

As the crew waits anxiously for a response, tension mounts inside the spacecraft, each member acutely aware of the gravity of their situation. The passage of time feels distorted, their sense of temporality warped by the cosmic journey they have undertaken. Though only a week may have passed for them, they understand that in the present time, much more could have transpired.

Their eyes fixed on the communication console, the crew holds their breath, hoping for a beacon of hope amidst the vast expanse of space.

Dr. Chen's excitement is palpable as she contemplates the potential of their discovery. A new galaxy represents a vast canvas of unexplored mysteries and hidden treasures, awaiting their exploration and study. With each passing moment, her mind races with possibilities, envisioning the scientific breakthroughs and revelations that could await them in this uncharted frontier.

Meanwhile, Lieutenant Johnson remains steadfast at her station, her fingers dancing across the control panel as she sends out signals into the void of space. Her determination to establish contact with any nearby outposts or civilizations is unwavering, fueled by the hope of finding a clue that could provide answers to their current predicament.

As the crew awaits a response, their collective anticipation hangs heavy in the air, mingled with a sense of urgency and excitement. For they know that their encounter with this new galaxy marks a pivotal moment in their journey, one that could lead to discoveries beyond their wildest imaginations.

Commander Hayes tasked Mark with checking the provisions.

With a heavy heart, Lieutenant Commander Mark

Thompson returned from his inspection, his expression grave, and his demeanor somber. As he approached Commander Hayes and the rest of the crew, his report weighed heavily on his mind.

"We're facing a critical situation," he began, his voice tinged with concern. "Our provisions are running dangerously low, especially our food and water supplies."

Commander Hayes's brow furrowed in worry as she absorbed the gravity of the situation. With their current predicament, rationing their limited re- sources would be essential for their survival until they could find a viable solution.

"What are our options?" she inquired, her voice steady despite the underlying sense of urgency.

Lieutenant Commander Thompson sighed, his gaze momentarily faltering before he continued. "At this point, rationing is our best bet," he explained. "We'll need to carefully manage our food and water intake until we can find a source of replenishment."

Dr. Chen and Lieutenant Sarah Johnson exchanged concerned glances, fully aware of the challenges that lay ahead. They knew that their journey through the cosmos had just become even more perilous, with the Specter of dwindling supplies looming over them like a dark cloud.

But despite the daunting odds, the crew remained resolute in their determination to persevere. With their unity and resourcefulness, they vowed to confront this latest obstacle head-on, trusting in their ingenuity and teamwork to see them through the trials that lay ahead.

As they grapple with the uncertainty of their situation, the crew is filled with a mix of anticipation and trepidation. They know that they are standing on the threshold of a monumental discovery, one that could reshape their understanding of the cosmos. But they also understand the inherent risks of exploring uncharted territory, where the unknown lurks around every corner.

As they assess their situation and process the implications of their new location, Commander Hayes wastes no time in convening a meeting to formulate a plan of action.

Gathering in the spacecraft's command module, the crew discusses their options and considers their next steps. They analyze the data collected from their instruments and consult their navigational charts in an effort to determine their precise coordinates and assess the characteristics of their new- found surroundings.

Dr. Chen, with her expertise in astrophysics and navigation, takes the lead in deciphering the data and interpreting their current position relative to known celestial bodies. She identifies nearby star systems and galaxies, noting any potential landmarks or reference points that can aid in orienting themselves within this unfamiliar region of space.

Lieutenant Commander Thompson, drawing upon his experience as a seasoned space farer, offers insights into the practical aspects of their situation, considering factors such as fuel reserves, propulsion capabilities, and the condition of their spacecraft. He advises caution and thorough preparation before embarking on any further exploration or travel through the unknown territory.

Meanwhile, Dr. Chen and Lieutenant Johnson assess the status of the spacecraft's systems and equipment, ensuring that everything is functioning optimally and making any necessary repairs or adjustments. They conduct thorough diagnostics and maintenance checks to address any issues that may have arisen during their journey through the black hole.

As the crew deliberates and plans their next course of action, they remain united in their determination to navigate this uncharted corner of the universe with precision, caution, and a spirit of exploration. Despite the uncertainty and challenges that lie ahead, they are ready to face whatever awaits them as they continue their voyage through the vast and wondrous expanse of the cosmos.

And so, with hearts full of determination and minds brimming with curiosity, the crew sets a course deeper into the unknown galaxy, ready to embrace whatever wonders and challenges lie ahead. For they are explorers at heart, driven by an insatiable thirst for knowledge and a boundless spirit of adventure. And as they venture forth into the uncharted depths of space, they do so with the knowledge that they are writing a new chapter in the annals of cosmic exploration—one that will be taught for generations to come.

Commander Hayes, her brow furrowed with concern, consults with Lieu- tenant Johnson, the expert on the spacecraft's systems. "Lieutenant John- son, have we used the backup reactor yet?" she inquires, her voice betraying a hint of urgency.

Lieutenant Johnson, her fingers flying across the control panel as she checks the power readouts, responds quickly. "Not yet Commander. The primary reactor is still operational, but power levels are fluctuating. We may need to switch to the backup soon if the situation worsens."

Commander Hayes nods, her mind racing with possibilities. They are far from home, navigating through unknown territory, and the last thing they need is a critical power failure. "Keep a close eye on it, Lieutenant," she instructs, her voice firm. "We can't afford any surprises out here."

With a sense of determination, the crew braces themselves for whatever challenges lie ahead, knowing that their survival depends on their ability to adapt and overcome. As they press onward into the depths of the unknown galaxy, they remain vigilant, ready to confront whatever obstacles may come their way.

Commander Hayes nods thoughtfully, her mind already racing through the implications. "Good work, everyone," she says, addressing the crew. "Activate a diagnostic scan on both reactors. We need to ensure they are functioning optimally after the extended operation. Lieutenant Johnson, keep an eye on our power distribution and consumption. Let's conserve energy wherever we can until we're certain both reactors are operating at full capacity."

The crew acknowledges her orders with brisk efficiency, each member turning to their assigned tasks with a sense of purpose. As the diagnostic scans begin, Commander Hayes cannot help but feel a surge of pride in her team. Despite the challenges they have faced, they have proven themselves resourceful and resilient, qualities that will serve them well as they navigate the mysteries of this unfamiliar galaxy.

Lieutenant Commander Thompson inputs the latest data from the ship's sensors into the navigational computer, his fingers flying across the controls with practiced precision. "I'm cross-referencing our current position with known star charts," he reports. "It may take some time to identify our exact location, but I'll do my best to expedite the process."

Dr. Chen leans over his shoulder, her expression focused as she studies the data. "We should also consider gathering additional data from nearby star systems," she suggests. "Their spectral signatures and gravitational anomalies could provide valuable clues about our whereabouts."

Commander Hayes considers Lieutenant Johnson's assessment carefully, recognizing the gravity of their situation. With limited reserves and an un- certain journey ahead, they must conserve energy to ensure their safe pas- sage through the unknown galaxy.

"Understood, Lieutenant," Commander Hayes replies, her voice steady de- spite the weight of their circumstances. "Initiate the switch to the backup reactor. We can't afford to take any chances out here."

With a series of swift commands, Lieutenant Johnson redirects the power flow to the backup reactor, seamlessly transitioning their spacecraft onto its secondary energy source. As the backup system comes online, the crew breathes a collective sigh of relief, knowing that they have taken a crucial step towards securing their journey home.

Chapter 21: The Saviors

Sarah said, her tone determined. "We'll proceed cautiously, scanning for any signs of communication along the way."

With the decision made, the crew adjusts their approach, slowing the spacecraft's pace to a steady crawl. Sarah takes her position at the communications console, her fingers poised over the controls as she begins scanning for any incoming signals.

The vastness of space stretches out before them, silent and vast. Yet, undeterred, Sarah persists, sending out radio signals into the void, hoping for a response from any potential nearby sources of civilization.

Hour's pass, each moment filled with anticipation and tension as they await a reply. But as the silence persists, the crew's resolve remains unshaken. They are determined to leave no stone unturned in their quest for answers, ready to explore every avenue until they uncover the truth about their cur- rent whereabouts in the cosmos.

With their energy reserves replenished, albeit limited, the crew presses on, their determination unwavering in the face of uncertainty. As they navigate through the uncharted expanse of the galaxy, they remain vigilant, ever mindful of the challenges that lie ahead.

As the crew works diligently to solve the mystery of their location, a sense of urgency fills the air. They know that every moment counts, and that their journey back to their home galaxy will be fraught with challenges and obstacles. But they also know that they are not alone—they are a team, united in their determination to return home safely, no matter what lies ahead.

Lieutenant Commander Thompson adjusts the navigation systems, calibrating them to analyze the surrounding stellar cartography in greater de- tail. Dr. Chen scrutinizes the data feeds, searching for any patterns or anomalies that might provide clues to their location. Meanwhile, Lieutenant Johnson ensures that the ship's power systems remain stable, ready to spring into action at a moment's notice.

As the crew works diligently to unravel the mystery of their whereabouts, Commander Hayes remains vigilant, her gaze fixed on the star map before her. She knows that they are facing a formidable challenge, but she also knows that they are a team, united in their determination to find their way back home.

With each passing moment, the tension in the cockpit mounts, but the crew remains steadfast in their resolve. They know that the path ahead will be fraught with uncertainty and danger, but they also know that together, they can overcome any obstacle that stands in their way.

And so, with hearts full of determination and minds focused on the task at hand, they press onward, ready to face whatever challenges the cosmos throws their way.

Commander Hayes turns to Lieutenant Commander Thompson, her ex- pression serious. "Mark, I need you to establish communication with any nearby star bases or outposts," she instructs. "We need to gather as much information as we can about our current location and potential routes back to our home galaxy."

Lieutenant Commander Thompson nods, understanding the urgency of the situation. He quickly navigates the ship's communication systems, scanning for any available frequencies that might provide a lifeline back to familiar territory.

"Radio frequencies locked in, Commander," he reports, his fingers flying across the controls. "I'm broadcasting a general distress signal and requesting assistance from any nearby vessels or installations."

As the transmission goes out into the void of space, the crew holds their breath, hoping for a response that will lead them one step closer to home. The seconds tick by, stretching into agonizing minutes, until finally, a crackle of static fills the bridge, followed by a voice—a faint yet unmistakable signal of hope in the darkness.

"We've got a response, Commander," Lieutenant

Commander Thompson announces, a hint of relief in his voice. "It's a research outpost. They're offering assistance and providing us with updated star charts for our region of space."

Commander Hayes exhales a sigh of relief, her shoulders relaxing slightly. "Good work, Mark," she says, her voice tinged with gratitude. "Patch me through to the outpost. Let's see what they have to say."

As the crew listens intently to the voice on the other end of the line, offering guidance and support, Commander Hayes exchanges a glance with Lieutenant Commander Thompson, silently acknowledging the relief washing over them. With each word from their newfound ally, the path back to their home galaxy begins to emerge from the darkness of uncertainty.

But amidst the reassurance, a note of urgency creeps in as the commander on the other end of the line reveals their own ship's dilemma. Commander Hayes nods, her determination unwavering despite the new obstacle.

"We're here to help in any way we can," she replies, her voice steady. "Please provide your coordinates, and we'll do everything in our power to assist you."

With the promise of mutual aid binding them together, the two commanders exchange vital information, forging a bond of camaraderie in the vast expanse of space. And as they work together to overcome their respective challenges, the crew finds strength in unity, knowing that they are not alone in their journey through the cosmos.

With the coordinates in hand, Commander Hayes wastes no time. She swiftly gathers her crew, their faces reflecting a mix of determination and concern as they prepare to assist their fellow travelers in need.

"Alright everyone, listen up," Commander Hayes commands, her voice firm with resolve. "We have a mission. We are going to navigate to the co- ordinates provided by our allies and offer whatever assistance we can.

Lieutenant Johnson, plot a course based on the coordinates we have received. Lieutenant Commander Thompson, prepare the engines for warp speed.

Dr. Chen, ensure that all systems are functioning optimally and stand by for any medical emergencies. Let us move with purpose but stay alert. We don't know what challenges may await us."

With their roles assigned and their objectives clear, the crew springs into action. As they work together seamlessly, a sense of unity and purpose fills the spacecraft, propelling them forward on their mission of aid and solidarity.

Lieutenant Commander Thompson's fingers move with precision as he in- puts the coordinates into the navigational computer, his eyes focused intently on the holographic interface. With each calculation, he ensures that their route is optimized for speed and safety, taking into account the vast distances they must traverse.

Dr. Chen works alongside him, her expertise in astrophysics invaluable as she cross-references the data with the latest astronomical observations. Her keen eye detects any potential hazards or anomalies that may lie along their path, allowing them to chart a course that steers clear of danger.

Meanwhile, Lieutenant Johnson diligently monitors the ship's power systems, her attention divided between the energy reserves and the demands of the journey ahead. With a careful balance of conservation and efficiency, she ensures that they have enough power to sustain their mission while also preparing for any unforeseen challenges that may arise.

"We need to tread carefully," Lieutenant Johnson advises, her voice steady despite the urgency of their situation. "Conserving energy is essential, but we must maintain a steady pace to reach our destination in a timely manner. Let's stay vigilant and focused as we embark on this journey into the unknown."

As the crew prepares for their descent, Commander Hayes orders a com- prehensive analysis of the planet's atmosphere and surface conditions to ensure their safety upon arrival. Dr. Chen and Lieutenant Johnson collaborate to assess the planet's environmental data, scanning for atmospheric composition, oxygen levels, and signs of water sources.

After careful examination, Dr. Chen delivers the findings to the rest of the crew. "The atmosphere is breathable, albeit with slightly higher levels of nitrogen than our home environment," she reports. "And there are indications of water reservoirs scattered across the planet's surface, which should provide a vital resource for both us and the stranded crew."

With this reassuring information, Lieutenant Commander Thompson adjusts their descent trajectory, accordingly, aiming for a landing site near one of the identified water sources. As they approach the planet's surface, the crew remains vigilant, ready to adapt to any unforeseen challenges that may arise during their mission to assist their fellow explorers in need.

As the crew's spacecraft descends towards the planet's surface, they quickly spot the stranded ship, the Venturer, lying on its side in an unusual position. Commander Hayes furrows her brow in concern as she observes the scene through the viewport, noting that the ship's orientation is not as it should be.

"Something's not right," she remarks, her voice laced with worry. "The Venturer shouldn't be lying like that. We need to find out what's happened and if the crew is still aboard."

Lieutenant Commander Thompson carefully guides their ship towards the Venturer, choosing a landing spot nearby that offers a clear view of the stranded vessel. As they touch down on the planet's surface, the crew prepares to disembark, their senses heightened as they brace themselves for whatever they may find aboard the distressed ship.

As soon as the crew's ship touches down on the planet's surface, Commander Andy Spear emerges from the Venturer, his expression a mixture of relief and concern as he approaches Commander Hayes and her team.

"Thank goodness you're here," he says, his voice tinged with urgency. "We've encountered some unexpected complications, and we could really use your assistance."

Commander Hayes nods, her demeanor calm and composed as she listens to Commander Spear's explanation. "Tell us what happened," she says, her tone reassuring yet firm. "We're here to help in any way we can."

Adverse weather conditions led to our mishap a decade ago, but we man- aged to survive by living off the land and preserving our supplies. How did you come across us? Were you dispatched to locate us?

Upon hearing Commander Spear's explanation of their predicament, Commander Hayes nodded thoughtfully, absorbing the details of their unexpected ordeal. "We weren't sent to find you," she clarified, "We ended up here after traversing through a black hole. And regarding the time discrepancy, it appears that time operates differently in different regions of space."

She then turned her attention to the matter of communication. "Can you not send a signal to Moon Base at all?" she inquired, hopeful that they might establish a link with their home base despite the challenges they faced.

"We lost communication with Moon base a while back, even before we stumbled upon this planet," Commander Spear clarified.

"Understood," Commander Hayes acknowledged, her expression grave as she processed the information. "We'll need to assess our options and determine the best course of action from here. First, let's focus on ensuring the safety and well-being of both crews."

With a nod of agreement from the others, they began discussing their next steps, mindful of the challenges that lay ahead in this unfamiliar territory.

All the crews gather in the Venturer, their spirits lifted by the presence of fresh food and drink, including hot meals cooked outside on a makeshift barbecue.

Both commanders stroll along the rugged terrain,

engaging in a candid discussion about the challenges they face. They share insights, ideas, and strategies, drawing on each other's experience and expertise to find solutions to their shared dilemma. As they walk, their conversation deepens, forming a bond of mutual understanding and respect that will serve them well in the days to come.

Upon returning to the Venturer, Commanders Hayes and Spear gather the crew to present their collaborative idea. Standing side by side, they address the assembled team with confidence and determination.

"Team," Commander Hayes begins, her voice firm yet reassuring, "Commander Spear and I have been discussing our situation, and we believe we have a viable solution to get the overturned spacecraft upright again."

Commander Spear nods in agreement, adding, "But we'll need everyone's help and input to make this happen. If any of you have ideas or suggestions on how we can accomplish this without causing further damage to the craft, we're all ears."

The crew members exchange glances, their expressions a mix of anticipation and determination. They understand the gravity of the task ahead but are eager to contribute their skills and expertise to the collective effort.

Lieutenant Commander Thompson's suggestion to utilize the Venturer's winches and cables garners nods of approval from the crew, who immediately begin envisioning the practicalities of the plan. Dr. Chen joins in, highlighting the importance of securely anchoring the cables to prevent any structural damage to the spacecraft. Her meticulous attention to detail earns her a round of appreciative nods from her colleagues.

Not to be outdone, Lieutenant Johnson proposes reinforcing the space- craft's hull with spare metal plating from the Venturer, a suggestion that receives enthusiastic support. The crew members exchange glances, im- pressed by the practicality and ingenuity of their fellow team member's ideas.

Then, Lieutenant Mary Spiers steps forward with a novel suggestion in- volving the Venturer's onboard drones. Her proposal to use the drones to provide additional stability and guidance during the lifting process sparks a flurry of excitement among the crew. Dr. Mira Lucas eagerly adds to the discussion, suggesting using the drones' cameras to monitor the operation in real-time, a notion that receives unanimous approval.

Dr. Robert Vaughan rounds out the brainstorming session with a proposal for a synchronized approach to coordinating the lifting process. His idea to assign specific roles to each team member ensures that everyone knows their responsibilities, fostering a sense of cohesion and efficiency among the crew.

Commanders Hayes and Spear listen attentively to the

additional ideas, impressed by the creativity and ingenuity of their crew. "These are excellent suggestions," Commander Spear acknowledges, his voice filled with admiration. "Let's incorporate them into our plan and make use of every available resource to ensure the success of the operation."

With a comprehensive plan now in place, the crew sets to work with renewed vigor and determination. Each member contributes their unique skills and expertise to the task at hand, united in their shared goal of restoring the overturned spacecraft to its rightful position. As they work together seamlessly, they know that success is within reach, fueled by their collective ingenuity and teamwork.

As darkness blankets the unfamiliar planet, both crews retreat to their respective spacecraft—the Explorer and the stranded vessel Venturer—to seek refuge and rejuvenation after a day filled with planning and preparation. Within the confines of their ships, crew members gather around makeshift tables, enjoying a hearty meal crafted from the provisions harvested from the planet's forest.

A silent understanding passes between Commander Hayes and Commander Spear, a recognition of the camaraderie that has blossomed among their teams. Despite the hurdles ahead, they draw strength from the unity and solidarity of their crews, knowing that together, they possess the resilience to surmount any challenge.

As night deepens, the crews settle into their sleeping quarters, their thoughts buzzing with anticipation of the tasks awaiting them on the mor- row. In the tranquil embrace of their spacecraft, they find solace in the shared bond of their community, united by a common purpose and unwavering resolve. As they drift into slumber, visions of triumph and adventure dance through their dreams, a testament to their indomitable spirit and un- yielding determination.

With the first rays of dawn illuminating the common area of the Explorer, the crew gathers for breakfast, their spirits buoyed by the sense of camaraderie forged during their time together.

"Morning already?" one crew member quips with a grin, eliciting laughter from the group. "I swear, I blinked, and the night was over!"

His observation resonates with the others, who chuckle and nod in agreement, united by the shared sense of disbelief at how quickly time seems to pass in the midst of their mission.

Amidst the cheerful banter and laughter, they fuel themselves with food and conversation, preparing for the day ahead with renewed energy and determination, fortified by the bonds of friendship and teamwork that de- fine their journey.

The crews gather under the open sky, the crisp morning air invigorating their senses as they discuss the plan for the day. They contemplate the first steps to restoring the stranded spacecraft to its upright position, reflecting on the importance of preparing thoroughly before taking action.

"It makes sense to strip the ship of any useful equipment before we begin," Commander Hayes suggests, her voice carrying across the group. "The winches, panels, and drones could all prove invaluable in our efforts."

Commander Spear nods in agreement, adding, "We'll need every ad- vantage we can get. Let's prioritize salvaging these resources and ensuring they're ready for use when the time comes."

With a collective nod, the crews set to work, meticulously dismantling, and organizing the equipment, their movements purposeful and efficient. As they prepare for the challenging task ahead, they know that careful planning and preparation will be key to their success.

Commander Spear expresses his concern regarding the reactors, stressing the need for their safe removal to avoid any potential damage during the spacecraft's repositioning.

"It's imperative that we take every precaution with the reactors," he emphasizes, his tone conveying the urgency of the situation. "We can't afford to risk any mishaps that could jeopardize critical components of the space- craft."

The crew members nod in agreement, fully understanding the importance of prioritizing safety above all else. They recognize the gravity of the situation and are committed to taking every necessary measure to minimize risks and ensure the success of their mission.

With a renewed sense of purpose, they add the task of removing the reactors to their list of priorities, determined to proceed with caution and meticulous attention to detail. Clad in radiation suits, they prepare to safely extract and relocate the reactors, with the collective goal of safeguarding both the crew and the spacecraft.

With meticulous care, they disconnect the power conduits and secure the reactors, ensuring that no loose components pose a threat during the ex- traction process. Working as a coordinated team, they carefully transport the reactors to a safe distance from the spacecraft, mindful of the need to minimize any potential radiation exposure.

As they survey their surroundings, Lieutenant Mary Spiers spots a cavern nestled among the rocky terrain nearby. "Over there," she calls out, pointing to the cave entrance. "That should provide a secure location to store the reactors until we're ready to proceed."

The crew members nod in agreement, grateful for the discovery of the cavern, which offers both protection and containment for the reactors. With synchronized movements, they carefully transport the reactors into the cave, placing them in a secure location away from the spacecraft and any potential hazards.

With the reactors safely stowed and secured, the crew can now focus on the task at hand: repositioning the spacecraft. With each member contributing their skills and expertise, they move forward with confidence, knowing that they have taken every precaution to ensure the success and safety of their mission.

With the winches secured and the crew fully prepared, the operation to lift the spaceship into its upright position begins smoothly. Under the watchful eye of the overhead drones the teams work in perfect coordination.

As the winches engage and the cables tighten, the spacecraft slowly begins to tilt upright, defying gravity with remarkable ease. The crews adjust their positions as needed, ensuring that the lifting process remains controlled and steady.

Despite the inherent challenges of such a task, the operation progresses with surprising efficiency. The combined efforts of the crews, coupled with the assistance of the drones and real-time feedback from the cameras, result in a seamless and successful maneuver.

With each passing moment, the spacecraft inches closer to its upright position, until finally, with a collective sigh of relief, it stands tall and proud once more.

The crews celebrate their achievement, knowing that their hard work and dedication have paid off, and that they are one step closer to completing their mission.

With the spacecraft now standing upright and the reactors safely rein- stalled, the crews turn their attention to ensuring the Venturer is in optimal condition. Working together, they conduct a thorough inspection of the spacecraft, meticulously checking every system and component to ensure it is safe for operation.

Commander Hayes and Commander Spear lead their respective teams, carefully examining the Venturer from nose to tail. They scrutinize the hull for any signs of damage, inspect the engines and propulsion systems for functionality, and test the communication and navigation equipment to confirm they are operational.

As the crews work methodically through their checklist, they communicate openly and collaborate seamlessly, pooling their expertise to address any issues or concerns that arise. They understand the importance of thoroughness and attention to detail, knowing that the safety and success of their mission depend on it.

After hours of diligent work, the crews complete their inspection, satisfied that the Venturer is in excellent condition. With a final round of checks and double-checks, they give the spacecraft their seal of approval.

Both crews worked diligently, filling their spacecraft with water and refreshments. Instead of the usual powdered or tablet rations, they opted for proper food sourced from the planet they had explored. Among the provisions were peculiar yet edible items, including a type of pink-colored banana and various other foods that differed from those found on Earth but were nonetheless palatable.

As the aroma of the freshly prepared meal filled the air, both crews gathered together to share a meal. Laughter and conversation flowed freely as they savored the unique Flavors of the local cuisine and exchanged stories of their adventures on the planet's surface.

After the meal, the crews retired to their respective spacecraft, feeling nourished and content. As they settled in for the night, anticipation buzzed through the air, mingled with a sense of camaraderie forged through shared experiences. Tomorrow held the promise of liftoff and a return journey home, but for now, they allowed themselves to rest, knowing that they were surrounded by comrades and filled with the satisfaction of a successful mission.

Chapter 22: Distress Signal

As the distress signal echoed through the vastness of space, Commander Spear aboard the Venturer spacecraft swiftly initiated contact with Commander Hayes on the Explorer. "Hayes, this is Spear. We have received a distress signal from the Voyager. They need our immediate assistance. Let's coordinate our efforts and head to their location."

Hayes acknowledged the urgency in Spear's voice, her response swift and decisive. "Copy that, Spear. I am adjusting our course to rendezvous with you. We'll work together to assess the situation and provide aid to the Voyager."

With their spacecraft hurtling through the cosmic expanse, Spear and Hayes synchronized their movements, preparing to join forces and assist their stranded comrades aboard the Voyager. In the face of uncertainty, their determination to aid their fellow astronauts remained unwavering, driving them forward on their mission of rescue and solidarity.

As the Explorer approached the coordinates of the distress signal, Lieutenant Sarah Johnson's surveillance revealed a sight that sent a chill down their spines. There, nestled amidst the rugged terrain, lay the abandoned Voyager spacecraft, its hull scarred by the ravages of time and space.

Commander Elizabeth Hayes and her team gazed in silent contemplation at the Voyager, Captain Ivanov's spacecraft, indicating that they had crashed.

With adrenaline coursing through their veins, the two commanders made swift contact, exchanging urgent updates, and formulating a plan of action. Dr. Emily Chen and Lieutenant Mary Spiers assisted Lieutenant Johnson in analyzing the Voyager's data logs, hoping to uncover clues about what had transpired on the planet.

Meanwhile, Dr. Mira Lucas and Dr. Robert Vaughan conducted scans of the surrounding area, searching for any signs of life or danger lurking in the shadows. As they pieced together the fragments of this interstellar puzzle, Commander Hayes and Commander Spear stood united, ready to face whatever challenges lay ahead in their quest for answers.

With their determination fueled, Commander Elizabeth Hayes decided to dispatch two reconnaissance drones from the Explorer to the planet's surface. Lieutenant Commander Mark Thompson and Lieutenant Sarah Johnson volunteered to supervise the reconnaissance mission, eager to uncover the mysteries surrounding the abandoned Voyager spacecraft and the enigmatic planet.

As the drones descended through the planet's atmosphere, tension mounted onboard the Explorer. Dr. Emily Chen monitored their progress from the control room, her eyes fixed on the telemetry data streaming in. Mean- while, Dr. Mira Lucas and Dr. Robert Vaughan continued their scans, ana- lysing the terrain for any anomalies or potential hazards.

Minutes felt like hours as the drones hovered just above the planet's sur- face, their sensors scanning the alien landscape below. Equipped with an array of sensors and cameras, the drones began their survey, scouring the area for clues about what had brought the Voyager to this desolate corner of the cosmos. As they ventured deeper into the unknown, they knew that every discovery could hold the key to unravelling the secrets of this mysterious planet and the fate of its previous inhabitants.

As Captain Ivanov's voice crackled over the radio, Commander Spear's tension eased slightly. "Copy that, Captain Ivanov," he replied, his voice steady despite the relief flooding through him. "We're preparing to land. Hang tight. Help is on the way." With those words, the Venturer descended towards the planet's surface, ready to aid their stranded comrades.

With the Venturer safely landed, the Explorer followed suit, descending gracefully to the planet's surface not far from their stranded comrades.

As the spacecraft touched down, a sense of urgency filled

the air, mingled with a palpable relief that they had arrived in time to assist.

Commander Hayes surveyed the landscape from the Explorer's viewport, her gaze focused on the distant site where the Venturer had touched down. Beside her, Lieutenant Commander Thompson and Dr. Chen stood ready, their expressions a mix of determination and concern as they prepared to embark on the rescue mission.

With the hum of the spacecraft's systems surrounding them, the crew braced themselves for the challenges that lay ahead as they stepped out onto the uncharted terrain of the alien planet.

Both commanders, Spear and Hayes, convened in the central command area of the Explorer, their faces reflecting a mix of concern and determination. With the Venturer's crew safely accounted for, their focus shifted to understanding what had happened to the Voyager spacecraft and how it had crashed.

Commander Hayes keyed the intercom, addressing Lieutenant Sarah John- son, who was monitoring the reconnaissance data. "Sarah, what can you tell us about the Voyager's crash site? Any signs of damage or external interference?"

Sarah's voice crackled over the speaker; her tone measured yet tinged with urgency. "Commander, the data indicates that the Voyager sustained significant structural damage upon impact. There are no signs of external interference, suggesting that the crash was likely caused by a malfunction or system failure."

Commander Spear nodded, absorbing the information. "Understood, Sa- rah. Keep monitoring the situation. We need to know what we're dealing with before we proceed."

With a shared understanding of the gravity of the situation, both commanders turned their attention to formulating a plan to assess the Voyager's condition and, if possible, salvage any vital resources or equipment that could aid in their mission to rescue the stranded crew.

In the midst of the tense atmosphere, all the crew members gathered in one place, facing each other with grave expressions. Captain Ivanov's revelation about the Pathfinder 2's distress call had drawn their attention, and now they stood in a huddle, exchanging urgent whispers.

Commander Spear, his brow furrowed in concern, addressed the group, his voice cutting through the silence. "We need to locate the Pathfinder 2 as soon as possible. Our fellow explorers could be in serious trouble, and every moment counts."

Commander Hayes nodded in agreement, her eyes scanning the faces of her crew. "Sarah, Mark, Emily, we need to mobilize immediately. We'll split into teams and scour the area, using all available resources to track down the Pathfinder 2."

Lieutenant Sarah Johnson, Lieutenant Commander Mark Thompson, and Dr. Emily Chen nodded in acknowledgment; their expressions determined. They knew the risks, but they also understood the importance of their mission. As they dispersed to begin their search, the fate of the Pathfinder 2 and its crew weighed heavily on their minds, driving them forward with unwavering resolve.

As the crew gathered inside the Explorer to strategize, Mark stepped forward with a suggestion. "Commander, I propose we deploy the pods for a thorough search," he began. "Emily and Sarah can each guide one pod, while I navigate between both pods to coordinate and provide support. What do you say, Commander?"

Commander Hayes considered the proposal for a moment before nodding in agreement. "That sounds like a solid plan, Mark," she replied. "Let's proceed with your strategy. Emily, Sarah, you will take control of the pods. Mark and I will coordinate from here and provide assistance as needed."

Commander Hayes swiftly relayed the information to Commander Spear over the radio, "Commander Spear, just an update: Emily and Sarah are currently using the pods to conduct a thorough scan of the site below. We're hoping to gather more information soon."

Commander Spear acknowledged the message, his focus shifting as he awaited further updates from the exploration team. With their plan in place, the crew sprang into action, ready to execute their mission to locate the Pathfinder 2 ship and its stranded crew.

As Emily and Sarah guided the pods over the planet's surface, conducting their surveillance, time seemed to stretch on endlessly. Hour after hour passed as they meticulously scanned the terrain, searching for any sign of the Pathfinder 2 ship or its crew.

Inside the Explorer, Commander Hayes and the rest of the crew anxiously monitored the progress of the surveillance mission. Each passing minute felt like an eternity as they awaited any updates from Emily and Sarah.

Despite the prolonged surveillance, the crew remained focused and determined, knowing that their efforts were crucial to the safety and success of the mission. They continued to wait patiently, hoping for a breakthrough that would lead them to the Pathfinder 2 ship and its stranded crew.

Commander Andy Spear's voice crackled over the radio, breaking the tension aboard the Explorer. "Commander Hayes, any luck with the surveil- lance? Have Emily and Sarah spotted anything yet?"

Commander Hayes keyed the microphone, her voice calm but tinged with urgency. "Not yet Commander Spear. They are still conducting their scans, but we have not received any updates so far. We're hoping for a breakthrough soon."

On board the Venturer, Commander Spear listened intently to Commander Hayes' response, his heart racing with anticipation. The fate of the Pathfinder 2 crew hung in the balance, and every moment counted as they awaited news from Emily and Sarah's surveillance mission.

No sooner had they signed off the radio, Sarah's voice crackled through the communication system, tinged with urgency. "Commander Hayes, this is Lieutenant Johnson. I have spotted something that resembles a ship down below, but I can't confirm. It's partially obscured by the terrain."

Commander Hayes's heart quickened at the news. "Copy that, Lieutenant. Can you get a closer look? We need as much information as possible before proceeding."

Sarah acknowledged the command and adjusted the pod's trajectory, aiming to get a better view of the mysterious object below.

As Sarah relayed her findings about the mysterious ship, Mark faced a crucial decision. With only one of them able to return to investigate further, they weighed their options carefully. Mark contemplated the significance of Sarah's discovery and the potential risks involved in exploring the unknown.

Ultimately, Mark decided to return to Sarah's location, prioritizing a hand - on inspection of the unidentified vessel. With his expertise in reconnaissance and analysis, Mark aimed to uncover vital clues that could shed light on the ship's origins and intentions.

Meanwhile, Sarah remained in control of the pod, providing support and additional observations from her vantage point aboard the spacecraft. Together, they coordinated their efforts to unravel the mystery of the alien ship, their collaboration serving as a testament to the strength of their teamwork and determination.

Mark hurried back to Commander Hayes, a sense of urgency in his stride. "Commander, it's confirmed. Not one of ours," he reported, his voice tinged with apprehension. "The shape, the crash—it resembles those old flying saucers from Earth's lore."

Commander Hayes absorbed the revelation, her expression grave as she contemplated the implications. The presence of an alien craft raised a myriad of questions, each more perplexing than the last. Was this linked to the distress signal from the Pathfinder 2? Or was it an entirely separate enigma?

With uncertainty hanging in the air, Commander Hayes

and Mark knew they had to proceed with caution. They devised a plan to investigate the crashed saucer, mindful of the potential risks and unknowns. As they geared up for this unprecedented venture, they steeled themselves for whatever truths lay hidden within the alien wreckage.

Commander Hayes swiftly radioed Commander Spear with the latest update. "Andy, it's confirmed. We have found an alien spacecraft—a crashed saucer," she relayed urgently, her voice conveying the gravity of the situation. "Mark believes it's not one of ours, resembling those old flying saucers from Earth's tales."

Commander Spear processed the information, a mixture of concern and curiosity evident in his response. "Understood, Liz. Keep me posted. We need to proceed with caution," he replied, his tone resolute. "Let's gather more intel before making any moves."

With their communication exchanged, both commanders braced themselves for the challenges ahead, knowing that unravelling the mystery of the alien craft would require precision, perseverance, and a careful approach.

Commander Spear's voice crackled over the radio, carrying news heavy with concern. "Liz, I've got tough news about the Voyager. It is beyond repair," he conveyed, his tone grave. "But there's a spare reactor we can salvage. It will bring you back to 100%. Note your location, and we will head over together. Also, prepare for two extra crew members, but return here first, and we'll fit the reactor."

Commander Hayes acknowledged the update with gratitude and resolve. "Copy that, Andy. Appreciate it," she replied, her voice resolute. "Looking forward to the help."

With their plan in motion, both commanders focused on the tasks ahead, knowing teamwork and resourcefulness would be vital in facing the challenges of this alien planet.

The pods were securely stowed onboard the Explorer, and the crew prepared to head back to the Voyager. As they descended and landed, a sense of purpose filled the air, driving them forward in their mission to salvage the spare reactor and ensure the safe return of their fellow crew members.

As soon as they touched down, a deluge of rain began. Commander Spear quickly radioed Commander Hayes, cautioning her to stay inside for the time being. This was not ordinary rain; it could react with their spacesuits, posing a potential danger to the crew.

As the rain cleared, the crews swiftly mobilized to transfer the reactor from the Explorer to the Voyager. With synchronized movements, they delicately extracted the reactor from its housing and loaded it onto the Voyager.

Simultaneously, preparations were underway to install the

salvaged reactor from the Voyager onto the Explorer. Despite the urgency, meticulous care was taken at every step to ensure safety and spacecraft integrity.

Commander Spear and Commander Hayes orchestrated the operations, guiding their teams with precision. With each maneuver, they progressed towards completing the crucial repair that would enable the Explorer to resume its cosmic voyage.

With the critical repair completed and provisions shared between the Explorer and the Venturer, Commander Spear proposed a plan to salvage any usable resources from the Voyager before departing the planet. "Let's strip anything salvageable from the Voyager and load it onto our ships," he suggested. "If we find the Pathfinder 2 damaged, we can use these resources to repair her and bring her back to Earth."

Commander Hayes agreed, recognizing the importance of making the most of the available resources. "Agreed. Let's gather everything we can and assess the situation with the Pathfinder 2," she affirmed.

With determination, the crews began the task of dismantling and salvaging components from the Voyager, carefully cataloguing and storing each item for future use. Amidst the debris, they harbored hope that their efforts would lead them closer to resolving the mysteries of this uncharted planet and its missing spacecraft.

With all salvageable components retrieved and safely stored onboard both spacecraft, Commander Hayes took the lead, her determination palpable as she prepared to embark on the next phase of their mission. "Alright, folks, time to find that flying saucer," she declared with a confident smile, her voice echoing through the command center.

Her words ignited a sense of excitement among the crew as they prepared to venture into the unknown. With Commander Hayes leading the way, they plotted their course, eager to unravel the secrets that awaited them on this enigmatic planet.

As they set out on their journey, the crew embraced the spirit of discovery that fueled their mission through the cosmos. With each step forward, they moved closer to uncovering the truth behind the mysterious crashed spacecraft and the fate of its occupants.

As they reached the site of the crashed spacecraft, Commander Spear's voice crackled over the radio, conveying a sense of urgency. "Commander Hayes, it's definitely not one of ours. Shall we land and investigate?" he queried; his tone laced with anticipation.

Commander Hayes considered the proposition for a moment before responding with unwavering resolve. "Affirmative, Andy. Let us bring her down," she replied, her voice steady despite the gravity of the situation.

With their decision made, the crew prepared for landing, their hearts racing with excitement and apprehension. Whatever awaited them at the crash site held the potential to reshape their understanding of the universe and the mysteries it held. As the spacecraft descended toward the alien wreckage, they braced themselves for the discoveries that lay ahead.

As the crews disembarked and approached the crashed saucer, Mark's voice cut through the tension. "Definitely crashed," he stated matter-of-factly, confirming what they all suspected.

The scene before them was surreal—a sleek, metallic craft nestled amidst the rugged terrain of the alien planet; its once-smooth surface marred by the impact of the crash. The air hummed with anticipation as they cautiously approached, their eyes scanning for any signs of life or clues about the ship's origin.

Commander Hayes led the way, her steps measured yet purposeful. With each stride, she drew closer to the saucer, her mind racing with questions about its occupants and the purpose of their journey. As they reached the craft, she gestured for the crew to spread out and begin their investigation, knowing that every detail could hold the key to unravelling the mysteries of the universe.

Chapter 23:
Flying Saucer

Commander Hayes raised a cautionary hand, halting the crew's approach. "Hold on, everyone," she instructed firmly. "We don't know what we're dealing with here. It could be radioactive. Let's use remote equipment to gather data—nothing that could potentially harm us."

Her words carried a weight of authority, grounding the team in a moment of sober reflection. With safety as their top priority, they deployed specialized equipment from the Explorer and the Venturer, carefully scanning the saucer from a safe distance.

As the instruments hummed to life, gathering data without risking their well-being, the crew watched with a mixture of fascination and apprehension. Each reading brought them one step closer to unravelling the enigma of the alien craft, while also ensuring their own safety in this uncharted territory.

With the craft deemed safe, the crew cautiously circled around, their eyes scanning every inch for a potential hatch or entry point. Commander Hayes led the way, her gaze sharp and focused as she surveyed the exterior of the alien craft.

"Keep your eyes peeled, everyone," she directed, her

voice steady despite the underlying tension. "We're looking for any signs of a hatch or opening. Stay alert and maintain contact."

As they moved around the saucer, their footsteps echoing in the silence of the alien landscape, they remained vigilant, ready to investigate any unusual markings or features that might offer clues to unlocking the secrets hidden within the mysterious vessel.

The crew's hearts quickened as they spotted a ship nestled within the forest, its design strikingly similar to their own. Without hesitation, they radioed Commanders Spear, Hayes, and Ivanov, urgently summoning them to investigate the discovery.

Racing against time, the three commanders swiftly converged on the site, their footsteps quick and purposeful as they approached the enigmatic craft. With a sense of anticipation hanging heavy in the air, they stood be- fore the mysterious vessel, their eyes scanning its exterior for any distinguishing features or markings that might offer clues to its origin and purpose.

As they examined the craft from every angle, a sense of awe washed over them, mingled with a gnawing curiosity about what secrets it might hold. With the fate of their mission hanging in the balance, they knew that unravelling the mysteries of this alien ship could hold the key to their survival and the answers they sought about the enigmatic planet they now found themselves upon.

Despite its striking resemblance to their own spacecraft, it was clear that the ship before them was not of their making. As they pondered its origin and purpose, the crew faced the pressing question of how to gain entry. With no visible hatch or entrance in sight, they scanned the smooth surface of the vessel, searching for any indication of how to access its interior.

Commanders Spear, Hayes, and Ivanov conferred quietly, exchanging ideas and theories about the best approach. They knew that uncovering the secrets hidden within this alien ship could hold the key to understanding their current predicament and perhaps even unlocking the mysteries of the planet they found themselves stranded on.

With determination in their hearts and a sense of adventure in their souls, they resolved to explore every avenue until they found a way inside. For the crew of the Explorer, the discovery of this mysterious ship marked the beginning of a new chapter in their journey—one filled with uncertainty, danger, and the promise of discovery beyond imagination.

Lieutenant Commander Li Wei's keen eyes spotted the opening atop the mysterious vessel—a potential entrance into its enigmatic interior. As the crew gathered around, they assessed their options for accessing the hatch. With no visible ladder or external mechanisms, they knew they would have to devise a creative solution.

After a brief discussion, Commander Spear suggested using a combination of ropes and grappling hooks to ascend to the opening. It was a risky endeavor, but with their survival depending on uncovering the secrets within, they were willing to take the chance.

With Li Wei leading the way, the crew secured the ropes and began their ascent, inching their way toward the hatch with cautious determination. Each member of the team relied on their training and camaraderie as they climbed, knowing that their success depended on seamless coordination and unwavering resolve.

As they reached the top and prepared to enter the unknown, they braced themselves for whatever mysteries awaited them within the depths of the alien ship. With hearts pounding and adrenaline coursing through their veins, they took a collective breath and stepped into the darkness, ready to confront whatever lay ahead.

As the team ventured further into the alien vessel, their senses heightened, and their anticipation grew. The dim glow of their helmet lights illuminated the path ahead, revealing a surreal landscape unlike anything they had encountered before.

Mark and Robert cautiously led the way, their eyes scanning the surroundings for any signs of life or danger. The eerie silence was broken only by the sound of their footsteps echoing against the metallic walls.

As they explored deeper into the ship, they encountered strange alien beings—lifeless forms with smooth skin, two eyes, and a mouth, but no nose.

The sight sent shivers down their spines, and they exchanged uneasy glances.

Alexei, undeterred by the unsettling discovery, pressed onward, his curiosity driving him forward. "I don't like the look of those two," he remarked, gesturing toward the motionless figures. "But we need to press on. There may be answers waiting for us deeper within the ship."

As the eerie silence enveloped the alien vessel, a strange device emitted cryptic sounds, echoing through the metallic corridors. The crew ex- changed perplexed looks, unsure of the significance of the alien communication.

Mark got his translator device out, its sleek design illuminated by the faint glow of the corridor lights. "This," he explained to Alexei and Robert, "is a translator device. We were given it when we were on the other side of the black hole."

With practiced precision, he activated the device and placed it near the source of the mysterious transmission.

Moments later, the translator device sprang to life,

emitting a synthesized voice that echoed the alien words in a language the crew could understand. The message was fragmented and cryptic, but it hinted at the vessel's origin and the fate of its occupants.

Alexei and Robert exchanged a surprised glance, their curiosity piqued by the unexpected revelation. "So, it's capable of translating alien languages?" Robert asked, his brow furrowing with intrigue.

Mark nodded, his expression solemn. "Yes, it's one of the advanced technologies we acquired during our journey," he confirmed. "And it seems like it's going to be invaluable in understanding the messages from this alien vessel."

With the translator device in hand, the crew felt a renewed sense of hope. Armed with this remarkable tool, they ventured further into the depths of the alien craft, eager to unlock its secrets and unravel the mysteries that lay within.

As the crew listened intently to the translated transmission, a sense of urgency filled the air. They realized that the answers they sought lay hidden within the depths of the alien vessel, waiting to be uncovered. With new- found determination, they pressed on, guided by the faint glimmer of hope that they were on the brink of a profound discovery.

Mark led the way, the translator device held firmly in his

grasp, its steady hum providing a reassuring presence amidst the unfamiliar surroundings.

Alexei and Robert followed closely behind, their senses alert for any signs of danger or discovery.

With each step, they encountered strange machinery and unfamiliar technology, evidence of a civilization far more advanced than their own. The air hummed with energy, and strange symbols adorned the walls, hinting at a complex system of communication and understanding.

As they delved deeper into the heart of the craft, they came upon a vast chamber, its walls lined with intricate consoles and control panels. In the center of the chamber stood a towering structure, pulsating with an otherworldly glow.

As the crew ventured deeper into the alien craft, Alexei's voice cut through the tense atmosphere like a beacon of caution. "We'd better not touch anything," he warned, his tone laced with apprehension. "We don't know what it will do."

His words hung in the air, a stark reminder of the unknown dangers lurking within the alien vessel. Mark, ever pragmatic, nodded in agreement. "Agreed," he concurred, his expression serious. "Let's proceed with caution. We can't afford to take any unnecessary risks."

Robert, his eyes scanning the alien technology surrounding them, nodded solemnly. "Absolutely," he replied, his voice steady. "We'll exercise caution every step of the way. We can't underestimate the potential dangers of this unfamiliar technology."

With Alexei's warning echoing in their minds, the crew advanced cautiously, their senses heightened as they navigated the alien corridors, ever mindful of the mysteries and perils that awaited them in the heart of the strange vessel.

Just as the crew delved deeper into the alien vessel, Commander Hayes' urgent voice crackled over the radio, breaking the intense concentration. "Alexei, we've got a situation outside. Can you and the team step out for a moment? There's steam emanating from the bottom of the craft," she relayed, her tone laced with concern.

Alexei's brows furrowed in concern as he processed the message. "Copy that, Liz. We are on our way," he responded swiftly, his voice projecting authority as he signaled for the team to halt their exploration.

With a sense of urgency, Alexei and his companions retraced their steps, their minds racing with the possibilities of what could be causing the steam. As they emerged from the alien vessel, they were greeted by a billowing cloud of vapor rising from the ground, a stark reminder of the ever- present dangers of their extraterrestrial surroundings.

As the crew emerged from the alien vessel, their attention was immediately drawn to the enigmatic flying saucer nearby. Without warning, a hatch on the saucer's surface creaked open, revealing a sight that sent a shiver down their spines.

A hand, unlike any they had ever seen, protruded from the opening, its appendages elongated and adorned with intricate markings. The crew stood frozen in disbelief, their minds racing with questions about the being that lay beyond the hatch.

With cautious curiosity, Alexei approached the hatch, his senses on high alert. As he drew closer, the hand retreated slightly, as if beckoning him to enter. Uncertain of what awaited him on the other side, Alexei hesitated, his gaze locked on the mysterious figure within the saucer.

Alexei beckoned Mark over, gesturing for him to bring the translator device. "Do you have the translator with you?" he asked urgently. "Ask them what they want."

With a nod, Mark activated the translator device and approached the open hatch cautiously. He spoke into the device, his voice amplified and echoed by the device's synthesized output. "Who are you? What do you want?" he inquired; his words directed towards the mysterious being within the saucer.

The beings inside seemed surprised by Mark's ability to

speak their language. "How can you speak our language?" they asked, their voices resonating with a mix of curiosity and caution.

Mark explained the translator device and reiterated his question, "Who are you? What do you want?"

The response from the beings was cryptic, hinting at their origins and their mission. They expressed a desire for peaceful communication and a mutual exchange of knowledge. Despite the initial tension, there was an underlying sense of curiosity and openness emanating from the beings within the saucer.

"We come in peace. Also, have you crashed your spaceship?" Mark in- quired, his voice conveying both curiosity and concern.

Commander Hayes, standing by Mark's side with her own translator device activated, listened intently to the conversation, ready to facilitate communication between the two parties.

"Yes, we were returning home when a ship crashed into us," the aliens responded, their voices echoing through the hatch.

"Was it this one out here?" Commander Hayes inquired, gesturing toward the crashed saucer. The alien crawled out and responded, "No."

Commander Hayes inquired, "Do you have radio communication to get in touch with your species?"

"All communication is broken, and all teleportation has ceased," replied the alien.

"Can we get a message to your species if you give us the coordinates?" asked Commander Hayes, her voice calm yet determined.

"The coordinates for the link, can you do it from here? Then I can tell them where I am, which would be better," the alien replied.

Commander Hayes instructed Emily to get the radio from the ship and bring it to her.

As soon as the radio was in Commander Hayes' hands, she inputted the coordinates, and the alien began to speak into the radio.

The alien spoke of the area where they were and of the help they had received from humans from planet Earth. Both Mark and Commander Hayes were taken aback when they heard that. How did they know we were from Earth?

Commander Hayes asked once the alien was off the radio, "How did you know we were from Earth?"

The alien, with a solemn expression, replied, "We have

been monitoring your activities in this sector for some time. Your technology and communication signals are unmistakably human."

The alien continued, "My kind will never forget this kind gesture of yours in helping a fellow space traveler. I believe your spaceship or one of yours crashed into ours and should be somewhere around. I hope they will be alright."

Commander Hayes, with a solemn expression, said, "Farewell, and I'm sorry for our spacecraft crashing into yours."

With a sense of duty and determination, the crew bid farewell to the alien and returned to their spacecraft. As they lifted off from the surface of the planet, their eyes scanned the horizon, searching for any sign of the Pathfinder 2 craft.

Guided by the coordinates provided by the alien, they navigated through the unfamiliar terrain, their hearts filled with hope that they would soon locate their fellow space travelers. Each passing moment was tinged with anticipation and concern, driving them forward in their quest to find the missing spacecraft.

Against the backdrop of the vast expanse of space, the crew pressed on, united in their mission to locate the Pathfinder 2 and ensure the safety of its crew. With each passing moment, their determination grew stronger, fueled by the knowledge that they were not alone in the cosmos. Together, they would persevere, forging ahead into the unknown with unwavering resolve.

The radio crackled to life aboard the Explorer as the transmission from the Venturer came through. Commander Hayes listened intently as the message relayed the news they had been waiting for.

"We've found it," came the voice from the Venturer. "We're preparing to descend."

Excitement surged through the crew of the Explorer as they prepared to witness the culmination of their search. With eager anticipation, they awaited further updates from their fellow crew members aboard the Venturer, ready to offer support and assistance as needed.

As the Explorer awaited the Venturer's reply, a collective gasp escaped the crew as they beheld an astonishing sight overhead. A fleet of flying saucers adorned the sky, their sleek metallic surfaces glinting in the sunlight.

Commander Hayes and her crew stared in awe at the unexpected spectacle, their senses overwhelmed by the surreal scene unfolding before them. The presence of the alien fleet added an entirely new layer of intrigue and com- plexity to their mission, stirring a mix of curiosity and apprehension within the crew.

Amidst the wonderment, Commander Hayes quickly

radioed the Venturer to alert them to the extraordinary sight above. With the fleet of flying saucers hovering ominously in the sky, the crew braced themselves for whatever revelations lay ahead, prepared to navigate the unknown with courage and resolve.

One of the aliens materialized onto the Explorer, catching Commander Hayes and her crew off guard. Before Commander Hayes could activate the translator to communicate with the alien, it spoke with a voice that resonated with a sense of gratitude and respect.

"Whoever contacted us on behalf of the Zendaran race, we would like to thank you," the alien expressed, its words echoing through the chamber.

Commander Hayes exchanged surprised glances with her crew, astonished by the unexpected recognition from the Zendaran race. The acknowledgment underscored the significance of their previous encounter with the stranded alien and emphasized the interconnectedness of their cosmic journey. With a sense of humility and wonder, Commander Hayes responded, expressing her gratitude for the Zendarans' acknowledgment, and reaffirming their commitment to cooperation and mutual understanding across the vast expanse of space.

Commander Spear's somber voice crackled over the radio, delivering news that cast a pall over the moment. "They're all dead, Liz. I am sorry," he relayed, his words heavy with sorrow.

The revelation hung in the air, a stark reminder of the fragility of life and the dangers that lurked in the uncharted depths of space. The Zendaran alien, bearing witness to the grim announcement, stood silently, its presence a solemn testament to the harsh realities of their shared journey through the cosmos.

Commander Hayes absorbed the news with a heavy heart, her thoughts turning to the fallen crew of the Pathfinder 2. Despite the sorrow that weighed upon them, she knew that their mission of exploration and discovery would continue, fueled by the memory of those who had ventured into the unknown before them. With a nod of acknowledgment to Commander Spear, she composed herself, ready to face the challenges that lay ahead with unwavering resolve.

The Zendaran alien, its voice solemn, expressed condolences: "We're sorry for your loss. We wish you a safe return to your planet." With a nod of gratitude, it continued, "We will be going now. Thank you again for your kindness." The crew watched in silence as the alien vanished, leaving behind a sense of solemn respect for their departed comrades.

Chapter 24:
Returning Home

With anticipation pulsing through their veins and the vast expanse of the cosmos stretching endlessly before them, the crews of the Venturer and the Explorer stand at the threshold of a new chapter in their extraordinary journey. Laden with supplies and fortified with determination, they prepare to launch their spacecraft toward the distant beacon of Moon Base, a bastion of humanity amidst the vastness of space.

Commanders Hayes and Spear, flanked by their trusted lieutenants and crew members as well as the extra crew from the voyager, stand at the helm, their eyes fixed on the shimmering stars that beckon them onward. In this moment, the weight of their collective mission bears down upon them, but so does the camaraderie and unity that binds them together. With every system checked and every contingency planned for, they are ready to face whatever challenges the cosmos may hurl their way.

As the engines hum to life and the spacecraft gracefully lift off from the surface of the alien world, a sense of awe washes over the crews. The beauty of the celestial panorama unfurls around them, each twinkling star and swirling nebula a testament to the majesty of the universe they traverse. In this vast and mysterious realm, they find both inspiration and solace, drawing strength from the knowledge that they are part of something greater than themselves.

Guided by the steady hand of their commanders and fueled by the bonds of fellowship that have grown among them, the crews embark on their voyage with hearts full of hope and minds open to the wonders that await them. Though the journey ahead may be fraught with peril and uncertainty, they know that together, they are capable of surmounting any obstacle and reaching their destination.

As they chart their course through the endless expanse of space, the crews of the Venturer and the Explorer become a shining beacon of human resilience and ingenuity, a testament to the indomitable spirit that drives humanity ever onward, toward the stars.

As the Venturer ascends into the sky, the crew reflects on the trials and triumphs they have experienced during their unexpected sojourn on the planet's surface. They have weathered storms, overcome obstacles, and learned to adapt to their unfamiliar environment, emerging stronger and more resilient than ever before.

As the Explorer hurtles through the void of space, the crew finds themselves grappling with the passage of time and the uncertainty that awaits them upon their return to Moon Base. A decade has passed since their last communication with the outpost, marking years of solitude and introspection during their cosmic voyage.

For some, the prospect of what they might find upon their return is a source of anxiety, their thoughts haunted by the Specter of loss and change. They wonder if the friends and loved ones they left behind are still waiting for them, or if the passage of time has scattered them like stardust across the galaxy.

Others find solace in the bonds they have formed with their fellow crewmates, drawing strength from the shared experiences and camaraderie that have sustained them through the long months of their voyage. They know that whatever challenges await them on Moon Base, they will face them together, united in purpose and resolve.

As the Explorer hurtles ever closer to their destination, the crew's emotions run high, a mix of anticipation and trepidation for the homecoming that awaits them. They brace themselves for whatever the future may hold, knowing that the journey they have undertaken has forever changed them, shaping their destinies in ways they can only begin to imagine.

Commander Dr. Elizabeth Hayes stood before her crew, her voice carrying the weight of their collective experiences as she addressed them one final time. With a mix of pride and nostalgia, she reflected on the trials they had faced and the wonders they had witnessed together.

"We've journeyed through the depths of space, encountering challenges that tested our resolve and discoveries that expanded our understanding of the universe," she began, her words resonating with each member of the crew. "Through it all, your unwavering dedication and courage have been the guiding lights that have led us through the darkness."

Lieutenant Commander Mark Thompson, sat beside her, nodded in silent agreement, his eyes reflecting the depth of their shared journey, Memories of countless stars and galaxies flickered through his mind, each one a testament to the bond they had forged as they ventured into the unknown.

"Together, we've explored the farthest reaches of space, pushing the boundaries of human exploration and discovery," Commander Hayes continued, her voice steady with emotion. "As we journey home, let us carry with us the lessons we've learned and the memories we've made, knowing that our experiences have forever changed us."

With a sense of unity and purpose, the crew listened intently, their hearts filled with gratitude for the journey they had shared and the commander who had led them with grace and strength. As they prepared to return to Moon Base, they knew that their adventure was far from over, but they faced the future with courage and optimism, ready to embrace whatever challenges lay ahead.

Dr. Emily Chen, Ph.D., sat in the chair in the cockpit, her

mind abuzz with the vast possibilities that lay ahead. As she anticipated the return journey, her thoughts raced with excitement over the wealth of data they had collected during their expedition. Each piece of information held the potential to revolutionize humanity's understanding of the universe, fueling her anticipation for what discoveries awaited them upon their return.

Lieutenant Sarah Johnson seated at her station; her fingers poised over the controls with a mix of emotions swirling within her. Excitement for the journey ahead mingled with a tinge of sadness as she prepared to bid farewell to the realm of wonders they had come to know as home. Memories of breathtaking sights and awe-inspiring discoveries flooded her mind, creating a bittersweet ache as she prepared to leave it all behind. Yet, amidst the nostalgia, she felt a sense of exhilaration, knowing that the journey back to Moon Base would mark the beginning of a new chapter in their adventure.

Lieutenant Commander Mark Thompson, diligently overseeing the status of the reactors, reports a critical issue to Commander Dr. Elizabeth Hayes.

"Commander," he says, his tone laced with concern, "one of the reactors is not functioning properly. We need to address this immediately."

Commander Hayes, concerned about the reactor situation aboard the Explorer, turned to Mark for clarification. "Mark, can you confirm if the reactor currently on the Explorer is the one salvaged from the Voyager, or is it our own?" she inquired, her tone reflecting the urgency of the situation.

Mark furrowed his brow, considering the question carefully. "Let me check the records," he replied, his fingers flying across the control panel as he accessed the spacecraft's maintenance logs. After a moment of silence, he looked up, his expression grave. "It appears to be the salvaged reactor from the Voyager," he confirmed, his voice tinged with concern.

Commander Hayes nodded, absorbing the information. "Understood. We will need to conduct a thorough inspection to ensure its integrity and functionality," she remarked, already formulating a plan of action to address the potential risks associated with the salvaged reactor.

With their focus squarely on resolving the reactor dilemma, the crew pre- pared to tackle the challenge head on, their determination unwavering in the face of uncertainty.

Commander Dr. Elizabeth Hayes maintains a composed demeanor, though concern flickers in her eyes. She knows that their journey home hangs in the balance, but she also trusts in the capabilities of her crew and their collective ingenuity. With a firm resolve, she addresses them, ex- pressing her confidence in their ability to overcome this obstacle and navigate through the challenges that lie ahead. Together, they will find a solution and persevere in their mission through the vast expanse of space.

"Thank you for the update, Mark," Commander Hayes responds, her voice laced with determination. "We've faced numerous challenges on this journey, and I'm confident we'll conquer this one too. Let's unite our efforts to restore the reactors and secure a safe passage back to Moon Base."

Emily Chen, Ph.D., pores over the data from the reactor systems, her brow furrowed in deep concentration as she analyses every detail. With keen eyes and a sharp mind, she navigates through the intricate web of information, searching for any anomalies or irregularities that may provide clues to the malfunction. As she sifts through the data, she remains focused and determined, knowing that the successful restoration of the reactors is crucial for their journey back home.

Lieutenant Sarah Johnson, monitoring the reactor controls with precision, nods in agreement. Her fingers dance across the console, adjusting parameters and monitoring readings with practiced efficiency. With a keen eye for detail and a steady hand, she ensures that each component of the reactor system is functioning as intended, ready to respond swiftly to any unforeseen challenges that may arise. As she works diligently to diagnose and address the issue at hand, her focus remains unwavering, driven by a stead- fast determination to overcome obstacles and ensure the safety of the crew.

Lieutenant Commander Thompson rushes to the control panel, his fingers dancing across the buttons and switches as he attempts to pinpoint the source of the malfunction.

Lieutenant Thompson's inspection of the reactors takes some time as he meticulously examines each component for signs of damage or malfunction. Despite the setback, the crew remains steadfast in their determination to overcome the obstacle before them. With a renewed sense of confidence born from their resilience and resourcefulness, they prepare to face whatever challenges may lie ahead as they embark on their journey back to familiar space.

Commander Hayes maintains a calm exterior as she coordinates the crew's efforts, her voice steady and reassuring over the intercom. "Stay focused, everyone," she says. "We've faced challenges before, and we'll overcome this one too. Let's work together to get our ship back on course."

Commander Hayes monitors the situation closely from her cockpit, providing guidance and support as the crew works to resolve the emergency. "Keep your heads clear and your actions precise," she urges over the intercom. "We need to address this issue swiftly and effectively to ensure the safety of everyone on board."

Despite their best efforts, the malfunctions persist, and

the crew faces a race against time to repair the damage before it jeopardizes their mission.

With determination and ingenuity, they persevere, their collective resolve driving them forward as they navigate the treacherous void of space on their journey home.

As the crew investigates the source of the malfunction, they discover that the emergency stems from an overheating issue in one of the spacecraft's critical systems. Lieutenant Commander Thompson and Dr. Chen quickly assess the situation, realizing that the overheating poses a significant risk to the safety of the crew and the integrity of the spacecraft.

Working swiftly, they deploy emergency cooling measures to stabilize the affected system and prevent further overheating. Lieutenant Johnson assists by rerouting power and adjusting ventilation to alleviate the strain on the overheated components.

With their combined efforts, the crew successfully manages to bring the overheating under control, averting a potentially catastrophic situation. As the emergency passes and the spacecraft stabilizes, a collective sigh of re- lief fills the air, and the crew is grateful for their quick thinking and decisive action in the face of adversity.

But it still seems to be malfunction with the reactor both Lieutenant Johnson and Dr. Chen are working like mad to find the trouble.

Commander Hayes monitors the situation closely from her position in the cockpit, providing guidance and support as the crew works to resolve the emergency. "Keep your heads clear and your actions precise," she urges over the intercom. "We need to address this issue swiftly and effectively to ensure the safety of everyone on board."

As the crew works tirelessly to restore the malfunctioning reactor, frustration mounts as the issue persists. Despite their best efforts, the reactor continues to falter, casting a shadow of uncertainty over their journey home. With each failed attempt to rectify the problem, tensions rise as the crew grapples with the possibility of being stranded in the unforgiving expanse of space.

Commander Hayes initiates communication with the Venturer, informing them of the ongoing reactor issue aboard the Explorer.

"Venturer, this is Explorer," Commander Hayes transmits over the radio. "We've encountered a problem with one of our reactors one salvaged from the Voyager and need to make an emergency stop. Can you provide assistance? Over."

"Explorer, this is Venturer. Copy that, we will stop and send a team over to assist with the reactor issue. Hang tight, we will be there shortly. Over."

Lieutenant Commander Thompson opens the airlock hatch to allow the crew from the Venturer to board the Explorer.

Amidst the urgent discussion about rerouting power from the non-functioning reactor, the crew members of both the Venturer and the Explorer deliberated on the best course of action. With time ticking away and the need to restore power growing more pressing by the minute, they knew they had to act swiftly and decisively.

"We should consider rerouting power from non-essential systems or those with redundant backups," suggested one crew member, her voice steady despite the urgency of the situation.

Another crew member nodded in agreement, adding, "That's a prudent approach. We need to prioritize systems that can provide enough power to sustain essential functions without compromising our ability to address the issue with the primary reactor."

Commander Hayes listened intently to their suggestions, weighing the options carefully as she assessed the potential risks and benefits of each course of action. With the fate of both crews hanging in the balance, she knew that their decision could mean the difference between success and failure in their mission to restore power and continue their journey home.

"Let's start by rerouting power from auxiliary systems such as onboard entertainment, secondary communication channels, and non-essential lighting," she decided, her tone firm and decisive. "Once we have stabilized power to essential functions like life support, propulsion, and navigation, we can then reassess and redistribute power as needed."

With their plan in place, the crew members sprang into action, working together seamlessly to reroute power and restore functionality to critical systems. Despite the challenges they faced, their determination and resourcefulness never wavered, fueling their efforts to overcome the obstacles standing in their way.

As they worked tirelessly to resolve the issue with the malfunctioning reactor, the crew members knew that their unity and cooperation would be their greatest assets in the face of adversity. And with each passing moment, they moved one step closer to restoring power and continuing their journey homeward, fueled by the unwavering hope and resilience that defined them as explorers.

With power restored and the reactors rerouted, both the Venturer and the Explorer resumed their journey homeward. The engines hummed to life, propelling the spacecraft forward through the vast expanse of space, their destination clear: Moon base.

As they embarked on the final leg of their remarkable

voyage, the crew members of both vessels felt a mix of emotions – relief, anticipation, and a touch of sadness for the challenges they had faced and the friends they had lost along the way.

Commander Hayes and Commander Spear each communicate via intercom convey their thoughts the trials they had overcome and the bond that had formed between their crews. Despite the uncertainties that lay ahead, they knew that they were stronger together, united by a shared purpose and a determination to return home.

As the stars streaked past their viewports, casting a warm glow upon the spacecraft, the crew members settled in for the journey ahead. They knew that they carried with them not just the memories of their extraordinary adventure, but also the lessons learned, and the friendships forged in the crucible of space.

And as they charted their course back to Moon base, they did so with renewed hope and a sense of camaraderie that would carry them through whatever challenges awaited them in the vast unknown of the cosmos. Together, they would face the future, ready to script the next chapter in their shared odyssey among the stars.

As both ships soar towards the stars, bound for the distant beacon of Moon base, the crew members find solace in the companionship of their fellow explorers. Together, they face the unknown with courage and determination, ready to confront whatever challenges lie ahead on their journey home.

Along the way, the crews encounter breathtaking celestial phenomena, from shimmering nebulae to distant star clusters, each one a testament to the beauty and wonder of the cosmos. Despite the vastness of space and the unknown dangers that lurk within its depths, the crews press onward with unwavering resolve, driven by their shared mission to reach Moon Base and reunite with their fellow humans.

And as the Venturer and the Explorer descend towards the lunar landscape, the crews brace themselves for the next chapter in their cosmic odyssey, ready to embark on new adventures and unlock the secrets of the universe that await them on the moon's desolate yet enchanting surface.

The long journey to the other side of the universe stretched before them like an endless expanse of possibility, each moment pregnant with anticipation and uncertainty. For Commander Dr. Elizabeth Hayes and her crew, it was a voyage into the unknown, a quest to unravel the mysteries of the cosmos and chart uncharted territories beyond the reaches of human imagination.

As their spacecraft hurtled through the void of space, they encountered wonders beyond comprehension— distant galaxies shimmering like jewels in the darkness, cosmic phenomena that defied explanation, and celestial landscapes that stretched into infinity. Each discovery fueled their curiosity and stoked the flames of their determination, driving them ever onward in their quest for knowledge and understanding.

Yet, amidst the grandeur of the cosmos, they also faced challenges and dangers that tested their resolve and pushed them to their limits. They navigated treacherous asteroid fields, weathered cosmic storms of unimaginable ferocity, and braved the icy depths of interstellar space. But through it all, they remained steadfast in their mission, their spirits unbroken and their determination unwavering.

As they pressed further into the depths of the universe, their journey became more than a mere exploration—it became a pilgrimage, a testament to the indomitable spirit of humanity and our insatiable thirst for discovery.

And though the path ahead was fraught with peril and uncertainty, they forged ahead with courage and conviction, knowing that they carried with them the hopes and dreams of all humanity.

For theirs was a journey of exploration, of discovery, and of wonder—a journey that would forever change the course of human history and illuminate the infinite possibilities that lie beyond the stars. And as they ventured into the unknown, they did so with hearts full of hope and minds open to the mysteries that awaited them, ready to embrace whatever wonders the universe had in store.

And though their mission may be nearing its end, they know that the lessons they have learned and the experiences they have shared will stay with them forever, shaping the course of their future explorations and inspiring generations to come.

Their mission may be over, but their legacy will endure testament to the power of human curiosity and the boundless possibilities that lie within the vast expanse of the universe. And as they set their course for home, they do so with a sense of fulfilment, knowing that they have left an indelible mark on the tapestry of cosmic exploration, and that their journey is only just beginning.

Chapter 25:
The Home Coming

As the Venturer and the Explorer transmitted messages ahead, Commander Hayes and Commander Spear worked in tandem to coordinate the communications with Moon Base. They ensured that their home base was alerted to their imminent return, providing essential updates on their mission progress and any unforeseen challenges encountered along the way.

They ensured that Moon Base was informed of the situation, preparing them for the return of the ships and the crew, while also mourning the loss of their fellow explorers.

The moon base was abuzz with anticipation and a touch of solemnity as the radio transmission crackled to life, announcing the imminent arrival of the two spacecraft. Excitement rippled through the base, tempered by the knowledge of the recent loss aboard Pathfinder 2 and the presence of additional crew from the Voyager.

The atmosphere at the moon base was charged with a potent mix of emotions, as the crew awaited the arrival of the spacecraft. There was an undeniable sense of hope and anticipation permeating the air, buoying the spirits of all who awaited the return of their fellow explorers.

Yet, amidst the excitement, there lingered a somber undertone of bereavement for the crew of the Pathfinder 2, whose loss weighed heavily on the hearts of those gathered.

As the minutes stretched into hours, each passing moment brought them closer to the long-awaited reunion. The anticipation reached a fever pitch, filling the air with an electric energy that crackled with excitement and joy.

It was a momentous occasion, one that had been years in the making, and the crew could hardly contain their excitement as they prepared to welcome back their comrades.

But amid the jubilation, there was a quiet solemnity, a poignant re- minder of the sacrifices made and the risks inherent in their mission. The loss of the Pathfinder 2 crew cast a shadow over the celebration, serving as a stark reminder of the dangers that lurked in the vast expanse of space.

As the spacecraft drew nearer to the moon base, the crew aboard the Venturer and the Explorer, along with the additional crew from the Voyager craft, braced themselves for the final approach.

They had endured countless challenges and overcome insurmountable odds, their journey marked by moments of triumph and moments of sorrow. But through it all, they had remained steadfast in their commitment to exploration and discovery, forging bonds of friendship and camaraderie that would endure long after their return to Earth.

As the Venturer approached their destination on the far side of the moon, anticipation rippled through the crew. It was a moment they had been preparing for, a milestone in their journey through the cosmos.

Commander Hayes seated and strapped in at the helm, her gaze fixed on the lunar surface below. The crew members were strapped into their seats, their hearts racing with excitement as they neared their landing site.

"We're almost there," Commander Hayes announced over the intercom, her voice tinged with anticipation. "Prepare for landing procedures."

With practiced precision, the crew went through their final checks, ensuring that all systems were primed and ready for touchdown. Outside the viewport, the moon's rugged terrain loomed large, a stark reminder of the challenges that lay ahead.

As the spacecraft descended towards the lunar surface, the tension onboard mounted. Every member of the crew held their breath, their eyes fixed on the landing site below.

Then, with a gentle thud, the Venturer touched down on

the lunar soil, its landing gear absorbing the impact with ease. A collective sigh of relief swept through the spacecraft as the crew realized they had safely completed their journey.

As the Explorer descended, it made contact with the lunar surface, its landing gear absorbing the impact smoothly.

Commander Hayes allowed herself a moment to Savor the accomplishment before turning her attention to the tasks that lay ahead.

There were still mysteries to uncover, discoveries to be made, and adventures to be had on the other side of the countless black holes scattered throughout the universe. And with their determination and courage, Commander Hayes and her crew were ready to face whatever challenges awaited them in the uncharted realms of space.

For in the endless expanse of the universe, there were still countless worlds waiting to be explored, mysteries waiting to be unraveled, and adventures waiting to be had. And with renewed spirits and a sense of pride in their achievements, the crew looked to the stars, ready to embark on the next chapter of their extraordinary journey.

For the Venturer, the sense of relief and joy is palpable as they approach their destination after a decade away and uncertainty and hardship on the distant planet. Despite the trials they have endured, they emerge stronger and more resilient, their bond as a crew unbreakable in the face of adversity.

With each passing moment, anticipation grew among the crew members, their thoughts drifting to the prospect of reuniting with loved ones and sharing the extraordinary tales of their odyssey through space.

Amidst the barren beauty of the lunar landscape, the crews pause to reflect on the challenges they have faced and the triumphs they have achieved. They are united by a shared sense of purpose and a deep bond forged through adversity; their spirits buoyed by the knowledge that they have made history together.

As they stand on the surface of the moon, surprised that so much has changed, surrounded by the vastness of space, the crews are filled with a sense of pride and wonder. They know that their journey is far from over, but for now, they take a moment to savor the fulfilment of reaching this monumental milestone in their odyssey among the stars.

And as they gaze up at the stars twinkling in the sky above, they know that their adventures are far from over. For as long as humanity dares to dream and explore, there will always be new horizons to discover and new mysteries to unravel in the vast expanse of space.

In their respective quarters, each crew member takes a moment to collect themselves after the exhilarating journey they have just completed. Commander Dr. Elizabeth Hayes stands before the mirror, her expression reflecting a blend of determination and readiness as she adjusts her uniform with precision.

Meanwhile, Lieutenant Commander Mark Thompson refreshes himself by splashing cold water on his face, the cool sensation helping to invigorate him and clear his mind for the tasks ahead.
In another part of the base, Commander Andy Spear takes a sip of cold water, the refreshing drink providing a brief moment of respite amidst the flurry of activity.

Dr. Mira Lucas and Lieutenant Mary Spiers, sharing living quarters, change into fresh uniforms, their movements purposeful and efficient as they prepare for the next phase of their mission.

Dr. Robert Vaughan, on the other hand, finds himself lost in thoughts of his family back on Earth, a longing for home tugging at his heart-strings as he contemplates the journey that lies ahead.

As Dr. Emily Chen meticulously reviews her notes, her focus sharpens on the scientific intricacies of their discoveries. She double-checks her data, ensuring accuracy and completeness, determined to present a compelling case during the upcoming meeting.

Meanwhile, Lieutenant Sarah Johnson takes a brief moment to collect her thoughts, mentally rehearsing the key points she intends to convey. With clarity and purpose, she organizes her ideas, readying herself to articulate the significance of their mission's achievements to the rest of the team.

In their individual preparations, both Emily and Sarah exhibit a shared commitment to excellence, each poised to contribute their expertise to the collective effort of the crew.

As all three crews gather in the conference room at mission control, they are met with a warm welcome from their colleagues and superiors. The atmosphere crackles with anticipation as everyone eagerly awaits the presentation of the crew's findings.

Commander Andy Spear steps up to the podium, his presence commanding the attention of everyone in the room. With a steady voice and a determined gaze, he begins to recount the remarkable journey of the Venturer and its crew stranded on the planet's surface.

"Ladies and gentlemen, esteemed colleagues," he begins, his words resonating in the hushed room, "I stand before you today to share the incredible story of our expedition to an uncharted planet and the challenges we faced while stranded there."

As he speaks, Commander Spear vividly describes the

trials and tribulations they encountered after their spacecraft, the Venturer, crash- landed on the planet's surface. He recounts their efforts to survive, the ingenuity they displayed in adapting to their new environment, and the solidarity that sustained them during their time of need.

"But through it all," he continues, his voice tinged with pride, "we persevered. We overcame adversity and worked together to overcome every obstacle in our path."

Commander Spear's voice resonates through the room, carrying with it a sense of gratitude and solemnity. "I must express my deepest appreciation to Commander Hayes and her crew for their instrumental role in our rescue. Without their unwavering support and resourcefulness, our stay on that planet may have been indefinite."

His words echo the sentiments felt by all present, acknowledging the invaluable contribution of Commander Hayes and her team in ensuring their safe return. Despite the challenges they faced, their unity and collaboration had ultimately led to their successful rescue.

However, Commander Spear's expression turns somber as he continues, "I am just saddened that we weren't able to rescue or get to Pathfinder 2 in time."

The weight of those words hangs heavy in the air, a stark reminder of the harsh realities of space exploration and the sacrifices made along the way.

Commander Dr. Elizabeth Hayes steps forward, her presence commanding attention as she addresses the gathered crowd. Her expression is a mix of pride for her crew's accomplishments and sorrow for the losses endured along the way. Yet, despite the weight of these emotions, her demeanor remains poised and determined, a testament to her strength as a leader.

"I must first express my deepest gratitude to my wonderful crew," Commander Hayes begins, her voice carrying with it a sense of sincerity and respect. "Their unwavering dedication and resilience have been the cornerstone of our success, and I am endlessly proud to stand beside each and every one of them."

Turning her attention to Commander Spear, she acknowledges his kind words with a nod of appreciation. "And to Commander Spear, I extend my heartfelt thanks for his generous praise. Indeed, I firmly believe that if our positions were reversed, he would have done the same for me and my crew."

A moment of somber reflection passes over the room as Commander Hayes addresses the tragic loss of the Pathfinder 2 crew. "I share in the sorrow of not being able to reach the Pathfinder 2 in time," she continues, her voice tinged with regret. "There will always be a lingering 'what if' in my mind, as I'm sure there is in the minds of many here today."

But despite the shadows of grief that loom over them, Commander Hayes' gaze remains steadfast, her resolve unwavering. "Yet, as we stand here together, we carry the memories of our fallen comrades in our hearts, honoring their courage and sacrifice as we continue on our journey through the stars."

She proceeds to recount the remarkable voyage of the Explorer and its crew, detailing their encounter with the black hole and their subsequent emergence into the uncharted territory beyond. With vivid descriptions and captivating storytelling, she paints a picture of the challenges they faced and the discoveries they made along the way.

"We not only traversed the black hole but emerged into a white universe, discovering a habitable planet where we had the unexpected privilege of sharing a meal with ancient natives, who were revealed to be related to the pharaohs of our own planet's distant past."

"It seems they were travelers through the black hole," Commander Hayes explained, her voice filled with a mixture of awe and concern. "But as we encountered, you cannot return through a white hole; it repels you. So, we had to come back through another black hole. You emerge through a white hole."

The crew members at the moon base listened intently, absorbing the gravity of Commander Hayes's words. The implications of their journey through the black hole and back were staggering, challenging everything they thought they knew about the nature of space and time.

Commander Dr. Elizabeth Hayes pauses, her gaze sweeping across the room as she gathers her thoughts. "And let us not forget the remarkable encounter we had with the beings from Zendaran," she continues, her voice filled with a sense of wonder and awe. "Their presence serves as a reminder of the boundless possibilities that await us beyond the reaches of our own world."

As murmurs of curiosity ripple through the crowd, Commander Hayes elaborates on the encounter with the alien race. "Their fleet of flying saucers, hovering in the vast expanse of space, spoke to the diversity and richness of the universe we inhabit," she explains, her words carrying a sense of reverence for the unknown.

"It is encounters like these that inspire us to reach ever further, to explore the depths of space and unlock the mysteries that lie be- yond," Commander Hayes continues, her voice growing in intensity with each word. "For in the face of the unknown, we find not fear, but an insatiable curiosity and a boundless thirst for knowledge."

Commander Hayes recounts the extraordinary events that unfolded when they stumbled upon the crashed flying saucer. "It appears that our fated Pathfinder 2 had collided with their craft," she explains, her words drawing murmurs of surprise from the audience.

"Moreover," Commander Hayes elaborates, "our astonishment peaked when we realized that the beings aboard the saucer could communicate with us effortlessly in our own language." She elucidates further, recounting how the crew's translator devices, acquired during their expedition on planet Bore, automatically facilitated seamless translation between languages, bridging the gap between disparate civilizations with ease.

"But that's not all," Commander Hayes adds, her voice filled with awe. "We also encountered fellow explorers from Earth, albeit from the year 2350." She recounts the marvel of meeting these advanced explorers, who boasted Antimatter Engines capable of faster-than-light travel.

As she concludes her recounting of these remarkable encounters, Commander Hayes's words are met with a mixture of astonishment and intrigue from the gathered audience. The room buzzes with excitement, with everyone eager to hear more about the wonders that lay beyond the confines of their own world.

As they processed this newfound understanding, a sense of wonder and curiosity filled the air. The crew members exchanged thoughtful glances, their minds buzzing with questions and possibilities. What other secrets lay hidden within the depths of the cosmos? And what adventures awaited them on the horizon?

Which left us disoriented and lost. We put out a distress call and probably about an hour later we got a radio message from commander Spear. If it were not for the distress call that Commander Spear and the crew of the Venturer intercepted, we might still be adrift in the cosmos. So, on behalf of the crew of the Explorer, I extend our deepest gratitude to the crew of the Venturer."

"But amidst the trials and tribulations," she continues, her voice unwavering, "we found strength in unity and solace in the knowledge that we were not alone in our endeavors. Together, we navigated the uncertainties of space and overcame obstacles that once seemed insurmountable."

Lieutenant Commander Mark Thompson steps up to the podium, armed with an array of data and analyses meticulously compiled during their extraordinary expedition. With precision and clarity, he delves into the wealth of information gathered by the crew of the Explorer, offering detailed insights into the mysteries of the cosmos.

"Esteemed colleagues," Lieutenant Commander Thompson begins, his voice resonating with authority, "I am honored to present to you the findings of our expedition beyond the black hole and into the uncharted realms of space."

He begins by outlining the methods used to collect data during their journey, detailing the advanced instrumentation and techniques employed to capture and analyzed the various phenomena encountered along the way. From spectroscopic analysis of distant stars to gravitational wave measurements from the black hole's event horizon, every aspect of their voyage is meticulously documented and scrutinized.

"Perhaps one of the most remarkable discoveries we made," Lieutenant Commander Thompson continues, his tone brimming with excitement, "was the presence of a habitable planet beyond the black hole's event horizon. Through careful observation and analysis, we were able to confirm the existence of a diverse ecosystem teeming with life, including ancient civilizations with ties to our own history."

He proceeds to present detailed analyses of the planet's atmosphere, geology, and biology, offering tantalizing glimpses into the potential for extraterrestrial life beyond Earth. Charts, graphs, and visual representations accompany his explanations, illustrating the complexities of the data and enhancing the audience's understanding of the discoveries made.

Lieutenant Commander Thompson's words echoed through the room, carrying a sense of reverence and determination. As he spoke, his gaze swept over the gathered audience, his voice resonating with a mixture of solemnity and hope.

"As we continue to sift through the vast troves of data collected during our expedition," he begins, his tone steady and resolute, "we are confident that further insights into the nature of the universe await us." His words are met with nods of agreement from those assembled, their eyes alight with curiosity and anticipation.

"Our journey may have reached its conclusion," Lieutenant Commander Thompson continues, his voice tinged with a somber note, "but the quest for knowledge and understanding knows no bounds." He pauses, a moment of silence hanging in the air as his words sink in.

"And yet, amidst the triumph of our return," he adds, his voice softening with emotion, "we cannot forget the sacrifice made by our fellow crew members aboard the Pathfinder 2." His words are met with a solemn hush, the weight of their loss palpable in the room.

"I knew some of the astronauts on board the Pathfinder 2," Lieutenant Commander Thompson continues, his voice tinged with sadness. "And I feel very lucky to have gone through the black hole not once, but twice, and stand here today." He pauses, his thoughts turning inward for a moment before he continues.

"But my heart goes out to my fellow members," he says, his voice filled with genuine empathy. "Like Lieutenant Emma Rodriguez and Lieutenant Commander Anna Patel, whom I had the privilege of serving with on a mission to Mars a few years back." His words are met with nods of understanding, the shared bond of camaraderie evident among the assembled crew.

As Lieutenant Commander Thompson concludes his remarks, a sense of reverence fills the room, a silent tribute to those who had bravely ventured into the unknown and to the enduring spirit of exploration that unites them all.

Dr. Emily Chen, Ph.D., stepped forward, her presence commanding the attention of all in the room. As an astrophysicist, she possessed an unparalleled understanding of the cosmos, and her presentation promised to unravel the mysteries of the universe.

With precision and clarity, Dr. Chen delved into the depths of celestial phenomena, her words painting vivid portraits of galaxies swirling in the void and stars being born and dying in cosmic explosions. Each slide she presented offered a glimpse into the vastness of space and the intricacies of its workings, captivating her audience with the wonders of the cosmos.

Yet, beneath her composed exterior, Dr. Chen carried a heavy heart. As she spoke of their journey and the discoveries made along the way, her thoughts drifted to

Captain Miguel Diaz, a colleague and friend whose absence weighed heavily on her soul.

"Like Mark, I too had the privilege of travelling with Captain Miguel Diaz," she began, her voice tinged with sadness. "And I feel sorrow for his family, whom I had the chance to meet." Her words were measured, her gaze distant as memories of their time together flooded her mind.

"I don't know if anyone knew," she continued, her voice trembling slightly, "but he was the most kind and caring person." A soft murmur of agreement rippled through the room, a testament to the impact Captain Diaz had on those around him.

"He was a wonderful father," Dr. Chen added, her voice barely above a whisper, "and I know his son will be heartbroken." A heavy silence settled over the room, the weight of their loss palpable in the air.

As Dr. Chen concluded her remarks, a somber mood hung over the gathering, a poignant reminder of the fragility of life and the profound impact one individual can have on those they leave behind.

Dr. Mira Lucas stepped forward, her presence commanding respect as she prepared to share her research findings with the gathered audience. As an expert in robotics and artificial intelligence, her work held the promise of revolutionizing space exploration.

With a heavy heart, Dr. Lucas began her presentation, her thoughts drifting to the colleagues she had lost aboard the Pathfinder 2. Despite never having flown with them, she had crossed paths with Dr. Hiroto Oyama at various meetings, and the news of his passing weighed heavily on her mind.

"As we look to the future of space exploration," Dr. Lucas began, her voice steady but tinged with sorrow, "it's important to acknowledge the sacrifices made by our fellow crew members aboard the Pathfinder 2." Her words echoed throughout the room, a solemn reminder of the human cost of venturing into the unknown.

"As I stand before you today," she continued, "I can't help but think of the contributions Dr. Oyama and his colleagues could have made to our shared quest for knowledge." A somber mood settled over the audience, the loss of their colleagues serving as a poignant reminder of the risks inherent in their work.

Yet, even in the face of tragedy, Dr. Lucas remained steadfast in her commitment to advancing the frontiers of science and exploration. Through her research on drones and autonomous systems, she hoped to honor the memory of those who had gone before her, ensuring that their legacy lived on in the pursuit of discovery and innovation.

Lieutenant Sarah Johnson approached the podium with a

sense of solemnity, her thoughts weighed down by the memory of the crew members lost aboard the ill-fated Pathfinder 2. As an engineer deeply invested in spacecraft operations, she could not help but feel a profound sense of loss for her fellow colleagues who had shared her passion for exploration.

With a heavy heart, Lieutenant Johnson began her presentation, her voice tinged with sorrow as she delved into her research on spacecraft propulsion systems and structural integrity. Each slide served as a painful reminder of the expertise and dedication of the crew members who were no longer with them, their absence casting a shadow over the room.

"As we reflect on the advancements, we've made in ensuring the safety and efficiency of space travel," Lieutenant Johnson began, her words measured and somber, "we must also acknowledge the sacrifices made by those who came before us." Her gaze swept across the room, meeting the eyes of her fellow crew members, each of them grappling with their own feelings of grief and loss.

"The loss of our colleagues aboard the Pathfinder 2 serves as a poignant reminder of the dangers inherent in our mission," she continued, her voice steady despite the emotion threatening to overwhelm her. "But it also underscores the importance of our work—the need to push the boundaries of human exploration in pursuit of knowledge and understanding."

As Lieutenant Johnson concluded her presentation, a sense of solemnity hung in the air, the weight of their collective grief palpable. Yet, even in the face of tragedy, there remained a glimmer of hope—a shared determination to honor the memory of their fallen colleagues by continuing to push the boundaries of science and exploration.

In the moon base's meeting room, Captain Alexei Ivanov, Lieutenant Commander Li Wei, Dr. Natalia Petrovna Ph.D., and Lieutenant Zhang Wei were joined by Commanders Andy Spear and Dr. Elizabeth Hayes, along with their respective crew members. The atmosphere was heavy with the weight of recent events as they discussed the fate of the Pathfinder 2 spacecraft and its crew—Captain Miguel Diaz, Lieutenant Commander Anna Patel, Dr. Hiroto Oyama, and Lieutenant Emma Rodriguez.

Commanders Spear and Hayes, flanked by their crew members, ex- changed grave looks for the loss of their fellow explorers weighed heavily on their minds, and the room fell silent as they reflected on the risks inherent in their shared mission.

Despite the somber mood, there was a sense of unity among the assembled personnel. Each member of the crew, from the seasoned veterans to the newest recruits, shared a common determination to honor the memory of their fallen comrades and continue the mission.

Captain Ivanov's voice, though tinged with sadness, carried a note of resilience as he addressed the room. He emphasized the importance of staying focused on their objectives and supporting one another through the challenges ahead.

Lieutenant Commander Li Wei, known for her unwavering dedication to her duties, nodded in agreement, her expression reflecting a steely resolve to press forward despite the loss.

Dr. Natalia Petrovna Ph.D., her usually stoic demeanor softened by empathy, offered words of comfort to her fellow crew members, re- minding them of the bonds that united them as they faced the unknown together.

Lieutenant Zhang Wei, the youngest member of the crew, listened intently, his determination bolstered by the camaraderie of his fellow explorers. Together, they formed a cohesive team, ready to confront whatever obstacles lay ahead.

As the controller's message neared its conclusion, a note of anticipation crept into his voice. "And as you prepare for your well-deserved break back on Earth, I have exciting news to share about the next phase of our mission. In the coming months, we will be launching four new spacecraft, each equipped with state-of-the-art technology and manned by expert crews. Among them will be esteemed professors specializing in hieroglyphs and the ancient Pharaohs."

The crew members exchanged intrigued glances, their interest piqued by the prospect of new discoveries and collaborations with experts in fields beyond their own. The controller's announcement underscored the boundless possibilities that lay ahead, reigniting their passion for exploration and discovery.

"As you embark on this next chapter of our journey," the controller concluded, "Know that you carry with you the hopes and aspirations of humanity.

Together, we will continue to push the boundaries of knowledge and explore the farthest reaches of the cosmos. Safe travels, my friends, and may the stars guide you on your path."

With those words, the crew members of the Venturer, Voyager, and Explorer felt a renewed sense of purpose and excitement for the ad- ventures that lay ahead. As they prepared to depart Moon base and return to Earth, they knew that they were not just pioneers of space exploration but ambassadors of humanity's insatiable thirst for knowledge and understanding. And with the promise of new spacecraft, new discoveries, and new horizons on the horizon, they set their sights on the future with optimism and determination.

With a collective sigh of relief, the crews express their appreciation for the opportunity to take some time off and unwind before considering their next assignment. They understand the importance of rest and recuperation after their arduous expedition and look forward to the chance to recharge their batteries.

As they discuss their plans for the upcoming break, there is a palpable sense of camaraderie and shared accomplishment among the crew members. They reminisce about their adventures in space, swapping stories and anecdotes from their journey, and marveling at the wonders they encountered along the way.

In the days that follow, the crews make the most of their time off, enjoying leisurely days spent with their families and loved ones. They relish the simple pleasures of home, from home-cooked meals to relaxing evenings spent in the company of friends and family.

As they reflect on their experiences and look ahead to the future, the crews are filled with a sense of gratitude for the opportunity to rest and rejuvenate. They know that another adventure awaits them in the vast expanse of space, but for now, they are content to bask in the warmth of home and the love of those closest to them.

All the crews found themselves thrust into the spotlight upon their return to Earth, with every television network clamoring for interviews and insights into their extraordinary journey. News outlets from around the world vied for exclusive access, eager to capture the firsthand accounts of these intrepid explorers who had ventured to the far reaches of the cosmos and back.

As they stepped onto the tarmac, cameras flashed and microphones were thrust forward, the air buzzing with excitement and anticipation. The crews, still reeling from the magnitude of their experience, graciously fielded questions, and shared anecdotes from their time in space, captivating audiences with tales of adventure and discovery.

From live television interviews to in-depth documentaries, the crews found themselves inundated with requests for appearances, their stories captivating the imagination of millions around the globe. They became overnight celebrities, their faces gracing magazine covers and their names trending on social media as the world marveled at their bravery and resilience in the face of the unknown.

But amidst the whirlwind of attention and accolades, the crews remained grounded, humbled by the enormity of their journey and grateful for the opportunity to share their experiences with the world. As they reflected on their time in space and the lessons learned along the way, they knew that their mission was far from over. For as long as humanity dared to dream of the stars, they would continue to in- spire and illuminate the path forward, one story at a time.

Epilogue:
A Cosmic Legacy

Indeed, the saga of these four intrepid astronauts is a testament to the unyielding human spirit of exploration and discovery. Their journey, spanning across the vast expanses of space, echoes the innate curiosity and relentless pursuit of knowledge that has defined humanity throughout history.

From the moment they embarked on their odyssey, venturing beyond the confines of Earth's atmosphere, they faced challenges that tested their resolve and ingenuity. Whether navigating the desolate yet mesmerizing landscapes of the moon or delving into the enigmatic depths of black holes, each step of their voyage illuminated new frontiers of understanding and pushed the boundaries of human capability.

Their courage in the face of the unknown, their unwavering determination to unravel the mysteries of the cosmos, and their willingness to confront the inherent risks of space exploration inspire future generations to reach for the stars and pursue the impossible.

As we continue to explore the uncharted depths of the cosmos, the saga of these four astronauts serves as a beacon of hope and a reminder of the boundless potential that lies within each of us to push the limits of what is possible and expand the horizons of human knowledge.

Amidst the stark tranquility of the lunar surface, where humanity's first steps into the cosmos were immortalized, the journey of these intrepid astronauts began. Against the backdrop of rugged terrain and the vast expanse of the lunar horizon, they forged bonds of camaraderie and determination, preparing themselves for the challenges that lay ahead on their cosmic odyssey.

Each member of the crew brought with them a distinct set of skills, expertise, and an unwavering resolve, united by a shared vision of unravelling the mysteries of the universe. Their time on the moon served as a crucible, honing their abilities to adapt and innovate in the face of the unknown, laying the foundation for the remarkable feats they would accomplish in the depths of space.

As the intrepid crew embarked on their voyage toward the heart of the Milky Way, they encountered a series of challenges that tested their courage, ingenuity, and resolve. Navigating through the boundless expanse of space, they were mesmerized by the breathtaking splendor of distant stars, swirling nebulae, and awe-inspiring cosmic phenomena. Each celestial sight served as a poignant reminder of the immense scale and beauty of the universe, fueling their sense of wonder and awe.

However, it was the tantalizing prospect of venturing into the mysterious depths of a black hole that truly captivated their imagination. The very notion of confronting the gravitational behemoth, where the laws of physics are stretched to their limits and the fabric of space-time bends and warps, stirred within them a fervent determination to push the boundaries of human exploration to their utmost limits.

Despite the inherent dangers and uncertainties that awaited them at the event horizon, the crew pressed onward, driven by an insatiable thirst for knowledge and discovery. Their journey into the unknown represented a bold leap into uncharted territory, where the laws of nature themselves seemed to defy comprehension. Yet, fueled by their unwavering spirit of exploration and armed with the collective expertise of their mission, they approached the black hole with a sense of reverence and anticipation, ready to unlock the secrets hidden within its enigmatic depths.

Entering the black hole's domain, the crew found themselves enveloped by a swirling vortex of darkness and distortion. Within this surreal realm, the very fabric of space-time seemed to contort and warp with every passing moment, defying the conventional laws of physics. Time itself became a fluid concept, and the once-familiar dimensions of space appeared to fold and twist upon themselves, presenting the crew with a disorienting spectacle unlike anything they had ever encountered before.

Yet, amidst the chaos and uncertainty, they remained

steadfast in their quest for knowledge. Drawing upon their collective expertise and unwavering camaraderie, they navigated through the treacherous cosmic abyss with determination and resilience. Despite the surreal and daunting challenges, they faced, the bond forged among the crew members only grew stronger as they relied on each other for support and guidance.

As they delved deeper into the heart of the black hole, they confronted phenomena that defied comprehension, encountering gravitational forces of unimaginable strength, and witnessing phenomena that pushed the boundaries of human understanding. Each moment presented new revelations and insights, fueling their determination to unravel the mysteries of this cosmic enigma.

In the face of the unknown, they pressed forward, driven by a relentless curiosity and a shared commitment to exploration. Forging a path through the darkness, they dared to venture where few had gone before, embracing the uncertainty of the journey with courage and conviction. And as they emerged from the depths of the black hole, they carried with them not only a wealth of scientific knowledge but also a profound sense of awe and wonder at the vastness and complexity of the universe.

Emerging on the other side of the black hole, the crew found themselves confronted not by the expected void of darkness, but by a realm of boundless light and energy.

Before them stretched a dazzling tapestry of colors and shapes, a celestial symphony that defied comprehension. It was a sight that filled them with awe and wonder, reminding them of the profound beauty and complexity of the universe that lay beyond their understanding.

As they gazed upon this celestial spectacle, their minds were filled with a sense of profound humility and reverence. The experiences they had undergone during their journey through the black hole had forever changed them, expanding their consciousness, and deepening their connection to the cosmos in ways they had never thought possible. They had witnessed the raw power and majesty of the universe firsthand, and in doing so, had come to realize the infinitesimal nature of their own existence within the vastness of space and time.

Yet, amidst the overwhelming grandeur of the cosmos, they also felt a profound sense of unity and interconnectedness. They understood that, despite the vast distances that separated them, they were all part of the same cosmic tapestry—a realization that filled them with a deep sense of peace and belonging.

As they lingered in this celestial realm, bathed in the glow of the cosmic light, they knew that their journey was far from over. There were still countless mysteries waiting to be unraveled, and they were determined to continue their quest for knowledge and understanding, guided by the timeless spirit of exploration that had brought them to this wondrous place.

In particular, the encounter with the inhabitants of the mysterious planet they stumbled upon in the White Universe left an indelible mark on their journey. The people of the underground city, led by the wise elder Ark, showed them a world illuminated by bioluminescent flora and nourished by advanced technology that harnessed energy in ways they had never imagined. Through their shared exploration and exchange of knowledge, the crew forged a bond with Ark and his community, a testament to the universal spirit of curiosity and cooperation that transcends the boundaries of worlds.

Equally remarkable was the unexpected meeting with humans from Earth's distant future, a testament to the enduring spirit of exploration that spanned across centuries. As they exchanged stories and shared knowledge, the crew glimpsed a vision of humanity's evolution and the limitless possibilities that lay ahead.

Emerging from the black hole, the crew of the spacecraft voyaged through the unfamiliar expanse of space, their senses attuned to any signs of life or activity. It was not until they had travelled a considerable distance that they decided to broadcast a radio call, reaching out into the vastness of the cosmos in search of any fellow travelers who might be in need of assistance.

To their surprise and relief, a response came swiftly, carrying with it a plea for help from another spacecraft in distress. Without hesitation, the crew sprang into action, their training and expertise guiding them as they prepared to render aid to their fellow voyagers. It was a moment of solidarity and camaraderie, reaffirming their shared humanity in the face of the unknown and reminding them of the importance of compassion and cooperation in the depths of space.

In the final moments of their journey, as the spacecraft glided gracefully through the vast expanse of space, the crew found themselves reflecting on the extraordinary encounters that had shaped their expedition.

Among the most memorable moments was their encounter with the Zendaran, inhabitants of the mysterious flying saucer. The crew marveled at the advanced technology and otherworldly beings, forging a bond of mutual respect and curiosity that transcended the boundaries of space and time.

As the spacecraft prepared to return to the moon, the crew carried with them a trove of memories and insights that would forever shape their understanding of the cosmos. Though their journey had come to an end, the lessons learned and connections forged would endure, inspiring future generations to reach for the stars and unravel the mysteries of the universe.

THE END

All the names presented in this science fiction narrative are entirely fictional and bear no connection to any living or deceased individual.

First, I would like to thank my family for putting up with me in writing this story and to my daughter Cheryl who has encouraged me all the way.

Thank You. Hope You Enjoyed reading it.

As Much as I did writing it.

Printed in Great Britain
by Amazon